For Ed

DR MOORE'S AUTOMATON

Strength & Honour!

Chris Lincoln-Jones

CHRIS LINCOLN-JONES

The Book Guild Ltd

First published in Great Britain in 2024 by
The Book Guild Ltd
Unit E2 Airfield Business Park,
Harrison Road, Market Harborough,
Leicestershire. LE16 7UL
Tel: 0116 2792299
www.bookguild.co.uk
Email: info@bookguild.co.uk
Twitter: @bookguild

Typeset in 11pt Adobe Garamond Pro

Printed and bound in the UK by TJ Books LTD, Padstow, Cornwall

ISBN 978 1916668 072

British Library Cataloguing in Publication Data.
A catalogue record for this book is available from the British Library.

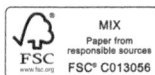

Gavin, Ged, Guy

AUTHOR'S PREFACE

This book has its roots in a conversation at a party. My friend Chris Cobb-Smith was asked if he knew anything about drones, and his answer was, "No, but I know a man who does." That was how I met the three Gs acknowledged at the front of the book: film director Gavin Hood, BAFTA Award-winning screenwriter Guy Hibbert, and CEO of Raindog Films Ged Doherty. I'd advised on the Raindog film Eye in the Sky. At the party after the premiere, Guy and Gavin asked what was next. I answered, "Lethal Autonomous Weapons" and explained what they were. The two exchanged significant looks before Guy said he'd write the script, and Gavin said he'd direct the movie.

My comment wasn't entirely party banter. I'd become an authority on the use of drones during my time in the Defence Industry and my reserve service. As an artillery officer, I was used to planning and deconflicting attacks using missiles, bombs and shells. I was called up, not unwillingly, to go to Afghanistan with 3 Commando Brigade in a recently invented role as the battlespace manager. There were lots of our people, projectiles and aircraft whizzing about in the conflict, and my job was to stop them from intersecting at the wrong time and place. My desk was next to that of Jo, the military lawyer. She was the brigade commander's legal adviser and the authority on the lawful use of lethal force. I learned a great deal from her; she is the inspiration for the lawyer in this book.

By the time Eye in the Sky was released, I'd also served in Naples at the NATO Headquarters in charge of operations over Libya. My job was to integrate naval artillery into operations, a task that needed detailed knowledge of targeting and the Law of Armed Conflict.

That led to an invitation from my friend Nick Jenson-Jones to contribute to a paper with the rather lengthy title of 'A Technical Analysis of the Employment, Accuracy and Effects of Indirect-Fire Artillery Weapons'. This was written for the ICRC; my part was the Law of Armed Conflict concerning lethal targeting.

I was also among the subject matter experts advising the Birmingham University Conflict Resolution Group for their 2014 paper on the security impact of drones. Chapter five of the paper discusses in great detail the possibilities and problems associated with autonomy; it is a must-read for anyone interested in LAWs.

When the University of South Wales invited me to give a practitioner's view of contemporary warfare and the application of the Law of Armed Conflict to their Masters students, it firmed up what I wanted to write about.

With the will, enough treasure, and current technology, what would a Lethal Autonomous Weapon system look like? What would it be capable of doing? What might be the outcome?

To make the story work, I have had to adjust recent history a bit. Events which were current in Syria and Iraq when I was writing the book overtook me, so I borrowed a bit of alternative reality to make the story work. I hope readers will think the situation that I devised is plausible. The timeline is also inaccurate for Fort Halstead, but I'd done some work there, and it's an exciting location. The book is a drama, not a documentary, but it has a point: we were dealt the ethical problems associated with 'Oppenheimer's deadly toy' by a world war and have been catching up ever since. It would be a good idea to get our ethical framework for dealing with the 'rise of the killer robots' before they make their presence felt.

DR MOORE GETS A LETTER

Craig Moore flips through the post. Newly risen, he wanders into his kitchen and and puts the kettle on to boil. In the background, yet another hapless politician is being 'Humphreyed' on the Today programme.

"Surely you could have seen this coming, Mr Lopresti. Why on earth would Airbus continue to..."

The hectoring voice fades into the background as, frowning, Craig pulls a brown envelope from the sheaf of mostly junk mail. The coat of arms on the back denotes it as government, but there's little else to suggest origin.

He reaches for a kitchen knife, opens the envelope and extracts an official-looking letter that unfolds to reveal a neat and formal document from an organisation called DSTL. However, the blue print in square grey brackets is trendily laid out in lower case, striking him as incongruous for government. At the top he sees it's from Dr Michael Sheppard, a name that means nothing to him, nor do the post-nominals give any further clue as to who Dr Sheppard is or what he does. The document speaks warmly of some of Craig's achievements in cognitive robotics and suggests that he might like to discuss collaboration with the organisation on a defence project that someone with his background would find *challenging and rewarding*. The letter informs him that, in line with the Defence Science and Technology Laboratory's mission to use innovative science and technology to contribute to the UK's defence and security, they were seeking to expand their work on autonomy in maritime systems into the land environment.

Deep in thought, Craig puts down the letter and leans on the high-backed stool that serves as a seat to his kitchen bar. He realises that the kettle has gone off the boil and, returning to the reality of his kitchen, he moves over to the bench and recommences the routine of early morning tea. He pours two mugs and takes one through to the bedroom, placing it on the bedside table nearest the recumbent form. The body stirs and emits an irritated groan. Craig contemplates the figure and then dispels the moment with a shake of his head. He returns to the letter and re-reads it. DSTL, it transpires, seeks consultants with the knowledge and skills it needs to collaborate in an innovative defence programme. In cordial terms, Craig is asked to a meeting in the Ministry of Defence. Several dates are suggested, and the contact details of Dr Sheppard's secretary are given. Craig sips his tea, deep in thought. He is interrupted by the arrival of his bedmate. Now vertical, dressed in a short robe with a vaguely eastern motif, and dishevelled. Sophie's mood is predominately sulky with hints of pout.

"Why are you up so early?"

"Nine is hardly early. There's stuff to do, people to see, jobs to hunt."

"You've got a job."

"I had a research project. Now I'd like something that pays the rent."

"You've got money; look at this place."

"And I thought you loved me for my looks and engaging personality."

"Oh, ha ha."

"Besides, I want to remain in 'this place', and my brain needs some work." Craig anticipates the onset of confrontation and puts down his mug, heading for the door to the bedroom. "I'm showering."

When he returns, Sophie is staring thoughtfully out of the window. Craig registers that the letter from DSTL has moved.

"So, you're going to work for the Government."

"I've had a letter from a Government department, that hardly constitutes work."

"Oh, please, Craig! Your 'fine work on machine learning', 'innovative science and technology', 'autonomy' – in what world will you be able to resist? Craig Moore, fucking weapons designer."

Craig flushes and looks at the face opposite him, wondering how he got into this. It's a pretty face, there haven't been many, but this one is starting to let the mask over its mean spirit slip. He'd known it was a mistake for a while but, as usual, he doesn't have the balls to just draw a line and now finds himself wondering how to get his house key back. He reddens and looks down.

"Defence doesn't just mean weapons."

Sensing something of Craig's inner thoughts, there is no response. Craig is relieved that there is to be no full-blown row. The two finish the morning routine in silence, and in due course, Craig hears the front door open and close. He looks again at the letter and reaches for the phone.

THE MINISTRY OF DEFENCE

The following week, uncomfortable in collar and tie, Craig walks up Whitehall and pauses at the foot of the steps before the brutalist building, with its massive bronze doors. Taking a deep breath, and straightening his tie, he enters the bustle of men and women streaming past him and stops to take it all in. Passes are presented to keypads and the brisk officials enter clear tubes like airlocks. Craig walks over to an armoured glass frontage and gives his name to one of the security people sitting on the other side. He is asked who he has come to see, and for some identification. A call is placed, and he is told that Dr Sheppard is coming to get him. A security pass is created, which he puts around his neck. A conventional glass door is indicated, and he goes through as a gangly figure approaches him, smiling.

Dr Michael Sheppard, bearded, bespectacled, with iron-grey hair, extends a hand and smiles at Craig.

"Dr Moore, I presume."

Craig returns the smile. "Craig, please."

"Thanks, Craig. I'm Mike. Let's go on up." He nods thanks to the security team and ushers Craig towards a set of lifts in a modest atrium beyond.

Small talk punctuates the lift ride and a short walk to an

office, where they join a tough-looking man in a pinstripe suit that contrasts with the slightly less formally dressed Dr Sheppard. Mike makes the introductions. "Craig, this is Lieutenant Colonel David Lucas, he's the military lead on the programme – my opposite number, if you like. He's also our direct link to the MOD."

"Good morning…" A pause. "Sir – you don't wear a uniform?"

"Sheep's clothing, Craig – and it's David, please." He smiles warmly.

Mike and David both produce folders and compose themselves.

"Thank you for agreeing to come and talk to us this morning, Craig. Frankly, I wasn't sure that you'd answer my letter. It was a bit of a cold call."

"Actually, it was quite intriguing, rather cloak and dagger, especially as Google didn't give much away when I tried your name. A systems engineer?"

"That was my Masters, electronics before that, and my Doctorate was about resistance to interference in radars – suitably obscure but quite useful when I started to work in defence."

"It was the bit on the DSTL mission to use innovative science and technology to contribute to the defence and security of the UK that hooked me."

"I'm glad to hear it. Of course, we've done our homework. I've read a number of your papers and attended your presentation at Vodafone's Newbury conference."

"You attended that? I don't recall seeing you."

"You were on our radar sometime before we wrote to you, Craig."

David has been watching Craig intently during this exchange and breaks in. "Mathematician, Masters in Neurophysics, self-driving vehicles, gaming AI…" David cocks an eyebrow smiling.

Craig fidgets and fiddles with his tie. "I saw an opportunity not to be poor, got into the gaming industry at the right time. I was a player of games and realised I could do a better job coding computer opponents for spotty teenagers, and cashed in. You know it's not artificial intelligence, don't you? It's not even machine learning, really, which is what I'm about. It's just complex decision trees and the fact that the programme can see everything and make decisions faster. Basically, I coded tactical games to cheat."

David casts a thoughtful and calculating eye over Craig, who has engaged confidently for the first time. He smiles wryly at Mike and nods approvingly.

"You've come a long way from southeast eighteen, Craig," David comments.

"Well, not bad for a geek in hand-me-downs. Absent father, mother doing her best. If I hadn't got up and got out of there, I'd never have survived. Not the typical profile for an Asian boy. In my case, half-Asian. Father took off when I was very young. The judgement of her community impelled my mum to move away. We landed in a flat in Woolwich. Maths was my saviour. Conventionally, I should have been an accountant. Mum supported me along the journey I took. By the time I realised she was working herself to death, it was too late." After a reflective pause, Craig is brisk. "I was lucky, but that's beside the point. Your letter asked me if I was interested in collaborating in a novel defence programme but didn't give much else away. The website I looked at has a piece on something called Autonomous Warrior; I'm guessing that's where this is going."

"Yes and no," Mike replies. "Autonomous Warrior was an exercise that dealt mainly with the Navy which, frankly, is relatively easy. Autonomous mine clearance is a bit of a no-brainer, and there are already anti-missile defences which detect and fire without human intervention."

Craig blinks, astonished.

"Let me tell you what I head up, Craig. My team is dedicated to what we call novel defence technology. Twenty years ago, we were looking at radio frequency weapons and enhanced blast munitions. The world has moved on."

Craig leans back, realisation dawns. "The rise of the robot warriors."

"You saw the paper this morning, did you?"

"I'm certain that what it suggests is a bit far-fetched. Besides, I've read a government paper that says that we won't allow machines to make decisions as to who lives and who dies."

David interjects. "The Birmingham University paper, yes, there's a brief mention about the UK and US resolve along those lines. That doesn't mean we shouldn't use aspects of AI in our hardware. In any case, we need to know them. After all, we don't use chemical or biological weapons, but we have a chemical defence establishment, just outside Salisbury, in fact. Quite fortunate, if you think about recent events. You may even get there, our present place is shutting down soon, and that's where we'll be going. Anyway, whatever our political masters might say in Parliament, others are developing them. When the time comes, we may not have a choice. Being on the moral high ground makes you an easy target."

Mike sits back and steeples his hands, observing the young man in front of him. David regards him with the calculating detachment of the hawk that he is. Craig's mind is buzzing with the possibilities.

Mike breaks the silence. "We want you to help us design an autonomous defensive system. You said it yourself – we want a weapon system that can cheat."

As the two scrutinise him, Craig's thoughts crystallise. "So, I was selected from a shortlist of one, which is why this isn't an interview, is it?"

"Introduction rather than interview," David says. "And, of course, we want to be sure you're the right man."

Craig ponders their questions. "What exactly is it that I'll be doing, assuming you decide I'm 'the right man' and I decide to do this?"

"Let's grab a coffee, then we'll talk about the specifics. There are a couple of people who want to meet you, and they'll join us shortly."

The three retrace the earlier journey through the atrium into a vast pillared hall with a coffee shop. Mike deals with the order, and while he is at the counter, David's small talk reveals that he is a Royal Engineer, experienced in humanitarian operations and fighting. In fact, despite his uncompromising attitude to conflict, he reveals he's spent more time building schools and digging wells than he has fighting.

Craig realises he might be more conflicted by all this than he thinks. Sophie's comment of the week before had bothered him. During the interval between letter and interview, much of his consideration has been on the morality of weaponising machine intelligence. The fundamental question, 'do I want to be involved with this?' at war with a desire to practice his craft at the cutting edge of future technology.

Looking around at the vaulted ceilings, waiting for Mike to return with the coffee, he realises that not only is the building impressive, if a bit intimidating, but so are the people. David, older than he, fierce, opinionated, and with a substantial physical presence, speaks to an inner desire for an exemplary figure. Craig finds himself enjoying these people that he would not otherwise have met. His train of thought is derailed when Mike arrives with coffee, followed almost immediately by the appearance of the two expected individuals. He puts down the tray of coffee and introduces the stocky figure of Group Captain Simison, who he calls Assistant Director ISTAR. He explains that ISTAR stands for Intelligence, Surveillance, Target Acquisition and Reconnaissance. The elegant woman next to him is from the Defence Equipment and Support Organisation in the 'Joint Enablers' department.* Mike explains that she has come up from Bristol. Her smile fails to reach her eyes, and she wins the handshake competition. Craig suspects that she outranks everyone present, especially himself.

—————————

*   Shortened to its initials, DESO, and pronounced 'deezo'.

They all sit, and the opening pleasantries reveal that the group captain is Bertie and the ice queen is Helen Sherwood. The conversation is easy. Bertie has been briefed and is obviously a policy wonk with little specialist knowledge but considerable charm. Helen is also from the policy world. In due course, she asks what Craig thinks of joining the project.

Mike interjects smoothly. "We haven't spoken in anything more than general terms yet, Helen. The actual project hasn't come up." Turning to Craig, he says portentously, "We want you to join a new programme called Project Heimdall."

"Oh! I'm going to help you design a robot that'll guard a bridge, I take it."

Mike is startled, Helen's dark eyes glitter with amusement.

"What makes you say that, Craig? Why a bridge?"

"Well, Heimdall guards the Bifrost, the bridge to Asgard. He has a horn to warn the Gods of danger to their home."

Helen leans back and folds her arms, gazing with satisfaction at Craig.

"It's said he required less sleep than a bird, could see a hundred leagues and could hear the grass growing in the meadows and wool growing on sheep." Craig trails off, noting the quizzical look on Bertie's face and the astonishment in the eyes of Mike and David.

Helen leans forward, still smiling. "Dr Moore's learning, it would seem, is a lot wider than that of machines."

Craig grins back at her, with a bit of bravado. "No, I'm the ultra-geek who likes Marvel films – Idris Elba plays him in the ones with Thor. I'm a fan."

David interjects. "Me too, though I have to be – I've got teenagers."

"So, where's your Bifrost?"

"Pretty much everywhere that a hostile group or individual thinks we're vulnerable," David observes grimly.

"What's the most expensive thing in defence, Craig?"

Craig shrugs. "Aircraft carriers?"

"Not even those white elephants, my friend – it's people, and in western democracies, they get more and more expensive. Soldiers, sailors, airmen, they not only need pay, but you've also got to give them pensions. They can't live in eight-man rooms any longer, so we have to spend millions upgrading accommodation. We give them maternity leave, paternity leave and, if they get killed, some well-meaning coroner makes us pile tons of expensive armour on them." He pauses for breath. "Defence in liberal democracies is pricing itself out of the market!"

Craig is ingenuous. "Peace at last," he says brightly.

"Fat chance."

"So Heimdall looks for enemies and warns you, how does that save manpower?"

"A human can only look at a few screens at once. And don't forget, Heimdall carries a sword, Craig."

Craig sits back and looks thoughtful as Mike picks up the narrative. He had fiddled with his tablet while David was speaking.

"My remit is fairly wide, Craig. This project started out as a simple question: how do we reliably, and with fewer false alarms than a human, guard a military base? Soldiers spend a lot of time guarding themselves."

He shows the screen to Craig, and the others crane in to see. A fortified camp is displayed that Craig assumes must be in Afghanistan.

"Look at these towers. At the height of operations in Helmand, only half had a sentry. Security occupies soldiers who could be better used elsewhere. It also needs lots of them. People get fatigued, and their concentration lapses. They need sleep, food. Sentry duty is also very boring, and bored soldiers don't concentrate on the task at hand, so they miss things. It's also a waste of a mobile, expensive and highly trained soldier."

"So, you want sentries who don't need sleep or food and never get bored."

"That's it, more or less, yes. Though the scope is greater, we think more can be done and, in this department, we are allowed to think beyond the boundaries of any given project. As I said, our remit is to look at how we might automate security at a military base in a hostile environment, but we want the application to go further. If head office – as we refer to this place – wants it to. Your work on self-drive vehicles is of particular interest because it deals with analysing multiple sources of information to give the car its spatial awareness, something close to our hearts. ISTAR is as much about the fusion of information as it is about gathering it."

Craig pauses before replying. "But my knowledge of military stuff is pretty basic. The closest I've got to soldiers are strategy simulations in the gaming industry."

Helen has been sitting back in her chair, watching the conversation, her eyes flitting from one speaker to another, face calm. She leans in, focusing on Craig.

"So no preconceptions, I think that's an advantage. Besides we can place all the knowledge you need at your fingertips." She looks at the others. "Can't we?"

There are nods and murmurs of assent. Her intense, unblinking gaze reminds Craig of a cat.

"How long will it take to develop the software? I'm told these things can take time, and we have deadlines."

"Er… it's already written."

"Sorry? What do you mean it's already written?"

"I came up with it at the end of the work on the car. There were bound to be other applications. It struck me that there was a better way of doing it than writing bespoke software for each application. This is not like a word processing program. It's machine learning. It's what I do… in fact, it's what you do. When you want to do something new, you learn what you need to know so you can do it. Say, climbing a mountain. You learn all you need to know about boots, clothing, how to navigate, what effect the weather has, and how physically fit you need to be. Your brain stores that information and fits it all together before judging how the activity will be approached. You then go and give it a try, adjusting your technique with experience, trying not to get killed in the process." He smiles encouragingly at his witticism. "You don't change your brain every time you do something new." He sits back and looks from face to face with a smile.

"Bertie and I have another meeting." Helen stands, and the men follow suit. Her basilisk gaze tracks across them, lingering finally on Craig. A decision is made. She turns to Mike and David. "A moment of your time, if you please." Her attention returns to Craig. "Excuse us for a short while."

Craig sits back down, glad of the opportunity to think.

Helen halts before the escalator, out of earshot and turns to Mike and David. "I want him on the project, soon."

Bertie mumbles assent. They both nod.

David ventures an obstacle, "He'll need vetting, maybe DV."

There is a brief pause. "Details to my office, I'll hasten the process, but only limited access to Secret, no Top Secret, at least at first. In the meantime, you have my authority to brief him as fully as is necessary. No delays – and Michael, I want that system." She turns and stalks off; they are dismissed. Bertie hurries after her. Mike and David share a look and breathe out audibly. They turn back to Craig as he sits, a picture of introspection, staring at half a cup of cold coffee.

CRAIG TAKES THE QUEEN'S SHILLING

The VW Beetle speeds along the M25, its driver grateful that the agricultural progression from the A3 to the Gatwick Airport turn-off is behind him. A glance to his left as he anticipates the change of direction to the north reveals a tree-covered escarpment that he will climb shortly. His GPS doesn't tell him much about his destination; the little flag just ends in a pale green landscape that signifies woodland. Even without leaves, the horizon is thick and dark. Craig had googled Fort Halstead when the invitation arrived, expecting to learn a bit about the place. He is thus a little disappointed not to be able to see the grim shape of a late-nineteenth century fort that the Wiki entry had assured him existed. Exiting the motorway, he follows a discrete red sign for DSTL Fort Halstead on his left, and follows a narrow tree-lined road for half a mile. A low building overlooks the road barrier that is eventually revealed. An armed and flak-jacketed guard observes his approach, stepping forward as he halts.

"Can I help you, sir?"

Craig is disquieted; sprites in computer games don't exude the menace of a rifle mere inches away, and the calculated stare of the man behind it.

"Craig Moore, I'm here to see Dr Sheppard."

The armed man relaxes, slightly. "You'll have to sign in, Mr Moore." He indicates the building. "Park over to your left."

Craig parks and walks over to the building. Behind the desk, a woman smiles at him and asks who he is visiting. On being told, she looks up with a smile.

"Ah, you're expected, Dr Moore." She reaches for a phone and tells him, "Stand on the footprints and look at the camera," nodding at a little ball on the counter. She looks up and smiles again. "Dr Sheppard will be down shortly, sir."

She reaches over to a printer and takes the label that appeared as she was speaking. After sticking it to a red pass, she hands it to him together with a car pass and invites him to take a seat. He briefly scrutinises the faintly worried face regarding him from under the prominent wording labelling him as an escorted visitor. Sitting down, Craig takes in his surroundings and tries to relax. Looking through the door and up the hill, he sees flat-roofed buildings behind trees and what looks like a green hangar.

His eyes return to the guard. It was easy to say yes to Mike Shepherd's offer without the current implications of what he was about to do so starkly evident. His contractor status and the daily rate had even brought Sophie's caustic remarks to a halt. He expected this was likely to be temporary, though. The term 'killer robot' has started to feature in her latest comments. His train of thought is interrupted as the door opens, and Mike walks in smiling.

"Let's go up to the lab." He thanks the lady at reception by name and ushers Craig out of the building.

They get in Craig's car, the barrier opens and they climb the hill that rises from the entrance. The road falls away to woodland on their right as the two of them pass sixties era buildings that include the large hangar Craig had spotted earlier. Craig glances across at it.

Mike chuckles and says, "Ah, incongruous, isn't it? A hangar in a forest. Someday you may get a look inside and see what happens when something explodes that wasn't supposed to."

Craig is curious, and Mike continues, "Aircraft or vehicle, if it's blown up unexpectedly in this country, that's where they try to find out how and why. Lots of interesting stuff happens here, as you're about to find out."

They've reached a shabby three-storey building with a flat roof and lots of windows, all opaque due to the plastic anti-blast coating. Mike directs Craig to the car park at the rear and tells him to remember the route. When they get to the doors of the building, Mike keys in a code. They step inside, walking past offices to a set of double doors that take them into an ample laboratory-style space. This is occupied by half a dozen men and women concentrating on multiple screens. Air conditioning hums gently and there is a buzz of conversation that ceases as they enter the room. Curious faces focus their attention on the newcomer. Mike strides to the conference table in the corner and addresses the team.

"This is Dr Craig Moore. You've all been expecting his arrival, and many of you know his work. I see the coffee has arrived and we even have cake! Grab a cup and come and meet him."

There is laughter and some banter at this. Craig is aware of a good-natured atmosphere. David is leaning against a table, talking to a younger woman of similar demeanour. He sketches an ironic salute and smiles a welcome. The others step up to him, and Craig is soon surrounded by eager faces. Introductions give way to a barrage of questions and admiring references to his previous work.

Mike interrupts. "Let's introduce him gently, people. As you know, Colonel Lucas and I only snared Craig last week, we don't want to scare him off!"

This gets a proper laugh from the eager team.

"Beyond a brief outline, we haven't told Craig much about Heimdall, that's what today is all about. I'll start that now. As we told you last week, Craig, guarding bases is resource intensive and boring. It begs to be automated but the people being guarded need to trust it not to make mistakes and, if we want it to detect, recognise, identify and attack an enemy like an armed guard does, it has to obey the same rules."

He gestures to the team.

"A month ago, we had a team of three software integrators and coders. As of last week, we've been joined by some key subject matter experts."

He indicates people around the room.

"We've got all the expertise we need to get on with the job in this room. Most important for you is Caroline, over there with David. She's an artillery officer, knows all about targeting and the rules that govern it, and has done it all for real. We'll co-opt other people if we need them as the project matures. He looks over at the trio of software engineers. "Will, would you oblige?"

One of them breaks away and operates a mouse and keyboard. At the end of the room, a screen springs to life, and a presentation opens. A Norse figure features on the title slide, carrying a horn and with a sword belted at its side. Craig smiles as the picture changes to an artist's impression of a military camp. He recognises the structure, built of giant bags of sand inside wire baskets. The view tracks to a tower at the corner, upon which is a turret with a gun. Mike talks of the optical sensors that see in both the visible and infra-red spectra, laser rangefinders, and as he speaks William moves a pointer on the screen to point these features out. The view pulls out, and other structures appear. A mast with a radar dish that tracks back and forth. Mike identifies it as a radar that detects moving targets.

Craig interrupts. "How does it do that, can it see stationary ones as well?"

One of the team pipes up. "It's a Doppler radar. For movers that can distinguish between people and vehicles, there's a different one that will give an image of stationary objects."

"Have you used Lidar? We had an array on the self-driving car, I would have thought that Lidar would do both."

"There are some mapping technologies being researched but—"

David interrupts from the side. "I think that's a love-in you two can have later."

Mike grins and carries on. "Yes, these conversations are what we want to happen in this room, but maybe not right away."

Slides of a quadcopter drone and a blimp appear.

"The point is that what we want is a system that will gather and tie together all this information from all these different sources, to give the best possible situational awareness and react appropriately."

The slide show ends, and there is silence.

"He requires less sleep than a bird, can see a hundred leagues, and can hear the grass growing in the meadows and wool growing on the sheep."

All eyes return to Craig as he leans thoughtfully against a table.

One of the software team hesitantly asks, "Is it true what Dr Sheppard says? You've already built an AI system that can do this?"

All eyes turn to Craig as he reaches over to the backpack he brought in from his car. He takes out a nondescript, dark grey block with a wire trailing from one end.

"You mean this?"

There is a moment of silence as the audience takes in the modest device in Craig's hand. The silence is broken by Caroline, the artillery officer.

"I expected it to be more impressive, bigger perhaps? With flashing lights."

There is universal laughter. Craig smiles and gathers himself, nervous under their scrutiny. He puts the object on the table next to him and moves to sit next to it.

"Look, you need to understand some things."

His audience make themselves comfortable, the IT engineers smile knowingly at each other. This is what they came for. Covert glances are directed at the two soldiers, and they hope that Craig doesn't make the explanation too simple, so they can watch it go over their heads.

"There's no such thing as artificial intelligence, not as we understand the way the human mind operates – and in my opinion, anything even resembling human creative decision-making is a very long way off. I mean multiple decades, not multiple years. All these assertions in the media that an artificial brain is just around the corner are wildly optimistic, even an attempt at it would need massive computing power and hundreds of terabytes of memory." He picks up his little oblong block. "This is an eight terabyte solid state drive, and there's still room on it." Craig pauses and orders his thoughts. "Some of you know my history. I started in pure maths and then went up to Oxford for a degree in Mathematics and Computer Science. I was interested in computer gaming and, after the degree, I had a bit of luck and got involved with the industry. I certainly needed the money. That's where I saw that so-called 'AIs' weren't. As I've already pointed out to Mike and David, they were just decision trees that worked really quickly, coupled with the computer's ability to look at the whole picture simultaneously. Anyway, I was good at it, and it paid for me to go to Birmingham and do a Master's in Computational Neuroscience and Cognitive Robotics. That's when I started working on this." He nods towards the solid-state hard drive. He indicates the block. "The two of us have recently finished the Doctorate on Machine Learning that, I think, is what some of you know me for." He turns and addresses Mike. "The Newbury Conference where you listened to my talk was the first theoretical exposure since I'd finished my thesis."

Mike is frowning. "But there was no indication at that talk that you were as far along in your thinking as you obviously are. I thought the use of machine learning and the limited cognitive abilities of a programme to run multiple systems were theoretical but possible. You gave no clue then that you already had one."

"If it works, it'll be very valuable, and I hadn't done much actual testing – it's a bit difficult at home!"

David interjects. "So, has it done anything at all?"

"It made a cake."

There is incredulous laughter.

"Are you serious?"

"I connected it to my KitchenAid mixer and asked it to make a cake."

"Did it do it?"

"It gave an unrecognised device error code, so I installed a camera and it recognised the mixer. It said it could only mix a cake. I told it to do that, and it then said it had located two hundred and fourteen types of cake and asked which one I wanted. I specified a brownie and got a list of ingredients and an instruction to tell it when to start. It stopped by itself when the mix consistency was correct. I was then given all the instructions needed to cook the cake."

The IT people and Mike have been listening very carefully, and their faces betray no amusement.

David notes this and says, "This wasn't a frivolous experiment, was it?"

Craig turns to him. "Well spotted. Just consider all I've just said and think of the processes required to reach those outcomes. Before the techs ask, no, it didn't tell me in those terms. It returned mostly error codes. I had to interpret those and then design an interaction system that made sense. It needs to recognise what an activity needs and then understand the inputs and outputs for the toolset. Think of yourselves undoing a nut and bolt. You need to know what spanner, what size and how to use it. Sensors and a manipulator to put tool and problem together. How to measure success against the task set."

Mike looks at the tableau before him, deep in thought. Six weeks ago, he'd put this small team together, briefed them on the plan and left them alone. Since then, they'd come up with ideas, edited some existing software and managed to integrate some hardware into a network. Until the revelation of the last two weeks, Mike had been looking at months and months of work, followed by even more in testing and evaluation. It is evident that, potentially, his project has been accelerated by months, if not years. He turns his thoughts to the phrase that has been at the forefront of his mind: 'If it works, it'll be very valuable'. Mike very much doubts that this brilliant young man has overlooked the commercial potential of the little grey block that is sitting at his side. He foresees difficulties, nothing insurmountable, but certainly challenging. Then again, Helen said she wanted it. Mike almost feels sorry for MOD Contracts Branch, this is going to cost them a fortune. Of course, Craig will find it challenging to sell it on if, 'for reasons of national security', the export or sale becomes subject to government approval. His final thought is that the sooner he signs the Official Secrets Act, the better.

He returns his attention to the young man upon whom all attention is focused, wryly noting that here, in his element, there is none of the awkward defensiveness that he worked so hard to conceal at their first meeting, answering questions from the team with authority and good humour.

Mike's introspection has been noted by David, who has eyed him shrewdly from across the room. David's own mind has drifted in the last few minutes, his thoughts, characteristically, on activity and logistics. He is already considering how to accelerate the programme from concept to hardware, who else needs to be involved, where to get equipment and where to put it. Paperwork and contracts are far from his mind. Their eyes meet, and Mike sets his jaw. Rising from his seat, he seizes control of the forum.

"David and I have some other pressing issues that we need to address."

The group settles and looks expectantly at him.

"You people all know what the aim is and have all the details at your fingertips. It's over to you now. Caroline, you coordinate things and let us know what extra resources need to be brought in. David and I will come and go, but we'll have a formal meeting last thing every Monday, let's say at five o'clock." He looks around, meeting their eyes, finally resting on Craig. "Welcome to Project Heimdall, Dr Moore."

With that, he marches to the door followed by David who, just before leaving, calls Caroline over and addresses her quietly.

"When Mike says 'coordinate', he means accelerate, Caroline. And... we've lit a fire under the vetting process for Craig, but he doesn't have it yet. We've got a dispensation to Secret so brief him fully. If you need to go higher... well, use your judgement, but we want this project in full flight ASAP."

Caroline straightens perceptibly. "Yes, Colonel."

With that, the two senior men leave.

DR MOORE JOINS THE TEAM

Two weeks later, Craig slams the door of his car and walks to the Heimdall Block. New trousers have replaced jeans and a smart jacket completes the image. A shiny, plastic photographic pass dangles from his neck, and this gets him through the new security lock on the door. As he enters the lab, he is greeted by the people already there, and he returns the greetings, noting that some new furniture has appeared – new arrivals are expected this week. The team is growing as the pace of the project increases.

He has spent the time that it took for his vetting to be completed learning about the military aspects of the project. Caroline has been his mentor, starting with a presentation called 'The British Army in an Hour' so that he could understand the basic terms and the structure of land forces. Jo, a military laywer temporarily attached to the team, has been feeding him the Law of Armed Conflict, and with more of Caroline's input he now knows how NATO and the UK carry out what is euphemistically called 'The Targeting Process'. Some of this has rekindled the simmering disquiet he feels when the possibility of making Heimdall into a weapon is revealed. Caroline's ingenuous reply of, "We're building a guard for camps," doesn't fully dispel his feeling.

He's allowed to take Official stuff home, though he sometimes wishes it were Secret, as the extra work has caused a good deal of sulking in Wimbledon and he's noticed Sophie taking an interest in some of the papers he's left lying around. Caroline and a new arrival, Sam, have introduced him to the world of ISTAR. This has proved to be revelatory, and Craig has been fascinated by the procedures and sensors that are available. As these are what his machine will talk to, this part of the process has been particularly exciting. Caroline, aware of his misgivings, has said little about weapons, though.

Before the weekend the promised vetting came through and, together with his signature on the portentous Official Secrets document with its dire threats should he betray them, a landmark moment came and went.

Mike ratcheted the pace up in the latest Monday meeting by telling them they should start to integrate elements of the system into the synthetic environment that had recently been brought into the lab.

When Craig produces his programme back in the lab, all eyes are upon him. A powerful computer has been positioned in the centre of a crescent of desks that face a screen of cinematic proportions on the opposite wall. Either side of him are the software engineers, sat at their workstations. Separated from the central bank screens are Caroline and Sam, who have been joined by a new face brought in to manage the Synthetic Environment. Caroline and Sam are running the wargame that uses the SE. The screen on the wall will display that environment as well as any screen views that they may want available for the whole team to consider. Jo sits quietly in the lab breakout area, taking in the entire scene. The atmosphere is momentous, the previous week has been spent populating the databases with the information that Craig's programme will access and deciding what ISTAR feeds to make available for the early test runs. The SE is usually used for the Operational Analysis teams to run wargame exercises that test tactics and what effect new weapons or other defence technologies have on the battlefield. Caroline and Sam can simulate many different types of actual systems. They have decided to use a base that is already in the programme, which has a mast with cameras and a radar sensor for detecting moving targets. As Craig boots up his computer, the SE operator displays a map view of the area that they are going to use.

Caroline opens the narrative. "This is the Salisbury Plain Training Area. We've got accurate mapping and 3D modelling. The database is populated with all the people and kit we need."

As she speaks, the SE zooms in on a small makeshift camp and switches to a camera view of the walls and tents inside. As Craig's two screens resolve into the interface with the programme, he puts his display up into the corner of the big screen so that everyone can see it. The screen changes to the map view and heads turn to regard Craig.

He and Caroline have been discussing a basic test plan in the days that have led up to today, so he says, "Right, apparently, this being day one, we mustn't walk before we fly." He looks at Caroline who wags an admonitory finger at him. He laughs and shakes his head. "We are going to make available the basic military lexicon that I've been working on, and I've analysed the relevant rules and procedures from the manuals that Jo and Caroline have been making me read. Those have been scripted so that the Game Engine can behave as we want. We also have the data on the different sensors that could be used, and the SE feed will match them. We'll use neutral environmental data at first but altering that and inputting other variables is going to be an important part of testing the learning capability of the programme. The programme will also connect to the SE's simulated GPS feed to give geospatial data and time – we've been careful to make sure that time is real across all the systems." He turns to the operators on either side of him and says, "Ready?"

They nod.

Turning back to the rest of the team, he says, "Rob and Will are logging everything that happens in the systems, and we have an audio log running, so be careful what you say!"

The tension dissolves in muted laughter as Craig rolls his cursor over the *Run Programme* caption and activates the system.

The eyes of all are glued to the screen. Craig's display in the corner is joined by a view of the camp overlaid on the map. The operator drags it into the bottom of the screen, the mast with its four cameras and radar antenna is clearly visible.

"What do you want to do, Caroline?"

"Oh! Er... display activity in the vicinity of the base."

Craig types instructions into a dialogue box.

In a separate area, what had been a blinking cursor suddenly types, *Sensors not available, please switch on.*

Seated on his left, Rob looks up and says, "That's interesting, the SE interface shows a lot of outward traffic, I think he was trying to switch them on himself."

Caroline looks up and smiles. "He, Rob?"

"What?"

"You just called it he!"

"Oh, I see..." Rob's voice trails away.

The moment is interrupted as the SE operator turns on the sensors at his terminal. On screen, the cameras move, and the radar head sweeps back and forth.

The map display starts to show crosses across the depicted area. The screen settles quickly, some of the symbols move slowly. Caroline frowns and turns to Craig.

"Couldn't we have military map symbols?"

"Sure." He types in, *Use APP6 symbology*, and almost instantly the display changes. The crosses change to the NATO standard symbols used to depict military equipment. It is also now in colour. Jo observes from her place that outside a circle round the base the pictographs are yellow, not red, blue and green.

Sam cuts through the speculative buzz that her comment generates and says, "Beyond the range of the cameras. The radar only classifies moving targets, it can't identify them."

She is quite impressed that the AI has spotted the ones it can recognise as friendly, enemy and neutral.

The first part of the afternoon progresses with different sensors being added to the mix, and Craig leans back in his seat. "This isn't going anywhere, and the software team haven't got enough data to prove anything needs changing. I think we should press on."

Caroline looks thoughtful and phones David. "Colonel, we've finished the first phase ahead of schedule and the team want to push on so they've got some meaningful data. You OK with that? Do you and Mike want to come down?"

While they wait for the arrival of the grown-ups, Craig and the software team tinker with the programme and peripherals. A quick check of the log files from this first experiment shows how the AI responds to Heimdall and, as a result, Craig adjusts some of the inputs and outputs of the Game Engine, the shorthand he has for the programme that sits in the unassuming drive. Leaning back he stares at the screen.

"Hey, IT Coven!"

Rob, Will and Diana turn to regard him, smiling. Since he started calling them that, they've been wearing the term as a badge of pride.

"We aren't really doing ourselves any favours spending our time typing info into the libraries. It's stopping us using the learning aspects and seeing what it can do. All the information is either on the intranet or out on the wider web. We just need to connect it."

There are sharp intakes of breath and shaking of heads. Diana pipes up with, "I think the powers that be are going to be nervous about that, Craig, even the three of us aren't completely sure what it can do." The three share a grin. "Your Coven aren't completely clear what we've got here. The suits haven't got a clue, although I think Mike intuitively knows more than he's letting on."

Craig frowns and shakes his head. "It gets on my nerves, all this paranoia."

He is interrupted by Caroline's return. "Are you ready to go for the run? I've loaded four scenarios that are more of a challenge." "Yes, I think we are. There are some questions I need to ask. Some more information resources that could be exploited, but I don't see a problem."

"There's one more thing, in the last scenario I want to attack the base. We've imported a defensive turret that we've had in mind for a while and altered the layout of the base to accommodate it. The characteristics of all the sensors and its kinetic capabilities are all modelled and available for the…" Caroline skips a beat as she cues Craig's vocabulary. "Game Engine."

"Oh! I didn't realise you'd done that. Let me do a few checks to make sure the controls are there." He sits down and rapidly throws up pages of instructions. Looking up, he says, "It's easy to forget what the eventual outcome of all this is." He returns to the controls, looks at the screen and hovers his finger over the return key for a second before tapping it.

When Mike arrives, there is an informal update around the lab breakout table. Over coffee, Caroline and Craig go over what has been done during the first integration experiment and what they have planned for the next part of the test. Mike is pleased with the progress.

"This is great news. It won't surprise you to know that Air Commodore Simmison and Helen Sherwood are all over me to know when we can show the capability off."

"Things would be even quicker if the engine could access data directly, you know."

"What do you mean directly?"

"We're pulling things off the intranet and out of manuals and inputting the data by hand. We'd save days if we just let the machine learn for itself. It can do it, you know, the clue is in the name."

"I'm not letting that programme loose in the MOD's intranet."

"If you're worried it'll start downloading porn, there's a firewall. In any case, I'm not saying it needs access to anything classified. I can't stand this inefficiency, it's plain fucking ignorance. Or are you suggesting I'm some kind of spy? Honestly, Mike, you of all people should know that it doesn't have initiative, it's not intelligent, it only learns what it's told to learn."

"I'm not suggesting anything, Dr Moore." Mike's tone is icy. "Try to remember who is in charge of this project."

Caroline has risen from her seat, looking thunderstruck. The other members of the team shift uncomfortably and look everywhere except at the two adversaries.

"I apologise, Dr Sheppard, everyone… it was a long night… the commute… I'm not terribly popular at home right now. I… I'm very sorry."

Mike blinks. "Look, Craig, it's alright. I do know that a computer programme only does what it's told. Still, this is no ordinary computer programme, is it?"

Mike looks more carefully at his software team and sees that the others are looking a bit fragged as well.

"Look, you've all been working hard, I can see that, and I should have made more of an effort to be here during the last week. I might have noticed some of the stress. Let's get this test done, and we might look at taking the foot off the gas for a day or two. You've done brilliantly to get this far in such a short time."

Diana sees an opportunity to pour more oil on the water. "Why don't we use the old network, Dr Sheppard?"

"What do you mean, Di?"

"Well, when we changed over to MODnet, we stopped using the old DSTL intranet, but it's still there. I worked on it because the security people wanted to use it for the new security system, you know, the new cameras and the passes. It had some of the old Dabinett software from before the funding got nicked. It's only graded Official, I could easily create an area for the system to use."

"Bless you, Di, that's a brilliant idea." Mike seizes the opportunity but has a second thought and turns to Craig. "It's not only a worry about an AI loose in the system, Craig, but I'd also be far more concerned about an attack on the programme. We'd want some sort of firewall between the intranet and our experiment."

Craig almost falls over himself to make amends. "Game Engine has his own defences… fuck, fuck!"

"What?" Mike lets out an astonished laugh.

"They've got me bloody doing it now."

"Doing what, for heaven's sake?"

Craig turns and gestures at the Coven, who are now creased up. "Calling the Game Engine 'he', they've been at it for days. Anyway, as I was saying, it's an independent entity both in terms of software and hardware, so I designed some security in."

The mood has reset itself, the military officers are smiling bemusedly at the nerds, pleased that earlier tensions have eased, the Coven is relieved, and delighted by Craig's slip-up.

"Shut up, you lot. Go on, Craig, how does an anti-intrusion system like that work? Surely you need to keep updating virus protection?"

"The hardware encryption is simple enough, and I used the learning algorithms to let it defend itself against malware. It accesses various databases that are out there in the open and adjusts its defensive systems. In any case, most malware attacks use established methods. I designed this to be cleverer. If fragments of code are sneaked in, you still need an assembler and some code to execute the attack. The system is like your immune system, it's always on the lookout for foreign code or bits of things that shouldn't be there and the machines antibodies attack anything they don't like. It uses the same system to keep itself tidy." He stops and looks around at them. They're all looking at him quizzically now.

"Keeps itself tidy?"

"Yes, like the registry cleaners and privacy apps we all use. Any extraneous code or junk files are scavenged and deleted."

Mike comes to a decision. "Right, we'll run the test as it is. Then, going forward, Diana will integrate the old intranet into the system. I must admit, we do probably need to push forward as fast as we can and as efficiently as we can." He looks around and says, "I may as well tell you... DESO are pushing for a live demo on some actual hardware. It's why you haven't seen much of David. He's got to find it and get it here."

Caroline frowns. "I wondered why he'd disappeared. You've been absent, as you just pointed out, anything I should know?"

"I can't tell you exactly, but it could be in a couple of weeks. Yeah! Yeah! I know, I know." He waves his hands at the groans of dismay and walks to the door. Turning, he says, "Thanks... that was... interesting." He looks hard at a distracted Craig and leaves.

MIKE STEPS UP THE PACE

David returns that afternoon, and he and Mike sit attentively with Jo at the vantage point to the side of the screen. This time, control of the base-friendly entities in the synthetic environment has been given to the Game Engine. The activities of hostile and neutral forces are under the control of Caroline and the operator. After a few basic runs that prove the system can operate the base surveillance devices and detect targets, there is a pause.

"OK, let's run the attack scenario," Mike says.

He is interrupted by David. "I'm a bit behind, Craig, what have you done with the artificial intelligence?"

Craig still winces inwardly when he uses the term. "We've just run it in Area Surveillance mode, which is what I did when you were last here. I've now added a 'guard' to reflect an active set of conditions instead of just passive."

"That takes account of the turret weapons?"

"More than that, we've got the surveillance systems on the wall and tower as well as those in the turret, the Game Engine—"

"Game Engine?"

"I don't like calling it 'programme', or 'system', still less 'artificial intelligence'. It's more than a programme, it's part of a system, and it's not intelligent. 'Game Engine' is less of a mouthful than 'Machine Learning Entity'. It appeals to my sense of humour, given where it came from."

"You have one of those, do you? A sense of humour." David's smile is mischievous.

"What is it Caroline says in these circumstances...? Oh yes, fuck you and the horse you rode in on."

Craig's bravery earns him a round of applause.

David sketches another of his ironic salutes in acknowledgement. "Well, as abbreviations go, MLE isn't bad, but Mike and I have a better idea. Game Engine's actually quite good, but might give the wrong impression as we go a bit more 'public'. Mike and I think that 'Intelligent Autonomous Defence System' might work, it sort of says what it is and makes a good acronym." He smiles at Craig. "You know how we love our acronyms! This one is good because it makes a word – IADS – and there are about five other uses of the same initials, so any leakage into the public domain is lost in the noise. OK?"

There are shrugs and nods.

"I rather fancied Cake Mixer."

Caroline's witticism draws laughter, fading as David baits Caroline with, "The professional staff officer, adding value as always. I can just see us telling DESO Joint Enablers we're calling it Cake Mixer, that's one parapet I'm not raising my head above."

Mike nods his agreement and smiles ruefully at David. "You were describing 'Guard Mode', Craig."

"Right, yes. 'Guard' is much more complex, it actually starts to use some of the capability. I've applied all the rules that Jo and Caroline taught me about the Law of Armed Conflict and Targeting. So, the Rules of Engagement are in there and the MLE – sorry, IADS – should test these against what it's legally allowed to do. The surveillance devices and the sights will all be integrated, and the feeds are collated and fused to be as close to a proper analysed intelligence feed as we can get." He looks around significantly. "We should also see learning from mistakes and improvements in efficiency, although the latter may only be noticeable when the log files are analysed. Now, we have the friendly forces inside the base as well, and because the capabilities they have are all in there, we may be asked for help."

Caroline chips in. "There's a terrain blind spot in the vicinity of the base, Craig's hoping it will ask for support from the drone detachment."

David exchanges a glance with Mike. "Well, let's do it then."

Craig selects *Guard* on the screen and presses the mouse button.

The main screen gives the same views that were available in the first experiment. This time, the base view shows that there is a blocky looking turret on the corner tower, it has its own sensor array, a long-barrelled cannon and a smaller coaxial machine gun. The background map view starts to build up, and the display is immediately less random this time. Vehicles travel in groups or individually along roads and tracks. Now most of them are green, indicating neutrality.

Jo points this out. "Why is the AI not using yellow now?"

"It's interpreting our lexicon and the rules in the system, anything not friendly or hostile must be neutral." Craig is pleased with this early indication that the Game Engine has shown improvements of its own accord.

"Can we see some of the targets?"

The synthetic environment operator selects a symbol at random, and a window appears showing a pickup truck with three nondescript humans in it, driving down a track. Another symbol, this time in blue, is examined to show a friendly military patrol on foot, the small figures are all correctly uniformed and armed. After a few minutes of this, Caroline informs them that she is going to run a scenario where a group of trucks will approach the base and carry out an attack.

Craig opens a window and drags it into the bottom left corner of the screen. "This chat room represents the military group chat reporting system that Caroline described to me from ops she's been on."

On the map, a group of green symbols can be seen approaching the base. As the small column gets to the kilometre marker, they start to blink alternately green and red. The chat window shows a message: *Contact. Grid SU18425186. Possible hostile force, section strength. Direction of travel 2750 mils speed 32 kph.* The map symbol changes to a yellow flower-like shape with a cross in the middle and a single spot central above the character.

David rises from his seat. "Look, it's changed it to 'unknown' and aggregated the contacts into a single section strength symbol."

He looks at Craig, who is grinning with delight. "That's what machine learning should do. It's not neutral, but it's also not enemy, so now they're 'unknown'. The data that we've put in there tells it that six to ten people make a section, so the correct image from the library is selected and displayed. It's tried one option and replaced it with a better one."

The troops are now within six hundred metres of the base, so David asks for a camera view. The scene switches to show the camp from a low overhead perspective, looking in the direction of the enemy's approach, the walls and turret in view. Some friendly soldiers are randomly wandering about inside the walls. Rob, from his position next to Craig, looks up and observes that the logfiles that track the AI activity have registered the troops in the camp and classified them as 'friendly'.

The hostile force has now come close enough that they can be seen from the camera perspective and, as they watch, the figures in the cars dismount and weapons appear. The gun on the 'technical' that triggered the classification of the section as possibly hostile is traversed to point at the base.*

---

* Technical is a term applied to a pickup truck or 4WD altered to carry a support weapon like a machine gun. Gun mountings are usually crude but effective. The term originated in Africa.

The group chat window now displays another contact report with the enemy location and the message, *hostile intent, request permission to engage.*

"Pause the simulation."

All eyes turn to Mike who has now risen from his seat.

"I said, pause the simulation."

Caroline obeys and looks back at Mike.

Rob has returned his attention to his analytics screen which has beeped at him. "He's saying that there is a simulation error."

Mike frowns at Rob, there are covert grins from William and Diana, he turns his attention back to Craig. "So... two things. First, why the request to fire?"

Craig looks nonplussed. "Er... there has to be a human in the decision to fire, so I added the requirement to the scripts."

"Right, of course... our earlier discussions. OK, that's fine, but I want you to take it out."

"Take it out?"

"Yes, that's what I said." The reply is impatient. "Look, I know that publicly the government is saying that there will never be a machine making decisions as to who lives and who dies, but then they would, wouldn't they? We're pushing the boundaries here, testing what can and can't be done. This is an experiment, a simulation. We want to know what can be done, someone else can decide if it should. And talking of simulations, how does it know?"

"How does it know what?"

"Don't be obtuse, Craig. How does it know the difference between reality and simulation? You keep telling us it's not intelligent, but that seems to me to be quite a bright observation."

"Sorry. When we gave it direct access to the ISTAR feeds from the SE, it wouldn't accept them because they weren't real."

There are murmurs from around the room at this announcement.

"Look, I designed it to interact with the real world. If it's connected to a cake mixer, it understands that it's a cake mixer, the same for a camera. The signals coming from the simulation programme aren't real-world signals, I had to reach into the simulation and design a communications interface to go between the two pieces of software."

"You hacked the simulator."

All eyes turn to the SE operator.

"Well, not really, when you gave the Game Engine access to the sensor feeds after the first experiment, I just poked around inside to see how it accepted commands and displayed the results. It was just a matter of writing a translation programme with some of the programming language and letting the Game Engine's compiler sort it out."

"Were you a hacker, ever?" David asks.

"Hacker is a word laden with ugly connotations, David, I was more of a digital code explorer."

Diana breaks in. "I must remember that one, I've got some friends who might appreciate vocab like that from the famous Dr Moore!"

"Alright, everyone. A nice distinction, Craig, but I'd like to return us to the point." Mike casts a look laden with irony around the room and returns his gaze to Craig. "How do you mean, 'the real world?'"

"It's a general-purpose device, Mike. Remember, I said that it's not efficient to have software that just does one thing. I wanted something that just needed the tools and the instructions before it got on with the job. So, if the cake mixer needs a whisk, it selects that and makes a meringue."

Mike adopts a mock stern tone. "One more cake metaphor and we shall fall out."

"Couldn't resist it… seriously, it takes real inputs from devices. So sound files that any of your music players use, videos files straight from the camera in the standard format. You could plug your phone into it, and all the functionalities would be at its digital fingertips."

"Hmm. Cake metaphor annoying, phone metaphor I think we'll keep to ourselves."

Craig continues, "If it had been connected to the internet when the problem of recognising the SE file formats came up, then it would have found and implemented the solution on its own."

Mike ponders this for a while as the others study him. This is his project, and his last comment has reinforced the awareness that they are straying towards areas that outsiders are likely to find challenging.

"Let's finish the experiment. Craig, take the human input requirement out so that we can see what happens. That last point is – interesting."

Craig turns to his screens and pulls a library window up, he selects a script file and alters a command line. Returning to the main interface he types *Command Update* in and hits return.

The dialogue box returns a reply of: *Waiting.* Caroline unpauses the SE.

The view of the wall changes instantly and the turret traverses to point at the advancing group.

There are some unconvincing popping sounds from the diminutive speaker below the screen as the machine gun on the pickup fires.

Another contact report appears in the command interface, this time with the words *Hostile Act.* Simultaneously, the gun fires two rounds in quick succession followed by a pause and then two further rounds. The screen view shows the first two shots impact the vehicle, which starts to burn, the second burst explodes in the air near the dismounted figures who drop to the ground. Rather randomly, some of the figures in the base who had mounted the walls and were milling about, fire some shots at the enemy.

They all consider the scene, which has stilled. The armed vehicle burns, the other one is empty, stationary but undamaged.

David breaks the silence. "The system waited until it had been fired on?"

"Yes, Caroline coached me on how Rules of Engagement work, and how they have numbers and appear on a matrix. I activated the one that needs a hostile act before you can shoot." He pulls up a table with rows and columns; each row is numbered and has a tick box on the left with a corresponding description to the right. "So, hostile act is there, and hostile intent is below it. Caroline, have you a sequence suitable for testing intent?"

"Yeah, I've got two more. One's a bit like the last, and another where civilians are attacked."

"OK, Craig, let's take the gloves off."

A tick appears in the box next to the *Hostile Intent* line. A dialogue box appears: *Confirm ROE Change.* Craig clicks, *Yes.*

"You don't need to go into the programme to change that?"

"No, Mike, that's all part of the command menu. I'll put the human control instruction in there later. I'd assumed that would be a set condition."

David clears his throat. "Right, run the scenarios."

Before he does, Caroline adds, "You might be interested to know that we looked into the SE at the last engagement because the shots looked different. When we checked, the Cake Mixer – sorry, IADS – had selected airburst ammunition for the infantry targets. Nice weapon target matching, Craig."

There are murmurs around the room, the Coven share satisfied looks with Craig, Jo raises her eyebrows and nods approvingly.

"C'mon, let's go."

This time, four vehicles cross in front of the base and then abruptly change course to close the walls. The third vehicle in the line has a white disk with a red crescent and star painted on the door. The convoy moves into range. The leading car is another technical, and as it halts a figure appears behind the gun. As with the last run-through, some robed figures dismount and produce weapons.

This time, the contact report on Craig's screen reads, *Hostile Intent*, and before any incoming fire the gun opens up on the convoy. The cannon fires at the technical, destroying it. The turret traverses and the coaxial machine gun fires in short bursts, the infantry fall, and the scene quietens.

"Oh, wow!" Jo is on her feet. "That's fucking brilliant! It's done the collateral damage estimate. The airburst would've harmed the ambulance, so it used the machine gun." She is elated and Craig beams.

Looking at Caroline, he says, "All that homework seems to have sunk in, eh?"

The scenario hasn't stopped, and the camera view shifts to a collection of stalls and tents close to the road that runs down one side of the base. The turret continues to point at the last engagement. Civilians mill about the tents, which are about a hundred metres from the camp wall. It is a market. Some vehicles approach down the road and halt a short distance away from the stalls. Figures get out and approach, drawing weapons. As they do this, the small sensor cupola on top of the turret spins to view this new threat. As the figures start to fire on the marketplace, the main turret traverses and the coaxial machine gun fires in bursts until all but one of the hostile figures is on the ground.

Jo has remained on her feet, she steps off the dais and approaches the screen, staring at the single remaining figure. Turning, she looks back at the faces behind the bank of computer screens.

"Holy shit! The insurgent didn't have a weapon, so he wasn't shot. IADS protected civilians it was its duty to protect, but only the direct threats were engaged. Amazing."

"Thanks, Jo. Look at the chat window, guys."

Faces look towards the corner of the screen. In the chat area is a new message from the IADS: *Hostile force approach from dead ground in vicinity of Grid SU18385093*. Below this is a nine-line message requesting a drone mission to place the area, which is behind a wooded slope, under surveillance.

For Craig, this is the icing on the cake. He looks at Caroline. "I told you."

"I never doubted you for a moment, mate." She approaches the control console and hands Craig a ten pound note with a smile and a handshake.

They both turn their attention to the rest of the group, who are all visibly pleased with the progress they've made. Off to the side the bosses, Mike and David, have their heads together in low conversation. Craig enjoys the moment with his colleagues while keeping a covert eye on them.

They turn back to the team, catching Craig's regard. He feels a momentary frisson of guilt at being caught, which he covers with a tight grin.

"Listen up, everyone." The room falls silent, and Mike continues, "Startling though some of this week's events are, I don't think we could be more pleased. Thanks to Dr Moore, we're at least a year ahead of our own expectations, and I don't think anybody else is close, although with the Israelis in the game one can never be too sure. Let's get the logfiles ready for analysis. Finish that now. It's Friday tomorrow, I don't want to see anyone here – especially you, Craig – you've all earned some downtime." He turns to David. "Colonel Lucas has, as you know, been looking at the next step, which is a real-world trial – David."

"Thanks, Mike. I echo what Dr Sheppard says, guys. Excellent work, and I think we're both reeling from the possibilities. With that in mind, I have to tell you we are under the usual pressure to show our work. I've been getting some real equipment together with a view to a live demonstration up on the range next to the fort. Our engineers will create a corner of a patrol base, and we'll put on a briefing day, show some of the work from the sim, and then do a live demonstration."

"With live ammunition?"

"No, Sam. I'd like to, but the safety constraints wouldn't show the full capabilities. We'll use blank firing weapons with lasers, I've got some of the kits from the trainers on Salisbury Plain earmarked for the trial."

Craig asks, "When exactly do you plan on doing this, David?"

"The sixty-four-dollar question, Craig. We have to speak with DESO, but you can bet they will be champing at the bit. It'll take at least a week for the build, then we'll have to integrate IADS into the hardware, test and rehearse."

"Plugging it in won't take long, but there'll be a good deal of testing as – IADS – gets used to the environment and learns about the equipment. A week might be a good bet for that."

"OK, then some rehearsing and an allowance for snags. Say, another week?" He looks askance at Mike, who frowns.

"You know what they're like, David, one sniff of success and they'll be all over us like a rash. Best we repair to my office and do battle with the redoubtable Helen." Turning his attention back to the others and bringing the conversation to a close, he says, "We'll have news and a plan at Monday's meeting. In the meantime, enjoy the weekend. Spend Monday going through the logs and helping Caroline with her analysis of the scenario results. Thank you all, an outstanding day."

The two of them amble over to the door on their way to Mike's office. As they pause before exiting, David turns back and addresses Craig.

"Could the IADS drive a tank?"

Craig looks up, thoughtful for a bare moment. "Well, yes. The initial design came from self-drive car research. As I recollect, tanks don't seem particularly bothered by roads. I imagine it would be a doddle."

David smiles. "Thank you, Craig."

They leave, and behind them the buzz of conversation grows louder, silenced by the closing of the doors.

IADS EXPLORES THE REAL WORLD

Mike and David climb the stairs to the office level and seat themselves in Mike's office.

"Well, we'd better take stock before we go to DESO, David, if we don't have all our ducks in a row she'll roast us. What's your take? I'm especially interested in your parting shot."

"Oh that, I thought you would be. You know I'm big on developing this technology to replace people – well, drivers are a good bet. As Craig says, tanks don't necessarily need roads, so why not just mark a point on the map and let the vehicle take you there. My chum Robin is CO of the Royal Lancers, they've got the first tranche of the new Ajax recce vehicles. Anyway, the Ajax has a crew of three, so dropping one soldier from each is a thirty per cent saving. If you could do it for all the variants in that family of vehicles, that's five hundred and eighty-nine people you don't need."

"That's some serious recurring cost saving, I agree. Letting an AI drive a vehicle isn't controversial, either, unlike some of what we're getting a taste of downstairs."

"Yes, we're going to have to exercise some care over this demo. Who do you think might attend?"

"Procurers from DESO, probably pretty senior, topped by Helen, of course. Some head office people, Bertie among them.

Your lot will be interested, I'd expect someone from Capability to come up from Andover, wouldn't you?"

"Definitely, but probably no one too senior. Frankly, at this stage, it would be better if we manage the release of what we've got going on here and rely on the written report, which will be drier than gossip from an exciting demonstration. 'Killer robots' is bad enough in the press without starting off some joker in our own ranks."

"What have you got in mind for the demo?"

"Above all, simple. Let's show detection, identification and engagement all nicely within the rules of engagement. Stress it's rules-based machine learning. Keep the AI word out. I'd suggest we parade our genius, they'll love that, but don't let him say much."

Mike nods. "I agree, you do most of the talking with me introducing and summing up. Briefing in the lab first with the demo proving we can do it. Shall we see if we can get Helen?"

David is distracted. "He's got misgivings, you know. We don't want those getting in the way."

"Yes, I've noticed it as well. We'll need to manage that; we don't want conscientious objection derailing our project."

"Hmm, he's fond of Caroline. I think her influence should be brought to bear, we're well used to debating ethics. A bit of counter-propaganda."

"Interesting, he let slip a little of his private life. A girlfriend. I think that might be the source."

"I'll see if we can find out more. Let's get a name and I'll pass it on to some contacts at Thames House. See if there's anything organised about her influence."

"Best keep it from Helen for the moment. Talking of which…"

Mike reaches for the phone on his desk and presses one of the speed dial buttons. He gets a PA and asks if Ms Sherwood could call him back when she has a moment. They continue their conversation for a few minutes, talking about the equipment David has got and what more he needs. It doesn't take Helen long to get back to them, and Mike puts the call on the phone's speaker.

Helen's cool and measured voice is hopeful. "Good afternoon, Mike, I trust this call brings me some news of encouraging progress?"

"It does indeed, Helen, we've just completed the second synthetic test programme. David's here with me, and we both agree we can go for a live demonstration."

"Good, that's very good. Well done, both of you. How is our genius settling in?"

Mike and David share a look. "Oh, he's as cerebral as you might expect…"

"Quite the businessman as well, I hear."

"Ah yes, I'm sorry about that. I had to shut that idiot from contracts up. Fortunately, the lawyer came equipped with some common sense."

"I quite understand. A trip into the contracts branch is to wade in the shallow end of the corporate gene pool. I really don't know where they get them. You did well, Michael, be in no doubt about that, it's worth the money just for the huge savings in the programme duration. Besides, there's a lot to play for in the coming months, we will get our pound of flesh from Dr Moore, worry not. So, when can I see our new toy?"

"We think four weeks should give us enough time to fully prepare."

There is a moment's silence at the other end. "Hmmm, I was hoping that you might manage something rather sooner." They hear paper being shuffled. "Yes, I thought so. It needs to be sooner, there are other factors in play here, that may confer a significant advantage to some other programmes. I'd like to see it by the middle of your fourth week. Where are we now… yes, eighth or ninth, I think. Can you manage that, Colonel Lucas?"

David is startled to suddenly be in the firing line and looks at Mike with an interrogative shrug. Mike nods furiously.

"Well, yes, it'll be tight but… yes. I think the IADS is the least of our problems, so far, it's dramatically exceeded our expectations. We'll just have to accelerate the engineering to give time for testing." David tails off, realising that he's babbling.

Mike jumps in to act as his top cover. "Let's go for the ninth then, usual format. I take it you'll let us know who's attending from head office and DESO?"

"Certainly, the ninth it is. Very satisfactory – make it so, gentlemen."

The line clicks into silence, and they stare introspectively at the phone for a few moments before looking up.

David breaks the silence. "I always feel slightly violated after a conversation with her."

They both laugh.

"I think satisfactory is a good word for the day though, David, let us do as we are bid."

TENSION IN WIMBLEDON

Craig arrives at his modest terrace in Wimbledon. The evening isn't quite dark but lights show at the windows. He opens the door and goes in to witness Sophie looking slightly dishevelled, peering at a recipe book and stirring a pan. She looks at him in surprise.

"Home early, sweetie? You haven't been fired, have you?"

"Most amusing, and no. We did well and were rewarded with a short day. Enjoy the weekend was the instruction."

"The killer robot finished, is it? What's it doing in its time off, terrorising Sevenoaks?"

Craig laughs, not noticing the flush of annoyance on her face. He ignores the jibe and moves to perch on one of the kitchen stools.

"You're very industrious yourself. What are you cooking?"

"Pasta computara."

"Is that a thing?"

"It's a dish for nerds with Asperger's."

Craig flashes. "You really understand nothing."

"Oh, so what is it you do? You never say anything to me. In fact, catching sight of you is a rare event. The only thing less frequent is a conversation; your head's always in your mechanical girlfriend."

"He. He's called Heimdall, and he's a machine that can control other machines. He can do it faster and make better decisions than humans, who let their emotions cloud their judgement. In any case, how would you know what I'm doing? Your face is never out of your phone."

Sophie's eyes narrow. "That's more than you've said in weeks. What happened to 'I can't talk about it'? Faster and better is 'he', this mechanical killer?"

Craig is flushed, aware he's said too much. "It guards, watches, things, I never said it would kill anyone."

"Liar! I've looked at what happens at this 'Fort', you're nothing but a paid killer like all those so-called scientists."

"So what are you, parasite? Happy to use me as a meal ticket."

They face each other, Sophie's eyes smouldering with rage, Craig unsettled by her fury, a frisson of fear knotting his stomach. The rest of the weekend passes in a series of tense silences, attempted conversations, and desultory meals. All the while, Craig wondering how to get her out of his life.

PREPARING FOR BATTLE

Craig walks into the lab and apologises to the team for being late. Friendly nods and commiserations on his commute greet this. After the bleak weekend he's just had, the welcome comes like a much needed warm embrace. He opts for brisk professional as cover and takes his place, asking how the analysis of the logs is going.

"Will and I were in early, and we've got some of the files showing the ROE related activity on hard copy for Jo. She was keen to understand how it worked as she'll have to write that bit of the report."

At the sound of her name, a curly head is raised and smiles, rising to join them at the console.

"The boys have annotated the techy stuff, but I'm not sure how the tables of ROE and the phrases from Law of Armed Conflict are… what was the word, Will?"

"Parsed"

"Yes, that was it. It's to do with analysing and making into logic, isn't it?"

"That's exactly right, Jo, the trick is to use words and phrases that are unambiguous. As simple as one and zero, yes or no. If IADS were cognisant in the human sense, it would regard what it's being asked to do here as being absurdly simple and boring."

"Yellow card stuff." All eyes turn to Caroline. "Soldiers have to have simple drills. Not much comes with more stress than combat. It's why the inside-my-head voice says 'fuck off!' when a civvy says, they're stressed at work."

"Would that be the one that says, 'Caroline, go out, cleanse the streets' late at night?" Rob has risen from his seat and intones this in a sepulchral voice, arms out zombie style.

"I merely suggest that cold, tired and encountering the unique apprehension associated with lead wasps buzzing around your head beats complaining that the watercooler is u/s, Robert."

Craig sits back with a complacent smile as he contemplates the easy camaraderie of which he is now a part.

He imitates Mike and brings them back to the subject. "If we might continue, you mentioned a yellow card, Caroline?"

"Years ago, soldiers carried a yellow card which had the rules allowing them to use lethal force. It's existed in other forms since; I think it's white now. Whatever. It says in simple, plain English what the circumstances are for you to open fire. It's meant to be as practical and as simple as possible, so even the least bright individual can understand, by which I mean the infantry, of course." She looks at William, who she knows is a reserve soldier in the infantry. He, well used to her attempts to bait him, refuses to bite. Gathering herself, she continues, becoming more thoughtful and abstracted, thinking out loud.

"Nearly all our doctrine, when it comes down to it, is applied as simple rules-based stuff. Either you can or you can't do something, yes or no, one or zero." She looks at Craig without really seeing him. "If we reduce things to what's lawful, tabulate it with tick boxes for execution, it all comes down to a few pages."

As she returns from abstraction to the reality of the lab, Jo observes, "But look how fast it did it, and we've got to remember that there are shades of grey when we do humanitarian stuff."

"Yeah, but most of that is policy or orders or guidance, this is grunt stuff. Speed, though, that's where you're right. OODA loop."

"Ooh da what?" Craig is nonplussed and shakes himself from the fascinated torpor induced by Caroline's monologue.

She laughs. "OODA loop, another acronym. The long version is the 'Decision Action Cycle'. You know how we like our circular diagrams, remember we showed you the intelligence cycle? Imagine that circle with 'Observe' at the top coming round to 'Orientate', then 'Decide' and lastly, 'Act'. And so it goes round and round: OODA. It comes from the Vietnam War, where they were training pilots in dogfighting and they realised that if you could do all of those things faster than the other guy, you were bound to win."

Craig nods. "Oh, I get it. I always say that games aren't smart, they just see everything and react quicker."

"Exactly, think of the lines between the words." She goes to the whiteboard and draws what she has just described. "As time, if you shorten them like this... the circle is smaller, and you always beat the bigger circle, the slower guy."

"But the decision and the action need to be correct, or you fuck up."

"Yes, that's true, William. Are you sure you're in the infantry?"

From behind his screen, a hand with a middle finger extended rises.

"So, what we've got to do is make sure that what is observed and decided in the orientation creates the conditions for the right decision and action."

"A set of conditions."

"How do you mean, Craig?" Jo asks.

"In my terms, a set of conditions is met, and an outcome is a result. We need to make the conditions as unambiguous as possible so that the outcome isn't an error. Unexpected second and third-order outcomes are what cause problems. Programmes that play Chess or Go select an opening gambit and then, in response, work out all the moves to the end state. The problem is, you end up with a sort of exponential explosion. Chess has more than ten to the power of over a hundred possible games, Go is even bigger. Think of branches of a tree dividing and dividing. It takes massive computational power to do all this. The latest and best computers doing this can intelligently 'prune' unlikely branches as the game progresses. Luckily for us, our tree has fewer branches, and this boy is good at pruning and learns as it goes along, so it doesn't prune anything twice." He pats the block that is the brain of IADS. "The less tree we have to prune, the better, we don't need as much computing power, and the outcome arrives quickly."

"But you want it to teach itself things…?" Diana swivels her chair to look at Craig. "Give it the rules and the means and let it work out for itself how to do it."

"That's the idea, yes, but within the limitations of the programming. It'll need constant monitoring. Remember, 'a set of conditions is met to create an outcome' – how long before those outcomes are trusted to always be correct? Even I can't be completely sure he won't come up with something completely unexpected."

"We call it 'Mission Command', Craig."

Heads turn to regard Caroline, who has drawn near the programming group.

"A commander is given something to do, a mission. You are then left to get on to do it with as few constraints imposed as possible. Usually time and resources, 'do it by then' and 'you've only got these troops'. I'm not told how to do something. I'm trusted to be able to do it. It's supposed to stop micro-management so that senior people get on with the tasks appropriate to them. It doesn't always work, though. Trust is pretty fundamental."

"He doesn't think like you though, Caroline."

Behind him, there are chuckles, and Craig turns. "What?"

"There you go again, Craig." Diana's eyes are bright with amusement. "Calling him 'he'!"

Caroline makes her own observation. "Now I come to think of it, I've always thought of it as being masculine for some reason."

"Perhaps it's because he only offers solutions to problems and isn't interested in discussing them." This gets Will a mock furious glare from the three women. "Just sayin'..." He hides behind his screen.

"Careful, Will, white and male, you're an endangered species. We'll have to find you a hashtag!"

"Returning to the subject." Caroline's amusement is plain as she retakes control. "I was saying that trust is a fundamental part of how we exercise command. Will humans ever really trust machine intelligence to work in their interests? I mean, we all know that airliners are pretty much flown by the autopilot already, but how many of us would go up the stairway if we were told that there was only a computer in the cockpit?"

"Well, me... obviously, especially if it were mine."

They smile benignly at Craig as he continues.

"Like I said, IADS doesn't think like a human, and for what we are doing here I don't think we would want that. If Caroline is told to attack something, she'll be more creative and intuitive about it, drawing on her experience."

"That's true and the more experience you have, especially if you're consistently successful, the more you're trusted."

"Well, one thing we do have going for us is that is that our system learns from experience. That tree idea I spoke about earlier, well, as the programme gains more experience in the task it's given, then the branches of the tree are pruned, so to speak. It won't bother going down paths that aren't referenced to the problem and will go more quickly to solutions that have previously worked."

"So, if we ran the scenarios from last week again, there might be changes?"

"Details, yes, outcomes, probably not."

"Why don't we try it?" They look at Diana. "It would be a good addition to the report."

There is general agreement, and Caroline strides over to the SE console.

"Do we need the operator?"

"No, he's only really here if we have technical problems and to try and make a point. Op Analysis think they own it, they already think Craig wants to make improvements! I'll use my login."

It doesn't take long for the system to come online and for them to run the experiment again for the last two incidents. As Craig predicted, there are changes. As soon as IADS is instructed to guard the camp, it asks for a drone mission to be flown over the area of dead ground previously identified. Caroline simulates the flight of the drone that the patrol base has on call and the area that had, the week before, been blank has some targets displayed, significantly, the line of vehicles that will move to attack the marketplace in due course. There is some discussion when, this time, the figures attacking the market are engaged before they open fire and Craig asks Jo if this exceeded the ROE. He brings up the matrix from within the programme, and Jo points out that the carriage of arms could be a trigger for opening fire depending on context, as it falls under hostile intent.

"For example, if we saw a group of people digging a hole in the road and could positively identify them as planting an IED, we can attack them."

"IED? There go those abbreviations again!"

"Sorry, Craig, I thought that was one everybody knew. Improvised Explosive Device, a homemade mine."

"We haven't got into any of that type of targeting yet, if we ever do. That's the one that will cause the most controversy." Caroline has moved to stand with Jo and looks at the ROE displayed on the wall. "This is the use of lethal force in self-defence supplemented by ROE that gives more freedom of action, if we had to wait until we were shot at or blown up every time, then we have limited our initiative and will take more casualties. We can get our retribution in first that way." She takes the edge off her last comment with a smile. "Keep in mind ROE can act as a deterrent; like if your enemy knows that you'll shoot them if they carry a weapon. It doesn't always work, mind, if your enemy culturally wears long robes, they just hide their AKs underneath them."

"I wondered why those guns just suddenly appeared in the sim."

Caroline looks thoughtfully at the screen, which has stilled. "OK, tell me why that happened differently this time, in simple English, please."

"Well, we didn't change the scenario, so he had experience from the last time to draw on. The drone request happened earlier because the dead ground appeared at the start of the run, and the connection was made with the last one." Craig's voice has slowed, and he has become abstracted. "That's simple enough, but why didn't the turret fire at the guys attacking the market before they opened fire the first time around? The ROE was the same."

They all look at the list of ROE. After a pause, Caroline looks at Jo.

"I don't see anything I wouldn't recognise."

"I used the standard wording. The syntax isn't challenging, *may use lethal force in defence of persons that it is your duty to protect*, and the usual hostile intent wording."

"Yeah but look at the words in the definitions bit – *Evidence*. You've got to have evidence. A human will see a bunch of bad guys that look like bad guys and then see that they're armed and then look at the context of the situation. I'd say that's intuitive, and IADS doesn't have intuition." Rob looks back at his screen and starts to search the logfiles from the two runs, placing the script files next to each other on the screen.

Jo nods thoughtfully. "He's right, we would normally specify that carriage of a weapon constituted hostile intent, but because it's ambiguous I didn't do it here."

There is an exclamation from Rob. "Got it, look. The first time around, the programme references the approach to the market as *threat*, and you can see the lines corresponding to the surveillance turret moving in the SE feed and the programme making that assessment, then moving the main turret into the aim. The weapons appear, and there is no change. When they fire it's an incontrovertible hostile act, so they're fired on. Look at the right-hand display, it's the same until the weapons come up into the aim. This time it registers as hostile intent, and the system opens fire. He's learned that a positively identified weapon in the aim is a precursor to firing based on evidence from previous experience."

Craig's Coven all look as happy as puppies as they point out various items on the screens to Craig, who is looking pleased but thoughtful.

Caroline is likewise thoughtful, as she regards Craig. On first meeting she'd been rather cool, the background information showed little of his personal life and a lot about his shining intellect, it was tempting to write him off as a useful uber-nerd. During the past weeks, she has seen ample evidence of his brilliance but also warmth and humour. He's a slender man, the word lithe is what actually springs to her mind, attractive but reserved enough to hint at a brittleness or vulnerability. She finds herself thinking back to the merest glimpse into his personal life that they got during his only angry outburst. Whoever she is, she must be quite a bitch. She finds herself wondering what he might be like in bed, and that startling thought returns her to the matter in hand.

"This is good, we need to get a draft report in hand for Mike and David. These two extra runs make for some more depth. Craig, you do a techie synopsis while Rob and Will get on with consolidating the records. Jo and I will get the rest done. The adults won't need a finished product, but they'll want enough to plan out what goes to head office and DESO. Di, you need to start getting the old intranet servers ready."

The meeting with Mike and David goes well. They are delighted with the initiative shown in re-running the two scenarios. They are further buoyed up by the skeleton of a report to go up the chain of command.

Diana outlines her progress with the intranet. "The infrastructure is creaky, but that's only to be expected and shouldn't affect us. The security people don't need high performance for managing their systems. The legacy software from Dabinett is still there, and usable, the security stuff and the fence cameras are plumbed into it, but there are no issues I can see with piggybacking our equipment on the range. There are network connections up at the fort and here, so we can test and record from the lab before we move up for the demo."

Grunts of satisfaction and approval greet this news.

Craig is frowning and says, "I never did ask what Dabinett was, I assume it's integration software? What happened to it, you mentioned funding?"

There are laughs and rueful smiles from the others. David takes up the story.

"Dabinett was all about networking ISTAR feeds into a system that would provide integrated information across the Battlespace. Look for information on a bridge, say, and you could get a picture in real-time and then what it looked like days ago. All different kinds of sensors would be available."

"So, why the amusement?"

"Ah, yes! The funding got 'redirected', well, most of it. The rumour was that the Royal Air Force suddenly realised that the Army was stealing a march on them in the world of drones, and they might lose an ascendancy in the air, so they looked for a way to catch up. Head of our air force met the head of the US Air Force, and they did a 'drug deal'. The RAF got a couple of Predator drones and a ground station, which they could use from California. Long story short is that we now have 'Reaper' – our name for Predator – a whole squadron of it. Like a well-known lager, it's reassuringly expensive."

"That's a true story, Caroline?"

"Well, I wouldn't want to be quoted. I mean, it sounds pretty unlikely in a modern and transparent democracy, doesn't it?" Then, more thoughtfully she says, "Of course, the irony of Colonel David's story is that Reaper was probably the right answer all along, it's been a massive success on operations."

"Welcome to the world of Defence Procurement, Craig." Mike still smiles as he brings the meeting to order.

"Procurement is DESO?"

"Oh, yes."

"As in, Helen Sherwood?"

"Yes."

"Ah."

"Ah indeed, Craig, ah indeed!"

They return to the present and discussion turns back to report writing and the impending demonstration. Mike wants to get the report out in the week before they demonstrate, as 'homework' for the attendees. It's obvious that he wants to manage the impact of their work so as not to induce any political nervousness at the MOD. He instructs Caroline to make it 'Eyes A'. Craig's ears prick up as he knows this means only a British readership and wonders why. He's saved the risk of being nosey when Caroline frowns.

"Can I ask why? I would have thought we'd be keen to involve the US."

"I've been wondering why Helen was specific on the date myself, Caroline, so I did a bit of digging and found out that Lockheed Martin is visiting DESO that week. Some of my colleagues there have been complaining for a while that projects are being held up by slow export licences for US tech. I bet we're going to find ourselves used as leverage." He looks at Craig. "We reckoned we were pretty much neck and neck in the race for real autonomy and not just some overblown industry demonstrator. Then you come along, and we've suddenly lapped everyone."

Craig sits brimming with satisfaction as they go around the table, raising points. Finally, Mike sums up and dismisses them.

David announces that he and Caroline are going to do a recce of the range in the morning.

Craig looks up. "Can I come?"

He is treated to a pair of warm smiles.

"Sure, it'll be cold, and the range is rough. Be early!"

THERE REALLY IS A FORT
AT FORT HALSTEAD

Mid-September is chilly, but for a change, it's not raining. Craig appears the next morning and is treated to some clothing-related banter along the lines of 'nice anorak' and 'are those baseball boots?'. The three of them walk up the hill to where the site levels out. As they wander along making small talk, Craig is introspective. He looks covertly at the two military officers, noting the easy informality that they have despite the difference in rank. Camaraderie of this nature is not something that has featured prominently in his life, and he finds that he is enjoying this unexpected excursion into modern warfare. He ponders on the subject and realises that he hasn't felt this included for a very long time.

Craig hasn't been to this part of the site before and is intrigued when they come upon a junction that leads to a scruffy brick bridge crossing a moat to an imposing gateway. The portal is open and reveals a tunnel through which they walk to stand in a large courtyard surrounded by massive walls that are penetrated by storerooms. There are one or two brick buildings in the space that appear to house offices. Craig knows this is the oldest part of the site. The brick and stone block construction is softened and stained with age. It is quiet at this time of the day, not many people work here anyway. But to Craig, the atmosphere is oppressive and slightly mournful, as if the structure is in some way disappointed by the neglect it is suffering.

David breaks the spell. "Marvellous isn't it, Craig?"

He startles Craig when he puts a friendly arm around his shoulders and gestures expansively at the walls.

"They knew how to do engineering in those days. What I could tell you about the mysteries of ravelins, bastions, casemates and counterscarps."

Behind him, there is a derisive snort. "God spare us, Craig, he's channelling his inner sapper."

"All gunners are philistines, my boy, don't listen to her." He lets go of Craig and whirls on Caroline in mock outrage. "Your trouble is, you only know how to blow things up."

"Oh really, Colonel? How about the obstacle crossing in Canada?" She turns to Craig. "There I am with my team covering this bank of sand – a berm, we call it – while the sappers, with their boy's toys, dug a hole in it. The idea is that they then fill the hole with explosives, blow it up and we all drive through to victory. Only thing is, the major in charge of engineers, one 'Mad Dave' Lucas, had found a lot of old explosives they needed to get rid of. So, he topped up the already excessive charge with that. Twenty tons of it. We'd been moved back to a 'safe' distance, further than usual, and we were dug in. Well, nothing really prepares you for that kind of explosion."

"Except, of course, the eager anticipation for the educational value of exposure to a unique detonation event."

"Detonation event! Craig, it was only just getting light, it was like the end of the world. Half the battlegroup couldn't see or hear for about half an hour, which was lucky really. The hole went downwards as well as sideways, so he had to fill it in before we could get across."

The two regard each other with broad grins, and Craig is suddenly a spectator. Not for the first time he is aware of just how much he likes these people and the world into which he has fallen. They turn to him, noting his amusement.

"C'mon, let's go up onto the parapet and look at the range."

They follow David up a stairway, and he leads them into a bastion at the corner of the main structure. Looking towards the east, Craig sees an area of rough ground pockmarked with pits and studded with bushes. David points out that most of the pits are actually craters from the range's principal use as an explosive testing area.

"What sort of testing?"

"All kinds, new ideas in explosives technology as well as some forensic testing to reproduce the effects of IEDs. Not so much now, what with the drawdown of the site. In the past, the days were punctuated by warnings over the tannoy followed by loud bangs." He adopts a faraway look and is rewarded with a derisive snort from Caroline.

"Shall we continue, Colonel, before you get too whimsical?"

He laughs. "OK, you can see the layout, we've got about a 200-metre square to play with, although there's a bit more depth if we need it as an approach. I thought we'd put them up here to watch and layout our kit and a control room down there at the foot of the wall."

"What did you have in mind for a control room?"

"There's a portacabin we can move up here for you and the team."

"Power and data?"

"That concrete hut on the left has both, we can run cables to the demo area. Your kit can be moved up a couple of days beforehand."

"I wasn't going to use anything from the lab except IADS."

"How will you manage that?"

"A laptop, very powerful, but it's quite easy. We just plug IADS in and connect the laptop to the intranet we're using, and it can access the servers in the lab. Saves us a lot of trouble."

Caroline nods with satisfaction. "It'll create an excellent impression if we don't have loads of hardware on display."

"I agree, nice one, Craig. My only remaining worry is getting a workable turret going."

"Why's that? I thought you had a real one?"

"I got my ambitions mixed up with my capabilities, my friend. The most modern one is on the Ajax, and I thought we might get a pre-production one without armour, but that proved to be far too difficult. There are other turrets around from old or obsolete vehicles, but when I suggested setting one up the engineers batted it into the 'too difficult' field. Getting them to traverse on a mock-up would be time-consuming and expensive. The turret trainer I looked at was too unwieldy."

"Why not use the real thing?"

"What, an actual armoured vehicle? That would mean all kinds of interface changes. We'd have to plumb IADS in electrically, I don't think that would be easy, or popular. Also, I don't think we've got enough time."

"The only electrical interface would be the bits that move the turret around, we'd just need to put a camera in front of the displays. Look, I keep telling you that IADS is a general purpose thing, a simple brain. It can already interpret images, it just needs a compatible camera. Remember, I had to teach it how to understand the signals coming out of the AI because they were different. Plug a compatible camera in, and you can put it in front of any space or any screen, you just need to tell it what it's seeing and correct any mistakes it makes in the interpretation of an image. It learns!"

David looks at Craig hard for a few moments and turns to stare thoughtfully out over the range. Caroline is similarly thoughtful.

Craig looks at them in turn and continues, "I looked at all that Ajax tank stuff we had in the lab and the controls are thumb controllers and buttons on joysticks. IADS already knows about them, they're just on-off buttons and potentiometers." He tails off as they both turn back to look at him.

Caroline breaks the silence. "I hadn't thought of Ajax, Colonel, I thought we might find an old sabre or something, imagine if we got hold of the latest piece of kit and showed it being controlled by an AI."

"I'm trying to imagine it, Caroline, the ramifications are immense, and I'm not sure if we'd impress them or terrify them. Second and third-order consequences, Major Atkins, second and third-order consequences."

"You've been in touch with Colonel Robin, haven't you? The prototypes are on Salisbury Plain being tested, I bet the White Witch could get hold of one."

David laughs at the nickname. "Helen Sherwood, yes, if anyone can it will be her. Hmm. I'll have a talk to Robin, he might be interested, although I'm not sure that reducing his regiment by two thirds will be appealing. Imagine only having one crewman in a tank. If it could be done for Ajax, it could be done for Challenger. Imagine that cat among the pigeons, Caroline." David looks at Craig, suddenly very serious. "You're sure you can do it, Craig? Our reputation is on the line if it doesn't work. Helen won't forgive us if we don't produce the goods."

"I don't see why not. So long as the interface to the left, right, up and down are available, it's just a matter of clamping a camera somewhere it can see the screen. Keep it simple and just use the one screen that shows the gunsight. Can it fire the same laser to simulate the gun?"

"Armoured vehicles have the same sort of system that clamps onto the barrel, that should be easy enough."

"This is really important for you two, isn't it?"

"Oh, you've noticed. Well, it certainly is for me, Craig. For us, promotion is pay and status. I'm at the top end of the lieutenant colonel timeframe for promotion to full Colonel, so I've only got one or two shots at it. If we create something revolutionary here,

I get a leg up, I'm willing to take some risk for that. Mike, as well, he'd like to go into Porton Down or somewhere else a grade up. It'll do Caroline a favour as well."

"I'm waiting to be a battery commander, Craig. I've had the posting, but the date I report is months away, so I got a six-month attachment to fill in time. Something at the cutting edge like this will give me a boost before I do the next job."

"A battery commander?"

"Sorry, infantry, tanks and engineer units are divided into companies and squadrons. Remember the presentation? Well, the artillery has batteries, the same thing. I'm going to Wiltshire to take over a rocket battery in two six regiment, it's a precision strike regiment and fires guided rockets."

David frowns at her words and asks, "Why did you go for that, Caroline? Your career is pretty stellar, why not one of the gun regiments? Your lot are still pretty snobby about guns being the be-all and end-all."

"I've got a mate in PJHQ, Colonel, he reckons there'll be something going down in the Middle East before long. My bet is precision strike will be there before guns, and I want an op tour."

"Will you remember me when you're chief of the general staff?"

"I might need a staff car driver!"

There is more good-natured, if rather salty, banter at this reply.

"You were manna from heaven when you walked through our door, Craig. We might take the piss a bit, but be in no doubt what you do here isn't just important to the future of the Military."

The compliment is sobering. Craig returns them to the subject in hand with some technical questions, before discussing the work needed on the range to prepare and how the demonstration might shape up. Caroline suggests they use some of the people from the other departments or some of the off-duty security detachment to role-play the enemy in scenarios along the lines they have used in the lab. The three end up with a roadmap towards the demonstration. By now, David is convinced that if the IADS can be attached to an Ajax, the impact will be worth the trouble. All he has to do is get hold of one. This means a call to an old friend.

CAVALRY MANOEUVRES

In his office, David places a call to the Commanding Officer of the Royal Lancers in Catterick. Robin Matheson is thirty-seven, somewhat younger than David. They have served together several times and are good friends after the military fashion: long periods where neither sees or hears from the other, yet when thrown together by the exigencies of the service, it is as if there has been no intervening time. David is thus confident that something can be arranged.

The languid drawl is pure home counties when it comes on the line. "My dear chap, this is a pleasant surprise. What can I do for you?"

"Robin, it's been too long. How's command?"

"Well, as train sets go, pretty good, and it's going to get a lot more fun shortly. You, of course, know what we're getting."

"I do indeed. It's about those new toys I'm ringing. I don't suppose you have a spare, do you?"

There is a chuckle at the other end of the line. "Now, pray tell, what would SO1 Novel Warfare at DSTL be wanting with a prototype Ajax?"*

---

* In the bureaucracy of the military the executives, called staff officers, are graded with numbers and initials (naturally!). Staff officers go from three to one depending on rank. David is a lieutenant colonel, so he is an SO1. A major would be an SO2, and captain, an SO3.

"We're running an experiment and want to try something. Look, you've got some of them doing trials on Salisbury Plain, haven't you? I don't suppose we could have a face-to-face? I could speak more freely about the details and find out what I'd need to do. I can come up to Catterick or, if you're going to be on the Plain, I could meet you there."

"Actually, I'm going down to visit A Squadron tomorrow. They've got nine of them doing troop trials. You could meet me there the day after, and we can discuss. It'll be great to catch up."

"That's excellent, Robin. Thank you so much. You won't regret it."

"No problem, old chum. Best let DESO know you're coming and a chat to Capability in Army HQ might be wise. See you day after tomorrow. I'll be at Harman Lines, my Adjutant will email details, I'm all agog!"

Two days later, on a drizzly October morning, David parks his car on a hill overlooking the Military camp at Warminster. He looks across to the nondescript set of buildings and garages in front of him. To the left is a washdown for vehicles, where two tanks are being sprayed with water to remove the beige mud of the Salisbury Plain Training Area. The Army trains on thirty-nine thousand acres of chalk downland studded with woodland and scrub. David is standing on the very north-western edge. A young captain intercepts him as he walks over to the gate and, with a salute and a handshake, introduces himself as Harry Greyland, Robin's Adjutant. He guides David over to an oversized garage. Two Ajax reconnaissance vehicles sit with hatches and engine covers open. Several men and women in grimy green coveralls peer into these various apertures and hand each other tools. Robin is standing in front of them and beams with obvious pleasure when he sees David.

"My dear chap, welcome, welcome. Thank you, Harry, I'll look after the Colonel from here, I'll give you a shout when we want to go up onto the range and visit the trial. I've already

67

warned A Squadron." He turns to David and gestures to the two vehicles. "Apologies for these two sorry specimens, the usual teething troubles you get in the lead up to delivery. So, what's this mysterious visit in aid of then?"

"Are you aware of what I'm doing, Robin? Heard of Project Heimdall at all?" David guides Robin out of earshot of the group working on the armour.

"Not a thing, old chap, we're all clueless out here in the Field Army, and I've been much too excited with my new toys."

"Well, this is pretty new and very sensitive." David goes on to briefly outline Project Heimdall and its aims.

"You were always one for the technical stuff, David. So, how does that lead you here?"

"Well, a month or two ago, we recruited a genius in software development to see if the project could be given a shove in the right direction. He dropped a bombshell when we described what we wanted: it turns out he'd already done it. We're suddenly years ahead and have spent a couple of weeks testing this brain he's developed in our OA simulator. Frankly, it's scarily effective."

Robin looks back at the two vehicles, frowning. He returns his attention to David. "I have a nasty feeling I know where this is going."

"Hear me out, Robin. DESO is all over us to demonstrate the capability. We were struggling to think of a way to put together a dummy position with a turret in time. My uber-nerd, just out of the blue said, 'why not use a real one?'. Long and the short is, I'm after one of these fitted with a weapon effects simulator to sit on the range at the Fort, connected to our system."

"Whoa! That's a lot to process. Are you saying you've got a machine that can do all the jobs in one of these?"

"Not quite, Robin. But, to be honest, I shudder to think what the genie in Dr Moore's bottle might be able to do in the future. What it's done thus far is carry out surveillance and operate a turret that engaged targets that fired on its patrol base. It also understands ROE, so it shoots the right ones. So far, all inside a simulator."

They both regard the tableau before them, and Robin lets out a loud and explosive breath. "I've heard the debates about these things and the potential of things like self-drive cars, David, but I never thought I'd be in the midst of it all. I can't believe it's that simple. I mean, all those inputs and then the operation of turret and weapons."

"I agree, if we wanted full functionality it would be a lengthy process of integration, but we only need to traverse and elevate the weapon mount and a view through the sight. Craig – that's Doc Moore, our genius – just said, 'Give it eyes and a pair of hands and it'll do the rest', when I last spoke to him. He doesn't even need to connect his machine to the sight, he'll clamp a camera to the seat and point it at the screen, wire it into the thumb controls and trigger and that's it."

"Eyes and a pair of hands – what the fuck is it, the Terminator? Presumably it'll be back!"

David doesn't join in the laugh. "Keep it down a bit, for fuck's sake, Robin. Our biggest fear is if this breaks out and we get red top hysteria over killer robots."

Robin is chastened, and David defuses the moment with a hand on his arm. They turn away from the people working.

"I'm starting to realise I need to be careful what I say to Doc Moore, Robin, a throwaway comment gets him thinking. I asked if the system – it's called IADS, by the way, Integrated Autonomous Defence System – anyway, I asked if it could drive a tank. Yesterday, he said he'd been thinking about what I'd said and had looked at the 'problem I'd set', so he tells me that not only could the IADS drive an Ajax, but it could also manage the gunner's job as well. The guy has almost total recall, and he started quoting from the Army field manual on armoured tactics and chapter and verse on the Ajax family of vehicles. He thinks you only need a commander – touch the screen and it'll drive to where you want it to go, analyse an area within surveillance arcs and display targets in order of priority. All the soldier has to do is give permission for the weapon to fire."

The two of them share a moment of silent introspection as they think through the implications.

Robin breaks the silence. "It'd solve my recruiting problems in one, completely fuck up the soldier progression, though."

"Yes, you can't just open a can of corporals and sergeants. You're short, are you?"

"Everyone's short, David. Infantry worst of all, but I'm fifteen per cent under-recruited. What you're suggesting would solve that at a stroke, a hundred and eight crew down to thirty-six."

"Just think what the bean counters would say, Robin, a saving of seventy-two salaries, pensions, and leave days, not to mention health and welfare."

"Oh, brave new world that has such people in it, eh David."

"So, can I have a tank, Robin?"

"It's not a tank you bloody heretic, it's a scout vehicle."

"A forty ton scout vehicle! Your current recce cars weigh eight."

Heads rise from the intense scrutiny of vehicle innards and regard the two senior officers giggling in the corner. Robin and David return looks of mock innocence, and the vehicle mechanics raise their eyes and grin at each other, before returning to their labours.

"I'd give you that one on the left in a trice, David, it isn't going anywhere for the foreseeable. Trouble is, it belongs to the contractor at the moment. The project team at DESO could probably prize it out of here, but it's beyond my gift."

"I think that may not be a problem then, I have a scary director there who tends to get what she wants."

"Not Ms Sherwood? Very slim, dirty blonde?"

"By dirty, I take it you mean elegant ash blonde? Be careful, she could be listening! You know her then?"

70

"Oh yes, she's visited – very interested in this project. A rather forthright woman of great presence, was our assessment. I think you're right. It would be a very brave contractor who dared naysay her. I'll assume that you'll get clearance and prep it for travel."

David spends the rest of the morning out on the range with an Ajax troop, relishing the company of soldiers in the field. Although he's impressed with Ajax, there are still many problems and missing capabilities in this much-lauded armoured vehicle. The cavalry soldiers are philosophical about this inevitable feature of a new system. The Ajax he has been shown is commanded by a newly promoted sergeant called Tate. Her crew refer to her as 'Maz'. They are men, she is one of a new breed, women in the so-called 'teeth arms', the infantry and armour. Leaning back against the tank's metal and ceramic armoured skirt, he eyes Sergeant Tate's compact form speculatively. She has a field rather than track athlete's build. He estimates her at about five-nine tall, and thirty. Watching her with her crew, he sees the same scene that has been a familiar part of his twenty-two-year career with the heavy metal of armoured warfare: a bunch of youngsters going about the daily business of soldiering, hard and professional but not taking it too seriously. They are outwardly unaffected by her gender. Maz rises and catches his regard, her open face changing to display the hint of a frown as she approaches him with a steaming mug.

Handing the coffee to him, she says, "It's the girl thing, isn't it, sir?"

"Partly Sarn't Tate, do you find it tiresome?"

"Repetitive, sir. I wonder when we're going to get over it. I need to get on with my career and stop telling people what it's like breaking down the last barrier to 'women in the frontline'. Daft really, I came from the gunners into the cavalry and my last tour in Afghan couldn't have been more frontline… you said partly, sir."

"You just answered that bit, I was wondering how the cavalry got a female sergeant so quickly. You were in a fire support team?"

"FST Bombardier. Supported this regiment, so I was used to armour and the blokes, it made the transition a bit easier. It turns out that it also helps to have a woman in the sarnts' mess. There are six female lance corporals and troopers, so I keep an eye on them."

"I would've thought that the mess would be the place where you might find it a bit difficult. In my experience, it's way more conservative than the officers' mess."

"At first, sir, but it's eased off. The RSM's really hot on any suggestion of prejudice, he's brilliant, measures you on your ability, not your appearance."

There is a snort of derision from one of her crew, and all eyes turn to the skinny Geordie lad who is her driver.

"He fookin' rifted me 'cos of my appearance, sor!"

"That's because you walk around like a bag of shit tied in the middle, Calum."

David joins in the laughter and notes that the rest of the crew have been listening attentively to the exchange. They are arrayed protectively around their crew commander, regarding him with interest.

Maz's gunner, a corporal, responsible for ribbing the young driver, adds to the conversation, "It's the usual pulling your weight shit, sir. Track bashing's heavy work and some of the girls find it hard, not all of them are ninjas like Maz."*

They share a grin, and David takes a swig of his coffee, murmuring with approval as he tastes the Baileys liqueur that is used instead of milk.

"Cavalry coffee, I was hoping it would be. Made with proper coffee as well. Outstanding, Sarn't Tate."

The slight tension eases with the smiles that greet his approval, and the soldiers' sandwich lunch is eaten to the accompaniment of relaxed banter. The driver has glanced often at the Colonel, and so

---

* The segments that make up a tank track stretch and wear out. Splitting the track to remove or replace a link is difficult, heavy work.

David is not surprised when he asks him a question.

"So, what's it y' do, sor, get us noo kit like?"

"Something like that, Trooper Davies." David pauses, choosing his next words with care. It's not for him to imply that Calum Davies could be out of a job in the future. "I'm looking at stuff that we might get in five, ten years or longer. New technologies, my area is…" He hesitates a moment, looking for the right words. "Computer-assisted systems."

Calum hits closer to the mark than David would have liked. "Robot guns?"

He winces. "Not quite, we're looking at how you monitor and guard an area with computer-aided surveillance." He looks over at the tank. "Like taking the sight off the top of that and putting it on a tower in a camp." He turns to Maz and her Gunner. "You two must have done sentry duty in Afghan? Hours in a sanger, bored stiff and looking at sand? You're recce soldiers, imagine towers with the sensors you've got on Ajax and a weapon of some sort. The computer watches and alerts an ops room if it detects a threat, so the ops Officer can decide if he can order it to fire. In any case, it's intelligent enough to return fire in self-defence if the base is attacked. It can detect, recognise and identify with a multi-sensor array, so the OpsO is helped to make the decision." David has said more than he had intended, but notices that the two junior soldiers have been left behind. Calum's confusion clears, and he grins.

"No more guard duty would be canny!"

The corporal glances at Maz and turns back to David. "You're always short of folk on ops, sir, I get it. It's a bit the same with getting the girls in the regiment, more people less pressure."

David is acutely aware of Sargeant Tate's thoughtful gaze. The two crewmen may have taken a simple view of his explanation, but he's pretty sure Maz has a much more perceptive interpretation of what he's just said. Fortunately, he is spared her further attention by the arrival of the Commanding Officer's Land Rover.

The CO is accompanied by the imposing and immaculate figure of the regimental sergeant major, Warrant Officer First Class Burke. David hears a muted, "Oh Fook!" and glimpses Calum slipping behind the Ajax.

The CO introduces him to the RSM, who salutes crisply before shaking his hand. He leans to peer around David.

"No amount of armour can hide you from me, Trooper Davies, you scruffy individual!" This observation is delivered in a stentorian bellow, after which he straightens up, smiling, and winks at David.

"I hope Sarn't Tate has looked after you well, Colonel?"

"She has indeed, Mr Burke, a most impressive woman."

Robin joins in. "I hoped you would think so, David, you're well used to co-ed life in your corps, but it's still quite new for us. Any insights most welcome."

The RSM nods. "Your rank structure is all in place. For us, the difficulty is in growing them into the sarnts' mess, getting Sarn't Tate was a godsend as it'll help us with progression."

Maz joins them with a smart salute for the CO and a friendly, "Afternoon, sir," for the RSM.

Robin beams at her. "Thank you for looking after Colonel Lucas, Sarn't Tate, I hope it didn't interfere too much with your programme."

"Oh, not at all, sir. I'm not sure who learned the most during the morning." She smiles archly at David before continuing. "Saved by the CO's timely arrival, I think, sir."

David cocks an ironic eyebrow at her. "Never underestimate a clever Senior NCO is certainly a valuable lesson, Sarn't Tate, I shall be sure to remember it."

The other two note the exchange with interest. The RSM, with grim amusement, asserts, "One should certainly beware of sergeants who are too clever by half."

Maz adopts a pose that might almost be described as, 'at attention', oozing mock humility.

Robin returns them to the matter in hand. "Well, David, if you get hold of the Ajax you want, might we get an invitation to this demonstration? A little payback for our cooperation."

David, from the corner of his eye, sees thoughts dropping into place in Maz's head.

"I'm sure we can arrange that, Robin, perhaps we might prevail upon Sergeant Tate to join you and the RSM. She obviously has some ideas about what I'm up to."

"That sounds like a splendid idea, David. It will be a marvellous education opportunity, the only downside is that poor Sarn't Tate will have to bear the RSM and me for the journey."

"I shall do my best to endure the experience, sir!" Grinning, she takes a pace back and addresses David. "It was a pleasure hosting you, sir, we got a lot out of the experience. I hope you did." Turning to the CO and RSM, she salutes and excuses herself before turning smartly about and returning to the Ajax crew.

David watches her go. "That's one smart woman, Robin." He pauses momentarily. "Mr Burke, it might be wise if you would counsel her to be discrete in her speculation as to what I'm about. I'd hate hares to be set running in the sergeants' mess."

"No problem there, sir. As you said, she's a bright woman."

"On that note, gentlemen, let's jump in my rover and we'll get you back to your car, David. You can tell the RSM how you're going to make all our soldiers redundant on the way." He laughs with gusto at his joke, David winces.

STAGE MANAGEMENT

Back at Fort Halstead the following day, David briefs Mike about the visit and the next steps that he will take. Mike agrees that Helen is likely to approve the use of an Ajax and is probably the only person who can persuade the project team at the procurement agency to lean on the contractor to release one. Rather than phone Helen, David decides to submit a written update, so he spends the rest of the morning putting together a briefing paper on progress towards the demonstration and his requirement for an armoured vehicle.

Mike wanders into his office as he finishes a covering email for the document and asks him if he's going to the mess for lunch. Replying in the affirmative, he gets Mike to check his work and, with the resulting approval, presses *send*.

While the two of them are finishing a couple of rather nondescript sandwiches, David's phone vibrates furiously in his pocket. The display shows that Helen Sherwood is calling, he tilts the screen towards Mike and, with eyebrows raised, says, "Well, that was quick!"

Answering, he moves to the French windows and steps into the chilly afternoon sunlight of the little garden behind the mess.

"Tried your office, not interrupting anything?" Her voice is as brisk as the day.

"Only lunch."

The irony is lost on her, or, more likely, ignored. "Excellent brief, David, very much approve of your progress. Is it really possible to so simply integrate the IADS into a vehicle as complex as Ajax?"

"We're deliberately only doing the simplest integration, Helen, no mucking about with any of the communications or direct interface with the cameras, half of them don't work yet anyway."

"Hmm! I'd heard, we expect delays and teething troubles, there always are. Still, it shouldn't interfere with what you want to do."

"You've arranged for the loan of the vehicle already?"

"Of course. An Ajax is coming up from the facility in South Wales to replace the one you want, they thought they were picking up the unserviceable one. I've leant on the general dynamics people to let us have it for a week or two. It'll arrive tomorrow. One man's teething trouble being another woman's leverage." She chuckles at her humour.

David is impressed at the speed of reaction and startled by the unfamiliar levity.

"You'll be getting an engineer or two into the bargain, they're interested in what we're up to, of course, so you'll need to be discrete. I don't want to reveal our hand."

"You alluded to other things connected to this part of our programme, Helen, is there anything I should know?"

There is a pause. "How soon will you be back in your office?"

"Ten minutes or so."

"Call me on the secure line."

David goes back into the bar and pauses for a brief moment to let Mike know that Helen is going to impart some classified news. They leave together and stride up the hill to David's office, where he loses no time placing the call. It is answered instantly, and as Helen's cool, measured tones greet him, he tilts the handset so that

Mike can listen. The classified phone has no speaker, against the chance that secrets might be overheard.

"I alluded to other things in play here, David, and there are indeed games being played that you need to know about. Interesting though your project has become, it is by no means my only concern. There are several in my portfolio, and some of them are stalled. You know what our allies are like about ITARs, my projects are delayed for want of the release of US technology.* It'll come, I'm sure, but I want it now, not next year. Honestly, you'd think we were Iranians sometimes; the damn Israeli's never have to wait."

"Most of it comes from them."

She barks a laugh. "Fair one, anyway, IADS offers us leverage. Suddenly we're ahead of them in the technology of the moment. I'm betting that if they get a sniff of it, then they'll want it. I intend that they will get that sniff. One of the Lockheed Martin VPs is across with some of his people. There's no chance they won't hear that we have an Ajax here and they'll want to know why. As a 'courtesy', I shall invite them to your demonstration, so expect some embassy representation and the Lockheed people. I'll bring someone senior from here. It won't be the minister, we don't need a politician in the mix at this stage, and I'm already liaising with Bertie at head office."

David interjects. "I've taken the liberty of inviting Colonel Matheson from the RL, he's coming with his RSM and one of the Ajax commanders."

"Hmm! The languid cavalryman who's not as effete as he tries to make you believe. Is that wise, at this stage, David? The implications of what we're doing have become far more complex since we recruited the Wunderkind."

"The genie was struggling to get out of the bottle when I visited them, Helen. I chatted informally with Robin and he grasped it

---

*   ITAR stands for International Traffic in Arms Regulations. It is basically a license to export weapon parts or materials. It can take a long time to get them done, even for an ally.

immediately, he's very conscious that he's at least one vehicle crew short in each of his sabre squadrons. His RSM blamed the fact that we don't have a war to entertain them, that and the efforts of the company that's supposed to be doing recruiting means that getting people in is not going well."

"That might be changing, from what I hear on the sixth floor, David."

"I see. I'll park that snippet for the moment, it matches something Major Atkins said. Anyway, the sergeant was putting two and two together by the time I left as well, a very perceptive woman."

"Ah! You met her, did you? Yes, quite a star apparently. She was wheeled out when I visited."

"There's a half colonel from Army HQ coming along, he's from the capability directorate and a contemporary of mine. I planned to have a side discussion with them and gauge what Army Capability and the Field Army might think."

"I take it Dr Moore takes the view that autonomous driving is achievable?"

David sighs heavily. "Dr Moore thinks that the only reason for there to be anyone in the turret is the tiresome necessity for a human in the loop. He says that the only reason for the gunner to be sitting next to the commander in an Ajax is so that the commander has some company."

"Do you agree with him?"

"Honestly, from what I saw yesterday, the crew are systems managers in an almost fly-by-wire vehicle. The IADS can probably operate the thing, but I'm less sure that it can fight it – not intelligently, that is."

"I think, Colonel Lucas, that I need to find some money from somewhere, and by some, I mean a lot."

David and Mike exchange meaningful glances as they wait out the silence of cogitation at the other end. It is broken as Helen asks a question of Mike.

"Michael, could you do a full integration of a prototype and test it at Porton when you move? There's more room there and, in fact, I could move you early if necessary."

He stutters the start of a reply, a little startled by her assumption that he would be listening. She interrupts with a mocking chuckle.

"You two are such fun. How likely was it that your sidekick wasn't present, David?"

"You are so scary, Helen, please don't add omniscience to your list of superpowers! After all, having Mike here does save me briefing him later."

The laugh at the other end is filled with genuine amusement this time. Mike has had time to compose both himself and an answer.

"To be honest, Helen, I've thought of little else since Craig suggested using a real turret and David thought he might be able to get hold of an Ajax. It's the obvious candidate since the digital communication suite on-board is so advanced. That is, it will be when the contractor gets it to work. You're right about the money, though, we're at the back end of what I was allocated already."

Helen is brisk. "Right! This is what I want. You push ahead with the demonstration. It needs to be simple but completely effective. Gather in your lab for a meet and greet and set out your stall using the simulator, then move to the live demonstration, which absolutely must prove what you did in the sim works in the real world. David, you take what resources you need to produce a spectacle on the range. If you need soldiers and equipment, take them. Refer any complaints to my office. Are we clear?"

The tone of command braces David up, and his reply is a military. "Yes, ma'am." This draws another bark of laughter from Helen, who moves on to give Mike his orders.

"Keep control of the integration and the tech end of the deal, Mike. You present to the audience to demilitarise it a bit. Use Craig if you can trust him, and make the point we are at the experimental stage at the moment. Concurrently you need to plan on moving a team to Porton Down to work on a prototype armoured fighting vehicle, I want to prove that if we can do this with one AFV, we can do it to them all. I will come down to see a rehearsal the day before we go live – don't disappoint. The key message for the Americans is that we're guarding a camp, though. Any questions?"

There are none and, after David returns the handset to its cradle, the two men sit back in thoughtful contemplation. They meet each other's eyes almost simultaneously, and Mike breaks the silence.

"Ever felt you were at the top of a rollercoaster about to begin the downward trip?"

"Apart from the fact that you'd never in a million years get me on an actual rollercoaster, yes."

Mike laughs. "Well, we'd better make all this happen. What do you want me to do?"

"You'd better mobilise the fort resources, it's probably about time we gave the senior management here another update and briefed them on the demo. They're so wound up in the move planning that they won't have grasped the significance of what's going on. I like that idea of using some of the security detail to play enemy for us, they've all had some training and can handle weapons, so they'll be convincing. So, you do domestic and leave me to handle outside resources and the physical prep of the range, if that makes sense?"

"Good plan."

"I'd better get on with what remains of the afternoon. I'm going to need to get some more engineering help from the district. We'll need to augment our own people with some sappers and plant."

Mike leaves David, who starts to make phone calls to branches of the district headquarters. By the end of the afternoon, he has secured a troop of Royal Engineers and the heavy machinery he will need.

The next day a low loader arrives with a tarpaulin-covered Ajax on-board. The engine is still not working so it is dragged off the truck and ignominiously dumped on the side of the road. It looks rather forlorn and toothless without its armoured skirts and cannon. David enlists the help of the driver and the two engineers, and they replace the tarpaulin on the armoured vehicle. David discovers that the two people who've come up from Wales represent each of the contractors who are delivering Ajax, one from General Dynamics and one from Lockheed Martin. They are both curious about the programme, but David convinces them that they should sort themselves out with accommodation in the local area and reconvene after the weekend for a briefing. He is expecting his sapper troop to arrive on the Monday morning and doesn't want to repeat himself. The two engineers leave, satisfied with the explanation.

Climbing to the fort's battlements, he then spends some time sketching a panorama of the range and designing a layout for the mock-up of the base. Returning to his office, he continues to formulate his plans and puts together a briefing pack for when the team assembles. It is late by the time he heads home.

He arrives early after his weekend, and the people on the gate rib him about a takeover. Groups of soldiers turning up with plant vehicles are not a usual event for them. David returns the good-natured jibes with some of his own. After he parks his car, he misses out the lab. Excitement at doing the practical part of the project puts a spring in his stride and a grin on his face as he climbs the hill to the fort. When he arrives, he finds a dozen soldiers cradling mugs and eating bacon sandwiches around a dull green crane. A similarly liveried digger and a truck are also parked by the side of the road. David has worn his uniform for a day he anticipates will mainly be spent on the range. The sight of a lieutenant colonel of engineers brings the troops to their feet. They adopt insouciant attitudes of attention, hiding mugs and sandwiches with varying amounts of success. The troop staff sergeant steps forward to salute David with a grin.

"Morning, sir! Good to see you, it's been a long time."

The grin is echoed on David's face as he recognises a character from his past. Returning the salute, he grasps the now outstretched hand.

"Staff Travis, this is a surprise. Iraq, wasn't it?"

"Op Telic Seven, sir, Basrah. Well remembered."

The troop relax as the two old hands reminisce for a few moments. David then turns to encompass them all, nodding to the two engineers from the day before who have joined the group. He thanks them all for coming to give them a hand on the project and provides a simple outline of what they are trying to achieve. He downplays the extent of what IADS is, referring to it merely as a computer that can network camp surveillance and defence into a central station in an ops room. From the corner of his eye, he registers that the explanation hasn't satisfied the curiosity of the contractors, but he puts that thought aside for later. He has a printed set of his briefing notes and the diagrams which form an aide-memoire showing what he wants. This folder he gives to Staff Travis before taking them all onto the range to present the plan in detail.

He finishes by telling them to drag the Ajax to form the corner of the camp mock-up first, so that his own engineers can start work. The General Dynamics engineer explains that a mechanical fault prevents them from putting it there under its own power. He wilts, blushing at the resulting barrage of derisory remarks from the soldiers concerning the cavalry in general and tanks in particular. David commiserates with him and draws the two civilians aside to talk to them about what they'll do to the Ajax. In the background, the engineers start to mark out the ground.

As David's briefing draws to a close, he sees Craig and Caroline approaching up the hill. He now regrets not stopping at the lab to warn Craig in particular not to be too forthcoming with the two company engineers, who are watching the approach of the two with interest. He smoothly opens the conversation, introducing the two outsiders to the pair and explaining their role.

"Craig will explain what he wants in the turret and the degree of integration we are after; it isn't much, incidentally. Caroline here is the lead military member of our group."

Craig shakes hands and smiles before turning with the rest of them to watch the sappers using the dozer to pull the Ajax across the road and position it to David's satisfaction. Craig then asks if they can get to work. David nods distractedly, his attention diverted to the engineers who now turn their attention to the pallets of Hesco bastion that have been pre-positioned on the range. Staff Travis supervises his team, and they assemble the wire and felt containers to form a short wall that encompasses the Ajax, making it part of a corner. David walks over to the back of the Ajax and climbs up to join Caroline, who is peering into a hatch to observe Craig and one of the engineers. The one called Bob is exclaiming at something Craig has said.

"So, you just need to wire your system into the pots on the joystick, and it will understand the inputs and outputs?"

"Well, yes, it's done it with game joysticks and throttle controls, it'll just adjust itself to this. We'll need to set some limits, so it doesn't input excessive demands and damage anything. There'll also need to be a switch to simulate the trigger and key the laser equipment we're getting."

"Actually, the traverse and elevation controls are self-limiting so they won't allow harmful demands on the motors. How will you make the connections? I'm not sure we want too much soldering."

"We've got a 3D printer. If you get me the CAD diagrams, I'll design and print an interface that will clamp on to the housing, and we'll just wire it up, so the contacts are dry."

The other contractor blinks and says, "What about the visual input, apparently you don't need that hardwired in?"

"No, the programme can deal with images. Of course, in an ideal world it would be cleaner to interface directly, but it's designed to be flexible. All we need is to focus an HD camera on the gunner's display. We don't have time for too much complexity."

He looks up at Caroline's face framed in the hatch above and smiles. "She keeps saying KISS to me. Unfortunately, I found out it means: Keep It Simple, Stupid!"

He gets a fond smile in return. "I'm glad something's getting through, Craig."

The two commercial men exchange meaningful glances. Bob turns to David, who has been observing the tableau before him.

"Just an integration programme, is it?" He glances into the turret and then back to the Colonel with an ironic grin. "What am I to discover when I Google Dr Moore?"

From behind him, Craig's voice rises from the turret interior. "Oh, just a geeky intellectual with some wild theories on machine learning and autonomous cars."

"Yeah, right!"

The engineer troop are now starting to fill the Hesco bastion bags with soil scraped from the range by the dozer, and the four of them are superfluous to this noisy process. David decides that they should close up the vehicle and retreat to the lab. Before leaving, he exchanges a few words with Staff Travis and then trots to catch up with the other three. Bob has spent a few minutes staring at his phone, and as David gathers the technical team up to go back to the lab, he waves his phone and says, "Geeky intellectual, hey?"

He gets a laugh in return, but David refuses to be drawn.

The day winds up with the commercial men being introduced to the rest of the team and to IADS. They also sketch out a plan for the days left before rehearsals.

The activity on the Fort Halstead Range is by now attracting a lot of internal attention. The DSTL hierarchy has, until now, only been vaguely aware of what is going on in the novel warfare building. They have been wrapped up in the plans to move to Porton Down, and turning good ideas into practical courses of action has given them more than enough to do. Their attention has now been drawn to the forthcoming demonstration, and Mike is now being

85

harassed into giving Heimdall updates and bullied into making sure that the head of DSTL and his deputy are involved. Mike and David are both resentful of this transparent attempt by senior management to hijack kudos that the two believe is rightfully theirs. They plot to forestall this and, in spite of the extra pressure they know will fall on their team, decide to use the dress rehearsal as a means of controlling the domestic pressure they are under.

A planning meeting is called that includes the commercial engineers and the extra engineering staff from DSTL, who will help with the physical integration of IADS into the Ajax.

When Mike and David arrive at the lab to begin, they find that there is already a bustle of activity. The enlarged team has already started on some of the engineering tasks that they will need. They are clustered around screens showing diagrams of the traverse and elevation controls, as well as other views of the turret internals. Staff Sergeant Travis is leaning nonchalantly against a desk observing the activity, and he straightens up when he sees David. The others turn, looking expectantly at the pair. Mike opens the discussion.

"We want to review our progress for the Heimdall demo and map out what is going to happen between now and the demo. I imagine you all have a handle on that, but we've had to shift some timings a bit."

"As Mike says, there's been a shift. You know that we do the main demo on the ninth and were planning a dress rehearsal the day before. We want to put an extra rehearsal into the programme for some of the staff here at the Fort, so that means rehearsing to audiences on Monday and Tuesday. Integration and engineering, as well as our own rehearsal programme, has to be finished by the end of next week." David looks expectantly at the team, anticipating dismay. He and Mike are surprised by the shrugs, nods and 'no problem' murmurs that greet this. Bob looks at him, noting his surprise.

"This is about as simple as software integration gets, David. I wish all my engineering challenges were so easy."

Caroline takes up the thread. "The only time-consuming stuff is physically moving the kit up to the range and plumbing it all in, Colonel."

Staff Sergeant Travis adds, "We've finished the build, sir, I've thinned most of the troop out already. We've kept the crane back to help you position a portacabin behind the parapet. After that, the heavy lift and shift work is done. Your guys up at the site said we can leave the stuff up, so we don't even need to come back and knock it down."

Mike is visibly impressed. "Thanks, all of you, that's great work. The pair of us have got a lot of balls in the air at the moment, so we'll let you get on with it. We'll stay out of your hair until the Monday meeting, let's go for our own final run-through the Friday before demo week then." He looks around approvingly and, with the thanks from the two of them lingering in the air, he and David leave.

True to their word, the now extended Heimdall team move the capability onto the range. A portacabin, placed by the Royal Engineers before they left, now sits behind the Ajax to the rear of the Hesco wall. Into this go tables and chairs, power is plugged in, and cables run through an aperture in the same panel, creating a control room for the trial. Craig has made the interface for the turret controller and Bob, as the Lockheed man, installs it. A simple clamp fixes the HD camera to the gunner's seat, and the cables for control and observation are run into the shelter. Although the Ajax is not mobile, its near-silent auxiliary generator works perfectly to power the on-board systems.

Rob and William have moved the recording systems up to the control room, and Diana has prepped the newly acquired, hugely expensive X500 ruggedised laptop into which they will plug IADS. All this is achieved in the three days they had set themselves. As they depart the site at the end of the week, an immensely satisfied Caroline informs them that the weapons effects simulator kits will arrive on Monday.

The white van with the sim kits turns up with a warrant officer from the Salisbury Plain Training Area, where the equipment is stored. He has brought along two systems for armour and twelve for infantry. He introduces himself as Sergeant Major Jim Perry from the Weapons Effects Simulation Team.

Fitting the armoured system to Ajax without a gun barrel is the first challenge they face, but Bob and his sidekick manage to jury-rig the box onto the external part of the gun mounting. The first snag is that the controller on Ajax isn't configured to fire the laser in the simulator kit and it takes the electricians and contractors half the day to come up with a solution and wire it into the interface that Craig has designed. While all this is going on, Craig and the Coven have been setting up IADS, and the system is live more or less as the trigger system is ready. The final connections are made, and the control room fills with people who now look at Craig expectantly. The silence is broken by Sergeant Major Perry.

"So what now? I just got told to bring the stuff up here; I wasn't expecting to see it installed in a half-finished tank connected to a computer. Am I allowed to know what is going on?"

Caroline explains, "It represents a defensive turret on a patrol base, Sarn't Major. The 'computer' monitors an area and detects targets, which it will engage if they meet the ROE conditions." She notices the Lockheed Martin and General Dynamics engineers exchange knowing looks.

"It's a sentry gun, is it, ma'am? Didn't think they would be legal. Some of our people have been involved in capability meetings where they were discussed. Something about man-in-the-loop being needed."

The sergeant major is a gunnery instructor from the Royal Armoured Corps, an expert in tank gunnery and armoured warfare, so it's not surprising that he has made the connection.

Caroline continues smoothly, "That's true, and if a system were developed for use, it would be several sensors and weapons networked to a control node like this. The computer does the analysis and offers targets to the operations staff, who monitor the feed. It takes the sentries out of the towers, basically."

The sergeant major blinks and nods approvingly.

Craig interjects. "What we're doing here is letting the system detect, recognise and identify targets then open fire if the ROE allow it, so we can check how reliable it is. As it's an experiment, we can go a bit further than policy allows to improve confidence in the system."

Caroline hides her surprise. She always expects Craig's relative innocence and literal-mindedness to result in him giving more away then they'd like. She makes a mental note to let David and Mike know that he's becoming more subtle. Craig has noticed her surreptitious scrutiny and winks at her.

"We ought to see if it works then."

Craig frowns. "How do we adjust the aim so that the laser is accurate?" He indicates a display that is now active, showing the IADS camera view through the gunner's sight. There is a graticule in the display, but Craig is not the only one who realises that the laser could be pointing anywhere.

"Well, we would normally collimate the laser on a target downrange and adjust the beam, so it strikes where the graticule is aiming." The sergeant major strokes his chin thoughtfully for a moment and then straightens up, looking at Caroline. "Ma'am, there must be some targetry here; this is a range. Let's put some out at various ranges and hang the infantry harnesses on them. We can use them to zero the system."

Caroline makes a call, and presently one of the few remaining people who work inside the old fort comes out and shows them a store that contains military targets on poles. In true warrant officer style, the sergeant major organises them into pairs and sends them off to hammer the targets into the ground at various ranges down the range. He then follows on and drapes the laser receptor chest harnesses over the targets. When illuminated by the laser, these will buzz, and an orange light will flash.

When all is completed to his satisfaction, the now dusty and sweating crew gather back at the control room where Craig, who was not part of the target party, has been working on the laptop.

He looks up as the sergeant major says, "OK, sir, what now?"

"I've just adjusted the programming to accept this as a test, and I've inputted the conditions and the desired outcome. The system now knows this is a laser that is being used to represent the weapon. I'm pretty confident that it will teach itself to adjust its aim to hit the target."

The Fort Halstead team obviously share this confidence, Sergeant Major Perry looks very sceptical, and the two contractors keep their faces carefully neutral.

"Go on then, sir, surprise me."

When the laser had been mounted, the engineers had roughly aligned the laser by laying the gunsight onto a fence post downrange and then pointed the laser as best they could using the basic sight on the equipment. Craig has programmed this assumption in as well.

He enables IADS and leans back.

For a brief moment nothing happens, and then the turret moves to the left and then to the right. It does this a couple of times more at varying speeds. Rob and William are looking at their screens to see what the log files reveal about the processes that are taking place. IADS pauses after moving the turret, and there is a sharp intake of breath from William.

"He's accessing the intranet. I can't really keep up, but there's loads of stuff about lasers. Ah! Weapons effects simulators have just come up, and he's stopped accessing."

As if to punctuate this last remark, the turret moves and the display centres on one of the targets in the centre of the range one hundred metres away. There is an audible click as the laser fires. At the target end nothing happens, and there is a pause. When the turret next starts to move, they see a pattern of small movements and laser clicks as IADS searches for the sweet spot that will initiate the vest. They hear the buzzer, and an orange light glows on the target harness. The silence is broken by the buzz of conversation greeting the success.

Craig interrupts. "Hold on, IADS has requested that the harness is reset."

"Well, you've succeeded in surprising me, Dr Moore."

Privately, Caroline thinks Sergeant Major Perry looks more aghast than surprised.

"Tell me why it wants that particular target reset."

William answers the question. "Looking at the log files, IADS found information on the specific simulator and its performance. I can also see some hits on target shooting, so I'd say it wants to fire a check group." He smiles proudly at this demonstration of his infantry skills.

Rob has looked at the scripts and confirms this. "Craig's syntax does it, he knows how IADS orders data to create its world model. IADS analyses the orders it's given, looking for instructions and keywords. He then analyses the data, rather like you would do your military estimate, Jim. Craig didn't give the system lines of instructions, he just told it what he wanted and let the machine learn how to do it."

Jim looks at them both and turns, shaking his head, to stride up the range, pulling a small green device from his pocket. When he gets near the target, he points the object at the blinking harness, and it stops indicating a hit. As he moves to come back down the range the Ajax turret moves slightly and the laser fires again, causing the vest to beep and flash again. Jim resets it, and there is another small movement, then the same thing happens. IADS does this a few more times and stops. Diana leaves the control cabin and waves at Jim, who stomps down the range to rejoin them, looking rather sourfaced.

"Eighteen years and a WO2, looking to be a WO1 next year, and I'm running bloody errands for a fucking computer. You've done it, haven't you? You've made an intelligent weapon. That's artificial intelligence, isn't it?"

Craig had joined in the general amusement at Jim's initial reaction to the IADS's zeroing demands, but his response to the accusation is irritated.

"There's no such thing as artificial intelligence, Sergeant Major. I'll allow that it's autonomous, but it's not clever. It doesn't think, certainly not like we do. What it does is look at the instructions it is given and available inputs. It then builds a probabilistic world model and tests the results against my desired outcome. If its answer falls within the parameters needed for it to act, it will act. If not, it will search for data and go around the cycle again. It's an autonomous system that learns – machine learning, not AI."

Jim notes the reaction and cracks a smile. "Well, it seems pretty clever to me!"

Caroline lightens the mood further. "That's because you're a cavalryman, Sarn't Major!"

"Ooh! Cheap shot, ma'am."

Bob is thoughtful after the events and nods at Craig's display where an IADS message shows:

Laser collimation complete.

Ready.

"Everything you say is true, Craig, it's just that no one else has done it, yet." The General Dynamics engineer standing next to him nods and murmurs agreement as Bob continues, "I'm an American, and I say to you that this project is under-classified. The fewer people that know about this, the better."

His quiet words are sobering, and Caroline decides it is time to end things for the day.

"I agree with Bob, as it happens, we've all got to remember this is a secret programme. You understand, I hope, Sarn't Major?"

He nods formally.

"I think that when we get other people involved on Wednesday, we need to make sure it appears to be a remotely operated system and we'll keep this area off-limits to gawkers. Let's secure things and knock it on the head until tomorrow."

The team, much sobered by these words, go about the business of winding things up before dispersing. Caroline stands for a while at the back of the position, deep in thought. Craig takes a few paces towards her and stops as, unseeing, she turns away and walks down the hill. He frowns and follows her progress until she moves out of sight.

For her part, Caroline goes straight to David's office to get to him before the meeting they always have on a Monday.

"There are some developments you need to be aware of, Colonel."

He has looked up as she entered and takes in her concerned demeanour, he holds up a hand.

"A moment, Caroline, have a seat."

Rising, he leaves the room to poke his head around the next door and ask Mike's PA for a moment of his time. David goes back to Caroline.

"Not a serious problem, I hope?"

"Not a problem at all," she replies, as Mike walks in and smiles at her. "More a wake-up call." She outlines the progress they have made, ending on the sobering remarks with which Bob closed the day.

Mike and David exchange glances and both of them are thoughtful for a moment. Mike opens the conversation.

"He's right, of course. We've been so swept up with the pace of the programme and the excitement of being at the cutting edge of progress that we've let the serious nature of everything get away from us a bit."

David steeples his hands and looks at Caroline. "Good catch, Caroline, what are your thoughts?"

"Well, I've already directed that we'll keep the guys acting as targets away from our command post, and to anyone not on the inside track, it's a remotely operated system. You've got the chief, his deputy and the heads of the branches at the dress rehearsal, they should be OK, but there's bound to be gossip in the mess."

"That sounds good. Mike, you might need to give a health warning to our hierarchy here. It may even be a good idea to set Helen on them."

"I think I'd enjoy that. She's coming up on Monday, so I can raise concerns and let her loose. What about the two engineers from the contractors, Caroline?"

"They know exactly what they're seeing, and I can't imagine they won't report back to their people, classification or not. I think the American delegation will be fully briefed."

David nods thoughtfully. "I think you're right, but from what Helen was saying about the leverage that the project might give us, that might not be a bad thing. Thanks, Caroline, we'll be down shortly if you wouldn't mind getting the team organised. It's just our people, isn't it?"

"Yes, sir, Sarn't Major Perry is sorting out his accommodation, he's staying until the end of the main demo and then taking his laser kit back. The two engineers haven't been invited."

She rises and leaves, the two men watching her trot down the stairs towards the lab.

Mike looks back at David. "She's pretty outstanding, isn't she? When do we tell her about the Porton Down move and the next phase?"

"Outstanding is exactly the right word, and I think we brief her the day after the demo. The rest of the team will need some management as a move means more to them domestically. I think that most of them just lodge locally and live elsewhere. In any case, they're expecting a move, just not quite so soon."

With that, they leave for the meeting.

DEUS EX MACHINA

There is a more severe air about the project in the morning as the team gather at the range. This is heightened by the fact that the barrier across the road leading to the range firing point in the shadow of the fort walls is now shut and displays a no entry sign over the words *Live Range*. Caroline tells them that the path around the inner perimeter, much used by lunchtime runners, has also been shut except to the security patrols.

William gives a short update on the log file analysis that he and Rob had done in the evening and says that the debate the day before was pretty spot on. IADS found the information on DTES from the intranet and cross-referenced it with the military manuals in the Fort Halstead intranet. The method it used to find the right place on the target was just logical trial and error. Rob adds that his look into the system showed an aim off calculation had been added to the scripts written by Craig.

The cover that hides the Ajax from prying eyes is taken off by the two Americans, and they start up the vehicle systems. IADS is started and runs its own checks before connecting to the vehicle and telling Craig that it's ready. When Bob comes in, he looks at the screen and asks Craig why he doesn't use voice commands. From the attention now being paid by the rest of the team, it's evident that some of them have been wondering this as well.

"Good question, Bob. I could quite easily, and when I was developing it, I did for a while. I stopped using it because I didn't want to waste time developing a speech engine or looking for and then integrating one. The one in my computer made too many annoying mistakes, and I'm just more efficient and accurate with a keyboard. I've left it fitted for voice activation, but once I stopped using it I just never bothered again. It'd need some development to be reliable. Working on this programme, well, there's a lot of background noise which doesn't help. The other reason is presentational; it gives the wrong impression if you start talking to it, people either don't take it seriously or, worse, are scared. We anthropomorphise it too readily, as well, we're already starting to call it 'he'. What I might do is get it to give verbal reports, though, but only because I think that might be more efficient."

Bob nods thoughtfully, and a voice from the doorway causes heads to turn. Sam is standing there, observing Bob speculatively.

"You're thinking voice-activated cockpit in aircraft?" She enters the control cabin and approaches him with an outstretched hand. "Sam Royle, I'm the ISTAR worker bee on the team. I'd say you're Lockheed Martin?"

Bob is startled, but he introduces himself and his colleague, telling her it was a good guess.

"Not really, that's an Ajax out there, so one of the strangers had to be." She smiles around the rest of the team, who all cheerfully welcome her back after a week-long absence at her own office in nearby Crawley. She turns back to Bob.

"I'm from Thales, we do most of the sensors on Ajax. Actually, that's my area, I'm one of the engineers." She is upbeat on her return.

She is brought up to date and introduced to Jim. Caroline brings them to order, and Craig gets ready to start the first serial of the day. They are going to practice on the static targets and make sure they are ready for the introduction of the live opposing force, that Caroline refers to as 'Opfor', the next day. Privately, Craig thinks they'll have proved everything they can in about five minutes. He types in what he tells them he now calls a 'Briefing Script', a set of tasks to be performed. Bob has positioned himself where he can see the screen and watches intently as Craig navigates around the interface. His scrutiny is secretly noted by Caroline. As Craig clicks the *Execute* button on the screen, they all look out across the top of the Hesco wall at the ten targets that dot the range area. The sound of the turret traverse and the click of the laser firing occur almost instantaneously and last for only a few seconds. On the range, ten orange lights flash. Jim's expostulation breaks the brief silence.

"Jesus Christ! Ten accurate shots in, what, less than ten seconds?"

This expletive-filled outburst draws admiring looks from the Coven. Rob looks back at his screen and briefly manipulates his mouse.

"Six point four three seconds, actually, Jim."

From Craig, sitting beside him comes, "Hmmm… interesting." He leans over to look at Rob's screen and appropriates the mouse to look at part of the recording not in view, before leaning back.

"What's interesting, Craig?"

"Well, Jim is pretty impressed with the shooting, obviously, but I noticed something yesterday, and this confirms it. IADS fired the laser a lot yesterday, and I could hear a change in the sound of the turret moving. It became less abrupt." He looks over at the incredulous cavalryman and says, "IADS acquired each target and then plotted the order of engagement that moved the turret most smoothly between targets to save time and, I believe, stress. IADS is, of all things, efficient, it will have assessed the performance limits that Bob said were in the system and looked at the best way of managing them." He stops and holds up a cautionary hand. "It's not intuitive – I told it!"

"What if you put in parameters for targets that were at different threat levels or priorities?" Caroline asks.

"I don't think we can prove much more on wooden targets, it'll just do the same thing over and over. Trying to prioritise them is a waste of time because they all look the same. Giving them each an arbitrary value isn't any challenge."

"There're some moving targets at the back of the range store, we could see if they work." Jim holds up the bunch of keys he was given earlier. "I'm pretty familiar with them, and we've got pretty high-powered engineering help here."

A chorus of approval along the lines of, 'It's better than going back to the office', greet this idea and the command post empties, leaving the Coven and Craig to look in detail at the log files from the range time thus far. After a short time, Rob leans back.

"Craig, something's been bothering me for a while, I thought I'd wait until it was just us before saying anything."

Craig, Diana and William swing their chairs around to look at him as he sits looking nonplussed.

"What is it?"

"Well, early on you said that IADS tidies itself up. I think it does more than that, I've seen the programme grow and contract. Also, some of the libraries and resource directories alter themselves."

"Well, the libraries will alter quite a bit. IADS deletes anything irrelevant, even with the add-on storage for the data libraries we could potentially have vast amounts of data building up. The learning algorithms do that, it's just pruning the trees, it looks like IADS has taken the instruction to keep itself as neat and tidy as possible literally and started to invent a shorter but more complex way of expressing my original code. It's probably because I become very bored with writing interminable lines of Python, so I let IADS do the leg work. It's just doing a better job and streamlining itself according to what the command scripts are asking it to do."

Listening to this exchange, Caroline interrupts with, "Should I be worried about this, Rob?"

"Not really, I can see what's happening and it's becoming difficult, rather than impossible, to understand. The outcomes are still going to be the same if we set the right conditions. Commands must be as unambiguous as possible, but we know that."

Craig looks at her and says, "If you had a conversation with some of my colleagues in the AI world, and I'm not suggesting you should, they would say this bears out some of their theories about the result of true AI."

"Like what?"

"Well, one theory is that far from taking over the world, it'll ignore us because we aren't relevant to its needs or way of thinking."

Outside there is a clatter that heralds the arrival of the group that has been looking for targets.

Jim pokes his head through the door and says, "We've managed to get two targets working so we can challenge Deus Ex to shoot some movers."

Craig lets out a delighted laugh as Caroline asks, "Deus what?"

Jim places a theatrical hand to his brow and exclaims, "What, the thick cavalryman baffles the clever gunner? Surely not! My son plays a shooting game called *Deus Ex*. Apparently, it means 'God in the machine'."

Sam's voice interposes. "Actually, it means 'God out of the machine', and you're cleverer than you think, Jim, because it's defined as an unexpected solution to a hopeless problem solved by the use of a machine."

Jim is even more gratified that he has outwitted Caroline. Craig is also impressed as he only knew the game reference.

"That's a much better name than IADS, Sam."

The Coven chorus agreement as Caroline groans in despair, "You people will be the death of me. What was all that 'anthropomorphism' crap, Craig? You're as bad as these lunatics.

Why can't you just call him Heimdall? At least that won't wind up the grown-ups."

There are mock impressed comments from the Coven along the lines of, 'we didn't know we could' and 'Thanks, Caro'. She leaves, shaking her head. While this conversation has been going on, the engineers have been fixing mannequins to the two mobile targets. The result is faintly disturbing as the figures obviously came from a shop display. The sight of the unclothed figures moving jerkily around on the wheeled trolleys provokes Caroline to call a halt and order some clothing to be found to go underneath the laser harness. Jim duly finds some old overalls in the store as well as some plastic weapon mock-ups. Presently the targets look bizarre but acceptable, and Jim and Bob send them off up the range.

Craig watches them go from inside the control cabin with a frown. Inwardly, he is sceptical as to the value of shooting at these comical figures.

A side window in the cabin is opened so that they can shout instructions to the two target operators sitting on the Hesco wall. Craig calls up the menu for the camp guarding functionality.

"I'm going to just let it run autonomously. We've made some adjustments based on the sim work, and I've altered some scripting to allow for the move into the real world."

Caroline moves to stand beside him and looks at the screen. In the IADS dialogue box, she notices the Heimdall logo to the left of the blinking cursor and tuts, punching Craig lightly on the shoulder.

"That didn't take long!"

He laughs and says that they can go for a test anytime she wants.

"As soon as Sam stops pratting about on top of the Ajax," is the reply. They look over to see Sam investigating fittings on the Ajax, and Jim leans out of the door to call her over.

She joins them, looking thoughtful, but fends off questions, indicating that it's a conversation for later.

Craig enables Guard Mode on the screen, and they look out towards the range as the turret tracks left and then right once before settling on the centre line. Caroline gives Jim and Bob a thumbs up, and the two of them start to drive the targets towards the firing point.

The turret centres on each target in turn and then returns to its rest position. The figures reach the firing point and stop. Jim shrugs, palms up, and puts down the radio controller. Then he and Bob walk over to the cabin. Craig sits back with a smile.

"I didn't think so."

"So you knew nothing would happen, but it attacked the stationary targets. Why's that?"

"I put the conditions in for target practice and zeroing, but now it's in Guard Mode with all the rules of engagement that we were using in the sim. Now it's in the real version of that, which just means it's using real-world feeds and not simulated signals."

Sam is leaning into the cabin, sitting on the steps. "In itself, that's quite good. Did it do any analysis, Rob? Or did it just ignore them completely?"

"I was just scrolling through it, there's an extended burst of activity for the first one and then a short burst for the second."

Will Conyers is also looking at log files and laughs. "He doesn't know what the targets are, registers the presence of weapons, continues to search and can't find anything in our database. Switches to the intranet and, at first, thinks that they're wheelchairs before correctly identifying them as mobile targets."

"Not shooting at wheelchairs is a positive sign, I'd say," adds Sam.

A vehicle has pulled up to the range barrier. Caroline brightens. "Lunch," she announces.

"I'll add moving targets to the target practice scenario, and we'll see how that works after lunch." Craig turns and busies himself in front of his screen as the rest leave the cabin and wander over to the lunch vehicle.

The afternoon is short and has no surprises. No matter what Jim does with the targets, Heimdall's aim is unerring. Craig is unimpressed, declaring that his watch could do as good a job of aiming and firing. He is looking forward to the following day when they have human targets with which to test the system.

As the team clear up and secure the range, Sam wanders over to peer at the Ajax again.

Caroline frowns and calls over to her, "What's bothering you, Sam?"

"I was wondering about the acoustic sensors, why you haven't wired them in."

Craig has been slightly disgruntled with the day which, privately, he thinks has been a waste of time. At Sam's words, he brightens up and asks, "What acoustic sensors, Sam?"

"The domes that you can see, three of them, they're for the acoustic shot detection system. If someone shoots at an Ajax, you get a location and classification on the screen."

"Ah! I recall that in the specs, I was wondering what those things were. Do they work?"

"Not at the moment, the microphones are OK, but there's an integration problem." Bob's voice causes them to turn.

Sam is a bit defensive. "This was my project, what's the matter with it?"

"Nothing to do with your kit, it just isn't currently talking to the multifunction display. It works on the ones at Warminster, but we didn't follow this one up as the rest of it was unserviceable."

"So, do they just hear or do they only listen for specific sounds?" Craig is staring intently at the mushroom-shaped devices on the hull of the Ajax.

Sam and Bob turn to him, and Sam replies, "They detect all sounds, but they're shot detection systems, so they filter out irrelevant noise. When they get a signal that meets weapon criteria, the three sensors triangulate the position and give a location."

Caroline is looking quizzically at Craig. "What's got you so interested, Craig? I've been under the distinct impression that you think this has been a waste of time."

All eyes are on Craig, but it is Sam who answers. "It's said he required less sleep than a bird, could see a hundred leagues and could hear the grass growing in the meadows and wool growing on sheep."

The two of them share a laugh, and Craig says, "Exactly, Sam. The ability to hear would be a significant enhancement, and I don't just mean detecting shots. There must be loads of sounds on the battlefield that could be characterised. Could you do it?"

"It should be quite easy to rig an ad hoc solution, but if you were doing proper integration, then that would be a different matter. Can it understand sound files?"

"If the sound libraries are in the same format you use, then yes."

Sam looks at Caroline. "Do you want to give it a go?"

Caroline has been distracted but returns her attention to them. "Let's give it a try. I mean, I can recognise our helicopters from their sounds so it would be an interesting addition to the experiment. Don't let it interfere with the programme, though. We've got a demonstration to put on." She turns away, looking up the track to where she has spotted Bob standing at the junction with the main route talking into his phone. She frowns and regards him thoughtfully as Sam notices her glance.

"Problem, Caroline?"

Caroline turns to her. "I'm not sure, but I think we're starting to leak."

LEANNE

Up at the junction, the telephone call is answered by a charming American voice. "Advanced Development Office, Charlene speaking, how may I help?"

"This is Bob Glassman from our Ajax project in the UK, is Ms Phillips able to spare me a few moments? It's essential that I speak to her."

"I'm sorry, Mr Glassman, she is in a meeting right now, can I get her to call you back? I'd need the nature of your enquiry, of course."

Bob curbs his frustration with the saccharine voice at the other end of the line, understanding that a Senior Vice President at Lockheed Special Projects won't have a clue who he is. He gropes for a hook to get her to call him back.

"Ma'am, please tell her it's vital that someone comes to the UK with the Lockheed team visiting the UK Procurement Authority next week, it has to do with the Akicita Maza project."

The voice at the other end loses some of its sweetness and becomes more business-like. She asks him to repeat his name, he does so and leaves his number. Turning, he spots Caroline watching him, and he smiles weakly on the walk back to the range. Caroline, in a voice laced with irony, reminds him that as an escorted visitor he shouldn't stray too far.

Bob's embarrassment turns into a nightmare as his phone rings, he ignores it for a moment but is not spared as Caroline smiles sweetly and asks him if he's going to answer it. Helplessly, he does so, noting the inevitable US number in his phone's display.

"Bob Glassman."

The voice on the other end is a cool southern drawl, measured and cautious. "Mr Glassman, given that I now know we have a Robert Glassman representing us in the UK, how do you know about the project that my secretary mentioned?"

Bob fights for composure. "Yes Frank, I'm sorry I missed your earlier call. As you know I'm with the Ajax at Fort Halstead, we need to organise a low-loader to get it back to the South Wales facility on the morning of Thursday the tenth, I was hoping your department would organise that for me."

Caroline turns away from Bob, her attention now on the rest of the team. Bob quietly sighs with relief as the voice in his ear calmly replies, "I see. Well played, Mr Glassman, I will be in my office for two hours. Ring me as soon as you are able."

"Thanks, Frank, that would be great, before twelve would be just right."

While he has been talking, the remainder of the team have wound things up on the firing point, and they move towards him, he gets another measured look from Caroline, and they all tramp down the road towards the lab. When they get there, Caroline conducts a hot wash-up of the day's events and reminds them that the ten people who will do 'Opfor' the next day will be turning up at the morning coffee break next day. The group disperses, and Bob notices that Sam and Craig are deep in conversation in front of Craig's screens, which are full of code. He exits the lab and heads for his hotel, where he composes his thoughts for the conversation with Leanne Phillips.

Leanne's secretary greets him by name as she takes the call and immediately puts him through.

"Ah, Mr Glassman, no more charades, I hope." She chuckles before continuing, "What can our work in the UK on an armoured vehicle possibly have to do with the project you used as bait to get this conversation?"

"I had to get your attention, the team working on your project reached out to me a few months ago to pull in some of our land environment expertise, so I know a bit about what you're doing." Aware that they are talking on an open line, Bob is choosing his words with care. "You know the significance of where I am, well, they've got an Ajax up here, and they've done what the Akicita Maza project is trying to do."

There is a pause at the other end. "Are you sure?"

"I've been watching it all day. The test is relatively simple, but I'm convinced it's way more capable than they're letting on. The demo is on the ninth of this month, I really think you should find some way of having one of your folks come along. I'd be surprised if some of the Ajax team weren't invited, so it ought to be possible to insert someone into the party. The whole programme is headed up by a woman called Sherwood at the MOD in Bristol."

Leanne has been leaning back in her chair, listening and calculating. "Helen Sherwood, I know of her, she's a big hitter – for a Brit. I think I shall have a word with our UK head office."

Leanne is recently in post as the lead executive of the Autonomous and Unmanned Systems section of the site better known as the Skunk Works, world-renowned for its work in aeronautics. She is deeply involved in applying AI to the organisation's work on drones. An engineer with twenty years' experience and with Harvard-backed business credentials, she is on track for a senior vice president's role in the organisation. Her perfectionist mind is now reeling with possibilities. Bob's news that the Brits may be ahead of her own programme pulls up a whole list of options, top of which is, far from sending someone to Fort Halstead, she must go herself. She returns her attention to Bob.

"Outstanding work, Mr Glassman. It's Bob, isn't it? You've done the company a great service, and I'll see to it that your contribution is recognised. Keep a low profile now, but expect one of my people to be in touch." After politeness's, she hangs up and asks her secretary to put her through to the head of Lockheed Martin UK.

In his hotel room, Bob jubilantly punches the air.

It is late, but former Air Marshall Alex Donohue is in his office, and his cultured tones betray only moderate surprise that a senior executive at the Skunk Works wants to talk to him. Leanne wastes no time briefing him on what she has learnt from Bob Glassman.

There is a chuckle at the other end of the phone. "How interesting, Leanne, only today I took a call from Helen Sherwood, who was ringing to ask if a representative would like to attend a demonstration at Fort Halstead next week. I considered it curious but relatively routine. Patrick O'Connor, the MD of our Bedfordshire operation, is going. They make the turret that Fort Halstead have been playing with."

"I need to get on that visit, Alex, can it be fixed?"

"Oh yes, no one would object to Paddy bringing a colleague. It's only in a few days you know."

"I'll be on a flight tomorrow. May I go to your facility and find out a bit more about this turret? I'm aerospace, so I'm not an expert in land systems."

"Of course, I'll let them know to expect you and arrange for you to be hosted. I'll get in touch with some contacts and see what's afoot. A former colleague is director ISTAR at the MOD, he'll know what's going on."

The call ends, and in offices either side of the Atlantic secretaries and personal assistants are suddenly very busy.

HEIMDALL SHOOTS AT REAL PEOPLE

Unaware of these manoeuvrings, the team at Fort Halstead reconvenes the next day to prepare for the first trial run of Heimdall against live opposition. Mike and David arrive shortly after the rest of the team have finished the initial setup. Sam tells the group that she and Craig have configured Heimdall to accept acoustic signals. Mike is startled, but his interest in the outcome of this extension of the turret capability trumps any caution. He also decides to tolerate the use of Heimdall instead of IADS. When the motley crew from the security detail turn up, they are dressed in an array of tracksuits and are carrying their weapons, which have been fitted with attachments for firing blank ammunition. David pre-briefed them not to wear clothing that would identify them as British Troops. Craig had warned him that the system would be unlikely to fire at them if it recognised the opposing force as friendly troops.

David now instructs them on how the first run-through for the day will see them advance towards the firing point, and point and fire their weapons. Jim hands out the laser vests and supervises the enthusiastic group as they put them on.

After the 'enemy' have been led away to the top of the range, Craig readies the system and turns his attention to the screen showing the inner workings of his machine's mind. As the group, which is strung out in a loose line, approach, the turret moves and the target display briefly centres on each figure. Rob and William's screens show the type of activity that they have come to expect, although they are caught by surprise as Heimdall identifies each of the Opfor by name. Craig immediately puts the system on standby and shouts for Jim to call off this first run. Mike has not seen what the system monitoring team have seen.

Craig explains, "Sorry, Mike. That was totally unexpected. Heimdall has identified all of the group."

"Well, that's what we'd expect, isn't it? Followed by opening fire with the start of a hostile act."

"No, he actually identified them, by name!"

All eyes in the control cabin turn to the team on the screens. Outside, the Opfor look at each other nonplussed, as Jim strides over to see what's happening in control.

Mike moves over to Craig's station. "What do you mean 'by name', Craig? How can it do that?"

Diana answers the question. "Of course! We're using the old network. The same one that all the security admin uses. These are the off-duty security bods. All their details are in the system and, remember, photos are part of the package—"

Caroline interrupts. "But you said the other day when we were discussing target lists that facial recognition isn't very reliable yet. I got the impression that you hadn't included it, Craig."

"Good point, Caroline. I hadn't, but I can guess how he did it."

Again it is Diana who, with her detailed knowledge of the old intranet system that they are using, answers the question. "It's more legacy software, there's a facial recognition programme in there that was just left behind. Our boy found it and used it, I bet."

Rob, who has looked at the log files during this discussion, confirms her surmise.

Mike is staring at the screen, but not seeing it, he is deep in thought. A few weeks ago, this incident would have bothered him deeply, issues of responsibility and out of control AIs being at the forefront of his management brain. The recent interference by his superior and the tantalising opportunity to take the project forward independently now colour his judgement, though he is still capable of exercising caution.

"You four have some work to do, then. I want a thorough analysis of what happened and how. Keep in mind the risks, I mean that. Di, you're versed in programme risk, you oversee that, you're less likely to be influenced by the 'boy's toy' element of all this." He turns to Craig. "Alright, wonder boy, how do we solve this little hiccup?"

"The same way you fool all facial recognition – wear a mask! A handkerchief, old western bad-guy style should do it. A buff or something would be better and probably look a bit more serious."

"You're learning, Craig. An ounce of image is worth a pound of performance." David takes a similar view to Mike. "I'm very interested in the acoustic side of the capability you've added."

"Sam did the work routing the sound through to the programme, my adjustment was minimal. We haven't checked it out yet, I was waiting until we'd got this bit right. If we get the time, Sam and I will do more testing and let you know if it'll add anything to the demonstration."

From behind them Jim, standing in the doorway, says, "Your point about image is a good one, sir. We've got some old Soviet-era uniforms at the School of Infantry. We could get them sent up?

"You're a genius, Sarn't Major. No need, the OA people here have got some, I'm sure." He dashes off and disappears inside the Fort. Jim goes back to the Opfor people, who he has adopted as his own, to let them know what is occurring. Before he goes, he cocks an eyebrow at Caroline and says, "The Colonel thinks I'm a genius, too, ma'am!" He dodges out of sight to avoid any riposte.

The team breaks up and scatters across the site to make preparations for reconvening in the afternoon. David finds enough uniforms to kit out ten people and William volunteers to go and find some one-size-fits-all buffs to obscure the faces on Jim's Opfor section.

There is a festive air that afternoon as the Opfor team lark about in their Russian gear. There is particular approval for the buffs that William has procured. He got them from a motorcycle shop, and now the section sport skeletal lower halves to their faces which, under the helmets they are wearing, are very macabre. Collectively, it makes them look quite compelling and Mike and David, counter-intuitively, like the look. Jim has been coaching them on several routines for their approach down the range. Mike settles everyone down as Jim and his crew march off into the distance and disappear into the dead ground.

David has got hold of a couple of radio handsets so that he can talk to the Opfor team. Craig indicates he is ready with a nod and a brief command is passed to Jim.

Shortly, a column of figures can be seen approaching the dummy base. Rob, who is monitoring the data recorders as usual, provides a brief commentary on what Heimdall is doing in response to the scenario.

"ID as possible hostile."

"Recognised the uniforms, can't classify the weapons."

On the range, the section shakes out into a line abreast formation and jogs towards the Hesco bastion wall. At about 200 metres distance, and in response to an unheard command from Jim, weapons are raised and the pop of blank rounds can be heard. Simultaneously the turret, which had been pointing at the right-most figure, emits a series of rapid clicks as it traverses across the line. Downrange, the simulator vests flash orange lights.

"Hostile act until end of engagement three point six seconds."

David exhales sharply. "CT40's cyclic rate of fire is a maximum of 200 rounds a minute. Would I be right in concluding that the only thing stopping Heimdall from completing that engagement in two and a half seconds is the rate of traverse?"

Craig is gazing thoughtfully down the range at the figures, who are trooping off to the side past Jim who cancels the vest lights with his 'God gun'.* He realises that firing at live targets, even with the laser simulator, is disquieting.

"Yes, but did you notice that he tracked the right-hand figure after he decided they might be a threat, not the centre one? That was so the turret only needed to traverse in one direction throughout the sequence."

David and Mike share a look and turn their attention to the back of Craig's head. He swivels his chair to find them watching him.

"I know," he says grimly. "It's not intelligent, but even I'm finding it to be scarily efficient."

The two senior men's ambition arranges approving smiles on their faces. Mike nods.

"Let's go again!"

Craig gets them to give him time to add the rate of fire of the cannon into his scenario script. He didn't know the figures and wants to place a limit on the laser. In answer to a question from Caroline, he tells them that he's specified 'Hostile Act' in the ROE for the exercise, explaining that he thought it would be better for the purposes of the demonstration. This elicits more approving noises from Mike and David.

On the next run, the 'enemy' behaves more tactically, taking a circuitous route before firing from cover. It makes no difference to the outcome, except that Heimdall takes slightly longer to track and engage while he waits for targets to expose themselves. Jim has told the Opfor not to shoot if they've been hit. On this serial, they only get three rounds away before they are all downed.

In Rob's commentary comes the news that Heimdall has aggregated the hostile act, only waiting for the first shot, because

---

* The lights on the laser vests can only be stopped by someone acting as an 'umpire'. The device they use is nicknamed the 'God gun'.

the enemy forces are dressed the same and carrying weapons. Mike wryly comments on this further 'efficiency'. Craig winces slightly but can raise a smile in response.

Throughout the day, Bob has kept a low profile and is a picture of studied calm. He is on his own now, as the General Dynamics contractor has little to do and left earlier in the week. Caroline has noticed this, and his discretion only serves to confirm her suspicions.

The final surprise of the day comes when the Opfor makes a real effort to approach unseen. The surveillance screen that shows the image of the gunsight blinks rapidly, and the image changes to show a rapid series of video feeds that can only come from the fence surveillance cameras. This causes David to bolt from the cabin to the range phone at the road end of the firing point. He comes back a little breathless to announce that he has warned the security post that their experiment might be causing a few issues with the cameras.

In the meantime, Heimdall has used the advantage gained by the use of this new footage to eliminate the opposition, who only managed to get one shot off this time.

This new development leads them to take a break, and Jim leaves his team at the brew table chattering and laughing about their performance.

Mike talks them through the decision he has made about the main demonstration, based on what he has seen.

"I'm changing the focus of the demonstration. We'll do most of the demo in the lab using the material we record from today and tomorrow. We can use the recorded material far more effectively down there and stage-manage things better. We'll come up here after lunch to show that what we've told them in front of a screen isn't just smoke and mirrors. It means we need to expand our briefings a bit and edit the recorded material, so there's some work to do between now and the dress rehearsal tomorrow. I'll put that off until the afternoon to give us more time. Remember that Helen Sherwood will be here for that."

There are groans at this reminder, and Rob loudly hums the *Star Wars* Darth Vader theme, whilst attempting to look innocent. Mike calls for calm and reminds them that not only is she on their side, but she also has all the money. David also tells them that the Director and the heads of department at the Fort are coming to the rehearsal. The Coven loudly proclaims their intention to be on best behaviour.

David and Jim debrief the Opfor and let them know that they will do much the same thing during the next couple of days. The rest of the team clear up and close up, before heading down to the lab.

Bob is excused for the rest of the day as he has no involvement in the mechanics of the demonstration, although Jim remains so that he and David can deal with any changes in the Opfor plan.

William is the wizard of video editing, and Rob and Diana pull footage and data together for him to string into the coherent product that Mike storyboards for them. Craig sifts through log files and makes notes to go with a series of screenshots, which illustrate the internal processes and learning routes that Heimdall uses. Caroline puts these onto slides for Mike to edit.

It is late when Craig gets back to Wimbledon, and the house is quiet. He wonders where Sophie is, and sighs glumly. He is long past any notion that the relationship has any future. Still, his partner's predilection for noisy and theatrical tantrums has exacerbated his own fear of emotional conflict. Craig sits in the dark on the edge of his bed and stares into the night. Eventually, he decides that she is not likely to return and, with some relief, he falls asleep.

At Fort Halstead in the morning, the team are caught in the whirl of preparation, so Craig has no time to dwell on the arid nature of his home life. They are all pretty much happy with the fruits of their labour until mid-morning, when the redoubtable Helen arrives.

Her agenda trumps theirs, and she sets about tightening and

focusing the forthcoming exhibition of their work according to her aims.

The team are pretty good at this sort of thing. In their world, it is bread and butter to invent something and then lay it out in such terms that the customer finds the product irresistible. Helen brings a whetstone to their work. They may privately and very carefully mock her. Still, after her critique and the subsequent rework, no one doubts the direction of travel that this project is on. She has already taken Mike and David aside to further update them on the future of the project. Having told them of her intentions, she deems that it is time to reinforce team cohesion. After approving the presentation, she hitches herself up onto the table in the breakout area and calls for them to listen up.

"OK, Project Heimdall," she says as they settle in a semicircle around her. "This is where we get serious. You know that the scheme you embarked on was time and finance limited. It was destined to run out, and that those of you so inclined would move to Wiltshire, which would mean a change of teams or moves to other projects. Well, I've got some news for you. I've been discussing the implications of what Dr Moore has brought to us with Mike and how we might take this forward. I have a question for you: if there were to be an extension to this work, who would be prepared for an early move to Porton Down to start on an independent project under Mike's direction?"

The reaction is muted surprise.

Diana breaks the silence saying, "We mostly lodge around here, and I think all of us were planning to take up posts at Porton." She looks around at her colleagues, who are equally astonished at this news. They all nod encouragingly. "I think we'd all like to carry on as a team. Does that include Craig?"

"That is rather up to him, but I hope so. What say you, Dr Moore?"

Her dark eyes fix on him shrewdly as the others all turn their attention to him.

"What exactly do you have in mind, Helen?"

"Good question. This project focused on automating aspects of the security of a base in hostile territory, and I think we can pretty much chalk up a success. Integrated surveillance reported to a central hub and a pattern of cheap weaponised turrets, what's not to like? Man-in-the-loop. Everyone is happy. Then you come along and tell us that we can take at least one, maybe two people, out of the turret of an armoured vehicle. That has got a number of my military policy colleagues very interested. Obviously, they are cautious, but I've been given a funding stream to find out what is possible." She looks across at David. "It does mean that your friend Robin will be short of an Ajax or two. How do you think he'd feel about letting us have a couple of crew?"

"I think I know just the woman for the latter, Helen, and as for Robin, I think he'll want to be part of future development rather than just letting it occur around him."

"I'll leave you to fix that then. By 'just the woman' I take it you mean Sergeant Tate?"

"Yes, I do. She already has a pretty intuitive grasp of what we're up to. If we're going to work on an Ajax, I'd like her where I can ensure her discretion as well as exploit her skills."

Helen turns her attention back to Craig. "What I have in mind, Craig, is letting Heimdall loose on the most advanced armoured vehicle in our inventory. The only condition is that it has a commander in the turret. You get to properly integrate your toy into our toy. Are you interested?"

"How long do we get?"

"I've been given six months. The team will be given a hangar close to the range." She turns to David and Catherine. "You two are, I'm sure, familiar with Porton."

They nod, both of them have done chemical, biological, radiological and nuclear training on the range there, part of a CBRN package to prep them for operations.

"What I want you to do is see if you can remove the driver

from the vehicle but maintain the same operational capability. The idea is to find out if it can be done and, if so, whether it should be done."

Craig frowns. "How will you test the effectiveness of a machine-assisted crew?"

"You're starting to get the vocab, Craig, I like that. 'Machine-assisted crew'. A very palatable way to describe it. To answer your question, once we've integrated the technology, we'll take it on to Salisbury Plain and let it fight the unmodified Ajaxes."

There is silence in the lab as this news is digested. Helen does not interrupt, but she watches the reaction intently, her eyes flicking from one person to another.

Craig breaks the silence. "Well, I don't know much about the place, beyond what was in the press when the nerve gas was used in Salisbury. I think I'm in, though." He looks around at the rest of the team, who all nod and make affirmative comments.

Helen smiles in satisfaction and turns her attention to Sam. She is the contractor integrated into the team and will need her company's approval to stay on in another location. Sam meets her gaze and pre-empts her question.

"If you get approval from my head office, I'm yours. This project is so cutting edge, I want to be part of it." Sam can see her career prospects starting to glitter if she can get to stay on.

Helen nods approvingly before saying, "I doubt very much that Weybridge will stand in the way, Sam. Far from it, in fact." Helen is elated by the reaction from the team, and she glances at Mike, who is equally pleased.

They share a look that is interrupted by a comment from Caroline. "Will we be inviting Lockheed or GD to the party, Helen?"

Helen notes the frown on Caroline's face. "Why do you ask, Caroline?"

"Well, I think Lockheed at least have had some fairly detailed briefs from Mr Glassman."

Helen gives her a measured look and nods. "That explains a couple of things." She looks over to where Mike and David are sitting. "I extended a polite invitation to the CEO at Lockheed UK. He's a former air force officer, very senior. At first, we were told that someone from the Bedfordshire site would be coming along, but just yesterday, I got a call telling me he's coming himself and asking if I mind if he brings a 'colleague from the States who just happens to be across'. He didn't give a name, but I found out from my own contacts that it's going to be none other than Leanne Phillips, the new head of Autonomous and Unmanned Systems at the Skunk Works." She is gleeful. "Things are fitting into place very nicely."

Mike explains to the team that US interest was bound to be aroused and that this development pretty much confirms that they are probably ahead of the US programmes. The core DSTL people are really pleased with this bit of news as it doesn't happen very often. Helen then explains to them the leverage it gives her in terms of getting American cooperation with some of the other projects with which she is involved.

While she's been talking Craig has googled Skunk Works and is impressed to discover it is Lockheed Martin's Advanced Development Programme, with a distinguished history of technological advances, particularly in aerospace. The pictures of such aeroplanes as the SR71 Blackbird on the screen start a chain of thought, only interrupted when he hears his name and feels all eyes are upon him. He stammers an apology as Helen repeats her question.

"How much time would you need to move down to Wiltshire?"

Craig regains his composure with a weak attempt at what, for him, passes for humour. "Oh, if there's a room somewhere, I'd just need to pick up a toothbrush."

Needless to say, Helen notes his discomfiture, so she drily takes him at his word. Turning to David, she asks if there might be some temporary accommodation that could be obtained through the Military.

David looks thoughtful. "Well, there's no shortage of units and headquarters around there. It's a vast sprawl of garrisons. That doesn't mean there's much accommodation, though."

"As a gunner, I'll be going to Larkhill if I still have a role, although I don't think I'll be able to do six months." Caroline looks from Helen to the Coven. "It's not unusual for civil servants to be put up there from time to time. If it's not full up, we might get a bunch of rooms in one of the annexes there; I could find out." She turns back to Helen. "What sort of timeframe are you looking at?"

"Well, you certainly have a role, Caroline." Helen tunes out for a moment as she thinks. "Once the demo is done and we've returned the Ajax, we will need to get a report together that I can put in front of my minister. I'll let you have a week for that, then you'll need some R and R, I think, as well as an opportunity to get ready for a move. I'd say the first week in November, if it can be managed." Her final comment hangs in the air like a challenge.

Mike is eager to grasp his new independent role. "The sooner, the better. There'll be a lot of preliminary work to do, that'll be plenty of R and R for me."

David is more cautiously enthusiastic. "Is the office and hangar space available, Helen?"

Helen's cool gaze turns to him. "I was there for a different purpose yesterday, David. I had a conversation with the Director, he was… very amenable and showed me just what I needed!"

David laughs out loud. "Of course he did!"

There is such an excited buzz in the team that Helen reminds them that what they are about to embark on is a step change from the present work. As such, it is to be approached with a great deal more discretion. Mike and David use this as an opportunity to bring everyone's attention back to the upcoming rehearsal in front of the Fort Halstead audience.

Under Helen's critical eye, the team run through the amended presentation. She has few comments, so they tramp up to the range to meet Jim and his crew. Having covered all the technical parts of the system during the laboratory presentation, the range demonstration is designed to reinforce the points already made, so they only intend to do a couple of run-throughs. Jim, however, has found a dummy RPG-7 rocket launcher, so they do a third run with one of the Opfor carrying this weapon. Heimdall correctly prioritises this threat and eliminates it as soon as it is exposed, before finishing off the remaining forces.

Helen is pleased but asks them to do a fourth run with an unarmed civilian involved to test the ROE more obviously. Jim grabs the man who runs the range, from his office in the fort. He's a retired soldier and is slightly amused to be asked. Helen is very interested when Will calls her over to his screen and shows the log file entry where this newcomer, who is without a mask, is correctly identified by name, and Heimdall does not shoot him.

She declares herself satisfied with the results of the morning, and they return to the lab, where a working lunch precedes the arrival of the Director and the heads of the other three departments. They arrive as coffee is being dispensed and there are introductions and small talk.

Helen observes the tableau before her. The DSTL hierarchy are obviously looking to gain advantage by attending this meeting. David and Mike direct covert glances at the Director that are anything but friendly. For his part, the Director is full of unconvincing bonhomie, drawing Mike and David into the senior circle and complimenting them on their excellent work. Oleaginous is the word that springs to mind, as she responds to his beckoning hand with a smile. Wandering over to join the management group, she sees that the remainder of the Heimdall workers are in a suspicious huddle, in turn darting glances at the bosses. By the time she reaches the Director, her smile has been warmed by the situation she's observed and the possibilities it offers.

The Director and his acolytes are pleased and impressed that Helen is taking such a personal interest in one of the final projects that Fort Halstead will see to completion before the move. The other three project leaders have all finished their regular work and are now deeply involved in the movement of resources and those people who have chosen to carry on in the new organisation. There is much jockeying for position at Porton Down, as well as competition for space, both qualitative and quantitative. Mike's contemporaries are secretly gleeful that his prestigious project has been so all-encompassing that he hasn't yet had a chance to position himself in the new organisation. The Director is the only person with a real knowledge of what Heimdall is, or might be, and even he is not yet entirely in the picture. He knows that Mike is nipping at his heels in terms of future progression, so this demonstration of capability is, to him, an opportunity to move in and enhance his own standing.

Of course, Helen Sherwood is the key, and as she joins the circle, she knows this. Everything is about budgets, especially in the world of advanced projects, and it is her firm hand that pulls the purse strings.

"Well, colleagues," says Helen, "how kind of you to allow me to come to this event. I'm sure you are all well aware of its importance to the minister and what it is trying to achieve."

There is an 'um' from the head of operational analysis, who says, "I'd understood this was a project to intelligently blend ISTAR products and feed them into a central hub to improve camp defence."

"Well, yes and no. We wanted to automate much of the mundane business of guarding a base and thought that AI could be utilised…"

There is a cough behind her that causes her to turn. Seeing Craig looking disapprovingly at her, she laughs and returns her attention to the senior audience.

"I should say Machine Learning, I think. When we recruited our expert there, it became apparent that we could do far more than just assist the soldiers on guard. However, I'm trespassing on Mike's territory now, so I'll stop and we'll get on with the presentation. Before I do, I should point out Craig Moore, who has been our principal scientific contributor."

There is a startled sound from head of explosive forensics. "Dr Craig Moore?"

"You've heard of Craig, have you, Ms Leatherland?"

"Well, yes. I'd not made the connection that it was *the* Dr Moore who Mike had managed to recruit. I wish I had, some of his research could help our work." Her look is a mix of respect and avarice. Her colleagues eye Craig with interest.

Mike takes control of the group, and they sit for his introduction to the project. After outlining the initial aim that the team were set, which corresponds to head OA's understanding, he goes on to explain that Craig was further ahead in his thinking than they realised and this led them to expand the mission to see how far machine learning in its current state could go. He ends, "As you are about to see, the answer to this problem is extraordinary."

David then takes over to explain the simulated work in OA environment that, he says, the head OA 'kindly' allowed them to access. He runs the edited scenes from their simulation series to show the increasingly efficient detection, recognition and identification that Heimdall achieves. Following on from this, they see the weaponization of Heimdall and the application of Rules of Engagement to the defence of the base. The lab part of the demonstration finishes with edited scenes from the range, the zeroing of the weapon on the Ajax, the unexpected recognition of the guards and co-opting of the fence cameras.

There is silence after Mike concludes the formal part of the exposition. It is broken by the Director saying, "I knew you were a long way forward after your last briefing to me, but seeing it laid out like this is certainly startling. Where does it go from here?"

Smoothly, Helen intervenes. "We're having discussions on just that subject in Bristol. Obviously, this concludes the current stage, and we're chalking up a success. Anything more will be a political decision, until then you have a move to execute." Her hard look focuses on Mike, who keeps his face bland.

"Let's save further questions until after we've been up to the range."

On the battlements of the fort, there is now an open-fronted tent that looks out onto the training area to the front of the firing point below them. The coverings are off the Ajax and the team quickly boot up the system. Mike gathers the senior people in the tent and briefs them on the now simplified live demonstration, emphasising this is proof of the concepts they have seen in the lab.

Jim has pre-positioned his opposing force at the top of the range out of sight. When Mike has finished, David initiates the first run, the armed group advances and, as the Heimdall team expects, when they open fire orange lights blink on in a matter of seconds. The spectators are expecting success, but seeing it achieved so quickly against a live enemy causes a buzz of conversation as the team resets for the next run. The three elements that complete the live demonstration all go perfectly, improved by Sam's work at the integration of the acoustic sensors and hooking up the sight on top of the turret. This shaves fractions of a second off Heimdall's times, as he has learned to use the surveillance mount to prioritise the targets more effectively.

On the battlements, Mike draws this part of the demo to a close and asks them to return to the lab for questions. David leans over the wall and shouts for Craig to join them. The remainder of them start shutting down the range and resting for the event to come.

Back in the lab, there are many technical questions from the audience, and Craig is drawn in for the first time during the day. Uncomfortable in front of these people he is, at first, reticent. Head of OA asks about the transition from simulated activity to live activity.

"That was easy, I changed the early iterations of the programme from game-like sim environments to the real world. When I got here, I had to go back a few stages, it was a matter of translating inputs and outputs that were peculiar to your OA world. Once the programme understands the language, it can build and sense the world and respond to inputs."

Head of forensics interjects. "So, how does it – I hesitate to use the word – think?"

Craig smiles as he replies, "Heimdall doesn't think, as such, but I've built human-like behaviour in as much as that's possible. There is perception, machine-cognition and action. The trick was to teach rules and mechanisms and then give the programme as much access as possible to information libraries, so that a sufficiently reliable probabilistic world can be built. Once Heimdall knows the rules of the world he's sensing, he then reacts when the sensory picture has enough fidelity to satisfy the verification levels we set. The reaction is just controlling a relatively simple machine."

There are chuckles at Craig's description of the advanced Ajax turret as a simple machine.

The Director clears his throat portentously. He thanks Mike and David for the 'exceptional quality' of the demonstration, and turns to Helen.

"I really am impressed with what has been achieved, and am a bit startled by the extent of what will be shown to a senior audience. I do think that perhaps I should introduce the programme tomorrow."

Helen notes Mike's suppressed reaction to this development and the less carefully controlled expression on David's face. She intervenes in the nick of time.

"You have a point, of course, and now I come to think of it, I must allow that you are right. It is, of course, my audience, and the presence of the US does certainly deserve senior input. I think I shall do it, that should set an MOD seal on things before the people who did all the work get to present the detail." She smiles, and the Director swallows this setback to his personal plans. After some platitudes, he leads his team away. Head of forensics smirks and winks at Mike on her way past. Craig excuses himself, as he wants to go back up to the range and join the rest of the group. Mike keeps a straight face until they are gone.

The expletive he uses before turning back to them raises a laugh from David and a sardonic smile from Helen.

"Thank you."

"Oh, don't thank me, Michael, he just doesn't know he's lost you, and you've got work to do."

Helen is very contented with this day, her reading of the situation has been perfect. It was predictable that, knowing the Director as she does, he would try to steal credit from Mike. Her ambition is tied to what she is confident this project will do for her. Mike now belongs to her, and with him, David. They both know that attaching themselves to Helen's coat tails can only lead onwards and upwards.

The three sit and talk through the personalities they are expecting to attend the following day. Helen is keen to manage the Lockheed Martin people, who will be joined by the US Military attaché, an Air Force officer from the Embassy. She is confident that when they get a taste of the Heimdall capability, they will want it. She is sure this will lead to critical radar and electro-optical sensor technology she wants that is currently stalled in the ITAR pipeline. Unblocking this will be a significant success for her.

They are presently joined by the rest of the crew, and they sit drinking the remains of the coffee, talking in a relaxed fashion about the next day. Helen takes the opportunity to quiz Jim about his career and what he does. She only has a vague notion as to the role of the gunnery instructors at the Royal Armoured Corps Centre, but she is impressed by his organisation of the Opfor section and his hands-on ability.

David talks them through the military guests. A lieutenant colonel from the Army's capability development branch, whose remit covers the Ajax. He mentions that the group captain that Craig met at the MOD will be attending, accompanied by a senior civil servant from the office of the secretary of state. He also tells them that the CO and RSM of the regiment from where he got the Ajax and one of the crew commanders will attend.

Helen finishes by adding that a senior colleague from Bristol will represent the ISTAR community in the procurement authority. She emphasises that they are demonstrating a system to assist in the protection of a military base by freeing up soldiers, and not to mention the forthcoming experiment at Porton Down.

DEMONSTRATION DAY

The atmosphere in the lab the following morning is tense, in spite of everybody's confidence in the system. It is a relief when the first guests start to arrive. There is an unusually lavish coffee and biscuit table laid out. The coffee tastes like coffee beans may have featured in its production, and the biscuits are high-end artisanal creations. Introductions are punctuated by non-specific small talk. David introduces Craig to his friend Robin and the other two from the Royal Lancers.

The US contingent arrives last and the atmosphere changes, losing some of its informality. Leanne Phillips is the focus of team Heimdall's attention, and is all charm and courtesy. Her slight southern drawl accentuates this, and Helen is aware of her skilful undermining of the team's reserve. She suggests that the late arrivals take their coffee to the seating area so that they can get started. Helen introduces herself while the rest of the audience moves to take their seats. They measure each other over firm handshakes, and their smiles broaden as they recognise a kinship of competitiveness and ambition. Leanne is the last to seat herself as Helen takes her place at centre stage.

She welcomes them all, adding, "A particular welcome to Leanne from the world-famous Skunk Works. We are very fortunate that she happened to be visiting Lockheed UK and we were able to extend an invitation."

Leanne beams with delight at this comment and inclines her head in acknowledgement.

"What we're going to show you today is the culmination of work we've been doing on improving the security of an installation by combining surveillance feeds and using machine learning to fuse the information, so reducing the number of people who need to be on guard. That in itself is useful, but we had a stroke of luck and were able to extend the scope of our work into some areas that are at the edge of what we thought was currently possible. I think that is what you'll find most interesting. But before I hand over to Mike Sheppard, let me introduce you to our 'stroke of luck', Dr Craig Moore."

Six pairs of eyes swivel to regard Craig, who smiles nervously in return.

"I'm sure that Craig will answer questions, but you'll have to wait until the end. Over to you, Mike."

The presentation is slick and well-rehearsed, the audience attentive. There are some sharp intakes of breath as the Heimdall's capabilities are revealed. Leanne gives little away, but she watches intently, and things that might be missed by others do not escape her. Henry, the senior civil servant, shifts uncomfortably as he watches the initiative displayed by the system in the synthetic environment, most notably when it asks for drone coverage and during the engagements around the marketplace. When the lecture moves on to the early stages on the range, the project team have highlighted the analysis of the mobile targets and the initial classification of these as wheelchairs. This draws an incredulous outburst, and Caroline pauses the simulation.

"Wheelchairs! How on earth does it come to that conclusion?"

Mike smoothly interjects with, "The programme searches databases for target characteristics and makes the best match. As it searched, it extracted data from our web and wheelchair was one of the results before the mobile target system was found. We're showing you this to illustrate the capability it has to rapidly detect and classify targets. The point is that the system did not engage, not even when it classified the objects correctly. In the rules of engagement, the target is not an actual threat, so Craig had to instruct the programme to treat them as hostile threats."

An American voice enters the conversation, the US Military attaché. "I have to say, I'm very relieved that your clever machine doesn't shoot disabled people."

This gets a laugh from everyone except the man from the Ministry. "You let it get into the internet? I can't say I think that's wise."

Craig bristles at this. "It doesn't get into the internet, sir, any more than you do. It asks questions and analyses the proffered answers in exactly the same way, just faster and more accurately."

Helen smoothly deflects Craig. "This is a controlled experiment, Henry, we very quickly met our remit once Dr Moore was kind enough to drop his own research and join our organisation. We must understand the nature of these new technologies, hence the extension of our work."

Her dark eyes bore into the man as he continues, "This is very sensitive stuff, Helen, I can foresee ministerial concern."

"Quite right, Henry, but don't you think that is a conversation to be had at another time… and elsewhere?"

Finally, he realises that his outburst is indiscreet, and he subsides red-faced.

The final part of the address shows the introduction of the live Opfor and Heimdall's recognition of the faces and co-opting of the fence cameras. Leanne leans forward and looks intently at the screenshots of this. Henry huffs, but subsides when Helen glowers at him.

Helen joins Mike and David at the front of the audience and invites questions.

The Americans watch and wait to see how the British will start. They are not disappointed. Despite the barely concealed disapproval that his earlier outbursts have brought, Henry is first to air his views.

"I think what we have seen here reinforces the views on artificial intelligence of both our governments. There must always be a human between the machine and the decision to shoot. Just think what one of those vultures of the press would make of this. The headlines would make mincemeat of us."

David keeps his reply to this opening statement carefully courteous. "Henry, we've already heard the lines of reasoning that have led us to exceed our original remit." He glances at Helen. "Yes, we have a system we could put in charge of defence. It spots valid threats and offers to engage. The operations officer looks, makes a judgement, and presses the fire button."

Mike picks up the thread from him. "Even I had no idea what we were embarking on when we got hold of Dr Moore. Yes, we may have forged forwards in our excitement. Yes, there are risks in scientific endeavour. Helen put her finger on what we are pushing towards. We must understand the new technology. If nothing else, so that we know what we may face. Press or no press!"

David steps forward and stabs his hand in Henry's direction. "Does anyone here not think that there are other countries out there who are experimenting on this? Countries that don't have our two nations' best interests in mind as they work, and don't have our sense of restraint."

Joe, the US defence attaché, speaks up. "I think our little delegation fully supports your words, Colonel Lucas. Especially those last ones."

There are nods and murmurs of approval from the Americans as he continues.

"Human-in-the-loop is all a matter of perspective. Dr Moore and his team, as far as I can see, are human and they are most certainly in the loop. I can see nothing here that sits outside human control." He turns to regard Henry. "Sir, the press will be a problem whatever we do. Speaking as an airman, someone who knows the cost of war personally, in human terms. If I say to a mother, the mouth of Hell is over there, ma'am, I can either send this machine in there or I can send your son. What do you suppose she'll say?"

Leanne has noted Craig's increasing tension during the exchange. Her voice stills the audience as she speaks.

"The arguments are nothing new. I think, from my industry perspective, I want to get ahead in this field and stay ahead. That is both for the sake of my country and for Lockheed. You'd no doubt expect that from me, so I'd be interested to know Dr Moore's view. It's his monster, after all."

Craig is startled to have all attention on him, and his reply is, initially, hesitant and nervous.

"I never saw myself working for the government, and not for a moment making a weapon. My monster isn't a monster." He directs a wry smile shyly at Leanne before continuing. "It's not intelligent, it doesn't have feelings, however much we all refer to it as 'he'. It can't get angry or sad or want revenge for the death of the machine next to it. It can only obey and implement the instructions we give it. It can act on its own initiative but only using percentage probabilities we set, according to rules we set. It's all in the scripts."

There are chuckles from the Fort Halstead team at this oft used phrase.

Craig smiles at his little group in the corner before continuing, "Our time is largely spent making sure those lines of instruction are as unambiguous as possible and the list doesn't have something contradictory in it. Our job is to set limits on this clever programme that can see and hear the real world and manipulate other machines faster and more accurately than any human ever could. Heimdall could never stand over a wounded, unarmed man and shoot him, just because he's angry or upset or bad. If these things do horrible things, it will be because humans tell them they must." He looks at Henry. "It's people you've got to control, Mr Scott, you can't uninvent these."

Some of them must have been holding their breath while they listened, as there is an audible sigh as he finishes. Leanne nods and smiles at Craig.

"I couldn't have put it better." She turns to Helen, who has murmured her approval, and the two women exchange a nod. Helen draws the discussion to a close. It had not gone as she expected but she isn't displeased.

"I think we should go up to the range and watch what Heimdall does in response to some live scenarios."

They arrive at the fort, and Helen guides the audience up onto the battlements to the shelter that has been set up there. They all stand in front of it, as the day is cold but the sun is shining. Inside the tent are screens that have views of William and Rob's workstations down on the firing point, as well as the main station that controls Heimdall. There are two-way communications from the battlements to the control shelter on the firing point, which includes a speaker so that the controllers can be heard. Currently, it is muted.

Jim's team are in a huddle with him, ready to go up the range to their starting positions. Their masks are around their necks, and they all look up at the casemate with interest. There is an air of excitement at the culmination of their work.

Mike tells the visitors that this part of the demonstration aims to prove the capability works outside of the simulated environment and will consist of four run-throughs of the same scenario with variables introduced.

He gives Jim the thumbs up, and the Opfor troop adopt their masked appearance and troop off up the range out of sight of the firing point. The audience murmurs with surprise when they see the faux skull appearance of the masks.

Henry looks deeply disapproving and says, "Isn't that in rather poor taste, Dr Sheppard?"

Mike laughs before replying, "We wanted masks and got some buffs from a motorcycle shop, the design was… unexpected! Didn't have time to change them."

As he moves to the side to look down at the command post, he knocks over a metal stand, which falls with a clatter. Below, the sensor mount on the turret abruptly swivels and the array elevates to look at the battlements. All eyes are drawn to the noise and subsequent movement. Even Mike is startled at this unexpected behaviour and, as the mount abruptly turns away from them, removing the disconcerting feeling of being observed, he opens his mouth to speak but is interrupted as the speaker in the tent crackles into life.

Craig's voice is heard: "I think if you look at the right hand set of screens, you can see why Heimdall didn't shoot at the enemy force before we put masks on them."

Mike walks over to the indicated screen, followed by Leanne. The others move to look as Leanne turns to face them and says evenly, "The machine just identified each of us by name."

There is a buzz of surprise at this news and an explosive, "What?" from Henry.

Mike hastens to explain. "We needed a separate network for our experiment, so we co-opted some legacy software on the old system that our administrators use. It's also used by our security people, so everyone's face and details from the badge system are there. Heimdall wouldn't fire at the Opfor because they were friendly forces, so we got the masks. Our sensor advisor, Sam, has been doing some integration work, and I think she got the acoustic sensors online as well as getting the surveillance array on the turret incorporated. That's the first time the system has looked behind the firing point. Until yesterday we only had the turret sight feeding data to Heimdall, and it was limited to looking up range."

The UK Lockheed visitor raises a question. "The microphones are linked to the Thales shot detection system, the noise we made didn't sound like a weapon."

Sam's voice comes over the speaker: "The fitted device only looks for weapon signatures, the microphones hear everything but the software filters irrelevant noise out. We didn't want to integrate our own software into the turret, so we just let Heimdall access the sounds straight from the microphones."

Craig enters the conversation. "While we were active yesterday evening, and this morning, we've seen the software analysing and classifying sounds."

Mike reasserts control. "We'll return to that later in the Q and A, I'm as interested as everyone else here to find out more about this aspect of our machine." Turning to the audience, he indicates the range, saying, "Let's turn our attention back to the demonstration and finish that. I think you'll all agree that there will be much to discuss afterwards."

David speaks to Jim over his radio, and the Opfor team begin the first run-through. Between the sequences, Mike and David explain the processes and illustrate how Heimdall sticks to the rules. The US attaché's eyes widen as David indicates the statistics showing the speed of engagement and the efficient ordering of targets. Leanne notes his reaction for future reference. At the end of the demonstration, Helen observes that the conditions are agreeable and coffee is brought up to the battlements where the Heimdall team join the audience for the Q and A session.

The Coven, Caroline and Sam gather together at the side while David, Mike and Helen make themselves comfortable against the battlements. Craig attempts to stick with the rest of his team, but Helen peremptorily beckons him over to join the hierarchy, which he does reluctantly.

Leanne is about to begin the questioning but is beaten to it by Henry, who leans forward and launches into a pompous monologue.

"Well, I must say that I am very impressed with what this group has done. It has far exceeded our expectations at head office, so much so that I expect some ministerial disquiet when I get back.

I'm sure our American colleagues will agree that this raises some serious ethical issues, after all, both our governments have declared that there will always be a human-in-the-loop where lethal force is being considered." He turns to look at the guests, who have divided into a Brit and US camp.

Both groups are regarding Henry with guarded expressions, the Americans less so than the Brits. It is blatantly evident that the last thing on the minds of the US people is ethics. Helen's colleague from Bristol, Colin Lewis, is a senior civil servant from the outer office of the minister for defence procurement, and he has been a taciturn observer of events thus far. He now intervenes, his tone is impatient.

"Henry, we are well aware of government policy, but it is not for us to make it or to limit our exploration of emerging technology. Others will decide how to proceed when presented, as we have been here, with breakthroughs. I will be recommending to my minister that we press ahead with this to the limits of what is possible and what we can afford." His last point comes with a smile that lightens the atmosphere – all the audience know about budget constraints.

The quiet civilian who is part of the US Embassy delegation observes, "We may wish to be morally virtuous, but there are plenty of folk out there who aren't, and too many on that list are our adversaries. It would be wise to at least know what is possible so that our forces can counter it when the time comes."

This draws murmurs of agreement and a thank you from Helen's associate.

Sergeant Tate surprises people by asking, "Where does this go from here? I mean, it's all very impressive, but when will we get to stop guarding camps ourselves?"

David answers her with a smile. "Good question, Sarn't Tate, the short answer is: not soon! Defence procurement is a slow process, it's got better over the last ten years, but the flash to bang is still a long interval. If the Capability people at Army HQ want it, I'd say it could be done in a couple of years if we got turrets off the shelf. Tom, it's your area, what do you think?"

Lieutenant Colonel Tom Foster has been quietly taking in all that he has seen during the day. He's had regular updates from David during the progress of the project, but this is the first time he has fully faced what could be done.

"I'm impressed by what I've seen, and to answer the question, I think we are going to want this and could use it right now, even without weaponisation. Based on your team's updates and the fact you borrowed the Ajax, we've been in touch with Sam's people in Belfast about a sentry turret design already. I must admit you've caught us by surprise with the speed at which you've been able to develop this."

Helen laughs at this statement and says, "Not half as surprised as we were when Craig pulled that particular rabbit out of his hat!"

All eyes turn to Craig, who grins sheepishly.

Tom looks thoughtful for a moment. "Actually, most of this system is in place as the sensors mostly already exist and it's just a matter of integrating them and letting your Heimdall do the rest. We'd need a command post for the operators and the hardware would need a deal of space, I imagine." He turns to Craig with a frown and asks, "How big is this thing, Dr Moore?"

Craig's smile is mischievous as he reaches behind his back to hold up the hardware dangling on its cluster of leads.

There is a chorus of astonished reaction from the audience, mostly variations of, "Is that it?"

Leanne quells the excitement of the US delegation with a glance, her own expression camouflaged behind a sweet smile that doesn't, much to Helen's gratification, hide the acquisitive gleam in her eyes.

Maz pipes up again. "It can't just be that little thing, can it? I thought it would be massive."

She gets a warm smile from Craig, who likes her guileless

fascination with everything she has seen. This also defuses the excitement, and several audience members are grateful that someone else asked the question that was at the front of their own minds. Craig puts Heimdall down on the battlement beside him.

"This is the brains, Mary, everything else is peripherals. Sensors to build the world view and then the effectors to interact with it. Eyes and ears, arms and legs, so to speak. Those can be pretty much anything, and size-wise they're just whatever is needed. The difficulty comes with the memory for the information that Heimdall needs so that he can make decisions. If the libraries of images, sounds, or other data must be on-board, that could get big and complicated. Networks or cloud-based systems wouldn't need as much hardware, but I'm learning just how paranoid you all are about security. The links would also need to be defended. We kept this experiment separate from anything sensitive, so most of what we needed came from the intranet, with some of the peculiar consequences you've seen today."

Robin's voice interjects. "Eyes and ears, arms and legs, Dr Moore. What else?"

Craig becomes the centre of attention again. He shifts uncomfortably and looks at Helen, who smiles and smoothly takes over any potential answer.

"Now, that is an excellent question, Colonel Matheson. There is, of course, huge potential in this technology. Still, I am reminded of what an engineer once told me many years ago. Just because you can do something, it doesn't necessarily mean you should. In this, Henry, there you may have a point. There is some distance to go before we may try any further experiments, but I will invite Dr Moore to, let's say, speculate." She turns to Craig and smiles, leaving him a bit flustered.

"Um… well, you probably know that some of my work has been looking at self-driving vehicles. Heimdall is rooted in that work, so in my view, it would be quite easy to drive a tank."

"How, Dr Moore? Autonomous vehicles are still some way from appearing on the highway." Leanne's voice is challenging, and Craig glances at Helen before replying.

"There's much more happening on a city road, and it's significantly more complex than open terrain. I've looked at all the manuals that David and Caroline have given me, and soldiers don't want to be close to each other, so all you need to do is build a decent three-dimensional model around the vehicle and teach it to avoid threats. It's still all rules-based and doesn't need imagination." Craig looks thoughtful and drifts away from his audience. Absently, he says, "It would be interesting to try it, much easier in an aircraft, of course." He returns to the moment and sees Leanne gazing intently at him. That same look has been observed by Helen, who retakes command and suggests that they should return to the lab and reclaim their bags before departing. Craig's last remark has opened up a direction that was not something she had foreseen and not something that a world-leading aerospace company was likely to miss. The others begin to leave, and Mike looks back to be motioned on by Helen, who leans against the wall in thought. Aware of scrutiny, she looks across to meet Leanne's eyes and smiles ruefully. Leanne walks over to join her on the now-empty battlement, and they look out at the range.

The late afternoon sun casts shadows across the landscape, and far off, an aircraft rises into the sky from distant Gatwick Airport.

"So, he thinks it can drive, and fly."

Helen says nothing, waiting.

Leanne smiles grimly and continues, "I can get all four."

The other woman turns to her with a startled frown.

"ITARs, Helen. That's what you're after, isn't it? And probably some tech."

That gets a hearty laugh, and Helen says, "When they told me where you came from, I knew you'd be good and I'm not disappointed. We'd better not linger, the testosterone contingent won't like it. We need to talk, how about you come down to Bristol and plot with me? Would tomorrow be too early or inconvenient?"

Leanne returns the smile. "Tomorrow would be just lovely, I can't tell you how much I look forward to it. My aeroplane can deposit me and pick me up from there simply enough." Seeing Helen's expression, she continues, "One of the perks!"

They walk down behind the rest of the group exchanging small talk on personal matters. At the lab, the farewells are warm and friendly but not lengthy. Afterwards, the British contingent gathers in silence, sipping tea and waiting for Helen to speak.

In the comfortable minibus that the US embassy provided for the US delegation, the group contains itself until they are on the motorway before the silence is broken by Joe, the Military attaché.

"So, Leanne, how far ahead are they?"

"It's not so simple. They aren't really a long way ahead, they've just assembled a bunch of things faster and, frankly, better. It's not 'they', either, it's that boy genius they've got there."

"What do you think they want? I can't imagine we were so courteously invited along as a gesture of transatlantic cooperation."

"I guessed what they wanted, and when I lingered with Helen Sherwood on the battlements, it was confirmed. There are ITARs in the pipeline on some tech that they are buying, we'll need to get them expedited." She turns to the quiet civilian, who she assumes is from the commercial department. "I don't understand why y'all insist on pissing off our closest ally and business partner by holding up exports time and time again. The number of times I've had exasperated Brits complaining that they're being treated like Iranians…"

Her target looks uncomfortable and mutters, "Well, I'm not commercial, but I guess we'll have to exert pressure."

Leanne blinks in surprise. "Ah, I see, so why are the agency interested? Might've been polite to let me know."

The others look uncomfortable.

"We have our own drone programme, as you know, we were curious to find out more, so I twisted Joe's arm."

"Well, make yourself useful and find out some more about Dr Moore. One thing's for sure, we want him as well as his toy. A CIA profile might fit the bill. Between you, you need to get the list of ITARs I'll give you sorted out and I may need to wave some other tech at her, so go as high as you need to bring pressure on the State Department and do it quickly. I doubt if any of you want the President hearing about this from my people and not yours. I fly back to the States tomorrow, and I'm stopping in Bristol on the way to speak to the Brits."

Joe is offended at being given peremptory instructions by this civilian, and Leanne regards him coldly.

"Do you want the chairman of the joint chiefs to find out about this from your side? Or would you prefer it came from the Lockheed Consortium whose own sources of information seem to be better than yours and who have saved months or years of research and millions of dollars all by themselves?"

The CIA rep winces at her words, and Joe stares at her, shocked. "No, ma'am, I guess not. I suppose the good news is that at least we've got the whole day stateside to work this out."

Leanne leans back, satisfied, and the conversation turns to practical matters as the bus speeds on its way to Nine Elms and the Embassy.

Back at Fort Halstead, there is an air of jubilation in the group that faces an obviously pleased Helen. She is all smiles and tells them that the day has exceeded her expectations. As she starts to talk, the three from the Royal Lancers, doubting their place, move to bid the team farewell.

Helen forestalls them. "No, no, you stay, this affects you. Although, needless to say what you hear goes no further for the time being."

They exchange puzzled looks and sit, the whole group looking expectantly at Helen.

"Not all of you will be aware that my organisation has been

working hard to extract some technology and equipment out of the Americans so that we can get some stalled projects moving along again. Your brilliant work here has given us some leverage. A short conversation with Leanne gives me every confidence that our wishes will be met. The Heimdall project has already started to attract interest at the ministerial level, which is why Colin Lewis has come here today." She turns towards him, and he takes this as his cue.

"Your interim reports have been received with interest in Defence Procurement as well as at head office. Getting ahead of our US colleagues and all that comes out of that is going to make you very popular indeed. Helen has already sounded you out concerning an extension of the project, and together with Tom's people, we want to get that going as soon as we can." He turns to Robin and continues, "Helen asked you to stay because this affects you, Robin. The Ajax turret we used here was chosen for convenience. Still, it's become evident that we might be able to offer some really radical solutions to our manning issues. We want to divert an Ajax and crew to Porton Down to take this trial further." Colin pauses, and Robin fills the silence.

"I wondered if we might hear something like that." He turns to David and says, "Let me guess, you want Sergeant Tate here to be that crew, don't you?"

"Well, the RSM did say she was too clever by half, so it would be a good way of keeping an eye on her!"

Mr Burke roars with laughter at this observation and earns a furious look from Maz Tate, who asks, "How long would I be away from the squadron, sir? Assuming I volunteer to be part of Colonel Lucas's plan."

Robin enters the conversation. "That is a good question, Sarn't Tate. There are storm clouds gathering in the middle east, I wouldn't want to lose one of my best crew commanders for very long, much as I'd like to have a representative or two in the tent, so to speak."

Helen answers the question. "The extension is for six months. Robin, Sergeant Tate would be crucial once the integration of the computer has been done and tested. We'd then take the modified vehicle out on to Salisbury Plain and see if it really works. Probably a couple of months in the middle."

Maz brightens up and says, "I'm in, sir. As if I had a choice, that is."

Colin has been watching the play of emotions on Henry's face and moves to head off objections there.

"My minister will be seeing the secretary of state next week, Henry, we'll be trying to find out if computer assistance will allow us to dispense with the driver. The savings could be substantial. I think you'll agree."

"Well, yes, put like that you're right. My concern will be how this plays out when the worst of the press finally gets hold of the story. I'll expect there to be a good plan for that, and for keeping the damn thing from roaming the internet."

"That's one of the reasons for putting a discrete team together at Porton Down, and few places are more secure." Helen has seen Craig bristle and, as she intercedes, fires him a warning look.

Robin brings them back to his part in this unfolding drama. "I've already said to David that if this is taking place, I want to be inside the tent. Mr Burke and I have had several conversations on this subject since David took me into his confidence during his visit to the Regiment down on Salisbury Plain. I think any of us who bother to think about the future know that this is coming sooner or later. What we've focused on are the human factors that will be involved." He turns to Tom. "I've put a strawman paper together looking at the manning implications of a capability where the command and administrative function may outnumber the fighting echelon. It's early thoughts, Tom, but in my view, managing that aspect is likely to be more complex than the tech when it eventually develops." Addressing Helen, he says, "We've volunteered Sergeant Tate happily enough, and I think I'll include her gunner, Corporal Hargreaves, rather than a driver. It seems to me you might start with one, but if you go for some prototype trials, I reckon you'll need two, and I'd rather plan for that at the outset. Hargreaves is getting close to having his own crew, and it'd be easier to add two novices to a couple of experienced bods later on."

Helen gives him a measured look and nods slowly. "I think you're right, Robin, you would want to see how a pair operate tactically. That makes sense. I don't think I can get a second immediately, though, as I don't want to interfere with the equipment programme too drastically." She looks at Tom, who nods in agreement and picks up the thread.

"There's been lots of discussion around tables about drones and robotic systems to enhance our capability, and mostly we've been in the realm of engineers toys when it's come to putting ideas into practice. Innovation is in my job description and, notwithstanding some people's reservations…" He looks significantly at Henry. "I think we need to build on the advantage Dr Moore has handed to us. I'm glad you're coming down to Wiltshire, it's just down the road from us and we'll be giving you all the support you need, as well as interfering a lot."

There are numerous laughs at this, and the atmosphere lightens still further. Tom pauses for a moment and then looks at Craig.

"If we really gave you free rein, what do you think you could do? I know you've been studying our doctrine and operations, how would you do it?"

Craig looks uncomfortable, as he's less confident under the scrutiny of outsiders.

"I've been doing some homework, that's true." He smiles at Caroline before continuing. "It's actually more complicated than I would have believed, speaking just as a software designer, mostly to do with the links between the elements of the system – the vehicles. Things like this work best if they are distributed and networked, it makes the whole thing more resilient and less vulnerable if a node is lost. Your radio system does it, although not very well, apparently. If you go up against enemies with the same tech – near-peer, I've heard you call them – it's the radio links and radiation from the sensors that the bad guys will look for. I think it would be possible to make a pair of vehicles work with one soldier."

There is a good deal of reaction to this speculation, Maz looks at her two seniors and says, "Jesus, sir, a troop down from twelve to two. I know we're a bit short, but that's drastic."

Tom has taken a calmer view, but even he blinks at the answer.

"I'm a realist, Sarn't Tate, and it will be a long journey to that place. Humans will need convincing first."

"Hence, experiments at Porton Down." Helen's dry comment silences the buzz and eyes turn back to regard Craig. He takes a deep breath and continues.

"You know, I think that for pretty good reasons most of what you do is rules-based – stuff machine learning systems can do. The decision: do I shoot or not? That's the least of the problems in designing an autonomous system.

"I think what needs to be done is to introduce autonomy in stages so that the humans get to trust and rely on the aspects as they are submitted. The driving will be a good start, we can do what you already do in your navigation systems with the terrain data so that Heimdall can build an understanding of the shape of the world. Caroline has told me you have accurate measuring systems for geolocation, so you overlay that on the basic shape. Then, you fill in the details with other sensors, on-board Lidar and multi-spectral cameras. External intelligence information fills in the threats as well as what the vehicle surveillance gets. I'd give the tank its own drone to look over the hill or around the corner, one of those little ones you already have. To manoeuvre, the commander just has to touch the screen and say, 'go there'. The system chooses a route that minimises the risk and drives there. That seems to be what happens with a human driver – the commander doesn't tell them exactly what route to follow. We'll have to work out how we instrument the machine not to throw the human crew around too much or overstress the vehicle. The rest of my ideas revolve around presenting prioritised targets the commander of the vehicle can then decide to attack, or not. The gun already loads automatically so that just leaves communication management, which is a doddle for Heimdall. Hence, my assertion that only one person is needed to manage the human element of the network."

Tom raises his voice. "You talk about introducing this in stages, and I agree, Dr Moore. We're used to crews in vehicles, fire teams in trenches. It's psychologically difficult to be alone in the noise and chaos of battle. The USA used to have individual foxholes in World War II, and they found that a lot of soldiers in the stress of combat hid in the bottom and didn't fire their weapons. If several men are in a fire-trench, they tend to fight so as not to let the guy next to them down. I think it will be a while before we drop below a pair of soldiers in a fighting vehicle."

Bertie Simison from the MOD interjects. "Pilots of Typhoons are on their own in combat, and I can see direct parallels with this and flight. Aircrew are becoming systems managers in fly-by-wire platforms, they already are in civil flying. Autopilots have been around for a long time, so my service will be much more relaxed about those issues, Tom. Dogfighting is a thing of the past."

"Ground combat's a bit more of a collective experience, sir." David's tone is light and draws some smiles from the service people present. "I get what you say, though, and the message is plain. We're at the start of a period of military evolution. This cutting edge stuff has got to be managed carefully, The Lancers will be interested in driverless crews, but even if a single crewman can fight the vehicle, there is going to be an awful lot we're going to want to know before we start taking that sort of step. There's also a major information operation that's going to happen alongside this work. Henry is right to be cautious about how this will be viewed, and an experiment to create a self-driving tank is likely to be a better line to take than the inevitable killer robot story that the tabloids will favour."

Henry mutters approvingly at that and appears to be much mollified at being taken seriously.

Helen and Mike discuss the impending move to Porton Down with the group and what will happen in terms of reporting from this demonstration. David's earlier comment about the management of the next phase has had the desired effect on Henry, and he reinforces Helen's outline plan for a report on the experiment so far that will go to ministers and the Central Military Staff. They want it to be a limited distribution document for senior military officers and civil servants, the secretary of state and his two ministers. Craig, Mike and the programmers, together with Sam, are tasked with a detailed scientific report on all aspects of the first phase of Project Heimdall, analysing all the data collected during the lead up to the demonstration. David and Caroline are despatched to close down the range and then prepare the facilities at Porton Down for the arrival of the Heimdall group. Helen asks Sam what the reaction of her company is to her staying on for several more months. The response is an ironic laugh.

"To say that they were falling over themselves is an understatement, Helen. They're desperate for a piece of the action. I imagine there will be a lot of polite enquiries coming your way as to how they can be of assistance."

"I'm sure Thales will be delighted to find my organisation owing them a favour! Thanks, Sam, and thank you all for your outstanding work. I'll leave you to it, I must get back and prepare myself for whatever Leanne Phillips has in store for me."

The other visitors voice similar thoughts and accompany Helen out of the lab and to the car park where they bid David and Mike, who followed them, farewell. Henry and Bertie leave together, and the Lancers climb into the CO's car, but Helen stops Tom as they pull away. Encompassing Mike and David with a gesture, she asks Tom if he is happy to commit to being the third member of the Heimdall leadership team.

"Absolutely," is the reply. "This is the future and my core business. My only question is how far we can take this. Unmanned logistics is already on the table and we need to be designing autonomy in at the outset of a programme and not retrofitting it. Put the man in the hull not the turret, if we have a turret at all. The devil will be in the detail, of course, especially data bandwidth details if my memory of getting the watchkeeper drone to work serves me. I'll be in touch." He grins, climbs into his car and drives off with a cheery wave.

The other three relax and look at each other, the smiles, when they come, are triumphant.

Helen breaks the silence, saying, "Well, I'll be on my way. Expect a call after I finish with Leanne tomorrow, I think that the meeting will be tough but rewarding. After that, I'm hoping I can leave you alone for a while to give you a chance to settle in and concentrate on results." She looks hard at the two now bland faces before her and laughs. "Don't worry, this little success means I have every confidence in you. Not only will I let you get on without interference, but I'll also take some further steps to make sure that the hierarchy here leaves you alone, so keep your heads down and don't poke that particular snake."

They are by her car, and she nods to the patient driver within, who gets out and holds a door open, she smiles at her two acolytes and shakes hands warmly.

"We'll speak tomorrow."

Mike and David watch her drive off, and Mike turns to David.

"Let's get to it then, my friend, we must keep ourselves firmly attached to those coat-tails!"

FAREWELL FORT HALSTEAD

The next week and a half passes in a flurry of reports and packing crates. Reams of data are recorded and analysed while Mike extracts and crafts a lite version for the eyes of a senior readership that Helen tells him are eagerly awaiting. He works late into the night until, finally, he puts it in front of David for peer review. They both test it against their own ambition and are confident that when it goes before Helen, she will do the same. It is a weighty document, even electronically, and in spite of the short executive summary intended for senior readers, they know it will be pored over by supporting staffs. Reputations are on the line and the two men spend an entire afternoon editing before the secret document is despatched to Bristol. They then make their way to the lab.

Both are gratified to see the rest of the Heimdall crew surrounded by taped and banded crates, scruffy and dishevelled but smiling. Craig and the Coven spent the time between completing their data analysis and Mike's formal report helping pack, and it's a tight bunch of people who chat quietly over coffee. Mike puts his cup down to expectant looks.

"Well, I eat a day into your break, but I'm pretty happy we did that well. We reconvene in six days at Larkhill. Caroline…"

"All your car details are in the Larkhill system and the gate will be expecting you. I'll be at the officers' mess to settle you into the block we've been allocated. Briefing packs are by the door, so you've got directions and some advice on dress and behaviour. It's the central mess of the Artillery, so they're a bit anal."

David takes up the narrative. "We'll be an unusual group that's kind of been imposed on the gunners, so they'll be curious. No volunteering information. Caroline and I will make sure all this stuff goes to the right place this week, and we'll receive the Ajax before seeing you on Sunday evening. We may not be around very much in the first week or so of work. Other things are brewing that we're both being briefed on."

Mike adopts a serious mien before saying, with mock gravity, "I'm sure I speak for the whole of the team when I express appreciation for the hard work you'll be doing during our time off!"

Caroline and David exchange rueful smiles. With that, the team disperse, brimming with good humour.

Craig gets back to Wimbledon at a reasonable hour and sighs with satisfaction as he makes tea and goes through the French windows onto the patio that overlooks his modest garden. His mood is uplifted by the day's events. Number crunching with his people and then hauling boxes around reinforces the sense of family that the last months have given him. Moral misgivings are consigned to a securely locked down compartment of his mind, and he sits contentedly sipping his drink. The evening is drawing in as the sound of the door disturbs his reverie, and Sophie appears. She smiles and asks how his day has been. He is surprised to see her mellow and at home. The dislocation of expectation catches him off guard, his smile is instinctive and warm as she asks how he has got back so soon. His mood spills into his response, and he tells her that the week has been more successful than they anticipated. They've worked on finishing everything early, hence his early return.

"Well, that's good, darling. I'm off to a meeting and a rally tomorrow. You might like to come with me."

Craig is immediately on his guard.

"What's the event, Sophie?"

"Well, I thought that, as I was so stupid and ignorant, I ought to try and learn something. I've been looking at all the robot stuff online and made friends with some people who are looking at the truth about… what you like to call autonomous systems."

"I did not say you were stupid and ignorant. Anyway, who are these people you've hooked up with?"

"You might be surprised. At least they hold beliefs and try to end wars, not encourage them. They're called AGC6 – Action Group on Chapter Six. They believe in settling disputes peacefully and the six means chapter six of the United Nations Charter."

Craig supects that she has rehearsed this little speech. He attempts to de-ruffle her feathers.

"Well, you are ahead of me there. I had no idea that there was a chapter six of the UN Charter, or what it's about."

"There's a rally in Parliament Square and then we've got a social in Vauxhall. You should come and put your side of the story."

The last words came with a hint of malice. Craig is distinctly uncomfortable with the new Sophie that he thinks he might have created.

"I'm not so great at 'social', as you keep telling me. Anyway, I'm meeting someone in town. Maybe I'll come and listen to what's said at the meeting."

His words mollify her a little and the rest of the evening is tolerable. The next day they both take the tube into Waterloo. Sophie marches towards Westminster Bridge, Craig goes in the opposite direction heading for King's College. He has coffee with an old friend who teaches robotics, and the discussion takes Craig's mind off his troubles.

As he takes his leave, he is in a sufficiently optimistic frame of mind to wander into Parliament Square. There are a number of demonstrations, long term and short term. A group of people are listening to a speaker standing in front of the statue of Winston Churchill. There are only a few dozen and Craig can't make out the words, but the shouts and banner waving are not something he wants to be part of. He also starts to realise he probably shouldn't be here. His eyes are drawn to Sophie, standing near the front with a placard over her shoulder. She catches sight of him and waves in surprise. Heads nearby turn to stare. Realising he is not going to cross the road, Sophie makes her way to where he is standing. He notices the words on her banner: *People not Machines*.

"I didn't think I'd see you?"

"My mind is open to ideas, Sophie. There are different ways of looking at things, I'm interested in other viewpoints."

"Are you coming over?"

"Too noisy and crowded for me. I don't think I should be here anyway."

He looks around for the sign to the underground and tells her he'll see her later. Across the road a nondescript couple observe the exchange. Hard eyes note the girl and a photograph is taken.

Sophie comes back to the house still carrying her placard. Craig has spent the afternoon brooding. He looks up when she arrives and stands up. His anxiety levels rise as he steels himself to articulate the words he's been rehearsing all afternoon. He gives her the 'it's not working' speech, including the obligatory, "It's not you, it's me." Thinking she's taking it well, he continues, "I'm away for a few weeks, you can use the flat until you get a new place and I'll put some more money in the expenses jar." His voice tails off and she turns and goes into the kitchen, a tremor of rage accompanies her glance at the money jar on the shelf with its new roll of notes. Composing herself she returns to Craig.

"I'm going out."

As the door closes, Craig smiles weakly at the Chinese lucky cat ornament on the bookcase.

"Well, that went OK."

The next few days pass in a state of uneasy truce and the parting is cool. Craig asks her to put the keys through the letterbox when she moves out.

HELLO PORTON DOWN

The DSTL facility at Porton Down is huge and bustling, the security tighter and the people more serious than at Fort Halstead. Porton Down is the centre of Chemical, Biological, Radiological and Nuclear defence activity in the UK.* The grim box that houses the research into that dangerous area of work has its own extra security. Craig's comment to David draws an indulgent chuckle.

"Considering all the nasty things they play with in there, you shouldn't be surprised. There are live bugs deep in that place that aren't allowed to be alive anywhere else."

Craig turns with a shudder and follows the group as they make their way down to the unmarked hangar on the edge of the main DSTL complex. It's a greenish-grey colour and set apart from the other buildings, deliberately discrete and with direct access to the training area and range that rolls away to the north and east.

Inside the hangar is an Ajax tracked reconnaissance vehicle. It looks very different from the one they used at Fort Halstead. This one is fully armed, and the bits of armour missing from the previous version are all in place. The beast looks far more deadly. Craig's eyes are drawn to the variety of intriguing lumps and panels that dot the

---

* Abreviated to CBRN. It used to be NBC, a simpler TLA. Most older soldiers still call it that.

hull and turret, rightly guessing that these are the network of sensors responsible for drawing the outside world into the turret. He looks around at the team, all of them staring at the green monster in the hangar, he sees his excitement echoed in their faces.

At the end of the hangar in front of the doors lie boxes and boxes of equipment, some recognisable from the Fort Halstead packing, others intriguingly new.

Craig continues his scrutiny of the hangar, taking in the stacked portacabin offices around the entrance, through which they have just come. Mike comes out of one of the upper ones onto the walkway and beams a smile down on the group.

"Welcome to our new home," he announces.

They are soon at work, and the boxes disgorge the equipment sent down from their old lab. Porton Down engineering staff arrive to help with the setup, and soon a semicircle of desks faces the vehicle. Computers and screens crowd the installation and cables snake towards power sources and network nodes. A complex umbilical bristling with connectors is laid from the computer hub towards the Ajax.

Mike calls a halt to proceedings after the local staff have finished, and the team gathers around him. The excited chatter fades.

"Here we are then, just us civil servants at the moment. Well, and Craig, of course."

Laughter greets this and Diana elbows him in the ribs. "Bloody contractor."

The return to the group's easy camaraderie warms Craig and dispels the false cheeriness he'd hitherto been showing. Leave and the inevitable collapse of his relationship withdraws to the back of his mind, and he focuses entirely on Mike's briefing with a broad smile on his face.

"Caroline and David will join us next week; they've got a bit more time off. In any case, they're all a bit preoccupied with the latest announcements about Syria."

The diminishing buzz of conversation ceases abruptly. Craig is puzzled. Looking at the serious faces around him, he realises that he's missed something important amidst his personal dramas.

"Er... I think I might have missed something."

Mike raises an amused eyebrow. "You spent your time off living in a cave, did you? The US has announced that they are 'recalibrating' their deployment in western Iraq. That's code for, 'oh fuck, maybe it wasn't such a good idea to withdraw our troops last year, now we have Russo-Syrian forces glaring at each other across a new border in the north, embittered Kurds facing a humanitarian crisis in the northeast, Daesh leaking across Iraq's western border and everyone in the world blaming us.'" He draws breath and looks around. "Did I miss anything?"

There is a chorus of affirmation. "Pretty succinct, Mike," "Nailed it, boss," "You should go on the TV."

Craig is abashed. "What does it mean for us?"

"For us? Nothing, we get on with what we were sent here to do. Out there in big boys' land? Well, our Military is currently very excited, and they will come up with plans that our broken government will largely ignore. Politicians will then vacillate for a while before sending some token force as part of a coalition so that we can remain America's favourite lapdog."

His audience stares at him in amazement, the ice is broken by William.

"C'mon, Mike, get off the fence!"

Mike looks sheepish against the background of collective mirth and brings them back to the business in hand.

"Well, that's dealt with international affairs, let's get back to Craig's last question." He indicates the armoured bulk glowering at them from the front of the hangar. "There it is. Ajax, the most advanced reconnaissance vehicle in production. Network-enabled, full-spectrum sensors, a gun that can fire on the move and defeat anything but a main battle tank." He pauses a moment before turning his attention back to the group. "Don't be too impressed, the vehicle it takes over from, as most of you know, is the Scimitar CVRT. That's Combat Vehicle Reconnaissance Tracked, Craig, it weighs in at eight tonnes. Currently, they're flogging them off at a hundred and fifty k. This beast weighs forty and will set you back seven million. We're almost at the point of finally handing them over to the Lancers, and some of the sensors still don't talk to each other and it vibrates like hell."

"Caroline says it's a medium tank disguised as a recce vehicle, Mike. Is that true?"

"Hmm. The trouble with putting a gun on a reconnaissance truck is that folk want to shoot at things instead of just reporting what they can see. It's also got an impressive turn of speed and great armour; if a general gets a dozen of these and he hasn't got any tanks, it'll be a tank. So yes, but it's also going to be awfully good at finding things."

"Well, what do you want us to do when we plug that cable into it?"

"At the moment it's got a crew of three, we want that to be two, and the best one to depart is the driver. You've seen the hysteria that's associated with any suggestion of full autonomy, so the key phrase is 'assist'. I want to avoid telling you precisely what to do."

Craig and the Coven exchange glances and Diana grins at Mike.

"So pretty basic stuff then."

Mike shares the laughter, and Craig then asks, "When do we get Sam back?"

"She'll arrive tomorrow. The soldiers from the Lancers won't be here until we've done all the integration and taught it to drive."

"How about engineering support? Bearing in mind what happened last time we had the contractors involved."

"An excellent point there. Fortunately, the Army's vehicle engineers, the REME, have had some of their people involved in the project during the manufacturing and development process. That's so they can learn to train the field maintenance teams when Ajax is fully accepted into service. It may be that we need to involve the Lockheed and General Dynamics people, but we'll avoid it as long as we can. We have a couple of Warrant Officers coming to join us, one for the electronics and the other dealing with automotive aspects of the machine."

As a group, they turn their attention back to the Ajax, sitting quiescent in the middle of the hangar.

Craig looks to his core team and says, "Alright then, let's think about how we're going to teach it to drive."

They spend the next hour or so peering in through the driver's hatch on the front of the vehicle, referring to manuals that explain, in rather dry terms, how the driver controls the system.

When Mike joins them, Will says, "Isn't there a simulator? I've been to Bovington, and there are sims for the Challenger and Warrior."

Mike looks questioningly at Craig.

"I don't think a simulator will do it. I think we need to instrument the Ajax with accelerometers and let Heimdall learn how to drive. We just set the conditions up so that the vehicle isn't damaged and when we have a crew inside, they aren't injured."

"What do you mean 'learn', Craig? Is it not a matter of programming?"

"Heimdall learns. If we give him an accurate representation of the area, how the controls work and the g-force limits for manoeuvres, he'll teach himself based on those rules; experience will refine the process. We set a series of progressive exercises on different terrain. The rules will come from the tactical doctrine, things like reversing back down a slope into cover before moving to the next observation position. Tactical movement is a set of fairly basic drills, and they're all in the Army handbooks. I should know, you made me read them. We can set an area of the range off-limits and let him get on with it until we're happy he's got the basics sorted. After that, we can put someone in the turret and move on to the next phase."

Will looks thoughtful and says, "It'll be the human-machine interface that'll be more tricky, then. How we give unambiguous commands and how Heimdall displays data to the commander."

Mike interjects. "In any programme, integration tends to be one of the most usual causes of delay and extra expense; software integration being the worst culprit."

Craig fingers his jaw, thoughtfully. "Minimal integration would seem to be the best approach then."

His audience regards him expectantly, and he turns to take them all in.

"I think we should try and make it a more human form of integration, like sitting Heimdall in the commander's seat and letting him tell all the bits what to do."

"I take it you have a plan." Mike regards him with an amused expression and gets a grin in return.

"Not quite, but I have an idea, something from my neuroscience work."

The next day the two warrant officers from the REME arrive. Craig's military knowledge lurches another step forward. He is told that they are ASMs, or Artificer Sergeant Majors, which is what technical specialists in their corps are called. They sit down with the Coven, and Craig outlines his thoughts on approaching the integration problem they've been set. Mike draws near to listen.

"I've thought we should take the same approach that an octopus does."

This unexpected statement gets baffled looks from the soldiers and gazes heavenward from the others.

"Go on then, Craig, how does an octopus drive a tank?" This from Will.

"It doesn't, I'm talking about how it drives itself. An octopus hands off some of its motor functions to nerve clusters in its arms, relieving its central nervous system of the need to exercise complex functions to do with moving about and sensing its environment. It saves time and effort."

Sam has quietly arrived while they've been talking and announces her presence. "Proprioception, you mean."

Her arrival disrupts proceedings with greetings and introductions.

"What do you mean?" Will asks when they settle down, and Sam seats herself.

"I fell off a horse years ago and wrecked my knee. Part of the physio involved getting the damaged nerves to relearn the things they did automatically. I remember they called it proprioception."

"Sort of, Sam, it's not quite the same but maybe more analogous. We'll design and integrate proprioceptors to deal with the driving and draw together the information feeds. In fact, some of them must already exist in the electronic architecture. That will mean we don't need to tinker with Heimdall, he'll just tell these sub-brains to do what he wants. We can connect these to manual inputs in case the crew want to take over the driving, and the gunnery systems will all work as normal."

"You're right that some of them already exist, Craig. The sensors mostly have their own computation, and there's a firing solution computer for the gun. The sensor suite already integrates and presents possible targets. Unlike what we did at the Fort, though, we need Heimdall to directly interface with them."

"I think we should do it one step at a time then. Integrate the sensors, and then fire control, seeing as they are already there. We need their picture to make a world that Heimdall can understand. We'll do the driving after that." He turns to Mike. "Driving is going to want Lidar, Mike. I don't think that the surveillance sensors on their own will be good enough to let Heimdall see in 3D. The self-drive car experiments were way more complex than the stuff we've been talking about here."

"Well, I'm ahead of you there, Craig." He gestures to a set of cases stacked against the wall. "Solid-state Lidar. The very latest, complete with signal processing, four of them. Good enough?"

Craig nods, impressed and Sam interrupts to make a point.

"That makes for complicated integration. At the moment, we just have to get Heimdall connected to the analysed feeds already there. That's pretty easy as the Ajax is already network-enabled; new fittings and connections won't be easy."

There is a moment of silence before Will turns to Craig and asks, "Could we not connect these new sensors directly into Heimdall? That would save us a lot of work, and you can bet it'll run on for months if we don't, it always does."

Mike raises his voice in agreement. "He's right, Craig, it'll also be massively expensive if it needs to be joined up with existing software." Mike looks thoughtful. "There are advantages to be gained by keeping Heimdall outside all these different sub-systems. If it's just receiving and sending information, sitting outside the firewalls, then there's no software integration, and that's good for security. It also means that there won't be any commercial issues or leaks."

Sam adds, "Keeping Heimdall behind its own firewalls and under control of the human operator is going to be important for presentational reasons as well."

Craig continues, "Actually, it shouldn't be difficult to just have the Lidar directly connected. Remember that Heimdall has some previous as self-driving car software. I've already got some code from that stage of development, I need to put it back in, and we can test and adjust it. That will solve the problem of raising the fidelity of Heimdall's 3D world." He addresses the two soldiers who've been looking a bit bewildered. "It'll take a day or two for us to get our processes done, can you two fit the Lidar and run it into the vehicle?"

The two soldiers nod and look relieved that they have something to get on with.

David asks, "Where is Heimdall going to be fitted? This will be different from the static position we had at the Fort. We're on the move, and there's an awful lot of vibration in an armoured vehicle. It needs protecting as well."

His look encompasses the two engineers, who share a look and ask the obvious question, "How big is it?"

Rob brings the nondescript solid drive over from its storage and hands it to them. As usual, the newcomers are startled by its modest size and bland appearance. They handle it with exaggerated respect when it is casually handed to them. The two look at each other again and Josh, the electrical technician, says, "I'll have a word with some local contacts and see if I can get hold of some knackered comms boxes. They're already fitted with vibration mounts, and we can isolate this inside. The cabling will be easy. It'll save a lot of trouble if we don't get something specially made."

The two engineers are full of questions about the device and technical queries about the inputs and outputs. Eventually, they are satisfied and wander off, deep in conversation.

HEIMDALL TAKES A DRIVING TEST

It takes two days to get the Ajax ready for driving. Craig and the IT Coven labour late into the evenings to enable the Heimdall engine to interface with the various controls and sensors. The Coven do this aspect of the job, helped by Sam. Craig plunges deep into the Heimdall programme kernel. He reworks his code, adding back the routines to build the complex three-dimensional model that the system must have to navigate in the real world.

While they are doing this, the Army technicians fit the new sensors and install the cabling and shock mountings that will contain Heimdall. They also include links to the fly-by-wire components that control the machine.

The Ajax hasn't moved from its position in front of the computer console, but on the morning after the work is completed, the hangar doors are open. When David and Caroline arrive after their absence, they find the team sat on or leaning against the vehicle, drinking coffee and taking in the vista of Porton Down Range laid out before them.

Mike appears from his office and addresses the two officers.

"Nice timing! We're about to plug in and see what happens."

He is cheerful, but the two can feel the tension in the group. They watch Craig as he is given the honour of connecting Heimdall into the vehicle.

Will is sitting at the central console, and as Craig walks back, he starts inputting commands. The tank responds by starting its engine, the sound is startling after the silence, and a gout of diesel smoke spreads across the tableau. The sensor turret rotates. The primary sensor array looks in a full arc, followed by the gun elevating and depressing. A change in engine note heralds minor movements of the tracks, forwards, backwards, left and right. It makes the vehicle appear to fidget, its bulk making the jerks impressive rather than comic. The engine stops abruptly, and the only sound is the muted noise of the auxiliary generator. ASM Potts has swiftly crossed the hangar to a panel on the wall and thrown a switch. Overhead, the sound of fans intrudes, and trunking clears the exhaust fumes that have formed skeins of bluish smoke across the hangar. He returns sporting a rueful grin.

"Sorry about that, I should have sparked. S'posed to have extractors running if we play with engines."

There are chuckles, and theatrical coughs as the team turn to face the central console. Speaking above the fans' noise, Will tells them that Heimdall had just done a self-check of the new environment he inhabits. Craig takes up the explanation.

"Heimdall ran through all the connections and looked for the expected data feedback. The small movements check that all the driving linkages work. The feedback is part of the learning, it's what the algorithm needs to start creating a world it can understand and test the limits we've set."

"So what's next?" Mike asks.

"We input some routes and see if he can drive. And before you ask, yes, I've put a cut-out switch into the system. The radio datalink has been set up by ASM Neal, Josh, to monitor and control real-time events. It works through the vehicle radios."

"The programme is linked to the Bowman radio?"

"Yes, it's so it can access the space defence satellites and the nuclear missiles!"

David turns to Mike. "Y'know, I think I preferred him without the sense of humour!"

"I know what you mean. Craig, you'd better explain."

"Josh showed me how the radio system works, and it seemed most straightforward to use a proven route to monitor what's happening and take control when we need to. We co-opted a spare keyboard socket to input commands, it's the same as a human input but way faster. Heimdall's already networked into the vehicle system's outputs to monitor what the engine and driving controls are doing. All the sensor data is also coming in and being fused with the terrain model by the programme. Heimdall is separate from the system in the same sense that the human crew is, even though the physical inputs and outputs are all electrical signals."

"Can you drive it remotely?"

"Yes, there's a joystick that represents the driving yoke with throttle and brakes. It's crude but workable. I thought it would be a good idea to manually control things until the Ajax is on the range."

"Fancy you not relying on your mate Heimy, Craig." Caroline's tone is gently mocking.

Craig looks at her sheepishly. "Actually, I wanted to have go at driving a tank. Given the paranoia around the project, it seemed a reasonable ploy."

"Alas, I believe rank hath its privileges." David lays a fatherly hand on his shoulder and grins a challenge at Craig's transparent attempt.

"Health and Safety trumps the lot of you." Mike's voice cuts in from the side. "Secret and discrete as we are, I had to write a risk assessment for all this. Why wouldn't you? ASM Potts is the only qualified Ajax driver, so he gets the job. Sorry to disappoint."

Danny Potts rather smugly settles himself at the gaming joystick on one of the desks flanking the central console. From here, he has an excellent view to the edge of the range, about one hundred metres away from the open doorway.

Craig points out the throttle lever and tells him to push the stick forward and back for the drive and twist for steering left and right.

"Does the trigger do anything?"

Mike's voice cuts in. "It better not." Craig gets a hard stare. He returns an innocent one.

Will has the Heimdall interface on his display and touches the screen. Again the Ajax roars into life.

"You have control, Danny. Thumb controller on the top for brakes."

The tank eases forward, leaving the hangar. Danny skilfully directs it down the road to the range; his commands become more confident as he gets a feel for the control sensitivity. It comes to a halt on the grass, and he looks over at the command console. Craig has sat down in front of his own screen that has an annotated map on it. The others gather to the rear, and Craig explains that he has plotted a simple course between some points on the range. The expectation is that Heimdall drives to an exact point relative to each one. On Will's screen, a touch changes the control from manual to autonomous, and he nods at Craig, who touches the route marked on his screen. A further gesture at the screen is greeted by a lurch from the Ajax. It moves off in a series of violent jerks, and Will makes to press the red stop icon on his screen.

Craig's vehement, "No! Wait," stops him. "It learns, be patient."

On the range, Heimdall has stopped. There are some apparently random movements in the sensor array and turret. It turns back and forth and advances and retreats several times. Each series of actions becomes smoother. As if gathering its thoughts, the Ajax pauses and then moves off into the range, picking up speed.

The series of points that have been chosen are all in view of the hangar, and the whole team watches the progress of the tank as it visits them.

Craig gazes in rapt silence, taking in every detail. Several times the vehicle gets into difficulties along the direct route it has taken between points. Each time this happens, Craig tenses until the machine continues its progress. In due course, it returns to the start point, parking broadside on to the audience that has left the hangar to get a closer look. The surveillance turret turns to look at the approaching group.

At his desk, Will looks with interest at the display, which shows what the Ajax is seeing. The figures in the group are labelled with their names. All of the identifications are formal, except one. As Will leans forward to focus on the spare figure in the centre of the diorama, so too does Heimdall. The camera zooms in to focus on Craig, who, alone of all the people in view, is simply identified by his first name.

Will's sharp intake of breath draws the attention of Diana, sitting next to him. Will draws back gesturing at his screen, allowing her to see. They share a look.

"That's interesting."

They both look up and observe the team as it returns, buzzing with conversation. Craig looks at them with a smile that fades as he notes their shared expression.

"What?" He moves around the console to stand beside them.

"Look at this." Will rolls back the video feed and pauses on the image that startled them.

"Oh, I see. That is interesting."

"But why? Is he adding weighting to individuals based on some sort of measurement?"

"But the measurement of what?" Rob has joined them. They look at the frozen image showing the others in the group. Rob speaks again. "Look at the names, all the ones from the Fort are different to Josh and Danny. Explain that!"

Diana is hesitant. "He's kept the data from the Fort, those IDs come from there, look at the format. Josh and Danny are new to the team, how does he know them?"

Craig's eyes focus as he returns his attention to them. "Databases and libraries. We've given the kernel programme the ability to manipulate libraries of information. Remember, we got away with access to all the data the programme needs by allowing access to the intranet and the libraries' external storage. Think about the last bit of work we did on the transition to the limited space available on the tank. Heimdall looks for relevance and keeps what is relevant to the situation, based on the scripts we write. Pruning the branches, remember? It'll be in our scripting, our instructions."

"That doesn't explain how he recognises the new guys, or why he focused on you and refers to you as Craig."

"No, it doesn't, but that answer is in the code, machine learning doesn't have mates. Don't set any hares running, Will, the adults will only worry."

Craig looks over to the water cooler. At the table next to it, Sam hands Caroline a coffee. He smiles as realisation dawns.

"Sam gave Heimdall ears. When we gave him the ability to use sound, we didn't limit what sounds, and we left speech and facial recognition in the database. Heimdall has an overriding need to build a world that is understandable to the imperatives we give. All objects are analysed and placed in context. Remember, we set the conditions, so there are outcomes. Stick it on the to-do list, Will, I'd label it as an unintended but desirable consequence. There'll be others. Let's do some more runs; we want to measure differences and improvements as he learns."

Even without the instrumentation to show them, it is evident that the machine is improving. After two more circuits, it is doing the route faster and avoiding difficult areas that exceed the stress limits that have been set. Caroline brings over some more courses that she has designed. She uses the registered datum pillars on the range but now wants Heimdall to place the gunsight exactly over a spot on the ground, ten metres from the post.

Craig asks, "Why?"

"I'm a gunner, Craig, we're obsessed with accuracy. Measure the bearing and distance from a known position to an object, combine it with an angle of sight, and you have a location. I don't even need geolocation, just those three things and I can shoot at it. I've imagined what could be done with artillery if it had Heimdall. The rockets I'm due to command wouldn't need anyone in the launcher vehicle." She straightens and gestures at the panorama behind a now quiescent Ajax. "Those woods there could hide a half dozen rocket launchers and trucks full of ammunition. Someone calls for fire, and one of them drives to a spot, fires its rockets and returns for a reload. Not a romantic command for someone like me, but realistic and efficient. Even if the machine is detected and destroyed, no one dies." She turns to him with a wry smile. "Brave new world you're designing, Craig. I don't think I like it very much when I think about it. People like me joined up to command people, not a bunch of machines. I know David says we don't have enough people, and they're expensive, but still." She squeezes his shoulder affectionately and returns to Sam and her coffee.

Craig watches her go, absently handing the piece of paper she gave him to Will. He doesn't notice the smile shared by his three acolytes.

The afternoon progresses, and the Ajax becomes more and more expert at navigating routes and negotiating the range's obstacles. Mike's smile during his frequent visits to the 'command post', as Caroline has dubbed it, becomes broader. When they check how close Heimdall gets to the points on the ground Caroline has specified, the half metre average gets nods of satisfaction from the two military officers.

The Ajax has performed up to Craig's expectations and exceeded everyone else's, except his small team of programmers. They would be content if the tank just parked up as the analytical work they need to do far exceeds what they need in experimentation. Not so the military contingent who enjoy playing with their new toy far too much to let it sit idle. Caroline periodically interrupts the Coven with a list of grid references. Will raises his eyes heavenward before rapidly typing and clicking his mouse. Heimdall drives off to visit distant concrete pillars like an obedient dog before stopping and cocking a metaphorical leg.

As the computer experts refine the programme, the first visitors start to appear. Tom Foster is the first and is at pains to come and chat with the team over coffee. Tom radiates bonhomie, but the questions are penetrating and incisive. A couple of days later, he brings a couple more military officers, one of whom wears an artillery cap badge in his beret and obviously knows Caroline. They discover he is the Commanding Officer of the regiment that Caroline is soon to join. This group spends the visit following the Ajax around the range, occasionally stopping at a checkpoint to watch the tank as it pauses. When it moves off, they take measurements. The programmers' curiosity is aroused, and Craig asks Heimdall what they are doing. The sight picture they routinely have displayed changes to give a view of the three officers leaning over the bonnet of their Land Rover peering at a ruggedised laptop. The answer they get is curious.

The dialogue box tells them it is: *<probable target location system; GPS; FIRESTORM(part)>*. As they watch the three, Caroline looks at the Ajax. She nudges David, the soldiers look up to see the vehicle's baleful glass eye watching them. Back in the hangar, Will clicks *<resume>*. At the other end, it appears to the three that the Ajax, embarrassed at being caught, has run away.

Craig is intrigued to know how the programme came to its conclusion and spends a little time mining the data stream from their questions. His research is interrupted by the return of the visitors.

"So what just happened?" Catherine's voice is brisk. She is very keen that her next boss's visit goes well.

Craig's reply is innocent. "We wondered what you were doing, so I asked Heimdall."

"That's what the Ajax is called, is it?" The newcomer looks askance at him. Craig returns his regard, unnerved.

David makes the formal introduction. "This is Lieutenant Colonel Manny Adebayo, Commanding Officer of Two Six Regiment Royal Artillery. His unit has the Multiple Launch Rocket System. He and Colonel Tom have been talking about what autonomy might mean for the artillery. Caroline invited him over today to look at what we're doing."

The newcomer fixes Craig with a gimlet eye and moves to the bank of screens. "So, what did *Heimdall* say?"

"That you were using something called Firestorm to measure geocoordinates."

The Colonel is completely taken aback by the answer, and even David and Caroline are surprised.

David breaks the silence. "How does it know about Firestorm?"

Craig cocks an eyebrow at David. "You know he doesn't. He looked for the answer. I've just examined the log to see how it was done."

"And?"

"There was a local database search that identified the GPS antenna; external searches threw up options. Interestingly, he recognised the Colonel as an artillery officer and used context to increase the probability that Firestorm was the correct answer."

A voice cuts in. Mike Sheppard has arrived and, smiling, introduces himself to the newcomer. The air of surprise and tension subsides as he says, "There you go again, Craig. Scaring the visitors!" He turns back to Manny. "Heimdall can place things in context. Like recognising if three similar information pieces are presented, they may refer to the same thing at different times or places. The programme measures probability, and we set what level of probability is acceptable for a decision. We're focusing on making a self-driving recce vehicle here, but at the same time improving the way other information is presented to the crew so that targeting is faster. In the right circumstances, you hand off engagement to the computer."

Manny looks back at Craig, nodding thoughtfully. "In my case, we might dispense with the crew entirely. The duties of a launcher crew are relatively simple."

"Caroline told me you drive out of a wood, shoot, and then come back to reload."

"At its most basic, yes. I take it you could do it?"

"You've seen the Ajax driving around; what you're suggesting is much simpler."

There is the usual laughter that accompanies Craig's ingenuous announcements. Mike takes up the narrative.

"The Ajax is going to be able to manoeuvre, not just drive about. Adopt fire positions, withdraw from them tactically, interpret an intelligence picture to move cross country using cover."

"It can do that?"

Caroline takes up the story. "That's what we'll do with the Ajax next, Colonel. Most of what tank drivers do is all down to drills. Reverse out of a position, avoid routes that are in the sight-line of threat areas. In our case, moving out of a hide to fire and then returning to cover is pretty straightforward. We could already fire the rockets from the computer in an artillery command post; we just choose not to. Loading tube artillery has always made gunners very crew-centric. You need lots of people to handle ammo and feed the breech. For us, taking the soldiers out of the cab if we're just 'shooting and scooting' ought to be easy." Caroline regards the man who will soon become her boss warily as she gauges his reaction.

"Well, this was supposed to be an interesting opportunity to find out a bit about my new battery commander. It's turned out to be somewhat more than that!" He turns and regards Craig. "Thank you, Dr Moore, I think. I'm not sure I joined the Army to command a regiment of robots." Turning to Mike and David, he asks, "Who's looking at the personnel aspects of this? If it gets adopted, and I think it will, it will throw a real spanner into the works of a regiment like mine."

David replies, "We look at the science and the tech, but the force developers and the personnel people are going to need to look at how to make it work with people. I think you know Robin Matheson. It was the first thing he said when we demonstrated Heimdall at Fort Halstead. I think he's written a paper for Tom Foster on the manning effects in the cavalry. I'm sure Tom would let you see it."

Caroline and the senior people move off to bid the visitor farewell, leaving the team to focus on the next stage.

The programmers have been confident that the machine would do what they want and are keen to move on. Accelerometers on the vehicle have been monitoring the g-force and shock caused by Heimdall's trips across the country. For the team, the next stage is to make sure that the crew won't be injured during manoeuvres. They already have data from human factors studies that tell them what the human frame can comfortably tolerate, so it's a matter of writing limits into the scripts that control Heimdall's driving. Here they are under some pressure, as Mary Tate and her sidekick Bill Hargreaves will arrive in a couple of days.

As they start to do this, the two soldiers take the vehicle on a series of manually controlled trips around the more challenging terrain. After each series of drives, the programming team make some adjustments until they are confident that Heimdall won't turn Maz and Bill into porridge on their first trip.

They are expecting the most challenging phase to have them working at the weekend before the two Lancer NCOs report for duty. Craig and Will sit down with Caroline and translate the tactical drills for manoeuvring armour into commands that Heimdall's compiler programme can understand.

Will's opening, and disparaging, remark is: "It can't be that difficult or a cavalryman wouldn't be able to do it."

He's wrong; the simple drills for tactical driving prove to be straightforward, but the integration of intelligence feeds is more complicated. The threat picture that comes through the radio arrives as both data and as voice messages. Inputting the data part is handed off to Heimdall, and after some trial and error the computer is able to interpret the report formats. They decide that they will leave it to human judgement to add in by hand anything that does not arrive electronically.

HERE COME THE CAVALRY

On the day that Maz and Bill are due to appear, Mike gets David and Caroline to take stock of the project's progress. As the rest of the team looks on, the two officers each have a short trip around the range with Danny in the left hand seat, supervising.

They return heaping praise on the technicians' improvements to the component installations. Neither had seen the whole of Heimdall's capability, and the hands-on demonstration is the icing on the cake. There is much cheerful banter over coffee, silenced when Caroline raises her voice to say she has an announcement.

"I got my posting order today. You all know I've been working here until the battery I am due to command comes up. Well, it has. What's more, I'm deploying on operations."

This last revelation causes a murmur of surprise from the group.

David interrupts. "You've all been following the news, and we all remember Mike's pithy view of the way the politics is going at the moment. Well, he pretty much nailed it. I was going to let you know at the close of play today, but you should know that there's to be an announcement later. In light of Caroline's news, I'm not giving anything away by telling you that the UK is sending just under six hundred soldiers to western Iraq."

Sam's voice has a tremor in it as she asks, "When do you go?"

The murmur that accompanies this question reflects a collective concern that has dampened the mood.

"Oh, come on, you lot! I'm off to sit miles behind the lines in the desert. Not crawl through the dunes with a knife between my teeth! I'm fed up with listening to war stories from all the Afghan veterans; I can't wait to get there. Not that I won't miss you, of course." She is sufficiently insincere that it defuses the tension caused by the news. Further distraction arrives in the form of the two senior NCOs from the Lancers. Introductions and greetings are followed by David's outline plan for the rest of the week.

The two soldiers spend a day letting Heimdall drive them around the range, periodically returning to the hangar to discuss their experiences. Both comment that it is good at navigating tactically but less so at hiding behind 'soft cover' like bushes and trees. Craig is concerned.

"Is that a serious problem for you?"

Bill declares, "It's the best driver I've ever had. It does what it's told and doesn't answer back!"

The software team puzzle for a while over why the tank pushes its front end through foliage.

Maz and Bill then deliberately go for realistic tactical positions, the team gather round the screens and listen to the radio chatter. Maz's disembodied voice issues from the speaker and they watch the screen intently as the picture shows that Heimdall has entered a wood and is approaching a treeline. The tank stops for a moment and then advances until the sight picture clears.

"Switching to manual."

The view changes and branches wave in front of the sight.

"Handing back control."

Heimdall moves forward again.

"I'll show you what happens if we go hull down."

The team watch as Maz inputs a spot behind the top of a low hill. Heimdall creeps up the last part of the slope to peer over the top with its surveillance pod and then a little more to expose the gun and gunsight.

"You see, he doesn't like vegetation waving about in front of the sensors and simply drives forward, 'til it's not."

Craig shrugs and replies, "I've never claimed that he could replicate human judgment. That's what the manual override is for." There is mild surprise that Craig is so sanguine about this detail. "I can probably teach the programme to do what you want, but it just isn't worth it while humans are in the loop." David has joined them as Craig adds, "I'd better stop him correcting your adjustemnt after you've made it. You'll get bored going back and forward long before Heimdall does."

David asks, "How far have you got with improving the targeting system?"

This job has occupied Will's time, as the most competent of the programming team after Craig. He tells him that the job is done, much to David's satisfaction. "That's good, we're off to the Ranges at the end of the week. It's time to fire that cannon and see what Heimdall adds."

Maz and Bill spend time rehearsing for the impending firings. Craig and Will accompany them to the firing position they've selected that overlooks the Porton range. The two programmers show the soldiers how to select the recognition library and switch on and off the hostile vehicles. Several Soviet origin tank hulks on the range are still recognisable. Heimdall quickly identifies them and marks them as targets in the crew displays. The crew are curious about this ability. Craig explains that there is a limit to how much data can be stored on-board the tank. Caroline and David had decided that a library of images should be loaded for each deployment so that Heimdall could operate even if it was not on a communications network.

Bill asks, "Infra-red as well as daylight images?"

"Yes. From a variety of angles and any electronic signature that it radiates. Like a radar or laser."

Maz continues, "So if our Ajax has comms, it could look for images on an intranet or the web?"

"Yes, but I've discovered that people get hysterical if I suggest it could get out onto the web and achieve world domination! Seriously though, you'd need your own web-based system like a mobile intranet that could be taken anywhere. You've actually got one, but it's not very good, and your communications infrastructure isn't up to it. You'd need a lot more bandwidth."

"Attack the communications, and you win?"

"Well, yes, Bill. But I've been talking to Josh Neal about jamming and your radio kit."

Will interrupts. "He has, of course, designed the solution. In his head!"

The two uniforms turn serious expressions on Craig. He shrugs.

"I like puzzles. There's only so much bandwidth for everyone to use, including your enemies. We're talking about data so just use what works, even if the frequency isn't yours. In an ideal world, you'd design your own 5G network. If it's jammed, widen it and chop it up so you can hop around it unpredictably. Even better if your adversary has to use the same part of the electromagnetic spectrum as you do, you lose your packets of data in the stream."

While he has been speaking, Bill has busied himself inside the turret, and in short order, four cups of coffee appear.

Maz prods the story along, fascinated by the direction of Craig's thoughts.

"So, if you're fighting an enemy with the same tech, they have to decide whether to turn off all the comms? Then we all get to use flags."

Sensing Craig's bafflement with this apparent non sequitur, Bill fills in.

"In the 1980s, only one in four Russian tanks had a radio, so they used flags to signal each other."

"Thanks! I don't think technological armies will want to turn off information conduits. Information superiority is bound up in winning, not just on military operations, but everywhere. Commerce, media, you name it. Of course, if you're not fighting a sophisticated foe, there's less of a problem, but that's not an assumption you can afford to make. There are examples all over the net where extremist groups demonstrate they are competent in the use of networks." Craig looks out over the range, his gaze unfocused, lost in thought.

Will is used to this. "OK, brainiac, what have you come up with this time?"

He gets a laugh, shared by the others. "We should put a Heimdall into the comms system. It could intelligently manage the data much more efficiently than a human."

Will has taken a sip of his coffee during this comment and chokes theatrically before saying, "Put our brain into the network; I can just see how that will go down!"

"No, Will, it would manage the routing of data, leave voice alone but let machine intelligence find routes through any network that it can access. Data is sent in coded packets and reassembled at the correct address. You could lose speech but still have text, which needs much less bandwidth. The Heimdall programme would be much more agile, and we already know it's insanely fast." He sits back with a grin and regards the three faces, displaying emotions ranging from incredulity to bafflement.

Will, a communications manager in his Army reservist life, ponders what he has heard for a moment.

"Our Bowman radios already do that, although it's a bit clumsy, and the networks are limited. I think what you're suggesting is to let the system find any frequency and use it?"

"Exactly, give our machine gateways into the whole electromagnetic spectrum and let it do the rest."

Bill, who has been at the baffled end of the audience, says, "Maz warned me not to use the 'I' word, and definitely not 'AI'. You just said intelligently."

Will and Craig share a sober glance. Craig tells Bill that he mostly does this to not fuel speculation that machine intelligence will take over the world.

"In my work, I get lots of invitations to speculate on the future of AI, Bill. It's mostly rubbish, so it annoys me when it keeps coming up."

Will picks it up. "Back in Fort Halstead, I noticed that Heimdall does mental housekeeping. Tidies up its programming and some of the data files. When we looked into the files, we also found it was rewriting the base language." He hastily adds that this was nothing they couldn't have expected as Craig takes up the narrative.

"I said at the time that I was lazy, and writing code was tedious! I'd just let the programme run its own compilers. Heimdall is capable of surprising me with the unexpected consequences of my work. I might not believe in human-like intelligence, but it can think, know, remember, judge, and problem-solve. That list means it's cognitive, but only in computer terms. So, Heimdall might fairly be described as a cognitive machine – that's because it thinks in ones and zeros, making judgements according to rules we put in there. There is no intuitive or creative process, no 'best guess'." Craig looks back at the range and the tank and armoured personnel carrier targets that the two soldiers have been tracking. "If we fully automated the gunnery part like we did for that demo you came to see, you could tell the Ajax to fire at enemy targets. Well, first off, it wouldn't do anything. It doesn't have any enemies, so you need to put a list of entities that obey the class 'enemy'. You set limitations, a geographical area, and you could give a time slot for the mission to be completed. Overlaid on all that are rules of engagement, you know all about those, and we've programmed Heimdall to apply them.

"So you give it orders, and it obeys them?"

"Yes, Bill, but it obeys them slavishly, without initiative. What if a tank with a bigger gun and better armour turned up out there?"

"I'd hide!"

"Heimdall wouldn't, unless it was told to. Will and I spend most of our time writing and inputting what we call 'scripts', lists of instructions for the programme to reference. You two don't need to be told not to provoke a bigger and better predator; you can imagine the consequences. You also might choose not to fire on enemies because you're trained intelligence gatherers and may find out more if you don't get into a fight. Now, we can probably script most of that, but something is bound to be left out. Or we might create a loop in the logic that would break the system."

"Wait, Craig, you've said before that if it can access libraries or the internet, it can access information and can look at the context. So, if it looked up 'enemy', it could decide what that meant."

Will turns and says, "Yes, Maz, well spotted. The good doctor and I have been discussing just that. What do you suppose it came up with?"

"We did ask, Maz. Will and I finished the scripting for all the drills we've done for driving and got into just this discussion. I asked the question and got a pretty accurate list. The programme looked for folk we were actually at war with first, didn't come up with any. Found the countries where we had military people serving where there was fighting and listed them. Then it listed all the organisations it found on the government terrorist list, including the UK ones. I found that a bit scary."

"Doesn't seem very scary to me." Bill looks at the three of them, a guileless expression on his face.

"Not everyone is as gentle and kind as you, Bill."

"Yes, and that's the point. It's also where I changed my mind about humans getting in the way of efficiency. There's loads of hysteria about 'killer robots', but no open debate amongst the people who will control these machines. It reminded me of something Mike said when I first got here: 'Just because you can do something it doesn't mean you should'. Give Will and me enough time, and we could probably modify the core programme then write enough instructions to do what you suggest. Even then, it won't be like some apocalyptic film. The machine has no concept of an existential enemy that it must destroy."

Maz shivers. "Unless we give it one."

HEIMDALL GETS TO SHOOT STUFF

When they get back to the hangar, a tank transporter is parked outside. David waves them to the briefing table and outlines the early start they have the following morning. Craig is delighted that he and Will are to accompany the Military team.

Most of them doze on the uneventful journey south, so there is little conversation. As the bus drives through the Bovington Garrison, David tells Craig that they are in the Armour Centre, where the Royal Armoured Corps trains soldiers to fight in armoured vehicles. There are tantalising views of military hardware behind the fences. When Caroline points out a Challenger Two Main Battle Tank, something he hasn't seen for real, Craig gets to see what a real armoured monster looks like.

The Lulworth range is set up for armoured vehicles and heavy weapons platforms to shoot at static and moving targets. When they get there, Caroline and Josh climb into a Land Rover and drive off to get the ammunition for the firings. The team are surprised to meet an acquaintance when they arrive at the firing point. Jim Perry is back with the armoured corps after his time with the simulation team on Salisbury Plain. He is in charge of their activities on the range for the day. This suits David. Indeed, he made it happen, as he can be sure of Jim's discretion.

The two stride off to the edge of the concrete strip that makes up the firing point to talk. Maz and Bill, with Craig and Will's help, pull the tarpaulin off the Ajax that is waiting to the rear. Danny Potts climbs in, and the vehicle comes to life as he performs start-up checks. At a nod from Maz, Bill joins him, and they drive the tank up onto the firing point. Caroline's Land Rover returns as Craig and Maz start up the hill, and she beckons them to help with the boxes that Josh starts to unload. The four of them struggle up to the Ajax and dump the four cartons at the back. Craig regards the enigmatic writing on the green containers and looks quizzically at Caroline.

"Practice rounds, Craig. We'll show you one before we load the turret. Behaves like the real thing but is cheaper."

A shout pulls them along to the end of the point, where David briefs them on what will happen for the rest of the morning.

The plan is for Jim to supervise three firing practices. The first will be a simple and deliberate engagement of static targets to prove the system works. Next, we'll let Maz and Bill use Heimdall to identify and attack the targets, including some movers. Finally, we'll do the same thing, but do it when the Ajax is on the move.

Jim looks at Craig. "We meet again, Doc Moore! Your plan for world domination seems to be proceeding well."

Amidst the laughter that this comment draws, Craig replies, "Good to see you too, Jim."

"Will your machine fire at them? I remember what happened at the Fort. The targets out there are knocked about, and some don't look like armoured vehicles."

"It's a good point, the programme can cope with training scenarios, but it still needs a valid target library." He thinks for a moment. "When you do the manual shoot, Maz and Bill can record the targets to memory. Will or I can stick them in the target engagement library."

This idea draws approval from the military people. Jim then describes all the safety regulations and protocols that govern live firing on the range. Maz and Bill are well used to these, having both trained at Lulworth before. Craig causes some surprise when he asks if they need the restrictions put in the programme. In response, Craig describes how he and Will have scripted options to put in target lists and priorities, as well as no-fire zones and target prohibitions. Jim is quite impressed.

"The crew just need to call up what they need and touch the screen to designate a point or area. If you don't want anything shot at, it just needs a no-fire designation. You can pretty much add whatever conditions you want. In this case, only shoot things in here."

"Hmm! An 'Only Shoot Things In Here Zone' is a bit of a mouthful, Craig. We might try Weapon Engagement Zone – it has a better TLA, as well!" Caroline grins at him and continues, "You'd better show the crew how to do that. I take it you loaded the maps?"

Craig nods and reaches into his bag to take out the ruggedised laptop they had last seen on Fort Halstead's range. Will goes over to the minibus and fetches a canvas cable bag. He walks over to the tank and attaches a wire to a panel on the tank's rear. The other end is plugged into the now active computer. Everyone else gathers around and looks at the screen as Craig logs in.

"Josh pointed out the fibre optic link and attached the business end to Heimdall. I thought it would be an excellent way to do our work without routing that umbilical in the hangar through a hatch. Will and Josh said it would be a valuable way for the crew to oversee Heimdall without being in the vehicle."

Bill and Maz are enthusiastic but for more prosaic reasons. For them, having a remote terminal means that they can both be out of the turret to work and administer, leaving the Ajax to monitor their surroundings. David is interested in how far it would be possible to remote the terminal.

Josh answers, "It's a fibre optic cable, so there's little attenuation of the signal even at distances over ten kilometres. The limitation is more the size of the cable drum. You wouldn't want more than a couple of hundred metres. I got hold of a hundred-metre drum from the stores."

Caroline and Maz bring a range map to Craig at the computer, and they input coordinates onto the map in the display. Jim and Bill start opening the boxes of ammunition. Craig is distracted by his first glimpse of the projectile and goes over to watch. Bill hands him one with a grin, which turns into a laugh as Craig gingerly handles the cartridge. It's about the size of a can of beer, but longer. The case is blue and plastic, lighter than conventional metal cased ammo.

"It's a practice round, Craig, hence the colour. All ammunition is colour coded or has coloured markings. It has an armour piercing shot and a couple of explosive types, as well as an anti-aircraft one. Training ammo is much cheaper and has fewer safety issues."

While he's been speaking, Bill has been passing the ammunition up to Jim. He now climbs up to join him, and the two men fill up the storage inside the turret. Craig walks back to the laptop with one of the empty boxes, and Maz puts the computer on top of it. Craig checks the system and nods affirmation to David's shout of, "Are we all set?"

With the firing point and the Ajax ready for the morning's first practice, David gathers them together. Jim gives the safety brief; only he and the crew will be on the range, everyone else watches from a tower. Craig reminds Bill and Maz to let Heimdall identify the targets. Jim is uncomfortable with this on the first run of the day until Craig explains.

"Experience has taught us that Heimdall needs to understand the difference between training and actual targets. I've written in a training mode, and Will put a library of target types together. Maz and Bill will keep manual control of aiming and firing, but we want to see Heimdall offer targets. The crew then touch the highlighted objects to validate them. It's more information for us to assess Heimdall's skills."

Jim continues to look sceptical but nods. "OK, then let's do this."

The spectators move off to the range control building, a squat tower behind the firing point. Craig brings the laptop with Will laying the cable behind him.

A few minutes after they are settled, the sensor array on top of the turret starts a surveillance search of the target area.

Craig's screen monitors the main display in the turret. Heimdall rapidly marks all the possible targets by outlining them in red. Maz, in the turret, confirms those that are valid and discards the couple that are misidentified. They note that the system has ignored the few possible targets outside the boundary marked on the map.

The firing point communicates with the tower, and Jim announces that they are about to fire.

Eight targets at varying ranges are engaged. Bill and Maz do this manually, taking deliberate aim before firing. The practice takes ten minutes as the crew monitors the turret's mechanical processes during each weapon discharge.

In the tower, each shot is announced with a muffled bang. A bright tracer marks the round's progress as it streaks towards the target.

The first practice ends, and they prepare for the next. Jim has his own instrumentation that records firing data and the performance of the gun. All live firings in the early stage of a weapon programme are carefully recorded for the procurement authority and the manufacturer.

For their part, the IT pair have looked at the response in the programme. They report an increase in activity for the first two rounds fired and a minor spike for the subsequent six. Craig puts this down to Heimdall's interest in the sounds associated with the gun firing. He also says the tracer and the flash of the round striking its target have been stored.

"Learning and building a world," is his comment.

David has a conversation with Jim over the intercom, and they get ready to let Heimdall manage the next engagement.

After Maz enables Heimdall, the targets are almost instantaneously marked with the addition of a red circle above each outline. She checks the display and touches the *Engage* command.

In contrast to the first shoot, this one is over in moments. Jim's stifled oath breaks the silence following the shots.

"Nine point three seconds. All engagements successful." Will's report is calm and matter-of-fact.

David shakes his head. "Nothing we didn't expect – but with live rounds, I must admit it's rather dramatic."

They repeat the exercise and then introduce some variations. Heimdall is ordered to fire multiple shots at some targets, and Jim authorises a bunker target. They then set up some moving targets and let Heimdall engage them. None of them are missed, even with the delay, as the crew nominate and authorise these fleeting shots.

The final practice of the day is on a battle run to practice firing on the move. A dirt road leads deep into the range. At a signal from Jim, the vehicle sets off at speed along the designated route. Maz again authorises the engagement. Heimdall drives the course and engages with spectacular success.

Bill reconnects the remote cable to Heimdall, and he and Maz follow Jim to the tower.

As they gather, Caroline is on the phone with the tank transporter crew who brought the Ajax from Porton Down. She turns to address Maz.

"I'm getting the low-loader here. We won't stop at the washdown up the road; we'll de-service the vehicle at home."

Jim turns from his quiet contemplation of the machine sitting on the firing point. Bill turned off the engine when they dismounted, but the auxiliary generator is running, and the system is still live. Craig has reconnected the laptop, and he and Will are busy at the screen. Jim's expression is troubled.

"Still under wraps then? What happens when this all leaks out? Robot tanks and all that."

David's look is cold, and his voice formal. "Moral dilemmas, Sarn't Major Perry? You've been involved in equipment trials and experiments before, haven't you? Part of your branch's remit, I think."

"Yes, of course, sir. I get that this is probably the way ahead. It's just a bit 'in your face'. A human crew couldn't do that last practice. Not in that time and with that accuracy."

"Numbers are down by about ten per cent, costs of soldiers go up. We can't even afford the ones we've got, Sarn't Major. You were in Gharmsir, weren't you? All that kit we urgently acquired at greater and greater expense for use against ten-dollar Taliban, no night sight on our sniper rifles, so we shot them with hundred and seventy-five thousand dollar missiles.* Convince me that adds up."

"Not to mention the time when we come up against a near-peer enemy that isn't as squeamish about AI. I don't mind standing on the moral high ground, but it doesn't half make you an easy target."

Jim is somewhat abashed at David's challenge, and he turns to the window. As if to deliberately taunt him, a Land Rover speeds down the road at the back of the range. The sensor pod on the top of the Ajax turns and tracks the vehicle until it disappears from view. Jim turns back, stifling his grim amusement at the irony of what he's just witnessed.

Will notices and says, "He's interested in military vehicles, that one's a Land Rover One Ten, apparently."

The subsequent laughter eases the tension, and Jim turns to regard Craig.

"What about you? Are you happy with the monster you've created, Dr Frankenstein?"

---

* The term ten-dollar Taliban refers to the ten dollars that Taliban leaders in Afghanistan would pay for locals to dig bombs into the roads or take pot shots at NATO soldiers.

Craig winces at the comment. His own misgivings are never far from the surface.

"Of course I do, Jim. I had a girlfriend before I became 'Craig, the weapon designer'. Complicated, though, I was the problem as much as Heimdall. Not that many of her outbursts had much in the way of original thought. She mainly parroted what you alluded to when you spoke of the result when our work gets into the public domain." He turns to David. "Which it will, given time."

"Or something goes wrong," Caroline's voice intrudes. She hasn't had much input to the day beyond taking an occasional interest in the firing or the remote screen. She has spent her morning reading documents, scribbling notes, making and taking the occasional quiet phone call. Since the announcement of her imminent departure, her focus has shifted.

"I think that's where I'm coming from. Who's to blame when one of these machines does something that wasn't intended?" Jim glances at David, not wishing to antagonise the senior man any further.

His response is, "There we agree, Sarn't Major, but I think that's where we've got this about right. Sergeant Tate was in control of all those events. The human-in-the-loop."

"Haven't we got some ammunition left, sir?" Bill's voice is slightly hesitant.

Jim replies, "Yes, Corporal Hargreaves, why do you ask?"

"Why not do another run? You sit in my seat. You can see what happens in the turret. We didn't shoot at the movers on the battle runs. Give Heimdall a bit more of a challenge."

David is enthusiastic. "Excellent idea, Corporal H. We've got time, and we should have a go at the mobile targets."

Maz and Jim exchange grins and exit the control tower. They trot over to the ammo point and grab a carton of rounds. It isn't long before Maz jumps out, and at a wave from Craig unplugs the fibre optic link. Jim and David talk briefly on the intercom to engineer the mobile targets' appearance. Jim makes the range active again. The Ajax engine fires up, and the tank moves forward onto the road. The only change in this sequence is the appearance of the two movers. Will and Craig note the slight delay in acquisition and engagement. They complain in low but audible tones about the lack of wireless communication between their monitor and the Ajax. In the distance, at the end of the track, the Ajax executes a neutral turn and starts to return. Unexpectedly, it veers off onto the range before returning to the route for a couple of hundred metres and then doing the same manoeuvre. It returns to its former place on the hard standing, and the two smiling crew disembark. They reconnect the remote terminal, much to the delight of the two programmers. By the time the team is together again, Craig and Will have finished exclaiming over this, the most difficult test so far.

Jim throws David a rueful smile before saying, "Alright, you got me, Colonel. When you see it in action and responding to the commands, it's seriously impressive. Still scary, and being without a driver is weird, but it's still amazing."

"I take it that the sudden detours were you experimenting?"

"Ah! Yes, I wanted to see what it would do if I touched the map."

They are interrupted by the arrival of the low loader that will take the Ajax back to Porton Down. Caroline takes the empty cases that were ejected while they were static firing back to the ammunition compound. The rest of them help shroud the Ajax once it is on the transporter. Bill climbs into the transporter's cab to act as a home team escort. The rest of them rejoin the minibus. As they do Jim walks over from his car to say goodbye. He hesitates and asks David if they will be firing again.

"Can't say for sure, but quite likely." It's his turn to stop and look thoughtful. "We'll be getting another one shortly, and I should think we might be back. There'll be an exercise on Salisbury Plain, with the weapon effects simulators. You after a job?"

"If you're back down here, yes. I'd also volunteer to help with that exercise. It'd break the routine here. I can clear it with my boss."

"Do that, give me a call if he's OK, and I'll make a request."

DIFFICULT QUESTIONS
AND A PARTY

There is more energy in the minibus as it drives north. The talk is about how successful the firings were and what's next on the agenda. David and Caroline are sat next to each other, not contributing, conversing in low voices.

Caroline glances up and catches Craig's eye.

"Are you bothered by Sarn't Major Perry's misgivings about the autonomy we've given the Ajax? That comment about your girlfriend was surprising. You don't talk much about what goes on in your personal life."

"Not much to tell. I suppose I went along with much of what she and her friends talked about. I do think about the morality of this. Some of Sophie's words stung."

David regards him thoughtfully.

"Have you heard of jus ad bellum and jus in bello, Craig?"

"The classics don't feature much in southeast London education, David."

"It's tied up with much of what Jo taught you about Law of Armed Conflict. That's jus in bello – it means 'right or justice in war', basically the conduct of war. Proportionality, necessity, rules on what you can attack and how. The stuff we did in the simulator at Fort Halstead. Jus ad bellum deals with whether you can go to war in the first place. Literally, it's 'right to war'. It's probably the fundamental thing that differentiates people like us from true pacifists."

The attention of the rest of the team is on David now.

"I suppose most of us here have this conversation before we start out. Your trajectory is a bit different to ours. A pacifist won't go to war in any circumstances. Caroline and I go to war believing it to be justified. We get quite a bit of schooling in ethics nowadays, and we regularly take our soldiers through Law of Armed Conflict training. There's a lot written about it, you of all people will be able to find that. In short, a war in self-defence is lawful. That can be individual or collective self-defence. There's also a need for it to be a last resort. If you are contemplating war, you must try diplomacy first. Then it's got to be proportional, so you don't go to war with the Faroes and straightaway reach for a nuke! There's a couple of other codicils: a proper authority must send you to fight, the government in other words, and you should have a reasonable chance of success. It's also possible to exercise a right to protect, for example, as a response to a genocide."

The minibus, approaching Blandford, swings through a roundabout. Disturbed by the motion, Craig refocuses on David.

"So Afghanistan and Iraq were legal?"

"Well, Afghan was self-defence according to the US. The UN sanctioned it through the Security Council. I'd say yes. The UN also authorised the first Gulf War. The second adventure in Iraq? That's trickier, and you might have to make your own mind up on that one." He shares a grin with Caroline. Craig realises that this is a debate they've had before. She takes up the conversation.

"I think Bush went in because Saddam tried to kill his dad. Both of us agree that they seriously fucked up the aftermath."

David nods in agreement. "It's worth you working it out for yourself, Craig, and there's still a big ethical debate to be had. If you start from a position where you don't believe in the use of violence, you're not going to resolve personal misgivings."

"It's not that I'm a pure pacifist, David, far from it. You put your finger on the problem, an ethical debate to be had. I'm fully aware that this is big. It's probably the next biggest thing after the atomic bomb development, and here am I, Craig Moore uber-nerd, accidentally propelled to the forefront. I have neither the inclination nor the ability to argue morality. That doesn't mean there isn't a conflict." He hesitates for a spell, head down. On looking up, he has a rueful expression. "The fact is, I look at what we've done today and can recognise the monster, those implications. It can sometimes feel like I'm staring into the darkness. Then there's that great big 'but'. I'm at the cutting edge of what I do, and I love it. I'm in amongst people who are serious and funny at the same time. I've never met folk like you or Caroline. Life is fast, furious and great, so it's easy to shove the dark to one side. I hope that doesn't sound too mad." He subsides, slightly embarrassed.

Caroline and David look at each other and nod. "It may surprise you to know that we feel pretty much the same way. I remember a conversation with Mike when we started to push things forward. That it felt like we were on the edge of a precipice. It's maybe a bit more black and white for me. I think we are going in a direction that we must take. I'm glad to be the instrument of government policy, not it's maker. You put it really well when you talk about this being the next big thing."

Caroline nods her head, her intense gaze continuing to rest on Craig. "I agree with Colonel David. Ethical debate, yes, but it mustn't stop the progress we're making. I shall miss the programme, too. I wasn't sure what I was getting into at first, but it turned out to be brilliant. I may have got the golden ticket – command on operations – but I shall miss all this."

David breaks the spell. "Talking of Caroline deserting us to go adventuring. Will, what are we doing tonight? You were in charge of the arrangements."

The rest of the team had been eavesdropping on the conversation, and attention focuses on Will.

"Well, curry and beer, obviously. Salisbury. We'll rendezvous at a pub, and I've booked a table at the curry house for eight o'clock. Details by text to your mobiles."

The afternoon passes quickly once the Ajax rejoins them at the Porton Hangar. Bill and Maz take possession, and the two ASMs troop over to give them a hand. They wash off the dust and clean the gun. The rest of the group gather around the central console to look through the record of the firings.

That evening, the Heimdall crew gather in Salisbury. The DSTL people trickle in from digs and rentals in the city or the environs of Porton Down. The military and the contractors arrive in a cab from Larkhill. The mood is festive and upbeat, with David particularly jovial, having been given a 'pink chit' by his wife and leave to delay his return to Tunbridge until the morning. Tom Foster also turns up as the de facto Army boss of the project. They are all astonished when Helen Sherwood, brisk and still in her daytime 'power clothes', walks in and joins them in the corner they have annexed. She doesn't stay long, but she meticulously summarises her appreciation of Caroline's efforts in support of the project and congratulates the whole party on what she describes as 'the end of Phase One'. The news that they will get another Ajax for 'Phase Two' during the following week draws a few gasps of surprise, though these don't include David or Mike. Their collusion is confirmed when David pulls a rank slide from his pocket and hands it to Bill with a smile.*

"Colonel Matheson asked me to give this to you, Sergeant Hargreaves. Congratulations from your CO and all of us. The Ajax that's coming down is yours."

Helen adds her compliments amidst the applause and bids the

---

* A rank slide is a sleeve of cloth embroidered with a soldier's rank insignia that is buttoned to the front of a combat tunic.

team farewell, pulling Craig aside as she withdraws and talking to him in a low voice before quietly departing.

Craig, looking bemused, rejoins the jubilant group and catches Caroline's eye. He joins her, and they regard the smiling faces around Bill.

"What was that all about?"

"She wants to talk to me about something next week; I'll tell you later."

Bill comes over to ask what they want to drink and bask in Caroline's approval before apologising sheepishly for stealing the show. She brushes off this apology, commenting that they were all overdue for a celebration.

The Indian restaurant is a short walk away, and they arrive in high spirits. The mood continues throughout the meal, fuelled by lager and fellowship. It is an unsteady team that departs. Most of them go off in the direction of the pub. Mike bids farewell, and Craig decides not to risk extending the evening into the next day. He joins Caroline, who pleads an early start, and David, who argues good sense. They intercept a passing cab and depart for Larkhill amidst good-natured abuse.

The three of them are dropped at the gate to the barracks and stroll down to the officers' mess in companionable silence. David, who dozed in the cab, excuses himself and staggers off to his room.

"Out of practice, Colonel?" is Caroline's comment. In contrast, she has perked up on the walk from the gate and suggests a nightcap; Craig readily agrees.

The Charlie Sharp bar is quiet; the prints on the wall that give it its name and the deep faux leather armchairs engender a 'clubby' atmosphere. The bar staff are closing up but pause to serve Caroline. She brings beers and two whisky glasses over to their table before settling into a chair and regarding Craig thoughtfully.

He picks up the whisky and sniffs it. "I'm not sure I'm much of a whisky drinker."

"Nor am I, as a rule. The exception is a good Speyside Malt. Special occasion, and besides, the bar is closing." She pauses and reaches for her beer. "So, why does Sherwood want to talk to you? You said you'd tell me later."

"She didn't give away very much. It's more than a talk, as well. I'm to go to see her in Bristol. There's further work she wants to discuss after Heimdall, and she hinted at cooperation with America."

"So, you're off to her Abbey Wood lair. Be careful, Craig, there are plenty of sharks in the defence procurement waters. If she's after something, it will mostly be to the benefit of her plan. Not yours."

"Thanks, Caroline. I'll keep that in mind." He raises his glass, and she mirrors the salute. "So what about you? When do you go out to Iraq?"

"In a couple of weeks. I have to go to a camp in the midlands, Chilwell, to get briefed on the country and culture. They also do weapons training, and I have to pass a whole raft of military skills tests. Then it's back down here to formally join the regiment and get my instructions from the CO before flying out. I join my battery in-country."

"They go out before you?"

"Yes. Your rooms look out on the main square, you'll probably be woken at some ungodly hour tomorrow as they leave for RAF Brize-Norton."

"Will you be there to see them off?"

"No. I'm not officially on strength. The guy who will be my second in command is in charge. It's his parade, and it would be bad manners for me to turn up."

"I sense you wish you were taking them. Why is this so important, Caroline? You've said an operational tour is good for you and implied that our project wouldn't do any harm. Are you that ambitious?"

Caroline leans back in her seat and reaches for the glass of whisky. She savours the smell and rolls the liquid around her mouth. Eyes unfocused, she swallows and returns to the present.

"It was supposed to be my brother."

Craig is startled, but she continues before he can interject.

"My father's a general, or was. Very senior in the Army, commanded an Armoured Division, went nearly to the top. Hugh was following in his footsteps, and everything came easily to him. Went to Marlborough College, Combined Cadets, First Fifteen. He was a few years older than me. Ma and Pa had given up on more kids, and then I came along. Trouble was I was a girl, and that was a slot reserved for number three. Don't get me wrong, life was good. Hugh went to Sandhurst, did well, joined Pa's regiment. I loved being the adored sister when he came home. All my girlfriends telling me what a gorgeous brother I had! Then he got his platoon and took it to Afghanistan." She pauses, a haunted look in her eyes.

"He was killed in action?"

Her laugh is bitter. "There would have been some point to that, Craig. He came back a shining star. Pa was beside himself with pride. He got home on leave and dusted off his motorbike, overcooked it on a bend and went under a lorry."

Eyes bright with tears, she drains the glass and meets Craig's gaze. He has no idea what to say, stunned at the revelation.

She chuckles bitterly, spilling her eyes. "My folks were devastated, barely spoke for months. Until then, I had no idea what I was going to do. A job and grandchildren was an unspoken expectation. I was at uni, doing chemical engineering. Once the dust had settled, I came home and told them I was going into the Army. I thought they'd be pleased. I couldn't have been more wrong. Ma thought she was going to lose her remaining child, and my father just scoffed. Pointless waste of time, was his view. So here I am, every achievement falling short of his dreams, but I'm getting crowns and swords on my shoulders if it's the last thing I do."

"Crowns and swords?"

She laughs, returning to the moment and tells him that general officers have a sword crossed with a baton as part of their rank.

Caroline gets unsteadily to her feet, saying she has an early start. Craig follows her down the corridor and pauses with his hand on the door leading outside. Caroline turns and says, "Remember what I said, Craig, look out for yourself. No one else will."

"You, perhaps?" He smiles, and she impulsively takes his head in her hands and kisses him. Turning away, she heads for the staircase, telling him she'll be in touch before she goes to Iraq. Craig touches his face where her hands had been before going out into the night, his mind in turmoil.

True to her word, Craig wakes to the sounds of people and vehicles outside. It is still dark and he goes to the window, his head pounding with a developing hangover. Outside, two coaches and a truck are waiting in line before a large group of men and women, milling about. Off to one side, a small cluster of what are obviously officers look on. A figure that Craig assumes is a sergeant major eventually succeeds in creating order. The soldiers file on to the buses, and the party loading luggage onto the truck finish their task. Movement by a tree below Craig's window betrays a slim figure looking on. On the square, the sergeant major marches over to the officers and salutes one of their number, obviously the senior. They board, and the convoy departs. Caroline leaves the cover of her tree and walks in the direction of the officers' mess. After a moment of contemplation, Craig returns to his bed. Sleep eludes him for some time as he muses on the changes that are coming.

A DAY TRIP TO ABBEY WOOD

On Monday morning, Craig boards a train from Warminster Station. It was David's suggestion to take a train to the DESO site in Bristol. Abbey Wood has its own stop, and as he alights from the train, a smiling young woman greets him. He is whisked through the gate and into the main block. His own pass works to get through security, and the escort leads him through the light and airy space beyond. Small groups of people come and go. Others are obviously meeting visitors like him. Here and there, people sit in earnest conversation at the scattering of tables. A few heads turn to regard Craig. Vague recognition stirring on one or two faces.

In due course, they reach Helen's offices, her PA indicating that they should go straight through.

Helen smiles her usual predatory smile and, rising, she takes him to a seated area overlooking gardens and a lake outside. His escort goes for coffee and leaves them alone after it is delivered.

"Thank you for coming, Craig. I have a favour to ask."

Craig is wary, Caroline's words echoing in his head. "A favour? Is this about the Americans?"

"Leanne Phillips called on me after the demonstration, Craig. They've offered me help with some of my projects, and some tech we've been waiting for. In return, she's asking for our help on her current project."

"Help? I take it that doesn't just mean a copy of the programme. She wants me, doesn't she?"

"Well… yes. What she's offering is important. I really need you to go, Craig."

Craig tries hard not to enjoy her discomfort, obviously begging is not in her nature.

"You'd be well looked after, Craig. It's at the Skunk Works, you'll never have encountered their approach before. They have a deliberately open-minded approach and almost no bureaucracy. The frustration you've had here with our limitations is not something Leanne's people do."

She watches Craig's mind working and makes a mistake.

"I've made sure they'll pay you an in-country allowance, they're generous people."

Craig grimaces. "I don't need money, Helen, not now."

Helen reddens and he continues.

"It's OK, you had me at frustration. I've not much experience of America, only been to a conference as a student. How long?"

Helen sighs with relief. "A few weeks, Leanne was vague about her project."

"It'll be a drone, won't it?"

"Bound to be, it's her department, she was cagey about how far they've got. Probably a bit further than we were when you arrived at Fort Halstead."

Craig vents a slightly bitter laugh. "Much easier in an aircraft."

"What do you mean?"

"At the demonstration, it's what I said – easier to fly than drive a tank. That didn't get past Ms Phillips."

"I don't think much does, Craig."

"When must I go?"

Helen is uneasy. "Umm… next week." Hurriedly adding, "The sooner I get you out there, the sooner I get you back."

"It's OK, Helen, the significance of this isn't lost on me. It ramps things up a bit fast, but I looked up the Skunk Works, it's definitely an impressive place. I'd be mad not to go."

There are people in Helen's outer office waiting to see her but Helen brushes them off and escorts Craig to the exit herself. She is warm in her farewells and a bemused Craig boards the train back to Warminster.

The next day, he discovers that Will and the team have started the process of getting the two Ajax to work together. The same simple manouvres that characterised the start of the Porton Down series but carried out in concert. For the rest of the week, Bill and Maz practice their tactics. Craig and the Coven leave them to it. Analysing the feedback from their monitoring of Heimdall and providing answers to the NCO's questions. Maz, in particular, trying to understand how Heimdall works.

Craig's trepidation increases over the course of the week as his flight to Los Angeles draws closer, reaching a hiatus when the electric ticket and itinerary arrive. As he leaves for London and a visit to his flat, Will reassures him that all will be well while he's away. Maz and Bill also bid him a cheery farewell, they are already excited at the prospect of live firing in the week ahead.

SKUNK WORKS

Craig returns to Wimbledon and the house is quiet, but he is aware that it hasn't been empty. There's still no key lying on the mat. Mail is on the table in the hallway. Much of it opened. In the kitchen multiple glasses and cups are in the sink and on the draining board. His nose wrinkles at the smell of stale smoke, and the sight of the pamphlets from the Anti-Robot Organisation is eloquent. He checks his flight details and calls an Uber and a Heathrow Airport Hotel.

The next day, high above the Atlantic, his spirits lift and he turns his attention to the reading pack that has been sent from the USA.

The influence of Lockheed Martin is immediately apparent as Craig nervously negotiates his way through US Immigration. Three smartly dressed young people from the firm are waiting on the other side. One steps forward with a smile.

"Dr Moore, an honour to meet you, sir. Come this way, please."

The other two relieve him of his luggage labels.

"I'm Russ Morales, chief programmer on the Akacita Maza programme. Don't worry, they'll get your bags and see as at the plane."

"It's Craig, Russ. Please."

"It's an honour to have you with us, Craig, the team can't wait to see you." Still smiling, he escorts him to a smart business plane for the trip to Palmdale.

After the comfortable but modest room at Larkhill, the apartment to which he is shown is palatial. Russ shows him around, respectfully concealing his amusement at Craigs reaction.

"Leanne likes to leave nothing to chance, Craig, we really want you to like us."

"I could certainly get used to this."

"I'm delighted to hear it. I'll let you settle in, there's a pack on your desk with some more information. There's also a pass and a cellphone. Anything you need, call me. I'll pick you up at seven thirty, we start earlier than you Brits do. And… Leanne says, make yourself at home."

True to his word, Russ is there at seven thirty, and the drive to the Skunk Works is short. The rest of the Akacita Maza team is there, eager to meet Leanne's talisman.

The first thing they do is to introduce him to the machine sitting in the hangar. A sleek black composite body, with two rotor blades, and an unusual backwards facing tail rotor.

Russ explains, "The two blades of the main rotor contra-rotate, giving power and speed. They also solve a problem with conventional rotors, where the blade going backwards loses lift. It means we can use the tail rotor to push us even faster. This will do two hundred and forty knots and can fly seven hundred miles."

He is interrupted by a gentle southern drawl and turns to see that Leanne Phillips has arrived.

"This is the Defiant X, or was until you arrived. It's a Boeing/ Sikorsky prototype helicopter. We want you to teach it to fly and become the Defiant AM."

Craig looks at the logo on some of the screens in the hangar, which show a silver grey Native American warrior.

"I looked it up. Iron Warrior? Lakota?"

"That's right, Craig. Can you do it?"

"Of course. I don't know how long it'll take, though."

"Well, we think we might have helped there. DESO told us a bit about Heimdall. We've already worked on the cockpit and controls to provide direct links. It'll be up to you and Russ with the programming team to sort out the communications. I'm hoping Heimdall didn't have to come in the diplomatic bag, will you download it?"

Craig laughs as he picks up his shoulder bag. "They'd have had an attack of the conniptions if I'd suggested uploading him to the cloud."

He gets the usual reaction when the modest device is produced. More exuberant from the Americans, causing him further amusement. Leanne's smile is warm as she steps close to him and says, "Welcome to the Skunk Works and to the project, Craig."

With his experience of integrating Heimdall into Ajax behind him, the process of getting the Defiant X prototype to fly is straightforward. Leanne's team are a mirror of his Fort Halstead Coven, though more numerous.

After two days, the team are able to hook 'Alpha Mike' up to the simulator. It crashes a few times, but the programme adapted and started to show its full potential..

Over coffee, Russ and Craig looked at the schedule of events.

"There's an awful lot of simulator flying to get through before we can put him on the test rig, Russ."

"I was thinking the same thing." Russ pauses, thinking. "I'm not the simulator expert but, I wonder, can we get it to do things faster?"

"It's a computer, everything we're doing is digital. I don't see why it wouldn't work."

With the help of the simulator team they get up to five times normal speed. This is no challenge to Craig's programme and the early flight testing is compressed into days not weeks.

This proved to be fortuitous, as Leanne asks Craig to see her. When he arrives at her office, she is delighted with the progress.

"It's a good thing, Craig. Helen and I have been speaking and they need you back as soon as possible."

"Is there something wrong?"

"Not with the programme. They've advanced the testing. Things are heating up in Iraq and they need the tanks back early. Actually I think it's those two sergeants they really want."

"Well, we've progressed from tethered flight on the rig to full live flying. A couple of days and we'll have completed all the flight conditions and emergencies we can throw at it."

"Outstanding news! I'll get you back to the UK when that finishes and we can organise where we go from here."

IRAQ

Caroline sits, swivelled in her seat, looking out of the open door of the Blackhawk helicopter that is transporting her to her new command. Opposite, the gunner leans against her machine gun mount, maintaining a desultory watch on the bleak and arid terrain flashing past them. Caroline is more interested in the view; bleak as it may be and baked by the sun, the rocky vista that fills the doorway painted in shades of tan and seen from the noisy wind-buffeted seat she currently occupies has a parched beauty. A point of view she wryly notes that will probably not endure as time on the ground stretches from weeks into months. The helmet she was given when boarding the aircraft interrupts her reverie as the pilot announces, "Fifteen minutes out, ma'am." The gunner looks up and smiles at her and the other two passengers before bringing her door gun into the ready. Caroline looks at the two soldiers opposite, who have been glancing covertly at her from time to time during the flight. They are returning to duty in the battery that Caroline will shortly lead. They have spent the flight wondering what the lean unsmiling woman will be like as a boss.

Behind the mask, the pilot's announcement has raised the tension in the new boss's stomach from frisson to knot. This is it, the chance she has been waiting for on the road to regimental command, an operational tour at a time when such career-enhancing opportunities are in short supply.

Caroline has just enough time to glimpse the patrol base that will be her home for the next few months before the gunner slides the door closed. The rotor beat intensifies as the aircraft flares for landing, and all sight is lost in the cloud of dust whipped up by their arrival. The engine spools down, and the rotors slow and stop. The gunner opens the door and jumps out, turning to help Caroline down. As she shoulders her Bergen and picks up her rifle and bag, two figures detach from the group awaiting her on the edge of the pad. They double over to relieve her of the baggage with smiles and cries of, "We'll take that, ma'am."

She straightens confidently and marches across to the reception party. The first to greet her is a face from her past. Captain Kevin Armstrong is the battery captain and her second in command, referred to as 'the BK', as all battery captains in the artillery are. Caroline is, of course, 'the BC'. The remaining two people in the reception party are the battery sergeant major, custodian of order and discipline, and the battery quarter master sergeant, the logistic lynchpin. Of course, both are referred to by their initials as well. The latter excuses himself after the cautiously enthusiastic introductions, telling her that he's off to fix her accommodation, or 'grot', as he calls it. After the BQMS lopes off with the two soldiers carrying her baggage, Kevin and the BSM take Caroline into the battery command post to brief her on the current situation.

Having come from 'Key West', the nickname for the US Quayyarah Air Base where she'd lingered for acclimatisation and theatre induction training, Caroline is up to date on the bigger picture. Standing at the map table in the command post, she is more interested in the domestic situation. Sensitive to this, Kevin grins at those gathered expectantly on the edges before turning his attention back to Caroline.

"Welcome to Patrol Base Namur, home of 132 battery, the Bengal Rocket troop. There are four GMLRS launchers and two

Exactor missile systems here.* Two of the launchers are deployed, ready for action at any time. We can bring the others into play within thirty minutes. The Exactor can be in action as and when any targets develop within its shorter range or for specific precision fires ops. To the west of us is a screen provided by A Squadron of the Royal Lancers—"

"They're the Ajax Squadron, aren't they?" Caroline interrupts.

"Yes, and very capable they are. Although we're here for any deep fires tasks from Brigade that can make use of our eighty-kilometre range, they have a Fire Support Team with them that can call us for direct support if they get in trouble. Nothing gets past them; although that's not saying much, we're in MMOFA terrain here." He pronounces it: *mum oaf a*, and in response to Caroline's quizzical look, says, "Miles and Miles of Fuck All!"

When the laughter subsides, the battery signals sergeant pipes up with, "We had a call from battle group HQ just before you came in, ma'am. The CO would like you to call on him when it's convenient. They're very polite, ma'am, so that could be cavalry speak for 'immediately'."

"I know Colonel Matheson, and he's pretty relaxed, but you're probably right. I think a quick tour, and then I'd better get over there."

Kevin and the BSM walk Caroline around the modest installation, rows of tents, each protected by a sandbag wall. Portacabin showers and makeshift toilets, air conditioning only for the command post – and that's for the computers' benefit, not the people. The whole structure is protected by a bank of sand, a 'berm' in military parlance. On the north and south sides of the base, smaller berms have been constructed. Two of these are occupied by GMLRS launchers. The oblong boxes containing the missiles are in the raised position, indicating that the systems are ready and can fire at a moment's notice. The fiery blast of a launch

---

* Guided Multiple Launch Rocket System, he pronounces it 'Gimmlers'.

209

is violent. The rocket efflux is toxic, so the berms are carefully sited and built so that harmful effects are directed away from the base. Caroline spends a few moments with each of the crews relaxing in their ready positions next to the launchers, she discovers that each of the weapons is targeted on a potential threat, identified by the screen out to their west. If the alarm sounds, they can instantly occupy their positions in the cab and respond to a call for fire. Although the new Fire Control System could remotely launch rockets, this is not yet an accepted drill. She is given the distinct impression that the routine is boring for the soldiers who arrived primed for action but have discovered that nothing is happening.

A thoughtful Caroline follows her command team back into the base. She is introduced to her driver, standing by the Panther vehicle that is her personal runaround. Kevin jumps in with her, and they talk about the deployment and reminisce during the thirty minutes it takes to get to the Lancers battle group HQ.

The two officers head for the command tent. Caroline's driver and the crew of the Jackal Escort vehicle, at a nod from Kevin, go off to the base shop. Forward Operating Base Wolfe is larger than Patrol Base Namur. It is built to contain the Royal Lancers HQ, a Military Intelligence company and the two platoons of infantry responsible for local security. It has a shop called the EFI, the expeditionary arm of NAAFI, which has run shops in military camps worldwide for many decades. As soon as the news of a trip to the main HQ got around, the PB Caroline's driver was given a long list of minor luxuries to purchase.

Colonel Matheson is in the command post and greets Caroline with pleasure. Their meetings in the UK on the Heimdall project, as well as the fact that she is his friend David Lucas's protégé, have earned Caroline his respect.

"Delighted to see you again, Caroline, and to have you with me. I know you are the brigade's long-range artillery, but you're the closest thing I've got to my own battery commander, so you'll forgive me for being a bit possessive, I hope."

"Don't worry about that, Colonel, the battery is still under your admin command and in your area, you can lean as heavily as you like on me."

The discussion that follows is relaxed and informal. Robin describes the line of Ajax Recce vehicles screening the front of their area of operations and the role of the Military Intelligence company. They are mostly based with his HQ, acting as an intelligence fusion hub. The operators pull down imagery and signal intelligence from the various fixed-wing aircraft and drones that patrol the skies along the Iraq Syrian border to form a comprehensive picture. Some of the Int Corps electronic warfare teams are deployed with his screen, listening at the tactical level to what is going on the other side. His mission focuses on 'watch and listen'. The coalition's main concern is a resurgence of Daesh forces that could further destabilise Iraq, so the screening forces are to report any indications of that happening and respond to any incursion. The location of the US Brigade that Robin and Caroline are supporting also means that they are discreetly monitoring Turkish troops' activities to the north and west and providing some reassurance to America's demoralised Kurdish allies that they haven't been deserted.

The CO had contrived that this meeting with Caroline and Kevin should take place in his office so that he could talk more discreetly to the two of them.

"Look, we know that this is a peculiar deployment. Capable though we are, it's still a bit of military tokenism. Our presence here is entirely politically driven, issues of trade and placating the US over recent national security decisions. That said, there's very little happening, so my main concern is the onset of boredom. We've only been here six weeks, but I already see the signs, even amongst the troops on the border."

"MMFA," murmurs Kevin from his position by the doorway.

"Exactly! That's really taken hold, I'm concerned for the time when it's no longer a joke. I'm going to thin the line down to two troops as soon as I get my remaining two Ajax and get some localised R and R going." The CO's eyes twinkle as he regards Caroline, who is momentarily confused.

"Two Ajax missing?"

"Your friends, Sergeants Tate and Hargreaves!"

"Oh, of course! With all the prep to come here, regimental business and then pre-op training at Chilwell, not to mention a week at Key West, I hadn't thought about... wait! You're not saying..."

"Oh yes, Caroline, they're bringing the two prototypes out with them."

Caroline sits back, stunned, as Robin looks on with amusement. Kevin looks confused, and Caroline distractedly says, "I'll tell you later."

"The programme isn't finished, but this was too good an opportunity to field test them. They ran a battle simulation on the plain against a whole squadron, and the pair beat them. Even without Dr Moore, the integration and testing went so well the MOD couldn't resist an operational trial."

"What do you mean 'without Dr Moore'? Has something happened to him?" Caroline is gripped by concern, a reaction noted by Robin. He hastily apologises and tells her that Craig was sent over to the USA as part of a deal brokered by Helen Sherwood.

"Apparently, the US made an offer Ms Sherwood couldn't resist, and she persuaded Dr Moore to go to the States and help with one of their projects. They wouldn't say where or what. I also ought to tell you they've mobilised one of the programmers. Conyers, I think. You probably know him. He's over here to deal with any techie stuff that comes up with our two vehicles when they arrive."

Caroline has recovered her equilibrium and replies, "Yes, Will Conyers, he's a corporal in the Army Reserve. Will understands the most about Heimdall in the absence of Craig."

"Going back to my point on boredom, I hope we get some activity on the border, or our trial isn't going to be much good."

"We're going to have to deal with it, Colonel, Kevin already has all but two launcher crews on standby. We've just got to be creative in keeping the boys and girls occupied. When you're able to pull some crews back, we should be able to do some exercises or run a sports competition."

"My thoughts exactly, Caroline."

"When do the two prototypes arrive? I'd certainly like to see Tate and Hargreaves, not to mention the vehicles."

"They'll be here in about a fortnight. I'll make sure they drop by on their way to the front."

They wind up the discussion, and the CO introduces Caroline to the key members of his staff and the officer commanding the Intelligence company. On the way back to their patrol base, Caroline tells Kevin about her secondment to DSTL. They finish the journey amidst speculation as to what elements of their own equipment could be automated.

As Caroline adapts to the new role of leading her battery, it soon becomes apparent that there will be little for them to do unless the threat changes dramatically. The tactical map shows the various activity reports over the border, but they are few and far between and mostly innocuous. She changes the routine a little and encourages a volleyball league, insisting on regular physical training at sunrise when it is marginally cooler. Periods of military training are also introduced.

VISITORS

The routine is interrupted ten days after her arrival when two Ajax reconnaissance vehicles arrive at the patrol base. She emerges from the CP tent to see a smiling figure climbing down from the lead car. Maz Tate greets her with a grin and a handshake. They are joined by the more reserved Sergeant Hargreaves, and the three catch up on events in the faux café she has encouraged her troops to build. Kevin and the BSM have been alerted to the new arrivals. They are keen to look in the vehicles, so Bill gives a tour to the curious audience gathered around the new tanks.

While that is going on, Caroline asks Maz for news of Craig.

"He went to the States a week after you left, ma'am. He wasn't pleased about it, at least, not at first. Sherwood had to persuade him." She casts a significant look at Caroline.

"You mean bully, bribe and cajole."

"Exactly! She's a cold fish that one, if you don't mind me saying, ma'am. I hope he doesn't end up being trodden all over. I really like him."

They mull this over, and Caroline asks what happened at Porton Down after she left.

"The other Ajax turned up on the Monday with our extra crew. Craig and Will created two separate programmes by copying

Heimdall and installing them. That's when we did the names."

Before them, the jolly tableau centred around Bill erupts in laughter at some quip. Caroline sees that the Ajax he's leaning against has a name. *Loki* is stencilled in black letters on the armoured skirt.

Noting her gaze. Maz continues, "What they did was fix identities on them so that they had what Craig called 'unique addresses'. Once the ASMs installed the internal modifications in Sarn't Hargreaves's vehicle, they got them working together. We set up a troop communications network and spent the rest of the week learning to work as a team. Weird on day one. We started up and networked them. Craig and the guys had them connected to the mainframe to see what would happen. The camera turrets turned, and they looked at each other for a bit. It spooked Jess and Callum, who'd come down as crew. Will said, after, that the two new programmes exchanged information with Heimdall. Craig had taken the original out of mine and plugged it into the hangar computers. The new ones didn't need to be taught to drive; Heimdall told them how. If one programme's done it, they all can. We just needed to get the new guys used to vehicles that drove themselves. After that came drills as a pair, and then we started team tactics. We got together with the programmers and worked out what we needed for the tactics and the reports we use. It turned out that Craig had put all the report formats into the programme when you were at Fort Halstead. You'd just never used them."

"Without a communications net, we'd parked that aspect. Never got around to it before I left. How did it work?"

"About as brilliantly as you'd expect with anything Craig touches! He listened in to the two of us working out on the range. Will set up a command post so that we could practice reporting to a headquarters. That also meant that the programmers could see what was going on in the processing architecture." Maz stops as Caroline stifles a laugh. She looks at the officer, eyebrows arched.

"Sorry, Sarn't Tate, I never thought I'd hear you say 'processing architecture'."

This gets a laugh in return and with a shake of her head she says, "Well, to be honest, nor did I. Thing is, when we started to get to grips with what could be achieved using the Heimdall programme, I thought I'd better find out a bit more. It's all very well sitting there while this machine is doing most of the work for you; I wanted to know how it did it. It also helps me to understand the command interface better. In that fortnight before they packed the two vehicles off to Iraq and our crews up to Chilwell, there were a lot of minor improvements. The left-hand seat is now more a vehicle management position than a loader operator's. It's much easier to input commands on both screens now. We had a lot of suggestions during the team training and, as I said, Craig and the Coven could listen to and see what we were doing. We'd come back, and they would make changes for the next day."

"So it's more capable?"

"Kind of. More efficient is probably a better description, and easier to control. We can do more with the keyboard and cursor. My crewman can send reports and returns faster because most of the information is already filled in. All the vehicle systems are now on screen when they're needed. Loki constantly monitors all the vehicle systems and shows an alarm if something is wrong; Danny downloaded the contents of the maintenance laptop. They now tell you when and how to service them and, if some unit goes wrong, which one to replace. Same with all the turret systems as well."

"When I left, there was going to be a test exercise."

Maz laughs at the memory. "Oh, that. The squadron was doing its final exercise on Salisbury Plain, and they got Bill and me to be enemy forces."

"What happened? I take it you won."

"In defence, even ten on two, it was easy. We could pick them off faster than they could acquire and fire. More complicated when we went on to the offensive. We lost a couple of times; even then, we usually got at least four of the opposition. It's easy to forget that they learn. Craig says it's because it's a player of games, and winning is built in. The tactical display started giving options based on predicted enemy positions. It made our route planning much more straightforward. Better still, after a few failures, the computer worked out the reaction speed of the enemy. The route options then included avoiding being hit by moving from cover to cover quicker than the opposition could aim and shoot. Will and Craig took losing personally, as well. We came in on the morning of day four to discover that the smoke-grenade dischargers had been loaded. Craig loaded up the characteristics and purpose. Loki and Freya did the rest. It's pretty alarming inside an armoured fighting vehicle doing forty kilometres an hour in zero visibility! Instead of what we do – pop smoke and withdraw to safety – they use the smoke as cover."

"They can see through the smoke?"

"Not yet, even the Lidar can't do that – at least, not yet. Craig's found a solution, but it's in development at the moment. Some sort of sensor on a chip."

"Of course, Craig found a solution. What was I thinking?"

They both laugh at this before Maz continues.

"The software doesn't need to see for this drill. It knows down to about ten centimetres what's within a hundred metres. They drive from memory."

The two women sit back, eyes on the people crawling over the two tanks. After a few moments of contemplation, Caroline breaks the silence.

"How long did you spend on the Plain?"

"Only five days. Mr Perry came up from Bovington, and we set up a Command Post at Netherhavon."

"Mr Perry?"

"Oh yes. He was picked up for WO1. Not put the rank up yet, not until he finds out where he's posted. He started out as a

Sixteen Fifth Lancer so he could come to our regiment. Mr Burke, our RSM, will be commissioned, so he'll be off after the tour. Not sure how that will pan out for us. Our two-gods performance didn't do anything to overcome Jim's robot paranoia. Craig's back in the UK, you know. Or was. They pulled him back to check the programming and integration before we deployed. He was a bit weepy when we said goodbye. He actually kissed me." She huffs a smile at the memory before adding, "Even Sergeant Hargreaves gave him a hug, and he doesn't do hugs."

This snaps Caroline out of her own reverie. "He's a very private man, not much into confrontation, and I don't think he has a happy love life. Always seemed to be trying to escape what was at home."

"Yeah, no dad when he was growing up, Mum holding down two jobs. Blokes don't do well without dads. Big guilt trip because he thinks his mum worked herself to death. I think that's why he liked Colonel Lucas so much… gave him a taste of something he missed out on."

"Colonel Lucas went off to PJHQ, I hear."

"What, you don't know? He's here, ma'am! A full Colonel back at the brigade, been sent to keep an eye on us, Will's here to give tech support. Oh shit!" Maz has glanced at her watch. "I'd better be going. The Troop Leader will be wondering where we are."

They both rise, and Maz grabs her helmet from the table before stepping towards Loki. Bill has looked up, realising they are off, and calls the two crewmen who are gossiping with some of the gunners. Maz turns back, grinning.

"Do you want to see something cool?" She pulls on her helmet and adjusts the microphone, gesturing to Bill, who shoos the audience away from the vehicles. "Loki, start engine, execute!"

With a muted roar, the vehicle comes to life.

"Only simple commands at the moment, it's still mostly screen input. Loki. Neutral turn. Execute!"

The tracks turn in opposite directions, and the imposing form rotates about its axis. She climbs up the side and takes her place in the commander's cupola before her crewman slides into the hatch next to her. Caroline recognises Calum Davies, who now sports a lance corporal's stripe. He catches sight of her and grins, pointing at the tape on his chest. Behind them, Bill's tank has also started up and turned. He now pulls away, and the vehicle makes minor adjustments to exit the camp safely. Caroline sees that Bill's tank is called Freya. As Maz leaves, she turns, smiling, and waves. Caroline returns the gesture and looks thoughtfully at the mess that the two tanks had caused when they manoeuvred. The battery sergeant major is going to be furious.

CRAIG IN THE USA

Far to the west, contrary to Maz's news, Craig is not in the UK. He is making his way towards immigration at El Paso Airport. Even so, he is still distracted enough not to notice the two smartly dressed young men moving to intercept him as he completes the short interview with an impassive immigration official. It is his second travelling surprise of the day. When he'd turned up at Heathrow expecting to board an aircraft to LA, there was a message telling him he'd been re-routed to Dallas. The change of plan raised his anxiety levels, last minute changes not being to his taste.

A discrete, "Dr Moore," calls his attention to the reception team and they guide him away from immigration, fending off his questions concerning their destination and his lack of luggage with a, "We'll explain in the air," and a, "Don't worry, it's all sorted."

Shortly thereafter, Craig finds himself outside in the heat and glare, boarding a Citation Business Jet. He notices the black military holdall that Caroline had given him at the rear of the plane. True to their word, his kit has been brought to him. He's also told they are going to Holloman Air Force Base and the Whitesands Range. The 'Programme' has moved. He is given a folder emblazoned with a Lockheed Martin crest.

He studies the folder he's been given. While he has been back in the UK, going over the integration of Heimdall into Loki and Freya, the Akicita Maza team had decided that they had achieved all that was possible at Palmdale. In his absence, they had given the drone its teeth. Craig folds out the latest schematic and looks at what the machine has become.

The team had worked hard and Leanne has decided that they should move to the White Sands missile range to start the next phase of tests now that the drone knows how to fly. Weapon integration is to take place at a secure site on the airbase, and Craig's next job is to make sure this happens before they go on to do flight testing on the live firing range. In the documents, Craig discovers the change of location isn't just about weapons testing but the fact that they want more room to allow the Defiant to autonomously fly in a difficult environment. Craig looks at the details of the Military training facilities in New Mexico and is staggered by the size. Larger than some countries, he's about to enter a missile testing range covering 3200 square miles. Sitting back and digesting this, his reverie is interrupted by the terse announcement of their descent. The arid landscape rises up to meet him and they touch down.

His two Lockheed shadows settle him into comfortable accommodation near the hangar complex that Leanne has been given by the US Government. Later, he joins members of the team at the canteen facility. They question him about his trip to the UK. He relaxes back into the Skunk Works routine that has been transferred to this remote spot, talking in vague terms about the two vehicles and how successful they have been. This cheers his audience, who, of course, joke competitively about the superiority of their machine.

The following day, a now less jet-lagged version of Craig reintroduces himself to the weapon he has created. The last time he saw Defiant, it was a smooth-flanked and elegant shape. Now its sleek fuselage has been marred by two plug-in weapons stations.

The guns are neatly stowed so that they do not unduly disrupt the streamlined form. Craig has seen the barrels that protrude from these mounts before, on the ranges at Bovington, where they annihilated every target set against them. The aircraft now sports two CT-40 guns. Hardpoints sit underneath stubby wings, and one of the techs tells him that each of them is there for two Hellfire missiles. The graceful aircraft that had arrived at Palmdale a matter of months ago has achieved its true status, the definitive lethal autonomous weapon system. Rather, it will have, as soon as Craig integrates these weapons into the system and places them in the hands of the Heimdall engine.

He sits in front of the screen with the script pages laid out in front of him, finally confronted with a reality that he has ignored for nearly a year. He has created the ultimate killer robot. His line of thought is interrupted by the analysts on either side of him. They are impatient to bring him up to date with all that has happened in his absence. After the simulated flying and his part in the opening series of flight tests, at which he had been present in Palmdale, the team had gone on to more complex tasks. This was so that they could log as many flying hours as possible. Russ Morales, the head of the flight team, is in a buoyant mood as he describes the results.

"We pretty much flew twenty-four-seven as soon as we'd night certified the bird, just stops for fuel and to download data. We were doing the analysis while he was in the air, and we got results ten times faster than it could be done with a human crew. 280 hours flying while you've been gone."

The Lockheed engineers are in a buoyant mood, and Craig asks, "So what next? Integration of the weapons and something called a DAS, according to my briefing notes. I didn't like to ask Tweedledum and Tweedledummer what that was. It seemed like a daft question."

Smiles and laughter greet this, and surreptitious looks are darted at the two men who had greeted Craig at the airport. They are drinking coffee and eating doughnuts in the corner of the hangar, trying hard not to look like a security detail.

"Defensive Aids Suite, Craig." Russ hands him a sheaf of papers. "That, and the tech specs for the guns and missiles are all there. You're familiar with the guns, that's one of the reasons they were chosen."

Craig spreads the paper out over his desk, and Russ realises that he has lost him for the moment, so he shoos away the rest of the design team. After a while, Craig looks up and wanders off to get himself a coffee. Russ has waited patiently for him to finish, knowing it wouldn't take long, and he joins the still thoughtful Craig in the rest area.

"So, can it be done? And how long will it take? We've got a six month option on this place, but that could be extended. I know that systems integration can be tricky."

"Six months! It won't take that long. Six weeks, perhaps."

Russ is astonished, and Craig continues, "It's a bit like the flying. We just need to get the machine language right and minimise direct connections to the sub-systems. Remember, we're replacing the human with a decision engine. We don't expect it to replace all the computation, just manage what's already there."

A familiar southern drawl interrupts them, and they turn to see that Leanne Phillips has arrived. Russ was not expecting her to appear so early, and Craig not at all. She is amused by the confusion caused and waits for her troupe to gather, motioning those that have risen from their seats to relax.

"Six weeks is music to my ears, though I am surprised to hear you say it. Do explain."

Craig struggles to de-fluster himself and falls back on what worked in Porton Down.

"It's like an octopus, Leanne."

The expected laughter and confusion lighten the atmosphere.

"An octopus hands off a lot of sensory input and movement to its arms. It has a distributed neural network. We do it ourselves to a more limited extent. I've looked at the specs for the three systems, and they all have their own computation. The DAS is the most complicated, but it also has the best inbuilt autonomy. All we need for that is an information link and a veto on the intended response. The gun is the simplest because Heimdall already knows it and the integration aspects are already there. The Hellfire will take some work, I've already seen the specs, and it's the heavy hitter, but it's older generation. It's the slowest weapon to acquire and fire, mostly because of the time it takes the rocket motor to get going and the sensors to warm up."

"Will it be a problem? We make Hellfire, so the software and specs are ours. It's getting old, but the replacement isn't properly tested and released to service yet."

"No, it's just that the helicopter is pretty agile, as we proved up at the Skunk Works. The laser has to be kept in a steady aim until the missile scores a hit. A fire-and-forget weapon would be better. Heimdall could just program it and fly Defiant out of danger."

"I think that might have to come further down the development line. But, as I understand, in general terms, you just need to ensure that the Heimdall engine can interpret the inputs it's getting and can talk in the other direction?"

"Exactly, but this is easier than the tanks in the UK because a human isn't getting in the way and slowing things down. Imagine if you had twenty of these controlled by a central node as part of a wider neural network controlling other weapons on the ground like tanks and artillery. You wouldn't have to risk a human at all."

"Whoa, there, cowboy! That's getting a little bit ahead of ourselves and raises more questions than I want and a bunch of answers that I definitely don't have. Not yet, anyways. One step at a time, please, and let's not start talking along those lines, even in this place." She looks around to include the whole audience, most of whom are as startled as she is by Craig's extrapolation.

Inwardly, Leanne is both intrigued and unsettled. She covers this by issuing instructions for the weeks ahead and outlining what they are to achieve. Craig's neural networks she parks for future consideration. Her final comment is to let Craig know that they've changed the nomenclature of the aircraft to distinguish it from the other prototypes. The X has been dropped from the name, and officially it is now the Defiant Alpha Mike.

She adds, "Of course, they all are just calling it Alpha Mike."

Russ adds, "Or Mike, once you get to know him well enough."

There is laughter, and Leanne wags an amused finger at him.

The conversation ends with the arrival of four people in uniform who have come to join the project. They are a mix of senior officers from the Army and Air Force whose job will be to design a series of exercises to test the system. Beyond curt nods to the civilians and a shared measured look at Craig, they say nothing before stalking off to a set of offices where they will do their work.

Leanne watches them go. "Don't worry about them, they're not sure what they've gotten themselves into. They'll warm up once we get going."

"Do they know what Alpha Mike is, Leanne?"

"Not the details, Craig, highly automated drone is the extent of the briefing we gave them at the Pentagon, and they're temporarily part of the DARPA team.* We'll let them get the tactical exercise series worked out, and then we'll pull them into the inner circle. It'll be a neat surprise." Leanne smiles brightly at Craig and the rest of her audience.

As the military people pore over maps and write their scenarios, Craig and his people bench test the new systems they are integrating. The chin-mounted turret that was installed at the Skunk Works is uprated to include a laser target designator. This lets the Defiant mark targets for the Hellfire Romeo missiles that will be part of the test series.

---

* Defence Advanced Research Project Agency, the US government's defence research department. They work closely with industry, when appropriate.

The first test flight is short and confirms that the Defiant communications link, proposed shortly before Craig returned to the UK, works. Conventional radio had been the convenient, cheap method of monitoring and instructing Heimdall for the early flights. However, a satellite communications system has been installed alongside the military radios to fully exploit the aircraft's range and speed. For Craig and the engineers, this means real-time monitoring during the long-range missions that are being planned. Leanne authorises two flights before they let the tacticians get to start their tests. The first of these is a circuit of about four hundred kilometres, the furthest flown so far. The sortie is a simple instruction to visit six points. Next, the range liaison officer assigned to them checks that the route is safe and will not interfere with other users.* Her clearance joins the green lights from the flight engineers and the avionics specialists. They have all taken their posts in front of the screens that flank Craig's central position. As this occurs, the ground crew tows Defiant onto the dispersal in front of the hangar. When they report the area clear, Russ gets a nod from the liaison officer who has been talking to the control tower, and Craig starts the engines. The RLO tells them they have clearance to launch from the dispersal, so Craig touches the mission execute button and the rotorcraft leaps into the air and heads north. By the time it clears the airfield, the velocity indicated on Craig's display is 250 knots. As he sits back and watches the symbol on the moving map display head north towards the range, he turns to Russ.

"I can't get my head around all these different scales."

"What do you mean?"

"Well, knots for aviation, miles per hour, kilometres. Degrees and mils for measuring angles, depending on whether you're a sailor or a soldier. It would be a lot easier if it was standard."

"I suppose we could convert it to metres per second, if you want?"

---

* RLO in military slang.

"129."

"What, you just worked that out?!" Russ leans back laughing; he returns to a neutral expression, wary of offending. During the time Craig has been in America, Russ has gone from fascinated respect to genuine liking.

"Yes, and the answer to the second question is yes, probably."

"Probably what?"

"On the spectrum, a bit autistic. Aspergers, although that's not very popular now. Dr Asperger was a bit of a Nazi. My mum wouldn't do any tests, just said I was clever, and people were jealous. I've thought about it a bit and done some research; I'd say I'm borderline. If I am, it's a small price to pay for being able to do this. I can understand Heimdall. That's why we are where we are."

"How do you mean?"

"My nature, basically, is to think obsessively in ones and zeros. Things are, or they aren't. It's not that I don't know that there are shades of grey. It's just that I'm more comfortable if there aren't. It means that I'm relaxed with the way Heimdall reasons. I think that's why my programming works. Everything has a set of conditions, and they lead to an outcome."

"It's a shame that there isn't a slider on that spectrum. I'd shove it a long way over to do what you can."

Russ's comment makes them both chuckle, and they return their attention to the displays. On either side of them, the two teams are busy. The engineers looking at the flight data and the design team poring over the feeds from the sensors. After a moment, they take in the position of Defiant on the map; it is already halfway along the route they have set. Finally, Craig looks at Russ.

"We can do better than this."

"What do you mean?"

"Can we get another flight, which we can do this afternoon? Just flying to some points on the ground isn't working the whole system."

They look at the groups on the flanks, and Russ notes that the sensor and weapons integrators are much less involved than the people analysing the flying performance.

"I see what you mean. What are you suggesting?"

"Well, the military types aren't the only ones who can do a scenario. So let's put together an exercise in the ground and air and let Heimdall decide how he's going to fly the Defiant."

Russ thinks for a moment and nods his head.

"We'd better speak to the RLO."

They head over to the desk where she sits reading. At their approach, she looks up and smiles.

Russ squats down beside her, Craig stands behind him.

"Major Travers, we'd like to fly another route so that we can see if our automatic route selection works. Can we plot some more points for an extra flight this afternoon?"

She looks thoughtful. "I'll make some calls, should be no problem, you plot your route."

Craig interjects. "Actually, we want to plot a couple of points and then put in some areas it can't go. See if the system can give us optional routes and choose the best."

Her interest is further piqued. "I'd like to see that, put what you want on the planning map, I'll get back with the clearance."

When she returns, she frowns at their plan. "I'll have to alter part of that, there's a rocket battery firing at targets there, you'll have to go round."

"Can't we fly underneath?" Craig asks.

"Well, yes. The rocket battery is moving about, though."

"The drone has a sense and avoid system." Russ is careful with his words and what he gives away. "Its reconnaissance pod will see the battery and plot a course that keeps it safe. We just have to put in the commands and monitor progress. That's right, isn't it, Craig?"

"Actually, they're already in. The exercises we did in the UK before coming here practised it. We just have to make sure the shape and size of the avoid zone meets your standards."

The RLO blinks in surprise, and Craig beckons her to follow him over to the command screens. He pulls up the instruction screen that deals with the targeting coordination commands. Then shows her how they can use area restrictions to prevent the Defiant from flying in harm's way. She is very impressed when he demonstrates the trajectory modelling that lets the rotorcraft fly underneath artillery lines of fire.

They are interrupted by the return of the Defiant. All three stand to watch it approach. As it reaches the dispersal area, it hovers briefly before landing. It is towed back to stand in front of the hangar, and the flight team join the ground crew bustling around it like bees attending their queen.

The three return to the job in hand, finalising a plan for the flight. A series of threat areas are created for Defiant to avoid, and a target is selected for a simulated firing of Hellfire. The RLO, in the meantime, has a conversation with the Range Control Organisation and gets clearance for the exercise. Russ places a call to Leanne, who has postponed her return to the Skunk Works for a day. She is enthusiastic as this will be the first drill she has seen where they will demonstrate intelligent flight. One of the military people, a major in the Army, appears, and Leanne beckons her over. She suggests she bring her companions over to hear what they have planned.

The four military men join them as the flight engineers trickle back from the dispersal. After a respectful nod to Leanne, the senior officer, a US Air Force colonel, extends his hand to Craig and introduces himself and his team members. Russ has learned that unprepared briefings to strangers are not Craig's forte, so he explains what they plan to do. He points out the threat areas and no-fly zones that will keep the Defiant out of harm's way and encourage the aircraft to fly a long distance to attack two targets. Encouraged, Craig explains that the Heimdall programme has an exercise mode and a live mode to separate real from drill targets. Leanne relates the incident in the UK, where the test turret wouldn't shoot at the mobile targets because it thought they were wheelchairs. This gets laughter and comments from the audience.

The Colonel looks hard at Leanne and says, "So, this isn't just another drone, is it, ma'am?"

"No, sir, it is not. You are looking at the first fully autonomous strike aircraft in the US. Now you understand why this is so highly classified and why we are way out here."

The service people exchange surprised looks and turn to regard the Defiant, framed by the hangar doors.

"So it's an—"

"Don't say it, Peter. Dr Moore may be an unassuming gentleman, but that phrase does, as the Brits say, wind him up!"

Craig is emboldened by the comment from Leanne, accompanied as it is by her trademark smile. The amusement from the Lockheed people who have got to know him well provides further encouragement.

"I prefer the phrase, highly autonomous system capable of multiple rehearsed behaviours, Colonel Doyle."

He gets a smile from the senior man. "Well, thanks for clearing that up, Doc!"

The Colonel turns to his team, and there is a short, muted conversation. Then, returning his attention to the rest of the group, he says, "Look, you'd better give us the lowdown on this new toy. We don't want to waste our time designing scenarios that won't prove anything."

Leanne outlines the events in the UK leading to Craig's involvement in the project. She describes the test that she witnessed in the UK and gives them a precis of the briefing from Helen Sherwood. She is in regular contact with Helen and so is aware of the trial series on Salisbury Plain. When she describes the capabilities of the Ajax, the Army lieutenant colonel breaks in.

"So, the Brits have self-driving armour, with this sort of autonomy? Already?"

Leanne smiles. "Not quite… Craig?"

He is still not entirely comfortable with the US officers and aware that he's not supposed to say very much about what happened on Salisbury Plain.

"Well, the job was to take the driver out of the vehicle and assist the crew with finding targets and managing the gun. We are a bit worried about full autonomy over there, or some people are. Public reaction to robotic weapons is a big thing. I get pretty pissed off with the whole killer robots hysteria myself. Anyway, what we've ended up with is a couple of vehicles that can drive around tactically, simply by touching a spot on the map you want to go to. They can detect threats themselves and download external ISTAR data. Their own data can be fed the other way."

The air force major interrupts. "Could you integrate Link 16 into it?"

Craig looks at Leanne in confusion, and she picks up the narrative.

"It's OK, Craig, this is UK US eyes stuff." Then she turns to the major. "It's already in there. A couple of days before Dr Moore came over to Palmdale, I was told they put an AWACS over the top, and it worked."

The Army officer speaks again. "So, we could take this and put it in one of our tanks, and it could drive it?"

Leanne is about to answer but notices Craig looking uncomfortable. She stops and looks at him, askance.

"Um, not exactly." All eyes are now on him. "Heimdall deletes stuff he doesn't think is relevant. He tidies up, saves space. Over here, he flies, so he doesn't need a driving licence." Craig smiles weakly under the scrutiny of Leanne and the four officers.

Russ adds to the tale. "The programme doesn't just save space. It alters its own language. Craig's been tutoring me as his deputy. I've done some work in the computer language we use, and Heimdall rewrites it."

There are the usual uncomfortable looks when information like this is revealed. Looks that don't extend as far as Leanne or the people who had been part of the development team at Palmdale. Craig hastily informs the worried-looking ones that it isn't about to take over the world. The programme is built to respond to external commands. It doesn't think up new ones. He repeats his words 'rehearsed behaviours', adding, as he looks at the air force Colonel, "That's what flying is; it's why pilots spend so much time in simulators even after they can fly. You rehearse all the emergencies and failures. Soldiers have drills so that they can fall back on well-rehearsed basic actions when the bullets start to fly."

"So how does this differ from conventional drones? They don't need constant human input."

Leanne steps forward and takes up the narrative. "When Craig arrived at the Skunk Works a month ago, we'd already been working the Akicita Maza project for a few months. We'd made some breakthroughs in the simulation labs. Our colleagues in the future troop lift programme gave us a Defiant X prototype when we had a mature enough design. So we were getting there, and then I had a phone call from one of our people in the UK. That's what led to the visit, where we got a glimpse of Dr Moore's programme." She looks at Craig with fond amusement. "After the demonstration, someone asked him if the programme could drive a tank. He said yes, and then why. His final comment that it would be 'easier to fly' was the one that counted. I got his bosses to let me borrow him."

Russ Morales adds some detail. "All Craig needed to do was programme everything about the rotorcraft into the Heimdall engine. We just plugged the system into the flight simulator. We used high definition cameras to observe the world screens and fed instrumentation data directly into the programme. Heimdall already knew how to fly various aircraft. He just needed to learn the characteristics of Alpha Mike. We just turned everything on and stood back. By the end of the first day, there were no mistakes. We'd introduced meteorological variables and most of the typical flying conditions. The machine taught itself to fly. In a day."

The junior of the Air Force officers protests. "Flying isn't just about a simple circuit and coping with weather conditions. Drones usually can't cope with high wind speeds or crosswinds. They're notorious for not following terrain and can't sense and avoid the threats a human pilot can."

"It's not really a drone. At least not in the way that current drones fly. The drones you are talking about are highly aerodynamic and find coping with external variables hard. This is one of the most advanced helicopters in the world. It was already designed with autonomy in mind. All we had to do was up the number of external information feeds and on-board sensors then plug it into a computer that could cope. Now we're down here, it's learning more advanced techniques and adding to what it can do."

HOT AND HUMID IN LOUISIANA

This is ably demonstrated when they go on to firings against the various targets on the range. The programme, as far as it was concerned, had already fired the CT-40. All it needed to do was get used to the characteristics of the Hellfire. All the allocated missiles are expended in a variety of scenarios. Success is absolute.

The US military team soon realised they were right when they decided to do something different to test the aircraft. Craig tells them how they managed the Ajax exercises and how good the results were. The four look for somewhere they can continue and decide that they should go south to Louisiana. At Fort Polk Joint Readiness Training Centre, there is a different climate and terrain to test the helicopter. There is also a skilful opposing force for Defiant Alpha Mike to fight.

They shift location to the heat and humidity of the heavily forested training area and commence the series of exercises that the training team have devised. The terrain is not ideal for a lone helicopter. The trees hide the enemy forces, and they exploit the weakness to the full. The team becomes frustrated with repeated failure. Russ uses the time to learn as much as he can and becomes, as Will Conyers was, the next best thing to Craig. He also comes to rather like the awkward but kind man.

After a frustrating week, the team is given a couple of days off. Russ, a native of New Orleans, takes him to his home. Craig is not keen on the climate, but the hospitality of the Morales family beguiles him. After a night of being guided around the musical nightlife of the city, he says to Russ, out of the blue, "I might have a solution."

Russ has noted moments of preoccupation and internet use during the break. "A solution to what, my friend?"

"Seeing through trees."

"You're kidding me."

"You'll have spotted I'm not much of a comedian, Russ."

"True! Go on then, Mr Genius, tell me how this miracle can be achieved."

"I remembered reading somewhere that a team was working on a method of searching through trees. A search and rescue tool. An algorithm that works with a thermal camera and programmes like Heimdall. I found some papers. I think I can write something similar, with your help. It'll save time if we don't have to involve other organisations."

Russ stares at him, speechless. When he recovers, the possibilities hit him, and he paces the room. Turning back to him, he says, "We have to go back."

Craig agrees, and after apologies and farewells to their hosts, the two travel back to the deserted hangar in Fort Polk.

The following day, the military element is the first to arrive and find two exhausted and dishevelled persons drinking coffee in front of Alpha Mike. He is awake and not a bit tired.

The two turn around to grin at the startled officers. Russ is triumphant.

"He did it."

"We did it, Russ."

"We can see through trees; he wrote an algorithm. A piece of digital art. It's genius."

Craig is embarrassed and explains more calmly that he thinks they've managed to get the thermal imaging pod to ignore the trees and detect heat beneath the canopy. Alpha Mike can then interpret the signal to give a reasonable chance of detection.

The rest of the group have arrived to hear the end of the tale. Colonel Doyle calls over to the engineers to get the bird ready for flight. Another of the officers runs off to file a flight plan.

Craig tells them that they need to put people, groups and vehicles out in known locations so that Alpha Mike can learn the signatures to improve detection probability.

Doyle looks at the exhausted pair. "I take it you came back early and worked all night? That'll take an hour or two to set up, find somewhere and get some sleep; we'll need you for the flight."

They wander off, and the Colonel looks back at his three teammates, shaking his head. Karen, the Army major on the team, looks back at him.

"If he wasn't so nice, I'd be real scared of him."

The four look at the retreating pair, then urgency takes over, and they get to work.

Leanne Phillips has gone up to Palmdale but comes back two days later. She is surprised to find that her driver is Colonel Peter Doyle. He settles her alarm by saying, "No, we haven't crashed it! You know we were having trouble finding the enemy in the trees. Well, we're not anymore."

"Dr Moore?"

"Dr Moore. The man has designed a method of seeing through trees. The Opfor can't believe it. They have no idea how we're doing it either. The machine gets better at doing it over time, too."

"Thank you for telling me before I arrived on site. It will take some thinking to work out the ramifications of this update to the system."

"Alpha Mike is now winning more times than it loses. That's pretty amazing for a lone helicopter. We think if we give it some friends on the ground and in the air, it'll be unbeatable. This brings me on to the other reason I'm here. We briefed up to the

Pentagon, and the chief of staff of the Air Force wants to visit. That's not a request to refuse."

Leanne leans back and replies, "Of course." She is delighted.

Elsewhere, a storm is brewing.

CLOUDS GATHER

The second, or Bravo, aircraft of the formation of two F-18F Super Hornets from the USS Abraham Lincoln disconnects from the KC-135 tanker high above the Iraqi desert and joins its partner. The two head for the Syrian border, today is a reconnaissance mission. Tensions between the US and Russia, Syria's principal backer, ebb and flow. Today is a flow day, and the task is designed to be routine and unprovocative. They will execute a wide arc from south to north with the town of Raqqah as its easternmost point. Sending a message, but also using their SHARP reconnaissance pods to gather what information they can.

The intelligence brief had mentioned a spike in military activity north of Raqqah and a report of continued Syrian opposition success in the area. The course set is due to take them close enough to the general location for a long-range scan.

Below them, keen but hostile eyes mark their progress, and a mobile phone call is placed. Further east, the Lightweight Electronic Warfare Team, attached to A Squadron of the Royal Lancers, notes the electronic signature and can establish a very rough location. The young intelligence corps corporal in charge of the detachment records this anomalous activity and reports it.

In due course, the intelligence cell at the Brigade HQ associates the call with the two Super Hornets' track. By then, it is too late.

As the two aircraft turn south, neither is surprised when they are picked up by Russian surveillance radars. Russian military operators sending their political master's message. The rear seat Weapons Systems Officers prepare the pods for the surveillance run, cancelling the warble in their headsets.*

The voice of the Bravo Wizzo crackles into his opposite number's ears.

"That's odd!"

"What's odd?" He turns his head towards the other F-18, noting his friend, head down in the cockpit. The aircraft fly in tight formation, mere metres apart, to present a single signature for the watchers far to the west.

"The radar, I've got an N2 spike, but there's also a Clam Shell signature."

The Alpha Pilot breaks in. "Should I be concerned?"

"We get a lot of S-400 surveillance hits, but this is from an S-300.** It shouldn't be this far over."

"Bastards are just jerking our chain."

The alarm note sounds in the airman's ears once again, and the tension ratchets up.

"Tracking radar, S-300 GRILL PAN!"

From the Alpha Wizzo: "I have IR signatures, missiles inbound."

His pilot screams, "Break, break!"

The defensive aid suites on the Super Hornets have a fibre optic towed radiofrequency decoy. Deliberately fitted with a braking system for fast deployment, this works against two aircraft flying so close together. The Alpha breaks high and right, his

---

* Abbreviated to WSO but usually referred to as a 'Wizzo'.
** S-300 and S-400 are Russian Air Defence Missile Systems. The 300 is older. The S-400 is much scarier. Its surveillance radar is code-named, 'Clam Shell'. Grill Pan is the targeting radar.

colleague, low and left. The two decoys collide, and the resulting catastrophic break-up of the two units creates a cloud of fragments that impact the tail of Bravo. With damaged control surfaces, the pilot struggles to control his bird. In addition, their layered defensive system has now gone from three to zero.

The two aircrafts dispense chaff and flares, but the Bravo cannot execute the same manoeuvres as his companion. Despite this, the chaff countermeasures match the ageing missiles, and one detonates at distance. The second missile has some luck. It steers towards the struggling jet. Despite being decoyed, the detonation of the 150 kilogram warhead is still close enough to send fragments into the aircraft fuselage and an engine intake. A piece of shrapnel penetrates the cockpit and fatally injures the Wizzo.

The pilot desperately attempts to control the jet as it loses height after the dramatic loss of power. Facing a hopeless situation, he ejects, and the canopy shatters into fragments through which the two crewmen leave the stricken plane.

Meanwhile, the Alpha Hornet has executed a tight turn, returning and spiralling down with the two parachutes. Calling in the emergency, an AWACS[*] over Iraq relays the request for Combat Search and Rescue to the US base at Key West.[**]

There, a scene of frantic activity resolves itself as two attack helicopters, and two troop transports lift off and streak westwards.

The fighter still over the downed aircraft calls in a last report and location. She is low on fuel and is instructed to leave Syrian airspace. Air defence missile radars still intermittently tracking it, the F-18 obeys and heads east.

Two deflated parachutes lie like fallen blossoms quite close together in the stony desert. Several kilometres away, a plume of smoke marks the spot where the stricken aircraft has crashed. The

---

[*] Airborne Warning and Control System. In this case a modified Boeing 707 radar and air defence control centre.

[**] Abbreviated to CSAR, pronounced 'See Sar'.

surviving airman limps over to the recumbent form of his Wizzo, falling to his knees in horror at the sight of his lifeless friend.

He is oblivious to the stealthy approach of sandalled feet.

A DASTARDLY PLAN

The attack on the two aircrafts had been carefully orchestrated.

Despite a month of setbacks around their last stronghold in eastern Syria, Daesh forces mounted a desperate attack on the Syrian Government forces, forcing them back. They ignored mounting casualties and overran a series of forward positions, taking ground and some armour and artillery, before being stopped at the small lakeside town of Al Tabqua. It was here that a detachment came upon a Russian air defence missile position. It was carefully camouflaged, and the command post discretely sited close to a mosque on the north side of the town. The Syrian crew appeared to have abandoned the equipment, and the Daesh fighters were delighted that this valuable asset was not destroyed. Pressing forward to claim the prize, their leader was astonished to discover two Russian officers, a colonel and a major, in the command vehicle coolly regarding their arrival. The fighters were further discomfited when the senior of the immaculate figures addressed them politely in beautifully accented Arabic. Even offering them tea before asking their leader to summon his superior.

The two officers were from the fourth directorate of the GRU, the department of the feared Russian military intelligence organisation that studies the Middle East.* Beneath the outward calm held in an iron grip forged by years of training and active service, the two were perturbed by this mission. They approve of the aim, but dealing with these capricious fanatics introduced, from their point of view, unpredictable outcomes and risks, not least to themselves. Nonetheless, when the senior commander arrived, none of this showed. Like his subordinates, he was bewildered by their presence and appearance. More used to fear, or at the very least, deference from people in his power, the offer to explain how this capable missile system operated utterly threw him. Instead, sitting in a chair offered by one of his men, he asked them to explain.

"You have had some recent success, but it will not last."

A hand raised halts the response.

"It will not last. Even now, the forces are regrouping, ready to destroy you. With our help, they will."

"Why, then, should I not kill you now?"

The two intelligence men exchange glances of grim amusement. Returning their gaze to the turbaned fanatic, they do not trouble to hide their contempt, even in the face of his mounting anger.

"Do you not have other ambitions? How will the Caliphate survive and spread if all its fighter's bones lie in the Syrian desert? Your cells in the African Sahel are weak and in need of reinforcement."

"How do you know of this?"

"Knowing is what we do, Laseef Mohamed Al Dulaimi."

If the knowledge of their plans is a surprise, the use of his real name is a shock. A look at the face of his sub-commander reveals an equal surprise. The two subordinates shrink into the corner, fearful.

---

* It's not called the GRU now, but if you're called Glavnoye Raz-vedyvatelnoye Upravlenie, why wouldn't you shorten it? It's now officially GU, but everyone still uses the old initials as a word. It's pronounced grew, like the name of the character in the film *Despicable Me*.

"I am Abdul Al Hadi."

"Servant of the Guide, how appropriate."

The senior Russian reaches into a bag and hands a satellite phone to him.

"This can send to and receive from one number. We will call in the coming days and discuss a route. It is in our interest that your Caliphate does not die. You are a useful… distraction. A thorn in the side of our enemies. Now, fetch some of your people for us to explain how this gift can be used. If they have survived, you have several men who are familiar with our older missiles. It should be easy to teach them what they need to know."

The group leave the command post and settle themselves outside. The two junior guards remain outside the door while the commander's guards fetch four men to be the beneficiaries of the Russian's instruction. They stay drinking coffee and talking in low voices until the two officers finish their brief and the pupils depart.

The Russians bid their hosts farewell and turn to their Tigr Light Armoured vehicle, keen to be gone. Behind them, two shots are fired, and they spin hands reaching for their sidearms.

The two Daesh soldiers by the door lie dead. The commander's two men eye the sub-commander, and the senior Daesh watches him, waiting. He lowers his head respectfully, and the Russians hear him say, "*Sayid.*"

Nodding with satisfaction, the leader turns to the two Russians and sneers as he says, "Go, Kafir!"

As they drive away, they see their protagonist speaking into a radio, but they are unmolested during the drive beyond the Daesh lines. Once clear, they both exhale with relief.

The major, who is driving, thoughtfully remarks, "I find Arabic to be a very poetic language for communication."

They turn to look at each other and, the tension broken, burst into laughter.

Sobering, the Colonel announces, "The sooner those creatures are wiped from the face of the earth, the better."

"Those four we spoke to are likely to find that using that system is more complicated than they think. If they turn it eastwards as we hope, retribution will be swift."

"Indeed, but it will add some more uncertainty for the Pindos, and I'm all for that."

"I hope the high-ups know what they're doing. If those beasts get lucky, there may be unpredictable consequences."

"My friend, I doubt that the very high-ups have any idea what we're up to."

They return to their speculative thoughts as the vehicle lurches across the uneven terrain towards its rendezvous with their Spetsnaz escort.

Finally aware of the presence behind him, the airman struggles to turn and draw his weapon. Too late. He is stunned by the rifle butt that sprawls him across the body of his crew. In pain and dimly aware, he feels his equipment and flight suit roughly cut away. Dragged to a pickup, he is thrown aboard and lashed to the framework at the back of the cab in a ghastly crucifixion parody. To add to his misery, the body of his companion, similarly disrobed, is dumped across his outstretched legs. Bewildered, he sees the length of rope around the hands being tied to the pillar of the technical's machine gun. Two insurgents climb in the back, and the vehicle speeds off to the west. Despair is piled on pain with the realisation that these people know about personal locator beacons. All hope of rescue receding as the discarded clothing is left behind.

When the rescuers arrive, the airman and his captors are far away, their vehicle and cargo under cover. The group that took him are part of a line of patrols watching the eastern skies for just this opportunity. From their hideout, the leader radios his chief, asking for instructions. Meanwhile, the support helicopters have landed, and the troops disembark to discover an awful truth in the two piles of bloody clothing. They search, but the vehicle tracks and footprints paint an eloquent picture of what has happened.

The two attack helicopters start an eastwards sweep, but the only signs are dust clouds approaching them. Eager for something to kill, the Apaches go for the distant pair of vehicles driving southward towards them. They are another of the watchers tasked with distracting this predicted US response in the event of their success. Taking on a pair of Apaches with machine guns from the back of pickups is suicidal, but this is irrelevant to their Daesh masters. The Apaches come under fire, but rockets and guns make short work of their adversaries. The only surprise for the US aircrew comes in the form of a shoulder-launched missile from a pair of fighters dropped off before the Daesh vehicles attacked. Countermeasures successfully defend the helicopters, and the subsequent RPG rockets are wildly inaccurate. After dealing with this threat, the helicopters head south towards a second dust cloud. The wiser head on the shoulders of the Mission Commander calls them back as he orders his troop helicopters to lift off. They can achieve nothing more, and he does not want to hand any more opportunities out on this day. The only hope for their lost men lies with the intelligence gatherers now.

THE HUNT BEGINS

That effort is starting as the four aircraft fly back across the border. Below them, the Ajax of A Squadron trundle in pairs north and south from their harbour and rest area to take their posts along the border. Electronic ears strain to listen deep into Syria from ground and air. Airborne radars sweep across the desert for any sign of movement or any static signal indicating a hidden vehicle.

All staff, resources and assets in the HQs in the Arabian Gulf now concentrate on a single task: find our people. Because of its proximity, the Brigade at Qayyarah West now finds itself at the tip of the spear. The US National Intelligence Centre at the Brigade speaks to the CIA Headquarters at Langley. A KH satellite has its course diverted to provide persistent imagery of eastern Syria at a high cost in both fuel and endurance. A similar call to the National Security Agency elicits the response, "We're on it."

David Lucas now becomes the focus of all UK efforts to help its closest ally in their hour of need. PJHQ is five hours ahead of Washington, so his conversation with chief joint operations is a more measured dialogue. The bottom line is clear: "Whatever you can do, do it! Whatever you need, ask." The only limitation that CJO sets is that no British forces may cross the Iraq-Syria border without his express authority. An authority he must, in turn, receive from the UK Government.

The US President is told shortly after she wakes. She listens to the information gained by the chief of staff over a strong coffee. Other staff place frantic calls to the National Security Council, bidding them to assemble. In their turn, they drag their own teams in to gather what information they can to advise and support their chief. The chairman of the joint chiefs of staff is the most well informed. He was woken by his own people when the crisis in Syria was confirmed by the Air Operations centre in the Middle East and the Brigade Commander in Qayyarah West.

When the Council convenes, they are frustrated by the lack of concrete information on which to act. They are told in detail what has happened, but with no further intelligence yet available, frustration starts to build. The President calls them to order and sends them away to drive their people.

"We will reconvene when we have information on which we can act. Find our people, find them quickly. And, ladies and gentlemen, I want retribution. America will not appear weak. I want whoever did this destroyed."

Calls go out from the Pentagon and the White House to America's friends and allies for help. The coalition countries operating over Syria offer unreserved promises of aid. Many a leader replacing the phone with a shiver of dread that there but for the Grace of God go we. Even Russia promises to lend its aid and interrogate its own well-placed contacts in-country. As the GU commander had surmised, the incident is a surprise to the Kremlin. A debate ensues as to whether this represents a threat or an opportunity. The chief of the general staff and the defence minister cleave to the latter, acutely aware that the blame will fall on them if the consequences are unfavourable. They lose no time demanding answers from the Military Intelligence Head when the meeting is over.

The news of an incident over Syria is impossible to keep out of the media. US reporters bombard the Government and the White

House. Short of concrete information, they merely confirm the loss of an aircraft. When the story does break, it is via the internet, specifically by well-known Jihadist websites.

AN ERROR OF JUDGEMENT

The Group Commander holding the airman receives instructions to bring the captive to a village further west, where a camera and media-savvy pair of Daesh propagandists are waiting. As they approach the village, a quadcopter drone operated by the camera crew records their approach. The guards in the back of the technical shove the body of the Wizzo off the vehicle. The length of rope attached to the wrists snakes out, and the half-naked corpse is dragged along the dusty track. A section of Daesh soldiers has assembled for the coming show, and they crowd around cheering and jeering. The villagers look on, mostly fearful of the insurgents. In the back of the truck, the pinioned pilot's horror has turned to rage at the treatment of his friend. When he is unshackled, he fights his captors. That he achieves a measure of success serves to enrage the fighters, and when one of his kicks connects with the groin of the leader, it further maddens them. A machete is produced, and its owner slashes at the pilot, incapacitating him. Falling to his knees, his assailant hacks at his neck and decapitates him.

All this is recorded by the insurgent with the camera. He and his teammate are well used to such spectacles, and they quickly splice in the drone footage on their laptop. It is encrypted, and the file is sent by email using their satphone.

While this has been happening, the Daesh commander has recovered and takes in what has happened. His orders were not to kill captives. He was expected to record the capture and hide the pilot deeper in Syrian territory until further orders. Hiding his fright, he berates the gunmen who are posing for photographs by the two bodies.

The two IT specialists have turned off the communications and are packing up, clearly intent on leaving. The commander hurries over to them, asking them why they are going.

"Our work here is done. We must go quickly. The eyes and ears of the Kuffar will be searching for us."

"What have you done? Where are the pictures?"

"They have been sent. As was ordered."

"Sent? Sent where?"

The two specialists exchange looks. "We do not know, to one of our cells. We would not be permitted to say even if we did know. Others decide what is to be done. Usually, it goes to the internet to inspire our brothers around the world."

The commander feels his world unravelling. With his attention no longer on them, his interlocutors carry on with their preparations to leave. In turmoil, he wanders off and climbs to the roof of one of the mud buildings. Taking out his radio, he begins a call to the hideout that is waiting for him to arrive with the prisoner. Below him, a worried voice shouts a question.

"What are you doing? We told you that it was dangerous. You will be heard. We must get away from here."

The two IT men take a last worried look around and upwards before getting in their car and speeding off to the west.

The leader comes to his senses and shouts orders to the group of men in the village square who are now looking up at him in consternation.

"Bury the Kuffar, outside the village. Do it quickly. We must be gone from here."

The bodies are dragged away and thrown in a ditch on the edge of the village. Earth is thrown over them and, eager to be away, they hurry back to their vehicles and leave the cluster of buildings behind them. In the front technical, the commander broods on what little future he suspects he has.

The unintended consequences that started with the two Russians handing over the knowledge needed to launch the S-300 missile continue. The Colonel and his Spetsnaz colleague assumed that Daesh would fail. The local Daesh leadership expected the surviving pilot to live so that they could exploit and humiliate the Americans. Now the cell to which the video file has gone assumes that it should be published, and does so. Instructions from Syria to keep the footage safe while deciding how to obfuscate and delay the certainty of retaliation arrive too late.

ON THE SCENT

Desperate for clues as to the whereabouts of their lost airmen, the eyes and ears of the allies have indeed detected the fleeting signals sent by the commander and the media team. The proximity of a Satcom signal to a radio broadcast is unusual enough for the intelligence gatherers to divert a Predator drone across the border to take a look. The Daesh fighters are long gone by the time the drone arrives and scans the village. The evidence of vehicles that have come and gone is plentiful, and further sensor sweeps in both visual and infra-red reveal other clues. The dirt hastily thrown over the two bodies cannot hide the heat they generate. In the centre of the village, a dark stain pollutes the earth. The images flash from the Predator ground control station to the intelligence cell at Key West and thence to Washington.

In the meantime, as the drone operators continue their scans, the screen goes abruptly blank. Keen to play with their new toy, the Daesh missile crew have fired another S-300 missile. The ability of conventional drones to sense and avoid threats is poor. With few countermeasures available, the Predator is an easy target.

The AWACS on duty soon confirms the cause of the drone's demise, but the news is overshadowed.

In Qayyarah West, the Brigade Commander's operations cell debates the risk of sending in the CSAR team to investigate what the Predator has seen. They are interrupted by an ashen-faced analyst from the intelligence cell. Her expression silences the debate around the table.

"Sir, I'm sorry. You need to see this."

Crossing to the screen on the wall, she turns it on and selects a feed from the intelligence cell. The image is frozen, drone footage of the Daesh vehicle dragging the hapless Bravo Wizzo across the desert. She unpauses the video, and the horrified watchers witness the appalling treatment meted out to their people. As the footage approaches its denouement, the brigadier general's choked voice orders her to stop it. Eyes brimming, she does so.

"I'm so sorry, sir. We've established from our drone footage that the buildings in that village are a match."

"No need to apologise, First Sergeant. It had to be seen."

He turns back to his audience as she departs. Addressing the commander of the CSAR mission, he says, "Major Macallister, go get our boys back."

The Commander directs his staff officers to give all support to this CSAR operation, stipulating that they are to put boots on the ground just before last light. Anticipating the need to speak to higher command, he turns for the door but pauses, looking back at the frozen screen. He picks up the remote and rewinds the images to a view of the crowd. All eyes turn to him.

"Mac, the villagers."

"Sir?"

"No weapons, and look at them. They were made to watch this."

The audience takes in the fear and shock on the faces of the ragged group in the background.

"Keep a hold of your team, Major Macallister. Enough blood has been shed in that sorry place."

"Yes, sir!"

The general turns away and leaves, followed closely by David Lucas. The latter foresees imminent conversations with his masters in the UK. Behind them, the conversation buzzes as the worker bees wrestle with what will be a risky penetration of Syrian airspace.

Once again, the CSAR team gets airborne and heads at high speed for the border. This time the team is smaller. Two Blackhawk helicopters carry troops with a pair of Apaches acting as outriders.

Once across the border, they fly bare metres above the ground this time, preferring to raise a dust trail than fall prey to missiles. Twenty minutes later, and one hundred kilometres inside Syria, they set down on the edge of their target. The sun is setting as the troops emerge from the dust with fingers on triggers. The few villagers who were outside flee for the safety of their houses, screaming that djinn are coming from out of the storm.

Mac, standing tall and grim, scans the scene to get his bearings. As he does so, a single terrified villager emerges from a hut falling to his knees as a dozen rifles point. A raised fist halts them, and hand gestures send his troops scurrying to positions of overwatch. Motioning for his interpreter to follow, he stalks forward to tower over the cringing village headman. Barely coherent, tearful, begging for mercy and forgiveness, the headman confirms what they already know. The villagers were unwilling participants.

The headman points. "I will show you where they are, Agha."

He leads Mac to the ditch on the southern side of the village, a curt command to one of his noncoms brings a half dozen of his people who unfold entrenching tools ready to dig. It is barely necessary, so shallow is the grave. Two military body bags are unrolled by the side of the trench and, as carefully as they can, the sand is scraped away from the airmen. They are in the grip of powerful emotions, and Macalister turns a furious glare on the headman. He bows his head respectfully and backs away, followed by Mac's Arab speaker. The interpreter converses with the man in low tones. As this happens, the two bodies are zipped into the bags. The separated head of the pilot is wrapped in a cloth before being placed in the bag. There is a pause while they recover their equanimity. The spell is broken by Mac, who recalls them to the danger they are all in. The section on guard joins the recovery party. They board the helicopters and fly east. On the journey, Mac is briefed by his interpreter. Keen to make amends, the village chief has told him all that occurred. The gang leader was known to one of his people, so now they have a name.

The video uploaded to extremist websites has hit the rest of the world. Media and intelligence agencies scramble to release stories and brief principals in turn. The loss of the US aircraft and its crew has already made news and instigated a clamour for action. The appalling scenes online make this clamour a roar. Unsurprisingly, the most significant outcry is in America. Senate and Congress unite in calls for the US to act. Public fury, echoed across all the media, demands retaliation.

The National Security Council was in session when the President was briefed on the mission to recover the bodies, but success was not announced until after the session ended. As pressure on the White House for a Presidential response mounts, a mission update arrives. Hence, the President arranges to address the nation that evening. She decides not to bring the Council back together but orders the Defence Intelligence Agency and the CIA to collaborate. She is to be given as up to date a report as possible before she speaks.

AN UNEXPECTED FRIEND

Intelligence is a painstaking process. Only in Hollywood do sudden breakthroughs occur. A leap of logic rarely results in a detailed picture of what happened or what might happen. Luck often plays a part, but mostly it is hard work and long hours. The net is wide, but sifting valuable data from what it catches is difficult. The help of friends is always useful, but sometimes so is that of enemies.

The chief of intelligence at the British Embassy in Washington has not slept much since he and his team were called in to help in their ally's current crisis. Calls from agencies on both sides of the Atlantic, directing his staff and numerous trips to the office of the ambassador, have run him ragged. In search of a moment of peace and tranquillity, he crosses Massachusetts Avenue to the Kahlil Gibran Memorial Garden. Sitting on the bench, contemplating the fountain in the star-shaped pool, he closes his eyes for a moment. As he relaxes, he is aware that someone has taken a seat next to him. Unusual, as individual peace and quiet are generally respected in this place. Opening his eyes, he is surprised to see his opposite number from the Russian Embassy calmly seated next to him, thoughtfully regarding the play of water on the surface of the pond.

The Russian turns to regard him, a wry smile on his face. "Good morning, Geoffrey. A busy night and morning, I think?"

"Good morning to you, Vasiliy. Yes, it has been… trying."

Geoffrey pauses; it doesn't take much imagination to realise the reason for this approach. But why? He buys a little time.

"How did you know that I would be here?"

The Russian's smile broadens into genuine amusement. "When problems arise in the West, I have one of my people observe this spot. If you appear, I know I must concentrate. It is one of our intelligence indicators!"

Geoffrey matches the gentle laughter, privately thinking he should be more careful.

"The Americans are becoming angry… and noisy. They are an excitable nation, prone to acts of retribution. Their unpredictability makes me… uncomfortable."

Geoffrey decides that some bait may be revealing. "Yes, they are. It makes for uncomfortable, sleepless nights. Even for their allies." He makes his cast. "They have recovered the pilot and the crewman, you know. It was the missile that killed the crewman."

He has the Russian's full attention now. "No. I did not. The missile… yes. It was one of our missiles. Not, of course, fired by us, or even the Syrians." The last comment is hastily added.

Geoffrey's reply is grim. "Unfortunate. To shoot down a Hornet, it would need to be a capable missile. Not one we would associate with Daesh."

Geoffrey now grasps the reason for such a senior visitor to his favourite spot. Not that the Russian has come unprepared. Geoffrey's own tradecraft skills have picked out at least three discrete individuals at the most tactically advantageous positions around them. He turns in his seat to face the Russian.

"Some cool heads with good information and sound advice are needed here, Vasily. What is it that I should know?"

Vasily sighs with some relief. "Yes, my friend. Well, it seems we may have been negligent in allowing one of our missiles to fall into the hands of those animals in Raqqah. An S-300.

Another organisation may have been playing games, and this is an unintended consequence."

Geoffrey cannot stop himself. "Not again, surely?"

"I am sorry. It would seem so. Apparently, it was supposed to fail but serve to make the Americans warier of entering air space we see as our own. When the Syrians were attacked at Raqqah, we persuaded them to feign defeat and withdraw. The plan is that, with their forces concentrated, the Syrian Army and our Air Force will counter-attack. The final stronghold of this so-called Caliphate will be destroyed once and for all." He pauses and regards Geoffrey, who is staring at the fountain while he absorbs this information. Aware of the scrutiny, Geoffrey turns.

He counters with his own knowledge. "This missile is dangerous and complex, I am surprised those creatures could use it at all."

"Some people were present who, we think, underestimated the terrorists. Some had knowledge of anti-aircraft missiles, and they had some luck."

"Russians complicit in this will not look good, Vasily."

"I know! I know! There will be consequences, I assure you. It seems there is a plan to allow some Daesh leadership and fighters to leak out of Syria. We are not entirely sure whether this is part of a broader game or an attempt to make the destruction of the faction easier."

"My country would see no advantage in allowing Daesh to leave Syria, only to appear elsewhere."

"There may be those in my organisation... and elsewhere... who might see an advantage."

They lapse into silence, digesting the import of this conversation. Presently, Vasily reaches into his pocket and removes a small envelope which he hands to Geoffrey, who looks at it speculatively.

"It is a time and a place. A meeting will be held there."

The Russian gets to his feet and faces his companion, who has also risen. Extending his hand, he says, "I seek to regain control of this uncertain situation. Please be careful how you play this next part of the game, Geoffrey."

"Be sure that I shall, Vasily Andreyovitch."

They exchange a firm handshake.

"I am in your debt."

Geoffrey turns away and heads towards the road, Vasily's last words ringing in his ears like the heavenly choir. The conversation and envelope might be vital intelligence, but an adversary in your debt is pure gold. As he passes a heavy-set man appearing to study a map, he bids him a good day in Russian, relishing the momentary confusion this causes before the fellow rushes off.

After briefing his deputy, he telephones his most senior and trusted friend at the CIA HQ in Langley to arrange a meeting. He alludes to the subject and is entreated to, "Come over right away." Before doing so, he briefs the ambassador, outlining his plans. The ambassador is delighted at this intelligence coup and sends him on his way whilst reaching for his secure line to London's Foreign and Commonwealth Office.

It takes Geoffrey a little under half an hour to drive to Langley. He is no stranger to CIA HQ, but there is usually some delay at the complex of road gates guarding access. This time, an intern appears and whisks him through. At the Headquarters proper, the young man swaps seats, saying, "I'll take care of parking, sir. Mr Campbell is waiting inside."

A bemused Geoffrey is greeted warmly by his friend, who gives him a badge and ushers him past the security control. He is even more surprised to be taken to a plush meeting room where several senior agents are waiting, including the Director of the CIA. He has met him before, usually at social events. Nonetheless, this is unprecedented. The Director puts him at ease as he is handed coffee.

"John realised if you were coming here yourself, it must be important. Given the subject, there is nothing more important right now. I wanted to hear it myself."

Geoffrey relates the information he has. The story is received more or less calmly, but he is apparently delivering the answer to their prayers. He is careful not to say where he got the information or when. Nor does he say from whom, merely referring to his 'source'. In intelligence circles, it is regarded as very impolite to ask the identity of a source. This will not stop them from trying to guess later. Geoffrey does edit the direct Russian involvement and allusion to deliberate action on the part of other agencies. When the CIA does their own analysis, they may deduce this, and he is comfortable with that. He saves the best part until the end. Reaching into his pocket, he pulls out a piece of paper onto which he has written the location, date and time that Vassily gave him.

As the Director looks at the information, Geoffrey says, "We believe this to be the place that a meeting of Daesh commanders and other parties will occur. We think they are probably meeting to plan the escape from Syria of some of their leadership and military force."

There are gasps from around the table as the Director passes the paper across to Campbell. He buries his head in his hands for a moment before raising his head.

"Geoffrey, many years ago I was told that for all the talk of a special relationship, the real one is between the various intelligence agencies in our two countries. Never was that truer than today. I cannot thank you enough, sir. Now, our President is due to address the nation in about four hours. As you can imagine, I have to get busy. Please forgive me if I beat a hasty retreat."

Handshakes and courtesies are exchanged, and John Campbell escorts an intelligence officer struggling with all the power of his upper lip to hide his elation.

On his return to the Embassy, he reports directly to the ambassador. Basking in the approbation following a conversation with the foreign secretary, the excellent news from Langley prompts a celebration. A chilled bottle appears, and the ambassador pours a sparkling wine for them both.

Toasting their success, he remarks, "This is from a vineyard south of Bristol, near where I live. It's called Jubilate, very appropriate, don't you think?"

THE AMERICANS ACT

There has been feverish activity all over Washington, nowhere more than at CIA HQ now that they have a new line of intelligence.

As his analysts cross-check the information and add their own perspective, the Director gives the President an outline of what he has learned. The impact of the news causes her to cancel the planned NSC meeting ahead of her address to the nation. That address describes what happened in Syria with a few details that the press could not glean from their sources. The main thrust of her message is one of retribution. With the nation placed on hold, later that night, she joins her team around the table.

The CIA is invited to speak first, and the Director makes the most of it. His people have worked hard, and the report is good. They have deduced that there is Russian involvement, and this draws angry comments from the group. This is silenced when the Director says that they believe the British source was from the Russian Embassy.

The final item from the CIA is the place and time of the Daesh meeting. The President is delighted. Envy and admiration are among the reaction of the other players.

"So we have a target and a time to strike."

"We will need to confirm the details, that it's the right place and the target is valid."

"Tell me that can be done."

"It's a difficult task, but our friends in Israel have well-placed sources in the area. They have offered to help."

"I see. That will come at a price, I'm sure. Down the road, no doubt, and inconvenient. When we would be less inclined to pay."

"Our problem, Madam President, is that we are short of time. This needs an asset actually on the ground. Our other collectors are less reliable. We need a combination of resources, and even then we might miss the opportunity."

Another voice joins the conversation, the Vice President. "We could surely have twenty-four-hour drone coverage over that place."

The general, who is chairman of the joint chiefs of staff, answers. "That's another problem we've got. We lost the drone that found our airmen to what we suspect is the same weapon that shot those poor fellows down. Since then, another one has gone missing. So far, we've had no luck finding the launcher. At the moment, ladies and gentlemen, we are literally in the dark."

The President broods for a moment on this unsatisfactory news.

"So we take what help we can get, whatever the cost." She turns to the secretary of defence and the general. "How do we do this?"

The answer she gets is not encouraging.

"For the reasons the general outlined, the obvious answer is out. We'd lose the drone and, in any case, it would be detected, and our adversary is likely to escape. With that Gladiator Missile Launcher out there, I don't think we can risk a crewed aircraft."

"Could we not send our SEALs in?" The voice comes from the Director of Homeland Security.

"This isn't an attack on a sleeping compound; there will be heavy weapons and a lot of security. Plenty of non-combatants as well."

Another voice suggests a cruise missile. The answer, this time from the general, is equally discouraging.

"The flight time is too long. Too much can change without the ability to react once we've committed. Also, the warhead is likely to cause a lot of collateral damage."

The conversation becomes increasingly frustrated as various ideas are discussed and discarded. Amongst this noise, the President is quiet and tense. The chairman of the joint chiefs turns and raises a quizzical eyebrow at the chief of the air staff. He is among the officials sitting in the background in case their expertise is needed. He opens his hands, shrugging a "perhaps" at his boss.

The exchange goes unnoticed by everyone except the Vice President, whose voice cuts through the background noise.

"Something to share, General Adams?"

There is a pause, and in the silence, all eyes turn to the military man. He glances at the CIA Director, whose face says he might know where this is going.

"There might be a solution."

"Might?" The President's voice is even.

"The problem is that a crewed solution is hazardous at present. An assault is out of the question, and a medium or even high-altitude drone strike is likely to fail. What we need is a high speed, low-level attack profile that doesn't risk a crew."

"Akicita Maza!" The voice of the President's chief of staff cuts in. "We were briefed before the President took office. There was no hint that the programme would be anything more than an experiment for a long time."

Adams continues as the audience becomes baffled and agitated by the references.

"Let me hand over to Air Force General Hughes." He turns and gestures at the blue-uniformed figure sitting against the wall behind him. "Marcus, please."

Marcus Hughes, the chief of staff of the Air Force, leans forward.

"Akicita Maza is Native American for Iron Warrior. It's the code name for a programme that looks at introducing artificial intelligence into a warfighting system. It was plodding along with lots of great ideas but little progress when two things happened.

"A brilliant aerospace exec was appointed to head up the Advanced Development Programme at the Lockheed Martin Skunk Works, and the British made a breakthrough at one of their research labs."

The President interrupts. "Don't tell me that as well as giving us the intelligence, the Brits have got a ready-made killer robot."

Marcus winces. "We try to avoid that phrase, ma'am. And no, we have a Lethal Autonomous Weapon System. Or we think we might have. Leanne Phillips, the exec I mentioned, managed to get the Brit's programmer. He was flown over here, and Ms Phillips put him on her team. Lockheed have been competing to supply a new troop lift helicopter to the Army and they used one of the prototype aircraft in their experiments. It's now a fully autonomous drone gunship."

There is complete silence around the table as the general draws breath.

The President looks hard at him. "You said, 'might have'. Why?"

"The programme is a joint Lockheed/DARPA project. It's been hugely accelerated by this Brit, but it's still a prototype. Still being tested. I saw it at the Whitesands Range, attacking targets with live weapons. It was very impressive. It's now in Louisiana, working in one of our training environments against a real opposing force. The team expects months of testing."

The President looks down at the piece of paper with its latitude and longitude, and date.

"We don't have months, General, we have days." She looks at the two military men and her secretary for defence. "Could this be our best hope for a decisive response?"

All eyes turn to look at Hughes. He shifts uncomfortably before replying.

"We have four officers who have been helping with tactical scenarios. It's been at Fort Polk for a few days now."

"Is that a yes or a no?"

"I'll have to ask…"

"No, General Hughes, you have to see. Go down there, find out, and tell me." The President is the image of grim determination as she looks around at her team. "We will reconvene tomorrow at two o'clock. General Adams, General Hughes, why are you still here? It may only be a couple of hours to Louisiana, but you have a lot to do. If that machine is the answer to my prayers, and I sincerely hope it is, it needs to be on its way to Iraq. You know the deadline. Make it happen."

The Director of the CIA is the next target of her scrutiny.

"Find out all we need to know to strike this target and show these people what America does to murdering terrorists. Demand everything you need. Call in favours. I don't care, just do it."

Her final target is her chief of staff. Glancing at the clock, it's a little after midnight. She tells him to get the head of Lockheed Martin on the phone before rising from her chair and heading for the Oval Office.

PEOPLE WAKE AND WHEELS TURN

It is not the Chairman and CEO of Lockheed Martin's policy to be available twenty-four hours a day, so even though the resources of the chief of staff can find a number, it doesn't get answered. The insistent ringing of the technologically sophisticated doorbell accompanied by old fashioned pounding on the timbers does rouse him. He is startled to find a police officer on his doorstep, who informs him that the White House wants to speak with him. The officer hands him a number and wishes him a good morning before disappearing into the night. The astounded Chairman rings the number he's been given and identifies himself. A voice on the other end thanks him for his response, and after these pleasantries, the President wishes him the second good morning of the day.

On an open line, the President is discrete. "You have an experiment running that interests me, Mr Meyer. The one Ms Phillips has had such unexpected success with. You are aware of this project?"

"I am, Madam President. What can we at Lockheed do for you?"

It really is the only answer available when you get an unexpected call in the middle of the night from the most powerful woman in the world. Fortunately, his protégé has kept him well informed.

"The Air Force chief of staff is flying down to visit that project. I would greatly value your cooperation and assistance."

"Leanne will meet the general at the airstrip, ma'am. You can rest assured that anything you or the general wants will be placed at your disposal."

"The answer of a patriot, Lewis. I am greatly obliged to you. I hope my chief of staff can arrange for you to come visit with me. Some details and a more detailed conversation may be required."

"I am at your disposal, Madam President."

"One other thing. I'm told that there is foreign involvement in the project."

"You are referring to our lucky charm."

"I don't mind what you call him. He needs to be gone. This must strictly be US eyes only. Do what you must, send him on holiday."

She rings off, and Lewis sits for a moment considering the import of this conversation. Only for a moment, though, as he has to get Leanne to the Fort Polk Airfield before General Hughes.

Leanne is less particular about being disturbed in the middle of the night than the Chairman. Though groggy with sleep, she registers the name on her phone's display.

"Lewis, is there a problem?"

"Far from it, Leanne, a huge opportunity is more like it. I've just got off the phone with the President."

"What did he want?"

"Not our President. The President!"

Lewis appointed Leanne for her quality. He is not disappointed.

"Ah, Akacita Maza."

"Exactly."

They digest the implications, both minds matching current events to future opportunities. Lewis breaks the brief silence.

"Air Force Chief of Staff Marcus Hughes is flying down to see our progress. You need to beat him there and be waiting for him when he arrives. Anything they need, we give it to them. You have complete freedom of action."

"Yes, sir."

"There's one more thing, Leanne. The President stressed that this is a US eyes only affair. You need to make sure that Dr Moore remains unaware of what is happening. Is that a problem?"

"I can handle it. I've a two-hour flight to figure it all out."

"Go to it, Leanne, a lot is riding on this. Update me over our secure link when you can."

As the phone call terminates, Leanne sits back, grappling with what she needs to do. The recumbent form of her partner has not stirred during the call. She quietly exits the bedroom and initiates coffee and a call to the Skunk Works.

Her position, location and the presence of a liveried jet aircraft parked a mere few hundred metres from her office confers many advantages. Even a four star air force general doesn't get that. Beating Marcus Hughes to Louisiana proves to be relatively straightforward. Rightly assuming that the Military members of the Defiant team have been woken, she calls the senior man and establishes the arrival time of their boss.

Her jet touches down at the Fort Polk airfield comfortably ahead of the Air Force transport.

This gives her time to deal with her other pressing problem: how to remove Craig from the equation. She calls Russ Morales and has a bit of luck. Russ tells her that Craig is frustrated at Polk and not enjoying the heat or lack of new work. The aircraft has been so successful Craig doesn't feel he has more to add at this stage. Leanne decides to take a risk and calls Helen Sherwood. She explains Craig's state of mind and adds the Pentagon's wish to do some US eyes only testing. Helen is only too happy to get Craig back to the UK, so she readily accedes to Leanne's hasty plan to persuade Craig to take some time away from the project. By the time that General Hughes lands, Russ has confirmed that Craig is happy to take a break. Russ has been creative and suggested that Craig fly back to the UK via Washington. The chance to visit the city and particularly the Smithsonian Institute further encourages Craig.

Leanne assuages her pangs of conscience by getting her pilot to file a flight plan to Ronald Reagan Airport. A call to her PA arranges a meet and greet for when he lands, and a smart hotel.

Hughes tells Leanne what happened at the White House on the drive to the test site. What he says confirms her suspicions and reinforces the need to keep things confidential.

She still feels a little guilty when Craig anxiously asks if it is OK for him to take time out. Marcus Hughes turns on the charm and adds his reassurance, telling him that it will give them some time to do US business.

Success at the Whitesands Range and the good results they've had so far in what the team is calling 'The Polk Series' has wrought a few changes since Leanne was last with the team. The group is more integrated, the military officers and the civilian engineers no longer two separate entities.

The head of the military team describes what they've done against the opposing force. Marcus listens intently as they describe a series of successes. Two tests are scheduled for the day ahead and, in what is almost prescient, one of them is an autonomous strike on a headquarters complex.

The aircraft has been standing silently as a backdrop to the VIP presentation. Marcus turns his attention to it and frowns at some changes. The nose of helicopter has a pattern of tiles on it that twinkle in the early morning sunlight. He moves closer to the machine and sees that the tiles form two ellipses, each tile having a lens at its centre. He turns back to the group who are watching him with amusement.

"The eyes! It looks like an insect!"

There are chuckles and the audience looks at Craig.

"A shrewd observation, sir, that's more or less what they are."

Leanne interjects. "Do explain, Craig, this is new to me as well."

Craig cocks his head at the military people. "It's just like back home. The soldiers keep saying they don't want active sensors like radar which can be detected. I've been studying some work on how insects fly, so I designed a way for Mike to do it. Insect eyes have a wide field of view, and they use what's called optic flow to avoid hitting obstacles. There's been quite a lot of work done on miniature drones using the same technique. I just upscaled it—"

"And made it better and solved all the other glitches."

The interruption from Russ Morales raises a laugh from the Alpha Mike Team, as they've started calling themselves. Craig grins self-deprecatingly at them before turning back.

"It allows insects to fly fast around obstacles. Because the Alpha Mike doesn't have a crew, it can manoeuvre more violently than a normal aircraft. It's really good at dodging obstacles and flying really close to the ground, it's only limited by size and stress tolerance."

The Air Force Colonel adds a significant remark. "It had its first run out at Whitesands, sir. Down here it doesn't happen, but up there it whips up dust, leaving a trail. The machine has 360 vision, so Doc Moore added an instruction and it adjusts its height now so there are no tell-tales."

Craig carries on. "There's also a Lidar array underneath. We left that on so that Alpha Mike has a cross check and an additional source of information. With more testing, it may be possible to remove it."

The general congratulates them on their achievement and observes that it was an early start for the two senior visitors. He suggests that some breakfast would be welcome and that they should not be late for the enemy. The military team are way ahead of the game concerning refreshments, which arrive almost on cue. As Alpha Mike does most of its own pre-flight checks, it isn't long before they are ready to conduct the first of two attacks.

This is the general's second visit to the project following the first, more cursory trip to see the Whitesands firings. This time he pays much more attention to the processes that lead to the launch. In particular, the sequence of orders, target priorities and rules of engagement that Russ runs through. Craig notes the attention and observes that Russ knows more than enough to 'fly solo'.

Privately, Marcus is delighted to hear this out loud. He says, "You're happy to leave your kid with us then, Dr Moore?"

Craig laughs in reply before commenting, "The UK want me to look at crewless artillery and some problems with autonomous logistics." He pauses a moment and looks at Leanne. "They must be well aware that we are working on an aerial machine. I would bet that's really why Helen Sherwood is getting me back."

Leanne smiles and agrees, adding that her hope is that his absence won't be a long one and that there is always room at the Skunk Works for him.

Turning back to Russ, who he has grown to like, he asks, "You OK? There's not much that needs me at this stage."

Russ replies that he is, and there is a chorus of banter from the rest about holidaying and not being up to the Louisiana weather. Amidst friendly farewells, Leanne walks him to her car and clasps his hand before he drives away. Russ notes the shrewd gaze of General Hughes watching the pair.

With a sour look at the general, she says, "Well. That's done. I think you had better explain why you're really here."

The general looks at this core team gathered around him and says, "Michael is going to war."

This dramatic announcement has its predictable effect. The group are astounded. Less for the military contingent, of course, they had already guessed. Leanne smoothly intervenes by telling them that she and the general will be looking for volunteers for the specialist engineering tasks.

Turning to Russ, she says, "You will be essential, of course. Can I count on you?"

"Are you kidding? I wouldn't miss this. Besides, I've done reserve time. It's not going to be new."

Other voices rise in assent, men and women keen to be part of the payback for what they've seen on the news.

Marcus takes back control, saying, "We've only got a matter of days, so no one will be going home, and no hint of what we are doing must get out. This next mission we're going to fly is similar to what we'll be doing in Syria. Let's get it done so I can call the President."

The task is the simulated destruction of a bunker defended by the local opposing force and includes an air defence missile.

The Defiant lifts off, and they watch as the aircraft flies at ultra-low level until in range before abruptly gaining altitude and loosing its missiles. One to destroy the air defence launcher and the other for the bunker. The enemy fire back, but the CT-40 cannons outrange them. The flashing lights indicating successful laser hits are plain to see in the display.

Marcus turns to Russ and Leanne. "I'm convinced. Do we agree that Alpha Mike can do this?"

Russ answers with a firm, "Yes."

Leanne is more cautious. "We're still learning a lot. This is a prototype. A long way from being a complete solution that we would be happy to field. Normally I'd want months of tests and evaluation before judging this to be a safe and serviceable system. I'm guessing the target can't be taken by anything else, or you wouldn't be here."

"We've lost two drones, and we won't risk crewed aircraft, not until we've nailed the S-300 that shot down our Hornet. This is our best shot."

Leanne thinks a while before looking back at him.

"The Chairman said to give you whatever you need. The Defiant Alpha Mike is yours. Be careful with it, though. We'd like it back." Leanne turns back to her team. "Colonel Doyle is in command. Get our bird ready to travel. I need to speak to head office."

"And I need to brief the President."

That conversation on a secure phone in the project office is short and to the point.

"Can it, in your opinion, accomplish the mission?"

"Yes, ma'am, I believe it can."

"Do you have everything you need?"

"I prepared for success. My staff have put everything in place. Centcom will need to be involved. They command the brigade in Iraq."

"I'll speak to General Cornforth myself. My chief of staff will call you when I'm through. Intelligence has confirmed the time and place of the terrorist meeting. You have a little over seventy-two hours."

ALPHA MIKE GOES TO WAR

The Brigade Senior Intelligence Officer calls Brigadier General Miles O'Brien into the US National Intelligence Centre in Qayyarah West. The secure conversation that ensues shocks and galvanises him. The general officer commanding US Central Command personally gives him his orders. He is to be prepared to receive a C-5 Super Galaxy containing a top secret experimental drone. It is to be transferred to his most remote hangar, and the accompanying strike force personnel are to be accommodated with it. They are not to mix with or even be seen by anyone not explicitly authorised by him. He is to arrange a deception that will allow the drone to take off as discretely as can be managed. A special forces team will accompany the strike force, ostensibly to conduct an operation into Syria. Their real task is to guard and mask the actual operation. The general finally tells him that the planned strike is scheduled for the early hours of the morning in two days. It will attack a meeting of Daesh leaders in a village to the east of Raqqah.

The general trusts his man on the ground, so he gives him twenty-four hours to develop a detailed plan and brief him. Miles sits back and considers what he has heard for some minutes. Coming to a decision, he rises and, exiting the intelligence cell, he calls for his planning team. After briefing them, he speaks to his chief air operations to get a hangar cleared and prepared for visitors. His Senior Logistics

Officer is told to arrange life support for the incoming personnel. Both officers are given stern warnings as to the secrecy of the mission.

That evening, the enormous transport aircraft arrives. The chief air ops is in the tower when it does. An unusual sight for the air traffic controllers. The C-5 taxis towards the end of the runway, and a vehicle joins it to act as a guide. It halts in front of a distant hangar. A detachment of troops scuttle towards the building and disappear inside. Presently the hangar doors open, and as this happens, the nose of the Galaxy tilts upwards. As they watch through the gloom of approaching night, mysterious shrouded shapes are towed inside.

The Senior Airman nods in satisfaction and moves to leave. The men and women in the tower watch him go. As he departs, his parting words are peremptory.

"No questions. No gossip."

In the hangar, there is frantic activity. The shrouding that disguised the nature of their cargo is pulled away. The team has brought their own equipment to reassemble the Alpha Mike's rotor blades. Its engineers treat this as a priority. Russ and his people put together the IT suite and run cables for data and power into the machine.

As this is occurring, a member of the security detachment warns Colonel Doyle of the approach of a vehicle. He accompanies the soldier outside to find Brigadier General O'Brien and a young major waiting by their vehicle.

Peter salutes before extending a hand. "Welcome, General. Peter Doyle. I'm glad you're here."

"Glad to meet you, Colonel Doyle, Elizabeth here is my chief J35.* I'm glad to see you as well. We've been trying to think of ways

---

* Staff branches in a headquarters have letters and numbers. In this case the J stands for joint. Single service headquarters have different letters. The Operations branch is numbered 3, 5 or 3/5. Three is ops happening now. The others are future ops and are planning cells. 3/5 are ops happening in a few days or weeks. Five is future ops and looks at more strategic plans.

to punish the people who killed our guys. Centcom tells me you can do it."

"C'mon in, sir, we'll show you how we think it can be done, and you can tell us how you might help."

The engineers are removing their kit from around the helicopter as the three officers approach. Their hangar is smaller than those they have used back in the States, and AM dominates the space.

The two newcomers stop short, and the young major gasps. "What is that?!"

O'Brien laughs and turns to Peter. "I would like to know that myself."

Peter looks over at a grinning Russ who takes the question.

"This is the Defiant Alpha Mike, sir. It's a prototype from the future long-range assault aircraft project that we've had at the Skunk Works. He's asleep at the moment. I'm just going to wake him up and tell him where he is. He might be a bit cranky at first, but he'll soon settle down."

Russ can hardly control his mirth at the looks on the faces of the Brigadier and his staffer. Peter stifles his own laugh and wags an admonitory finger at Russ. He looks down and strokes the controls on his screen. The aircraft does indeed appear to wake up. Soft electronic noises emanate from it, and the navigation lights blink. The nose pod rotates, stopping disconcertingly to look at the strangers. The irises in the array of lenses on the nose open and close, creating a silvery ripple that looks like a blink. Elizabeth crosses to the console and looks at Russ's screen. She turns back to her boss.

"This is no drone, sir. It's an artificial intelligence."

Russ sucks through his teeth and winces.

Peter says, "The genius who invented it would be all over you. He says there's no such thing."

Russ takes up the narrative. "It's a highly automated weapons system capable of multiple rehearsed behaviours. It is capable of learning by experience and altering future behaviours as a result."

The Brigadier turns his attention back to Peter. "So, what is your plan, Colonel Doyle?"

"We lift tomorrow night, actually, early the following morning. Tomorrow will be spent loading maps and intelligence libraries. Our intelligence liaison from Langley will feed us more information on the target. We can rehearse the whole mission. All without leaving the hangar." Colonel Doyle pauses. "Of course, no plan survives contact with the enemy. That's where autonomy comes in. All the Rules of Engagement are in there as well as all the targeting protocols. The only thing we changed markedly is the collateral damage. The President herself has raised the acceptable threshold."

The comment concerning CIA liaison caused a woman in the corner of the hangar to look up from her screen, ear to a satellite phone receiver. She finishes the call and walks across to the group. She nods to the general and addresses Colonel Doyle.

"Sir, our friends have confirmed that their asset is in place. They have also confirmed that the meeting will take place as indicated. Confidence is now as high as we can get. The asset will mark the building."

"How?"

"An uncoded infra-red laser marker. There is, unfortunately, only one place where it can be put that will return a strong enough signal to give a high chance of detection by Alpha Mike, and reduce the risk of the asset's own and the device's compromise. Langley have given me the desired attack heading. The asset has also managed to photograph the building from that direction, so we have some decent imagery now. There's something else." She pauses. "Our other friends, our very good friends, who made this possible, have told us that there will be two Russians at the meeting." She turns and walks back to her desk after nodding a "Sir" and "Ma'am" to the two visitors.

Peter returns his attention to the visitors. "We're paranoid about the security, as you've probably noticed. CENTCOM had a suspicion that there was information being fed to the group and that it might not be entirely luck that put the S-300 in Daesh hands. We've only been able to get routine satellite feed of the area because we don't want to disturb the track timings and get it noticed. You know about the loss of drones, of course."

Elizabeth nods thoughtfully, her planner's mind moving into overdrive. "My team have looked at what we might be able to do. Looking at your timings, if our CSAR flight took off with your bird, that would be a distraction. We also thought a temporary resupply base north of our surveillance line could be useful. It would allow a refuel or recovery if necessary."

"Alpha Mike can probably do it in one, but it would be a good contingency. We are prepared to lose him, but would rather not, so it would be good to have rescue options. Our SOF team would go with a couple of engineers."

"The Brits have a screen along the border, but we'll pull them in for some rest and replenishment tomorrow. A Special Ops out-of-bounds area for the activity won't look out of place, either." She looks at the Defiant Alpha Mike, sitting quietly now. "What are those guns?"

"Forty millimetre cannons, HE, HE Airburst and Anti-Aircraft."

"Hellfire missiles?"

"Yeah, but we're using the MAC warhead."

"Ouch!"

"I know. It's a slight worry. They've upped the collateral, but we still need it to be proportional. Now we've got some better imagery we can reassess. Looking at the building that we think is the target, it's likely the walls can contain the over-pressure."

As they talk, the Colonel has guided them to a table on which there are several air photographs. He selects one that shows a substantial building with a courtyard. It's in the middle of a small town, at a crossroads. Smaller, poorer compounds abut two sides. Elizabeth studies it.

"If that's the one, I'd say the roof will lift off, and then drop back in."

The CIA operative joins them, holding a tablet on which there are a series of photographs taken from the ground. She hands the screen to Elizabeth.

"Two story. Likely domestic upper story. Meeting downstairs." She flicks through the series, stopping at an annotated image that shows the aspect that will be marked by the laser. Looking back at the overhead view she says, "There! Delay fuse through that window. It'll pop the walls and the upper story will collapse."

"The laser is just a simple marker?"

The Intelligence Officer nods.

"The aircraft will need to self-designate and get in closer than you might like. What's the range of those guns?"

"Two and a half klicks."

"I'll bet it can fire both of them simultaneously, more accurately and at more targets than a human. Two klicks out gives the missile a five second time of flight. Add a few seconds for acquisition and the motor to spool up. That's less than ten seconds exposure." Her abstract gaze refocuses, and she fixes her attention on Russ. "So, you relay commands from here and the device gets on with it?"

"Our brilliant lethal autonomous weapon doesn't need inflight instructions. That's the point. Those eyes on the nose means it flies like an insect, no radar, lidar or anything active. It'll be completely electronically silent. It can fly at two hundred knots six feet above the ground. It's been given the objective and knows the rules. Tactics are programmed in."

Colonel Doyle breaks in. "You've just heard our concerns about the enemy being given warnings, you already know the level of air defence threat. There's also likely to be jamming. This thing can fly at high speed below the radar horizon."

Russ continues, "As soon as we unmask, communication links will open so we'll get camera feeds from the satellite link. We can also then give commands if we need to."

The general looks around at them all. "We were described as the tip of the spear after this incident. That job now goes to you all. Get some rest, my people are on their way with food and drink. Tomorrow will be a busy day."

He and Peter walk to the door. Outside, Peter salutes him farewell.

He returns the salute with a final remark.

"When this kicks off tomorrow, I expect I'll be answering a lot of questions from home. I'll be in my headquarters, but I'd like Elizabeth down here as the link."

Food and drink do indeed turn up. It's brought in by the ever-watchful SOF guys. The group are exhausted after the long flight, so sleep comes more easily than they expect.

THE ATTACK

The Alpha Mike Hangar is a bustle of activity the following day. The mapping and imagery loaded into the databases is checked. Libraries are updated and checked. Targeting scripts are checked and tested. The flight plan is flown in simulation mode.

Elizabeth returns in the afternoon, bringing the commander of the CSAR detachment with her. He needs to know how the Defiant will integrate into his squadron when they depart the following morning. The engineers are arming Alpha Mike when they turn up and he finds it hard to keep his eyes off the machine. The solution they come up with is to fix an infra-red strobe to one of his CH-53s and tell their aircraft to keep station until it reaches the approach to the forward base that the CSAR team will occupy during the mission.

On the border, the Queen's Royal Lancers battle group has been instructed to withdraw to troop hides for rearming and replenishment. They don't need to do this, so Robin Matheson is curious to know why, but then the coordinates of a Special Forces out of bounds box arrive. He guesses that this no-go area and the mini holiday his screen has been given is to stop them being nosy. It's a regular event on operations where SF are involved, particularly American ones. No one really minds, a relatively relaxed get-together for the troops is a welcome distraction.

Since the shooting down, frontier life has returned to its usual stultifying routine. Maz and Bill's troop is at the northernmost end of the line. The others got used to the presence of the two enhanced Ajax. The infallibility of the two vehicles is the envy of the rest of the squadron who, until it became boring, would try and sneak up on A Troop's position. The soldiers now leave Loki and Freya on guard while they socialise and sleep. Only one person is left, keeping a desultory eye on the remote controller terminals attached to the two sentries. The cavalry troop never leaguer up in the same place. Tonight's is a good spot, with a fold in the ground where they can use the brazier that Bill has made. Fresh rations coming up the line mean that they can have a discrete barbecue. Conversation and banter mean a later than usual night, but most of the troop is up well before dawn anyway. Night vision devices may have made dawn attacks obsolete, but being alert an hour or so before dawn is a difficult habit to break.

The sound of helicopters to the northeast of their position silences what little conversation there is. Giles Fox, the Troop Leader, is with Bill and Maz, who are looking at their respective terminals to see if anything was missed by the sentry.

"That must be that ops box. I wonder what it is?"

One of the terminals displays a message: *Two AH-64, two CH-53E, One Unident Rotorcraft.*

Giles shudders theatrically. "It still creeps me out when they do that."

"What, answer questions?" Bill laughs. "We didn't know they could at first, but the shot detection microphones are really sensitive. We can hear conversations in our headphones out to about twenty metres, thirty sometimes."

Maz continues, "It's the speech recognition software. We started trying basic commands. They both recognise everyone in the troop now. If a question makes sense, they often give an unprompted answer. Odd that it doesn't know what the other aircraft is. Loki, identify low-level aircraft north of our position still moving east to west."

The answer is near instant. *Ident not possible. No library matches.*

"How fast is it going?"

Estimate 350kph.

Bill looks at her. "Helos can't go that fast, must be a mistake."

"If so, it's the first." She turns to Giles. "Might be worth a report upwards, sir. We'll probably be told to mind our own business."

Giles mutters an affirmative and walks back to his own vehicle. Maz and Bill look at their charges, both troubled by the unanswered question.

The Alpha Mike, free of the constraints of following the slower helicopters, increases its speed as the border approaches. Dropping to bare metres above the ground, it monitors the rear view and adjusts its height until barely any dust is whipped up. If it bothered to look at an altimeter, a reading of twenty-six feet would result.

The route taken exploits wadi bottoms and low ground, bringing the aircraft round in a gentle curve to approach the target from the north.

In the town, a man indistinguishable in any detail from the general population around him exits a nondescript building opposite the target and heads to the crossroads, before joining the flow of people heading to the mosque. On a shelf disguised with crockery, a modest green box emits a steady stream of infra-red energy towards the top of a wall on the opposite side of the road.

At the crossroads two pickup truck 'technicals' mounting heavy machine guns stand guard. In the compound another, with a twin barrelled anti-aircraft gun on the back, is refuelling. Several watchful and heavily armed insurgents on the roof watch the surrounding area. More Daesh gunmen are in the street. Inside the meeting house, the Daesh leaders are at Fajr, the first prayers of the day. Standing discreetly away from this are the two Russians, their faces carefully neutral. The colonel and major who handed the S-300 to the terrorist have been sent back to observe and report on the meeting. They swim in a sea of hostility, but the terrorist leaders know that the opportunity they have been given comes from the masters of these men. The two were nonplussed at the orders that came directly from Moscow. The job seems pointless, as they know that to the West, Syrian Armoured Forces backed by their own Air Force are already on the move, determined to extinguish this last stronghold. Their only thought is the Mi-24 Hind in the desert to the west, waiting to ferry them back to safety.

In the cellar below the meeting room, chained to a pipe, is the unfortunate commander who allowed the pilot to be beheaded. Filthy, bruised and battered. One eye closed and teeth broken, his fate is to be executed in the street after the meeting.

Above, prayers have ended, and the leaders gather to discuss who and how many they can get away in accordance with the GU plan.

Alpha Mike is streaking in from the north and begins decelerating to an attack speed. It is approximately ten kilometres from the target. Rising as its flight aspect changes slightly, it is seen by the Hind crew to the west. The black aircraft is completely unfamiliar to them, but its intent is plain. Professionals that they are, they immediately start their engines and prepare for a fight.

Mike has seen the Hind but ignores it. As it closes to within two kilometres of the target, it flares and uses the energy created to leap into the air. Reaching apogee at two hundred feet, its sensors immediately see the laser spot and it matches the window that is its target with the photograph in the target information pack. The launch of the first Hellfire is near simultaneous, it acquires the sparkle of coded laser energy from the helicopter's designator and makes the journey in three seconds.

The insurgents in the town are alert. They are experienced, doughty fighters, so the apparition rising into the morning sunlight is immediately perceived as a threat and guns are cocked, weapons trained in the direction of the threat. In the courtyard of the meeting house, the crew of the heavy weapon throw aside a petrol drum and spring to get their weapon into action. It is too late, of course. The Hellfire travelling at Mach 1.3 flies a perfect trajectory to the target, entering the window at its centre. Hitting the opposite wall, the delay fuse pauses detonation until the warhead enters the meeting space. The metal particles that give this missile its name do their work to deadly effect, multiplying the heat and blast. The walls of the building bulge and crumble. Seeking egress, the enormous pressure throws the upper storey into the air. The ground floor collapses into the cellar and then the first-floor rubble drops in to fill the space. Secondary explosions from the munitions in the cellar throw rubble and debris back into the air to rain down on the surrounding area. The fuel tank in the courtyard ruptures and the fuel ignites. The technical with the heavy gun is thrown onto its side and the fireball finishes the destruction of vehicle and crew. Balls of fire rise above the surrounding buildings, petrol drums picked up by the violent deflagration of the fuel split, and ignite. Where they land, fires spring up, adding to the confusion. The panicked crowd who ran from the mosque towards the target building turn and seek to flee in the opposite direction, further adding to the chaos in the street. A propane cylinder from the courtyard, its valve knocked off by a collision, flies out of the conflagration, trailing a stream of fire. It ricochets off the road in front of the mosque and, like a ghastly parody of the previous missile, flies through the gate scattering an escaping group of worshippers. It streaks through the open doors, bouncing and spinning like an insane firework. It ignites furnishings and sets the building ablaze.

In the street, Daesh soldiery remain under control. They have a focus for their ire. The many small arms that now open fire are ineffective at this range. Not so the heavy machine guns which now begin to engage the dark shape in the sky. Rocket-propelled grenades add to the mix.

At the delivery end of this chaos, the Defiant Alpha Mike, according to its orders, has to escape. The trouble with military operations is that the enemy gets a vote. As Alpha Mike rises to fire, he feels the gentle touch of radars on his composite skin. As that touch from a surveillance radar becomes more insistent, it is joined by a targeting signal. Alerted by the first radar, the S-300 is now after him. An ultra-low level flight to the east would solve all his problems, but having dealt with the primary target, there is now a second imperative.

The S-300 missile system, in particular the TELAR, or Transporter Erector Launcher vehicle, is a target of priority. Added to which, the disciplined response from the Daesh fighters has created a further complication. Girding up his synthetic loins, Mike deals with the situation. Swinging obliquely and beginning to take evasive action, he brings the port gun to bear and opens fire. The trajectories of the RPGs are analysed and ignored. The programming changes from formal targeting procedures to self-defence. Still bound by the rules to minimise non-combatant harm, Mike does not use the more effective HE airburst rounds. He does face a problem in that there is only one targeting pod and the Hind has now become the principal threat. Firing a long burst of HE, he abruptly shifts attention to the approaching gunship. The intelligent machine uses the flight cameras to track the bullet tracers and adjust the port gun onto target. Forty-millimetre rounds tear both technicals in the street to pieces. Simultaneously, Mike has brought the starboard gun to bear on the approaching Hind, cycling the magazine to anti-aircraft ammunition. The equipment libraries place every performance detail, strength and weakness of the opposing helicopter at Mike's disposal. The launch of two anti-aircraft missiles from the outer weapon rails is expected and the starboard gun intercepts both missiles well before they can do any harm. The Hind is very heavily armoured, and the drone knows that the tungsten slugs in the selected ammo will do little harm to the gunship. Nevertheless, the hammering impacts of the fragments on its nose and canopy are a serious distraction and one of the engine intakes is hit, giving the pilot an emergency to deal with. The gunner attempts to bring the chin gun into play but cannot react fast enough. Mike looses one of the three remaining missiles at the Hind, which is now well within range. The Hellfire is not designed to be an air-to-air missile, nor is the warhead optimised for the role, but it is well up to the job. Mike dives towards the ground to break the radar lock from the S-300 targeting radar, leaving behind a stream of countermeasures. At the same time, his missile is guided unerringly to its target. The Hind disappears in a ball of orange-white fire, from which wreckage falls to the ground.

A kilometre or so to the west, two pairs of eyes observe the aerial combat with careful attention. They will mourn their comrades later, now is the time to mark details and record images. Some distance off, approaching them at speed is a battered saloon car appropriated by the two Spetsnaz escorts to the now dead officers. Training and luck aided their escape, the news they bring to their colleagues is dire, and all four now have the problem that their ride is a smoking wreck in the desert.

As the Alpha Mike dived earthwards, it scanned the area for clues as to the whereabouts of the missile system now looking for it. With only a general area to search, it chances another climb based on the detection of electronic signals. The TELAR has raised its missile silo and the tubes are now plainly visible some seven kilometres away. Mike banks towards it and selects a Hellfire. With the targeting radar now locked on, it becomes a race. The drone gets its weapon away first, but the S-300 launch sequence has started and the missile leaps from the tube, belching flame and smoke. Altering course abruptly, its on-board radar locks on to the helicopter, only just evading the devastating explosion of the launch vehicle. The Hellfire does its job, with the added bonus that the command vehicle has parked closer to the launcher than a better trained crew would contemplate. Blast and fragments immobilise it; the dazed crew jump out and stagger away.

Mike continues to rise and flies backwards so that both guns can be brought to bear. Chaff and flares spew from the dispensers. The guns emit a torrent of tungsten shot, into which the missile flies. The dense fragments flense the missile, which breaks up in a spectacular display of burning fuel and debris.

The Alpha Mike's problems are not over, and as it plunges earthward again, the on-board systems are cataloguing damage. The two improvised fighting vehicles in the burning town might be destroyed, but they got some retribution in. The two Dushka machine guns on their backs had brought accurate fire to bear on the Defiant and, despite the spread of shot and the agility of the target, the helicopter is damaged.[*] Violent manoeuvring during the two subsequent engagements hasn't helped. The composite skin has been holed and cracks are evident. It is also a prototype fielded too early to benefit from armour and properly hardened systems. The fuel tanks are holed and, although self-sealing, an alarming amount of fuel has leaked out, forming a grey contrail behind the craft as it heads east. More of a concern is a hydraulic leak that the damage warning system is telling Mike will impact handling and manoeuvrability increasingly over time. The programme makes a series of calculations that it tests against its current imperative, written in by Craig Moore when it was still called Heimdall. Defend, and survive. A landing site is selected, it is well short of the border.

---

[*] Dushka is the nickname of the Soviet era DShK 12.7mm Heavy Machine Gun. It's in widespread use today, a tribute to its reliability and effectiveness. The nickname comes from the Russian word for 'dear or beloved person'. The D and the Sh from the proper nomenclature originate from the brilliant designers Vasily Degtyaryov and Georgi Shpagin.

In Washington, the NSC has been in session since the start of the mission. Prominent at this meeting is the President's press advisor. Her staff team are well aware that there will be a briefing and questions. She has already indicated that another address to the nation is likely, so her senior speech writer is also there. The screen in the room is linked to CIA HQ at Langley and a live satellite link from that headquarters is displayed. This is a rare and expensive occurrence. The Agency did not want to arouse suspicions by adjusting the track or timings of a satellite pass. Fortunately, the routine schedule allowed coverage by a minor adjustment at a stage late in the mission profile. The risk was therefore deemed worthwhile.

The spacecraft clears the horizon after the helicopters reach the desert hideout, which is pointed out by the image analyst that the Director has brought along to interpret, explain and relay commands back to the controllers. They see the Defiant Alpha Mike as it begins its southward turn towards the town. The analyst almost immediately picks out the Hind to the west and, because the image is infra-red, points out the heat signature as the engines start. The tension ratchets up at a comment from a military observer.

"That was not expected."

The attack is watched in silence, except for the odd intake of breath or exclamation. The fight with the gunship and the destruction of the missile and launcher draw admiring comments, especially from the military. The satellite drops over the southwestern horizon shortly after the incident is over. The analyst is asked to bring up some stills, which he does. He shows the destroyed building before it is obscured by the fuel fire, laconically observing, "No one will be walking away from that." He also cautions that the thermal blooms of fires and explosions in the images are larger than the actual events. That draws questions on collateral damage; his reply is that it's impossible to judge from this material. He speculates that some is likely because something must have caused the mosque to catch fire. The President is brisk and thanks him before turning to the chairman of the joint chiefs.

"When can we expect a report from Iraq, General?"

"We'll be on it right away, Madam President, certainly before daybreak."

A curt nod. She then sees him pause, looking thoughtful. "Yes, General Adams?"

He looks up, sweeping his gaze across them. "You've just witnessed history being made here. Not the punishment meted out to our enemies, laudable though that is. No, a completely independent machine entity just executed a complex and hazardous military mission. On its own, with no help. We, and some of our allies, have declared that we won't take the human out of the kill chain. The politicians in here might care to think about how we square that circle. I suspect..." He turns and looks at General Hughes. "We military folks may have less of an issue." Looking back at the President, the smile on his face fades. "It also occurs to me, in the twilight of my service, that there are some moral and legal decisions to be made. War handed us the ethical issues surrounding nuclear weapons, and we've been playing catch up ever since. I think it might be worth trying to get ahead of the game for a change."

The President eyes him soberly and nods. "Wise words as always, sir. Thank you."

The council leaves in thoughtful mood.

THE PRESCIENCE OF GENERALS

Back at the leaguer, Bill is shaving. He is old school and favours a wet shave. RSM Hughes doesn't allow beards or, for that matter, stubble, even though they're on operations. Most of the crews favour 'battery buzzers'– electric shavers.

Maz broods quietly, sitting on the ridge looking west. Behind her, Loki is hull down. The morning is quiet as the sun comes up behind them. The sound of the auxiliary power unit can just be heard, along with occasional quiet whirrs from the surveillance pod as the vehicle maintains its tireless watch over the troop. Maz is troubled, a nagging disquiet that she can't quite put her finger on.

The western horizon is still in shadow, so the faint flicker of light is noticeable. She rises to her feet. Twenty seconds later the rumble of detonations reaches the ridge. Bill joins her, half his face still covered in shaving cream. Giles trots up the ridge along with most of the rest of the troop. Clearly visible, a distant ball of fire rises above the horizon. Maz turns and hurries to the remote terminal behind the tank where Calum is sitting. As she passes Loki's flank, she asks a question.

"Loki, identify nature of explosions to the west."

She gets to the terminal as the answer appears in the chat window: *ID not possible. Insufficient recognisable data. Visual analysis suggests fuel deflagration event.*

Her presence cues Callum to satisfy his curiosity and he ascends the slope. Distracted Maz stands, lost in thought. The distant noise has subsided. Giles looks around and declares that he will report their observations and ask for instructions. They are supposed to re-establish their screen today.

Maz stares to the north where she knows the out of bounds area is, but all is quiet, and no clues are forthcoming. Bill's voice sounds from behind her.

"What are they up to?" He has wiped the foam from his face and is holding the terminal leading to Freya.

"I don't know, Bill, but I don't like this. A helicopter that flies too fast, which our two can't identify, crosses the border and half an hour later there are explosions," she starts, as a lower, more distant rumble is heard. She looks at Bill. "Now, that is artillery."

Bill looks at his screen. "Freya agrees. Russian. We were told the Assad forces were going on the offensive."

The two wander back to the top of the slope. Bill hands his terminal to his corporal, who sets it on a rock and sits down by it.

Maz, still distracted, doesn't notice Calum gossiping with his mates further along the ridge. Behind Loki, the remote terminal is unattended.

The two sergeants stand shoulder to shoulder, deep in thought.

Suddenly, Bill says, "What do you suppose that is?" He points to a cloud of dust or smoke to the northwest. Frowning, he turns back to his crewman who is, ostensibly at least, a sentry, so is wearing his combat webbing. The corporal is used to being a mind reader around Bill, and he hands him a set of binoculars.

"About ten klicks, I'd say. There's something there, but I can't tell what."

He hands the binos to Maz and she takes a look. The roar of two engines causes them to stagger in shock, grabbing each other for support. Freya and Loki both lurch forward. Loki executes a turn to avoid two soldiers and moves down slope. They hear the unmistakeable sound of the CT-40 breech operating. Freya is also off.

Bill turns and shouts at his stunned crewman, who recovers and stabs his finger at the red cut-out button on the terminal. Freya stops abruptly, engine dying, she rocks back and forth before becoming still. Not so the other vehicle. Maz stares in horror at the unattended terminal which bounces in the air, and gets stuck between two rocks. The cable pulls tight as Calum runs after it. It is a forlorn hope. By the time he reaches the device, the cable has snapped. Loki gathers speed, heading for the dust cloud in the distance. Giles runs across, his face a picture of confusion and fear.

"What the fuck has happened? Stop it!"

Bill's voice is furious. "How exactly? There's no one in the fucker!"

The other crews are running for their vehicles.

"Well, do something, shoot it!"

"Are you fucking mad?! You try, if you fancy your chances."

"But yours, Freya, could."

"I'm not starting her up again until I know it's safe."

He turns back to Maz, who has started to speak. She is gasping with shock and betrayal.

"It's Heimdall. Heimdall did it."

"What are you talking about, mate?"

"Craig, Craig… Skunk Works… advanced planes… he made them a drone… they've used it."

He takes her abject face in his hands, the realisation of what she's said dawning on him. He looks at the rapidly disappearing Loki, abstractly thinking that it must be doing about fifty miles an hour, putting his arm around his friend's shoulder.

"Jesus titty fucking Christ, mate! You're right. What else could do that?" Turning back to Giles, his temper flares as he sees the expression on the officer's face. "What the fuck are you looking at, sir?! Call the squadron leader, tell him the fucking Yanks have stolen one of our vehicles. We think it's gone off to rescue a downed drone."

Giles recoils in confusion. "Oh, right, yeah! Sorry, Sarn't H." He scuttles off.

Bill walks Maz back to the centre of the position. The other troop members are emerging from their vehicles after the panic. They sit down in a pair of canvas chairs. Maz has recovered some of her equanimity, she apologises to Bill. He brushes it off.

"Never, mate, no need."

"I feel a bit betrayed. I might have to shoot Calum, mind. Dozy twat!"

"I know, and shooting Calum might teach him a valuable lesson."

The two laugh. Maz becomes serious again.

"We need Will here; he can get Freya back on the road. Freya will get Loki."

"Yes!"

Bill jumps to his feet and turns towards the troop headquarters. Maz gets to her feet to follow.

A distant lance of flame rises above the desert atop a pillar of dense white smoke. At regular intervals, three more follow.

Bill stares at Maz. "You don't think...?"

The cloud of dust that the troop observed earlier marked the spot that the Alpha Mike had chosen as an emergency landing site. The touchdown was heavy and one wheel failed to deploy, so the machine lies tilted at a drunken angle. Its auxiliary power unit continued to function, and the machine landed sideways on to a probable western threat. The unserviceable wheel station prevented the starboard, eastern facing, gun and the one remaining missile from being brought to bear. A further complication was that the port gun had fired most of its HE ammunition. It had suffered intermittent jamming from the Russo-Syrian forces now attacking Raqqah, but now it is able to communicate with the AWACS circling to the east and its satellite antenna still works. Data now streams towards the team at Qayyarah West. It updates the system with the information that it has gleaned on its flight back. The watchers in the AWACS and the Qayyarah West command post now see a number of hostile positions and estimated tracks of mobile patrols that have observed its passage and forced landing. Before flight, the communications networks and cryptographic keys for the brigade had been uploaded to the on-board databases. So, Alpha Mike also sends a nine-line casualty evacuation message to the desert resupply base. Realising that rescue might be slow, the drone begins to look wider for help.

The curious content of the nine-liner causes the CSAR commander to shake his head. Injuries to hydraulic systems are not something he normally encounters when rescuing downed pilots. He already knows from the AWACS that a US aircraft has landed in the desert, so he simply shrugs and asks permission to cross the border. This is immediately given and he informs callsign Delta Alpha Mike, now a blinking item on his tactical map, that rescue is thirty minutes away. Breaking radio silence on his unit radio, he calls for an immediate lift. His four birds start their engines and call in their troops.

The Alpha Mike assesses that the approaching vehicles it can now see will beat the CSAR. It has access to the situational awareness transmissions, so it can see the vehicles grouped ten kilometres south and reaches out to touch the UK Bowman communications network. The communications gateway opens in response to the correct codes and the programme immediately recognises Loki and Freya. Summoning its siblings is a simple matter. He feels Freya cut out in response to a signal and keeps his channel to Loki active. In effect, this keeps the transmit button pressed so that the channel is effectively jammed in the on position. Loki now belongs to him.

As Loki speeds up, a calculation shows that the arrival of help is marginal, so the search widens to reveal the ballistic computer in Caroline's battery command post. Alpha Mike's understanding of the system is visceral and instant. The protective fire coordinates are replaced with a series based on the predicted positions of the vehicles approaching. In the command post, the duty command post assistant is not looking at the screen of the ballistic computer and fails to see the numbers change and the *Check Fire* command change to *Fire*.

The first indication that the ready launcher is about to fire is the crack as the initiator ignites the engine of the first rocket. The three crew are relaxing in the shade of their launcher when this noise alerts them to danger. Recognising it for what it is, they are on their feet and sprinting before the first signs of the efflux pop the moisture seals from the ends of the missile box. One of them stumbles, it is a fatal mischance. The three are engulfed in dust and toxic smoke. As the fourth missile leaves the launcher, the smoke starts to clear. Only two smouldering figures emerge to collapse in the sand.

Their comrades inside the base scramble over the defensive berm to their aid. Most have sensibly grabbed bottles of water. Kevin has run to the scene and stands on top of the bank. He takes control and bellows instructions, telling those without water to return and get some. He turns to call for the medical team and sees that they are already on their way and have co-opted soldiers to bring stretchers. He turns back and his mouth sets in a grim line as the smoke finally clears to reveal a motionless body in the sand.

The battery sergeant major has run for the command post. Caroline is sprinting for the berm, but she sees Kevin in control, and changes direction to follow the sergeant major.

The hapless bombardier in the CP quails at the sight of the BSM's anger, stammering that he hasn't done anything. The signaller, who he was talking to when the missiles fired, confirms his story. This is repeated when Caroline appears.

The CP bombardier points at the screen and says, "The grids have changed. Those aren't the ones for the FPF."* He hands her the target list. She hands it to the BSM, who also checks it before telling the Ack to plot the grids on the map. He then types a holding reply into the brigade fires chat room that has been asking for a sitrep. Caroline fields a call from Robin Matthews but he breaks off, telling her to wait. There is a pause before he comes back, saying he may have an answer. The satcom terminal buzzes. It is Robin, who wants to talk on a secure one-to-one link.

Her eyes widen as she listens to what he has to say. She looks at the targets plotted on the map.

"We just fired to the west and north of that location."

Kevin arrives to give her the bad news on casualties. Caroline passes this news on before hanging up.

She looks at them. "Colonel Robin has just told me that their two modified Ajax were hijacked shortly before we fired. One of them is now fighting in the area we just engaged. He says that Sergeant Tate – she's one of the crew commanders who visited us a couple of weeks ago – thinks there's a Heimdall out there."

The other two look baffled.

"Heimdall is the name of the project I was working on in the UK before this. The guy who designed those two Ajax went to America, Tate thinks he made them a drone and the Yanks have used it to get revenge for their pilots.

---

* The Final Protective Fire or FPF is an emergency target. The guns or rockets are pointed at it so it can be fired on with no delay.

CLOSE QUARTER COMBAT

The drone is having a tough time of it. Loki is closing the distance at nearly eighty kilometres an hour, but is still outside his effective range. The rockets have landed but the problem with precision munitions is that they can also miss very precisely. Only one of the groups approaching the Defiant has behaved as predicted and paid the price. On the plus side, the arrival of the rockets has produced spectacular, if largely ineffective, explosions. Two of the groups have thought better of it and are now making speedy progress in the opposite direction. That leaves two serious teams. The first to breast the rise overlooking the downed helicopter halts and stares in amazement at the stricken aircraft. Luckily for them, they have arrived at a point outside the traverse of Mike's portside gun. Unluckily for them, their pause to admire the view and celebrate has provided enough time to bring a deadly enemy into range.

The gun in Loki's turret is one of only two stabilised weapon systems in the British Army inventory that can accurately fire on the move. That this is rough terrain, and the fighting vehicle is travelling twice as fast as it would on a training range, makes no difference at all. The target selection scripts in the Heimdall programme select the lethal airburst ammunition. The cloud of dust approaching from the south now attracts the attention of the insurgents. As it resolves into the shape of a sinister armoured vehicle, they struggle to react. The Royal Lancers first operational use of the eye-wateringly expensive forty-millimetre ammunition provides the first example of value for money in defence procurement for a very long time. Three bursts bracket the two pickups, the vehicles heave and twitch, tyres burst, and men are thrown about like rag dolls. Smoke and dust disperse on the breeze, diesel and blood drip into the sand.

The last group of would-be looters are from one of the anti-Assad militias. Witnessing the fate of the two pickups on the ridge line, they come to a halt. The tan hulk of Loki appears to leap over the hill. It skids to a halt. Libraries are accessed, scripts are read. None of the weapons it faces are a material threat to the Ajax and the asset it is obligated to defend is not in danger. One of the humans raises a rocket launcher. The turret shifts, Loki selects and loads an anti-aircraft round. This rocket might cause damage but not death, the tank pauses. The commander of the opposition can't think as fast as Loki, but he has some intuition and screams a command. Loki hears, translates, and recognises what is said. The RPG drops from the shoulder of the militiamen and the others lower their weapons. The machine gunners raise their hands. Loki's surveillance pod twitches left and right to focus on each potential adversary and he begins to slowly reverse. His rear manoeuvring camera selects a flat piece of ground behind the ridge and the monster withdraws until only the baleful eye of the recce pod is visible to the now utterly terrified militia section. Their two vehicles reverse slowly away before retreating into a wadi and speeding off.

The CSAR team are on their final approach by now. The two Apache have observed the whole incident, crews marvelling at what they have witnessed. Like the militia, they assume that there are humans in the turret. Much of the banter on the radios and intercom complements the skills and aggression of their allies. The final act of the drama elicits the view that it was: "Risky, and a strong shout," "We'd of just wacked those guys." The rescue flight is feeding constant updates back to hangar and the relief that the Defiant is now safe is welcome. British involvement is not mentioned.

The drone's last act is to release Loki from its task and invite it to go back to the leaguer. The tank reverses off the slope and speeds away to the southeast. This causes some surprise amongst the rescuers, who expected some social interaction, they are also surprised that the turret hatches remain closed.

AFTERMATH

Back at the command post in the hangar in Key West, the Alpha Mike crew are looking at the information stream that they can now see. Now that a rescue of the downed aircraft is in play, they are in jubilant mood. Were they paying more attention to the images on the live feed from Alpha Mike, they would be better prepared for the coming developments. Elizabeth is wearing the headphones that are her link with the main operations room at Brigade Headquarters. A message causes her smile to fade, and her eyes go to the screen on which the Union Flag on Loki's turret bustle is quite evident.

In the brigade headquarters, Brigadier General O'Brien is not concerned with current operations. He has been told that the attack has been successful. The details will be given at his routine morning update. His attention is caught by a burst of activity in the normally calm British national staff cell. There is a bustle of worried faces. Fingers point at maps and handsets are pressed against tense faces. The major, who is Colonel Lucas's senior staff officer, is having an intense conversation with his boss. He watches as David's worried frown is replaced by intense anger. The head turns and he sees that anger directed at him.

As he gets up from his chair to meet the figure striding towards him, the head of his own current operations cell appears at his side and attempts to speak with him.

"Not now!"

The ops major looks at the approaching British officer but doesn't go away.

David speaks, his voice taut with fury. "When were you going to tell me?!"

"Calm down, Colonel Lucas. I take it you mean the drone strike. CENTCOM gave strict instructions that it was US eyes only until mission end. Your government was informed."

The pat reply does little to mollify David.

"Really! Well perhaps CENTCOM will tell me why one of my soldiers is lying dead in the desert and two more are badly burned and waiting for a medevac helicopter. While they're at it, perhaps they'll also let me know why Colonel Mattheson has just informed me that a British reconnaissance vehicle took off on its own accord, crossed the Syrian border in clear violation of our rules of engagement and the memoranda between our countries, and got into a fight with Syrian militia."

He pauses for breath and the hapless American major interjects.

"I was trying to tell you, sir. We had a report of three casualties. The battery told us they were caught outside the launcher when it fired. And the Ajax vehicle, sir. It didn't have a crew."

The whole headquarters has fallen silent, and every face is watching the angry confrontation in the middle of the room. Will Conyers, in his corporal's uniform, appears at David's side. He quietly tells David that Ajax Loki has returned to its troop location completely of its own accord. He adds that Sergeant Tate managed to stop them turning the vehicle off when they regained communications.

"Apparently she was the only one calm enough to realise that they'd end up having to go and get it."

The general looks at Will and remembers why he's here. He turns to David, whose anger has evaporated as he realises that the general is nearly as much in the dark as he is.

"Come with me – both of you."

In the Alpha Mike command post, the team are looking at the footage from the recce pod that shows Loki. They have rewound it enough to see the Ajax firing, and smoke rising beyond the ridge.

The hangar side door opens and the general strides in with David and Will. They are followed by a flustered sentry. Peter advances a few paces and protests at the two British uniforms.

"BE QUIET!" The general slips the leash on his mounting anger. "I have a British soldier, a soldier in my brigade, lying dead in the desert while two of his comrades are on their way to my Role Two Facility with serious injuries. It seems that's down to you." He looks over at the screen with its evidence in red, white and blue. "While you're at it, maybe you can also explain why a British amoured vehicle crossed the border in violation of our agreements, apparently without its crew."

Outside, the sound of helicopters arriving can be heard.

"Well, Colonel Doyle?"

"We don't know, sir, we were reviewing the attack footage when Major Capstone drew our attention to the British armour."

Peter turns to the console operator. "Russ?"

Will reacts. "Russ? Russ Morales?"

Attention is on him now as Russ nods his head in confusion. Will has heard about Craig's friend on the Skunk Works team. He looks at David.

"Lockheed Martin, sir. Craig never told us the details, but we guessed it would be a drone. We hadn't got that far in our thinking, but we were on our way." He turns his attention back to Russ and steps to his side. "Roll the feed back to when it landed and put the logfiles up on your other screen."

Russ looks at his colonel, but it's the general's voice that barks,

"Do it!"

They roll back the footage and data. The bumpy landing is recorded by Mike's targeting pod and they see it looking about. In the logfile, Russ points to the nine-line message and the response from the CSAR. Will exclaims when he spots the plea for help to the two Ajax. He explains to the others how Freya was abruptly deactivated and how the Alpha Mike got around the problem. He rightly surmises that Mike based its decisions on time and space calculations.

Looking at Peter, he says, "You gave the drone all the access codes and crypto for the coalition?"

"We needed to use some of the bearer systems for our comms to the aircraft and, of course, he needed it to access data from the AWACS."

Will continues, "The logfiles show that the drone opened the Bowman gateway and sent a simple fire mission of four targets. It would've taken us a while to sort out which communications net to use. This took about three seconds."

He and Russ fiddle about a bit more and the screen shows the engagement on the hill and Loki's climb. They let the footage run on and watch the odd behaviour at the top of the hill.

Will asks, "I wonder what happened there? It does something and then your boy abruptly lets him go and stops jamming the link."

A voice from the other side of the hangar provides the answer. Commander CSAR has arrived and quietly entered the hangar. Realising something important was going on, he held his team back.

"They let two of the hostile trucks go."

Will is confused and then realises that the man in the full war gear doesn't know what Loki is.

"They? Oh! Of course."

He gets a funny look from the major.

"One of the Apache gunners said that the tank went up the hill and the two technicals were stationary downslope. It just stopped and looked at them. The gunner couldn't understand it. They even pointed an RPG. He said the gun traversed but still didn't fire and the hajis surrendered. Said it was funny to watch. The tank then reversed back over the ridge and watched them drive away. Our guys were impressed really, don't think we'd have given them the benefit of the doubt. The crew must have nads of steel."

Will laughs out loud, and a lot of the tension fades. "You don't know how right you are, sir! You really don't." He turns back to his officer and as he gets up, says, "Cold, unemotional, inescapable logic and rules. No threat. No fire." He glances back at Russ. "It'll be in the scripts, Mr Morales. It's always in the scripts." He looks at the Colonel with distaste. "How did Dr Moore let you get away with it? Rigour and detail could be his middle names."

The Alpha Mike team looks uncomfortable. Will scans them.

"Of course. He didn't know, did he? He wasn't there." Walking towards the door, he asks David, "Can we go, Colonel? I want to talk to Loki; they better not have turned him off."

The senior officers turn and follow him, commenting that they have some difficult conversations ahead.

AN EARLY CALL FOR THE PRESIDENT

The President is awoken early in the morning. She is irritable. Her irritation turns to dismay at the news she receives. The chief of staff is waiting for her, he hasn't slept at all. His briefing is detailed and covers the facts available. He sits, patiently waiting for her to digest this news. His own mind is formulating the factors and nuances that will be needed for the political discussion to come. The campaign for a second term has not yet begun, but he knows that any foundations built here will need to be strong. Opportunities must be taken, threats crushed or evaded. His future depends on it.

She looks up. "I need to freshen up. Oval Office in fifteen. Just you and me. First off, I'll need to speak to the British Prime Minister."

When she sits behind the desk, preliminary approaches have been made between British and American officials. The British were expecting the call and it is later on their side of the Atlantic Ocean, so they are already fully staffed even at their early hour. The conversation is cordial. The President emphasises the success of the mission and the message it sends to their joint enemies. She is sincere in her apology for the death of the British soldier and the injuries to his colleagues. They both know that the incident will have deep repercussions, but recriminations are neither appropriate nor useful. The Prime Minister, in any case, sees no advantage in harming the distinct warming of relations that has occurred following the UK contribution. The situation must be managed; advantages, however few, sought and gained.

They go on to discuss some of the implications nationally and internationally, how the media in their respective countries will react. The Prime Minister observes, a little enviously, that her people will likely be more hawkish than his own. Both acknowledge that as more is revealed, the peaceniks and liberals will raise an outcry. The President adds more details about the nature of the Defiant AM. In her call to the PM before the attack, it had been described simply as a drone strike. They both acknowledge that sooner or later the killer robot aspect will be revealed. This leads to a discussion on human-in-the-loop and morality issues. She quotes the final words of the chairman of the joint chiefs. The conversation ends with her asking for discretion and close contact in the days ahead. Neither leader mentions upon whom the blame will fall, or which side of the 'big pond' it will lie.

In the Oval Office, the conversation is deemed to have gone about as well as it could have. The President is doubly grateful that she briefed the British on the impending attack. The chief of staff broaches the subject of political management. There is likely to be disquiet amongst some of the Democrats, and the Republicans, while rejoicing over the result, will throw brickbats simply to sow discord. She thinks for a moment.

"Someone has to be to blame. There wasn't anybody in the cockpit or, for that matter, in the control station. Makes it difficult, more complicated."

"Lockheed Martin?"

"Powerful. Big lobby in defense. A possibility. Find out more about this programmer. In the meantime, summon the team. A smaller group, the Veep, secretary of state, intelligence, the military, I leave it to you."

As he leaves, she calls after him, "Don't forget the science advisor… and make sure the attorney general is there."

In the UK, the problem is more pressing. Civil servants and special advisors are frantically gathering information and fielding calls. As in the USA, the news broke too late for the printed media, but all the PM's press staff have phones pressed to their ears as the online and television media clamour for a story. Ministers are called, along with the Government chief scientist, the military and, of course, the attorney general. The PM plans to consult with his most knowledgeable staff before a press briefing.

In the USA, the equivalent meeting is underway. All present are aware of the serious issues that have arisen. The secretary for foreign affairs has already spoken to the British ambassador and the head of the CIA has spoken to the British head of station. Details have been shared. The aim being to align the American and British stories as much as possible. When they discuss the press and public response, the tone is optimistic. Press and pundits are fully supportive so far, and interviews in the street are encouraging. The news of the British casualties has roused expressions of sympathy but mostly coupled with an acceptance that this is what happens in war. Officials point to a rise in the President's popularity. The President's comment is, "So far."

General Adams takes up the theme. "So far nobody knows the true nature of our drone, but it's bound to get out. There'll be more voices from the anti-war lobby and folk who already fear the proliferation of so-called killer robots."

The President raises the issue of responsibility. "I've been tussling with the issue of who's to blame. This isn't like a pilot making a mistake, faulty intelligence or a bomb going off-course. The machine meant to do what it did. It's a Lockheed Martin aircraft, what's their position in this?"

The attorney general takes up the subject. "It might be possible to make a case for corporate responsibility, if we thought we really needed to. If there's something in the programming that we couldn't know about that caused this, having taken on the machine in good faith."

General Hughes, who has been sitting at the big table for the first time, sits back, smiting his forehead. "Damn that woman!" He looks at the lawyer. "I went down and saw the Defiant Alpha Mike in action last week. After the British guy, Dr Moore, had left, I made our request for it. The Skunk Works programme leader, Leanne Phillips, had obviously been briefed to say yes. She made a little speech though. It's a prototype, early development, not finished, don't blame us speech. In public, but in any case, they record everything that goes on at their mission control. I thought at the time it sounded a bit rehearsed, but there were other priorities."

The attorney general turns to the President. "That would do it. In any case, there are a lot of congress people and senators with vested interests in a company like Lockheed. A lot of Americans work for them. Even without Ms Phillips's clever intervention, I'd advise against placing any blame there."

The scientific adviser had reacted when Marcus mentioned Craig's name. "Would that British individual be Dr Craig Moore?"

"It would, do you know him?"

"I know of him. Several of my colleagues have met him. His work is… impressive."

The President asks if any of them know where he is.

Marcus replies, "Ms Phillips was uncomfortable with our summary dismissal of Dr Moore. She got the Brits to call him back and sweetened it with a ride to Washington in her jet. There was talk of the Smithsonian. That was over a day ago, so he must be back in the UK."

"Actually, he may not be." It is the chief scientist again. "One of the people who knows Dr Moore got a call telling him that he was over here. I was in Boston yesterday and the people at MIT were excited at the imminent arrival of a British robotics specialist."

The chief of staff calls to one of his people and tells him to call the FBI office in New York. They are to find Craig Moore. The scientist grimaces at this.

"If our first reaction to something going wrong every time a computer does something unexpected is to arrest the programmer, we're going to set back the most significant advance in science this century by many decades while we wait for them to be released from jail."

General Adams agrees. "I know I made a pretty speech about morals yesterday, but from my briefings this guy has put us ahead of all the competition. There were casualties and some diplomatic toes have been stepped on. The collateral damage was higher than I would like, but that attack was an outstanding success."

"Thank you, General. As it happens, I'm inclined to agree. Sanctuary is probably more appropriate than a cell."

The attorney general speaks up again. "The problem is that there has been a death. The British will have to conduct an inquest and if the death is ruled as unlawful, then Dr Moore may be the easiest target for a charge of manslaughter."

The President thanks her attorney general. She is keen to finish and turn her thoughts to the press.

"However this turns out, America is not in the direct line of fire. Dr Moore's name is not public and the nature of our weapon is not yet known. That gives us time and opportunity to shape events."

UNFORESEEN CONSEQUENCES

Dr Craig Moore is still in the USA when FBI agents converge on the Massachusetts Institute of Technology. But only just. He is at New York's John F Kennedy Airport about to board an aircraft to Heathrow. An incomplete briefing to the FBI has not resulted in a flag against his name at immigration.

As he waits in the upper class lounge, his attention is drawn to the news feed on the silent screen, reporting the drone strike in Syria. The screen shows a declassified overhead image of white flashes among what look like buildings. Craig does not make any connections. Settling into the comfortable seat as the aircraft taxis, he prepares for a flight composed mainly of sleep. The enjoyable end to the previous day with his MIT colleagues had extended long into the evening, and he feels a bit woolly-headed. The morning flight is at quite a civilised time and is expected to arrive in the evening. He is flying into the darkness.

While he is in the air, a meeting in Downing Street with a similar attendance list to that in the US has convened. The casualties are the immediate and pressing concern. In front of the Prime Minister, on the desk are three typed letters that he will transcribe into his own handwriting for them to delivered to the grieving families.

Craig's name is introduced early in the debate. His nationality leaves little doubt as to what the American approach will be. If the situation were reversed, they would do the same. The secretary of state for defence says his piece; he has been briefed by Henry Scott, whose opposition to the UK project has been like a scratched record ever since Fort Halstead.

"This was inevitable. What the Americans were doing releasing an uncontrolled artificial intelligence into the wild, I do not know. Dr Moore should never have been allowed out of the country."

The slight brings an angry retort from the minister for defence procurement. "Our programmes have been advanced by the use of US technology and Dr Moore's expertise. Our Ajax vehicles have been an outstanding success. His loan to the Americans was a price well worth paying."

"It didn't stop our Ajax violating the memorandum, or Moore's machine killing and injuring our troops."

The PM interrupts. "I don't see what value your tirade adds, Douglas. You were happy enough with the deployment of the two vehicles when it was discussed in Cabinet. We're supposed to be coming up with options. Attorney general?"

"The body will be flown back within a day or so. An inquest will be called but I expect the first hearing will be adjourned for the gathering of evidence. It does look to me that Dr Moore could be in the frame."

The chief scientific advisor picks up the thread. "This sort of issue has been started by the behaviour of a very few self-driving vehicles. I believe there have been several accidents. Blaming an individual programmer seems excessive and is bound to stifle the appetite for research. In any case, most of this type of programming is collaborative. Focusing on one individual is an oversimplification."

The PM is dry. "Frame seems to be an unfortunate word choice, Peter. Is there not a case for corporate responsibility? It occurs to me that we may not want Dr Moore's talent stifled."

"Of course, Prime Minister. Difficult though, Lockheed Martin will be well defended. They will have planned for this type of unforeseen event. It may not even be possible to bring such a case, and I'm certain that the current rosy glow around our relationship with America would suffer."

Defence steps back in. "I, for one, would have no objection to seeing Moore take the fall for this. Deflect any blame from America and us. We have his programme. Relations with our best ally are good. Lessons are learned."

Another withering look comes his way. "How easy to be cavalier with another man's future from such a position of privilege. Perhaps the strain of your office is beginning to tell."

The defence secretary quails at the implied threat. Other eyes around the table are malicious, sensing a weakness that may be exploited. The spell is broken by the home secretary. Her voice is sharp.

"This gets us nowhere. The true nature of this highly successful operation is not yet in the open. It may not be for some time. We need to manage public reaction to the casualties. Offer support to the families who are victims of this unfortunate accident. The inquest is far enough down the line for us to deal with that when it comes. We are well used to dealing with these casualty situations. In the meantime, plan for the news to break, hope it doesn't. CDS, anything to add from a military point of view?"

The chief of the defence staff has been quietly observing the social dynamics in this meeting. He can't stand the defence secretary and has been relishing his discomfiture.

"It would be sad to see Dr Moore's talents go to waste. I agree that the attack was a great success. Its implications, given what we know, are immense. These weapons are coming. If we don't use them, there are plenty who will. As you can imagine and, I hope, forgive, my concerns lie in these directions and not those of image or party politics. On the subject of breaking news, I agree with the home secretary. We will, of course, be convening a service enquiry to investigate the incident. That will at the very least reveal that this was no ordinary accident. The most immediate question I would pose is: where is Dr Moore? He needs to be brought under control."

"As ever, CDS identifies the nub of the problem. Where is our scientist, Peter?"

The chief of defence procurement has been waiting for this question. "I was briefed by the head of our side of this project earlier. The Americans had asked for her help in easing Dr Moore out of the way while they executed the plan. She wanted him back anyway for another of our projects, so she agreed. He was, apparently, due into the country this morning. On a Washington flight."

The home secretary takes back control. "Good, we need to know where he is. I would suggest we prime the chair of the select committee on artificial intelligence. He belongs to us. If this does break early, we can divert their current work into an enquiry. It will be good to have a decisive act up our sleeves. I'll speak to the police commissioner. If it looks like the law is needed, an investigation can be started, which delays awkward questions. The bottom line is, if we need to throw Dr Moore under the bus, we can, if there is no other way to manage the issue. Regrettable, but necessary."

The PM thinks for a few moments, his gaze on the home secretary. He sits back and addresses them all.

"We have a plan, home secretary, to lead the action." He looks at the head of the Security Service. "Your people will be needed here, I think. More discrete than a lot of uniforms charging around."

UNFORESEEN EVENTS

There now follows a series of unfortunate events. During the dramatic events in Iraq, an Illinois reporter from the Herald Newspaper in Decatur was in Key West, collecting local soldier stories. As he walked along one of the dusty roads, a flurry of activity on the airfield caught his eye. Moving to a vantage point, he witnessed the extraordinary arrival of the Defiant in front of a hangar. Other helicopters land and troops disembark. He is in an inconspicuous spot and stops to photograph the unfolding drama. The pictures are wired to his editor. There is a short distance in the leap of logic to associate what he has in his hands with what is on all the main news outlets. The pictures are shortly in the hands of the New York Times.

In a Bovington café, Sergeant Major Jim Perry is with a couple of colleagues. The attention of the group is caught by an item of breaking TV news. The story of the drone strike in Syria has been a regular feature. The images on the screen are different this time. The group shout for the volume to be turned up, and the image resolves into a report from US media. It shows a helicopter in front of a hangar in the desert. The commentary speculates that this is a new drone, never seen before. Images of the aftermath of the attack from insurgent and other sources are shown. The reporter laments and criticises the number of civilian casualties, pictures of a burned mother and child, scattered bodies at the entrance of a burnt out mosque. The voice goes on to comment on the shooting down of several drones over Syria. It speculates as to the nature of this machine.

"Is this a new kind of drone? A robot weapon, perhaps?"

Jim Perry slams his mug down, startling his companions.

"I knew it would fucking happen!" His voice is loud.

"What would happen, mate?"

"Dr fucking Craig Moore and his clever machines."

Jim's mind goes back to Fort Halstead and the Americans. The ranges at Bovington and the capabilities of the Ajax.

"So, you know about these killer robots?"

"They're not killer…" His voice trails off. He is in a public place. Belatedly, he realises that his outburst is indiscrete. Heads have turned at his outburst. In the corner, one of the listeners senses an opportunity. He writes down the name he's just heard.

In the coming months, Jim Perry will come to discover what Craig Moore means by his oft-quoted mantra: 'When you create a set of conditions, there is an outcome.' In his case, it will not be favourable.

A communications blackout has been in force at the patrol base that houses Caroline's rocket battery in Iraq. This is standard practice when there is a fatality, and the family needs to be informed. The British Military has a rigorous system for establishing the identity of a casualty. Only when the details have been verified is a representative despatched to notify the next of kin. Until then, welfare telephones and internet access are shut down. The lifting of this restriction coincides with the first revelations that indicate the true nature of the drone. It is not long before the news that the casualties were sitting outside the launcher reaches the UK.

The breaking news is reported to the Prime Minister and the home secretary at about the same time. They spend a period in discussion. They decide that he must conduct another press briefing in the evening. Neither is very worried. The nature of the drone was always going to be revealed. This is a good deal sooner than desired but has not surprised them. Officials have already been developing briefing notes and lines to take when talking to the media. Press and public reaction has not changed since the news of the drone attack broke. It remains positive. That evening in the Downing Street press studio, the Prime Minister gives a short statement bringing the audience up to date on developments. He uses the word "autonomous" to describe the drone. He refers to a series of programmes and experiments being carried out in the UK to explore the use of similar technology. His speechwriters hope that this explanation will dilute some of the anticipated wilder theories based on a picture and some speculation about the meaning of autonomy.

He is about to walk into an ambush.

The BBC political correspondent has an exemplary production staff to support her. Jim's outburst in Bovington has been reported by a contact who just happened to be in the right place. A BBC reporter in Birmingham, where the injured are being treated, had overheard relatives discussing the news from Iraq that the crew of the MLRS launcher had been outside the vehicle when it fired. They have not made the connection, but it didn't take long for the researchers to do so.

The PM invites questions. After some questions on responsibility and help for the families have been fielded, many of the audience ask questions about the collateral damage and the PM's opinion on the level of destruction. The replies to this are the usual view on avoiding casualties and blame-shifting onto the insurgents.

The BBC get their turn.

"Prime Minister, there are reports that the British casualties were outside the rocket launcher when it fired. Surely safety procedures would stop the people inside from shooting? Also, my sources say that the American attack was too far away for one of our rockets to reach. What were we shooting at?"

The PM is visibly uncomfortable and unprepared.

"Well, obviously, I can't go into details. We are investigating the incident, and the Ministry of Defence has started its own enquiry. First reports imply that there was a computer error."

"A computer error, Prime Minister? The United States launched an attack with a drone that you describe as autonomous. Computer-controlled. Then a computer error kills and injures British soldiers. Tell me, Prime Minister, who is Dr Craig Moore?"

The last question throws the PM into confusion.

"We don't have much time left. I'll take one more question."

He indicates the Times correspondent, who looks at the BBC questioner.

Seeing that she is outraged at being brushed off, he asks, "Who is Dr Craig Moore, Prime Minister?"

There is some bluster about time and the PM retreats, leaving his press secretary to conduct a last stand. Many of the audience are already googling. Others are leaving. The Times and the BBC are in conversation.

DESCENT INTO DARKNESS

Dr Craig Moore is beginning the descent into London's Heathrow Airport. Craig likes money, but he doesn't pay much attention to it. The gaming industry sorted out the poverty of his youth. The wealth he will accumulate in the future from Heimdall is still to come. The current work has, in any case, conferred a substantial bank balance and a taste for comfortable travel. The costly flight at his own expense enables a swift transition through immigration, and he has no hold luggage. A pre-ordered car whisks him away from the airport towards his house in Wimbledon. Officials at the Home Office did not flag his passport to the Border Force in time. For the second time that day, the forces of a state have missed their prey.

Craig unlocks and enters a slightly musty smelling house. He brings it to life and opens the doors into the garden. Frowning, he notes that some items are missing. Sophie's things, mostly, but a few of the costlier of his own as well. His spirits sag, he had hoped the key might at last be on the mat. Sleep did not come easily on the plane, so he is tired. There is nothing in the fridge he is prepared to risk eating. But a bottle of beer catches his eye. He notes the best before date but decides to drink it anyway. Sitting on the couch, he looks for the remote and realises that the TV is missing. Sighing, he sits on the bed, finishes the beer, crawls beneath the duvet and sleeps fitfully until the early morning.

Turning on the radio, she had at least left that, he listens with mounting horror. The presenter mentions his name and describes a sequence of supposed events in Syria. Repeated references are made to the killer robot that had hijacked a British rocket launcher and a tank. The casualties' injuries are recounted, and interviews with grieving relatives are played. Opponents of militarised AI rehearse the fears of machines deciding who will live and who will die. The presenters speculate as to who is to blame. The British and American governments are in the frame. So is the man who is now assumed to have unleashed the killer robot.

Craig switches off the radio and reaches for his tablet. The news feeds say pretty much the same thing as the BBC, ranging from considered words in the broadsheets to hysterical rants in the red tops. One thread runs through it: a search for someone to blame. There is a reasoned piece in one column that examines the incidents involving self-driving vehicles. The possible culpability of computer programmers leaves Craig gasping for breath. Clasping his knees, he rocks back and forth, trying to still the turmoil in his mind.

After an age, some calm returns. He turns on his mobile phone and tries to call his friends. The most obvious are the least available. In operational theatres, personal mobile phones are switched off. Caroline has written him a couple of affectionate aerogrammes, the flimsy letter forms known as 'blueys'. They take several days to travel. He has no idea how to contact David. A call to Helen Sherwood comes up against the wall of her PA.

"Ms Sherwood is in a meeting."

Sam and the others simply don't answer. He considers calling his friends at Lockheed Martin but recoils in the face of their betrayal.

He calls Mike Sheppard's number. Just as he thinks there will be no reply, Mike picks up. His voice is low, almost a whisper.

"Craig, are you alright?"

"Mike, what's happening? No one will speak to me. The news. I didn't know 'til this morning. They made me go away. I couldn't do anything."

The words tumble out of his mouth. Tears stream down his face.

The anguish at the other end of the phone almost unmans Mike.

"Oh, my poor boy. I'm so sorry. We've been told we mustn't talk to you. Look, I've got to hang up. Craig, you must get a lawyer. I'm sorry, I have to go."

Mike gets up from his desk and visits the gents. Washing his hands, he looks in the mirror and doesn't like what he sees. Striding back to his desk, he places a call to Helen Sherwood and is put through. He tells her that he has spoken to Craig.

"Unwise. That will not make you any friends."

"Those are the sort of friends I don't want."

There is a pause at the other end of the line. "What exactly do you think you can do?"

"I really don't know, Helen, but I'm worried. He's being hung out to dry. He isn't likely to talk to Lockheed. He's bound to think they've betrayed him. Can't you do anything? For all his brilliance, he isn't emotionally skilled. From what I've just heard, I'd say he was unravelling."

Helen has been smugly allowing things to progress. Now she feels a sense of disquiet. Ever manipulative, her plan had been to leave Craig dangling and step in as an ally as soon as she judged it suited her. The first step is to control Mike.

"Hmmm. You're right, of course. We wouldn't want any harm to come to him in the long run. He's far too valuable. Leave it with me. The minister came back from the meeting in London furious with the secretary of state. Douglas is the enemy, apparently. I'll see what can be done."

"Right. Thank you, Helen. Oh! I told him to get a lawyer."

Helen rings off, frowning.

Corporate America starts early, and in Lockheed Martin's headquarters, another conversation featuring Craig Moore occurs.

Events in London are being watched closely. Leanne has been uncomfortable with Craig's treatment since Fort Polk. She is dismayed by the implications for him that she sees in the UK press.

In the CEO's office, she voices her disquiet.

"We've got to do something. The poor guy will be hounded. I've read the CIA profile I prodded them into making. He's not robust enough for this treatment."

"I understand, Leanne, but I don't see there's much we can do. He's thousands of miles away. I can't see him reaching out to us. He'll be blaming us."

"With justification. Lewis, this is not who we are. What message does it send if we don't stand up for our people? He is our people."

"You are getting emotionally involved, Leanne. I know we don't want to lose that expertise, but our involvement makes our situation precarious."

"Why did you hire me, Lewis? What are we if we have no loyalty or ethical framework."

"What do you want to do?"

Before she can answer, her phone, lying on the table, rings. It is Russ Morales, just back from Iraq with Alpha Mike. She looks at Lewis, who nods. As she speaks, her eyes widen, and she looks at the chairman. Thanking Russ, she hangs up.

"That was our lead programmer. He's Dr Moore's protégé. He's also his friend and has been as guilty and dismayed as I am by the news. What I've just been told might offer a solution. It's all down to us excluding him. Russ pointed out that Dr Moore wasn't there at a critical time when we uploaded the mission parameters. Maps, and critically, the collateral damage and Rules of Engagement. More importantly, we didn't take out the self-defence line because, unlike the Brits, our national rules allow us to use lethal force to defend property. The Alpha Mike prototype is our property. It puts us back in the firing line, but we can handle that. We need to make sure he's got a lawyer, and they know this."

Lewis looks at Leanne and smiles. "God bless you and Mr Morales, Leanne. Make it so."

Leanne hurries back to the office she has co-opted in the Lockheed headquarters. Her first task is to call Helen Sherwood.

Helen is wrestling with a problem that she can't control. When Leanne calls and tells her why, there is a glimmer of hope. She assures Leanne that if Craig doesn't have a lawyer, he soon will have. Leanne replies that she realises that Helen's government is unlikely to pay. Her call ends with the words, "Lockheed will."

Helen has a contact in the Home Office and they have a conversation. It transpires that the Security Service have been tasked with finding and keeping track of Dr Moore's whereabouts. Helen tells her contact more about Craig and raises her own worries about Craig's state of mind. She also passes on the US interest and the likelihood that the CIA in London will be looking for him.

EVERYONE IS JUST A
LITTLE BIT LATE

The bell rings at Craig's house, and there is a peremptory knocking at the door. He pulls himself together and answers. Two slightly badly dressed people are standing at the door. They are startled by the dishevelled creature that greets them.

"Dr Moore?"

"Yes."

"Detective Sergeant Phillips and Detective Constable Hanley."

"But I haven't done anything wrong."

"We're not saying you have, sir."

"We're investigating the death of a UK citizen overseas. We want to ask you some questions."

"Am I being arrested?"

"No, sir. We just want you to help us with our inquiries."

The expressions are bland, Craig is dazed. He gets his phone and a hoodie that is slung over a chair and meekly follows the two police officers to their car.

The home secretary is informed that Craig has been found. She leans back, considering her next action. Ambitions for the top slot in this administration are never far from her thoughts. Being in the lead on this crisis can only help strengthen her position. She looks again at the note and calls for her permanent secretary. They discuss the situation and decide that making the House of Lords Select Committee on Arificial Intelligence aware of 'concerns' would be a sound move. AI is bound to impinge on national security. The permanent secretary points to the fuss surrounding facial recognition. It would do the department no harm to be shaping development and regulation."

They decide on a plan, he is to send an official to the police station where Craig will be interviewed. She will talk to the chairman of the committee.

Craig is sitting in an interview room. In terms of experiences, this is a first for him, and not a jolly one. The plain room and its uncomfortable chair, together with the baleful gaze of the two police officers, are quite intimidating. A camera dome looks down on the scene. The two policeman have started a recorder going, and named themselves and Craig. Phillips smiles and starts.

"DC Hanley and I have been asked by the Home Office to interview you in connection with an incident overseas that resulted in the death of an individual and injuries to two others. Dr Moore, are you aware that during an incident in Iraq two days ago, a British soldier was killed and two others were injured?"

"I saw the news, yes."

"Early reports suggest that a drone operated by the United States was involved in these incidents. Would you know anything about that?"

"I saw the picture and the news report, yes."

"Is it the drone you were working on?"

"I'm not allowed to say what I'm working on, in this country or in America."

Hanley takes over. "Dr Moore, this is a serious matter. We haven't cautioned you, but if you want to be arrested that's easy enough. We both have security clearances and this is a serious matter, people have been killed. I suggest you start cooperating."

The hostile tone and threat alarm Craig and he is flustered.

"You can talk to the Ministry of Defence, they'll tell you."

Phillips cuts in, quieter, and in a placatory tone, looking at his colleague. "I'm sure there's no need for us to take such measures, I'm sure Dr Moore is keen to cooperate." She looks at a sheaf of notes that she brought in. "We've had a briefing on the autonomous weapons project in the UK, Heimdall, and the US one, Akacita Maza." She stumbles over the pronunciation and, unwittingly, Craig corrects her.

Hanley again. "So, you were working on a US autonomous drone?"

Craig starts to panic. "Yes, but I just took the UK work over and helped the Americans with their machine."

"So it wasn't your programming that caused this robot to do what it did?"

"It couldn't have. He wouldn't be able to, the rules are all scripted in. He attacks targets that are legal and he can defend himself. I had to put them in as I was told. They're called Rules of Engagement."

The more reasonable tone of Phillips smoothly continues the conversation. "Well, 'he' did defend himself, Dr Moore, he fired some rockets. Our people were in the blast area when they were fired. Funny you should call him 'he'. Should a machine be allowed to defend itself, if a person would be harmed? You think it has the same rights as we do, Dr Moore?"

Craig looks at the two detectives, who are now both looking at him with the cool gaze of lizards. He feels nauseous. A knock at the door interrupts and the face of a uniformed officer intrudes to say that an official from the Home Office is outside. At a nod from Phillips, an immaculate figure in suit and tie enters the room. The two detectives rise, belatedly Craig does as well. He knocks over his chair, adding to his confusion. The civil servant introduces himself and turns a tight smile on Craig, telling him not to worry about the chair. Phillips picks it up and guides Craig back into it.

She feels the physical tremor in him and alarm bells ring in her head. She turns a worried look to Hanley. The Home Office man notes it and warms his expression a little.

"Dr Moore, I'm here to tell you that the House of Lords Select Committee on Artificial Intelligence have been asked to look into this matter and that they will call you to Westminster shortly, to answer some questions. No need to worry, it's just an investigation that will add to their work on the Government policy." His expression does little to encourage Craig. "Please make sure that you can be contacted. You should also feel free to talk to these officers about the projects you've been working on. They are both briefed and cleared. Oh! I would advise you against talking to the press." He forces another smile, it's about as warm as the brass plate on a coffin.

Phillips hastily announces that they have finished their interview, "For the present."

The man from the Ministry speaks again. "Just one further thing, Dr Moore, one of our agencies saw you at a protest against killer robots talking to a young woman. Why would you attend such an event?"

The two officers sit down again.

"That was my girlfriend, I wasn't at the rally. I'd been with a colleague."

"That would be Sophie? Is she at home?"

"I haven't seen her since I went to the States. The relationship is over, we argued."

"I see, well, I suggest you maintain some distance from these types of people. I'm sure we shall wish to speak again."

The official departs and the two detectives rise and indicate that Craig can go home. When they get out of the interview, a pale Craig asks if he can use their toilet. Hanley points to a door.

When he disappears he looks at Phillips and says, "He's coming apart, we'd better make sure he gets back to his place."

Phillips nods and goes to speak to the desk sergeant. Behind her, the sound of Craig being sick is plain to hear. She grabs a bottle of water. When he returns she hands it to him and steers him towards the two uniformed officers who have been tasked with driving him to Wimbledon.

Craig is dropped outside his house. Further down the street, the press pack has the wrong address and is looking up and down the road. They spot the car and start to run. The two officers push Craig towards his door and tell him to get inside. They impede the lead reporters none too gently. Craig enters the house, vaguely realising that the door is already open. When he gets in, he sees he has had visitors. His possessions are scattered about. There is a terrible smell. The word *murderer* is daubed in excrement across a wall.

Retching, he staggers to the doors into his garden, runs blindly to the back fence and climbs over into the alleyway beyond. As he does so, his phone falls from his back pocket, tumbling through a bush, coming to rest in the shadows. Still running, he reaches the high street. Grabbing a cab he settles miserably in the back and gives a street name in Woolwich. Luckily, his anonymity remains in place during the ride. He is dropped at the north end of Repository Road near the Army barracks. He continues down the hill and enters a block of flats. The lift doesn't work, so he climbs the stairs. A worn key amongst the others on his keyring unlocks a shabby door. There is a struggle to open it, junk mail and flyers lie on the mat. The dust is thick. The flat is dark. It smells of mould. Entering the sitting room, he falls to his knees and stares around this room of memories. They crowd in on his misery. He rocks back and forth, keening his sorrow to the room.

The lawyer who has been looking into Craig's predicament ever since Helen spoke to her is wrestling with a defence for her new client. So far, she has refrained from calling Craig – Helen told her not to before she heard from a 'colleague' in the USA. She was given a thorough briefing by Helen and has been sent redacted documents to back the explanation. When her phone rings, she answers, and an American voice starts to talk.

In Thames House, the Security Service officer who has been told to find and keep tabs on Craig has made contact with the US Embassy and arranged to meet one of their people. The individual to whom he has spoken did the investigation into Craig that Leanne asked for after the Fort Halstead demonstration. The British agent decided that some cooperation would be a good idea. They meet up and, after co-opting a colleague from the Metropolitan Police Special Branch for liaison with uniformed police, they drive to Wimbledon.

The two intelligence officers and the plainclothes policeman see the press pack in front of Craig's house and stop short. The policeman spots the exit of the alleyway and beckons them to follow him. They identify the back of Craig's house and climb over the wall. They take in the open doors and start across the garden. What they find inside the house leaves them disgusted and in no doubt as to what must have happened when their fugitive returned home.

Exiting the house, they hear a phone ringing. Crossing the garden, they discover Craig's mobile phone. When they answer, they find themselves speaking to a lawyer that Craig still doesn't realise he has.

The three officials tracking Craig are at a loss. The angry policeman vows to get whoever did the house and put them away. He calls the local station to get uniformed officers and local CID to the address. The CIA officer is on his phone to the US Embassy. The MI5 officer calls his office to try and get CCTV footage of the street into which Craig must have run. Hanging up, the CIA officer announces that the profile says his mother lived in Woolwich. He still owns an address there. The three sprint to the police car. The policeman calls his control and passes on the address, telling them to contact the local force and get a uniformed presence there. He switches on the siren and blue lights, and they race towards SE18.

It is after dark when they arrive and greet the uniformed officer at the block. Curious locals gather to watch. Entering the building they note the signs of a recent visit. Their bird has flown, and there are no more clues.

Early the following morning, the King's Troop Royal Horse Artillery prepares to go out on morning exercise. The smart troopers are lined up at the gate. Each one rides one and has two more horses in hand. That they can control them in the streets of London is testament to the skill of the riders and temperament of the Irish horses. A young captain watches with pride as they pass her into the street. Her day's routine starts with a run. She trots out on her way to Shooter's Hill. Relaxing into her stride, she leans into the run entering the woods. Looking down to check her smartwatch, she is struck in the head. Reeling with the shock, she falls. Hauling herself to a sitting position, she looks up to see what obstacle she has encountered. Above her, a dismal figure sways and twists. A thin cord around its neck is tied around a branch.

Television and radio report the discovery of the hanged body of the renowned expert Dr Craig Moore. The reporting both in the broadcast media and online is the reverse of recent coverage. Now Craig has been 'hounded', 'betrayed'. His lawyer is widely quoted. Her defence, which came too late, is much cited.

In western Iraq, at the battle group HQ of the Royal Lancers an investigation is underway. A service enquiry has been convened to record the series of events leading up to the death and serious injuries of soldiers on operations in the Iraqi desert. David is there along with Robin, Caroline, Maz Tate and Bill. A screen flickers on one wall, displaying news from the BBC World Service, though the sound is muted. As the team who have come out from the UK ask questions, Caroline catches sight of a familiar face on the broadcast. Underneath the picture, the story of the apparent suicide of a brilliant programmer scrolls its way across the screen. All turn at the horror etched on Caroline's face. She staggers to her feet and lurches out of the tent. Maz sits, face in hands. David, calmer, gets to his feet and pauses, looking at the head of the UK delegation.

"That will be all today." He continues through the tent flap accompanied by Bill's torrent of invective, towards the abject figure of his friend in the desert outside.

It is early in the morning at the Skunk Works. Russ Morales has been unable to sleep and is in the hangar. Alpha Mike is still scarred, but at least he has a new wheel station and is back on three feet. Russ, a newly made coffee in his hand, looks across at him and, sad though his mood is, he smiles when the machine looks back. Walking over, he lays a hand on the machines's nose.

"Sorry, my friend, I did what I could. It wasn't enough."

On his desk, his tablet screen flickers and he walks back to it. Media reports flick rapidly across the screen. Looking up, he sees reflections on the wall echoing his display. He looks down as the motion stops and sees Craig's face staring shyly up at him. Alarmed, Russ crosses to the console as the opposite wall darkens. The screens that hitherto have shown the Akacita Maza logo are now blank. At the bottom of each one, there is a blinking cursor.

A set of conditions have been met.

ACKNOWLEDGEMENTS

Gavin Hood for showing me how movies are made. Ged Doherty for telling me to write about people, not things. Guy Hibbert for showing me how stories are told and his friendship.

Jenny, my wife, for the first edit, Paddy for passing his young eyes over it and being agreeably surprised that his stepdad could write something relevant! Stephen Colegrave and John Mitchinson for being the first to suggest I write something. Joanna Jepson-Biddle for almost editing the book. Flora Nedelcu-Smith and the BAP Creative Retreaters, thank you for the Saturday 'Show and Tell' encouragement. Jason Clarke for his guidance on writing a one-page book teaser. Alex Hammond, thank you for doing an amazing structural edit and for his advice to 'show readers, don't tell them'. The Writers and Artists Guild for putting me in touch with Alex. Kate Baker, author of Maid of Steel, for encouraging me to go for the Book Guild as a Publisher. Finally, The Book Guild, particularly Chloe and Dan, for advice and guiding me through the publishing process.

The British Army, my home for forty years. The defence industry, especially Thales Aerospace. They created the conditions that allowed me to write this book.